ENDGAME CONTENT

ENDGAME CONTENT

An MMORPG novel by

Thomas Goose

ENDGAME CONTENT

Cover designed by Tomasz Guzewicz, realised by Dilan P
Editing and correction by Tomasz Guzewicz
Typesetting and formatting by Tomasz Biernat (tosiewyda.pl)

Characters and events in this book are mostly fictional, and any resemblance to actual persons, living or dead, is sometimes intended.

ISBN: 978-83-969936-0-1
First published as paperbound in 2023

Preface and acknowledgements

Thank you for taking the time to read my book. It is my first novel and if you are an enthusiast of online gaming, particularly MMORPGs, then this is a story for you. It uses my own memories and real people I have met online over the years of gaming, as well as stories I heard from others on forums or on evening wiping sessions on that one boss that just won't die.

Special thanks go to my friend Faye who, like a few of my other friends, was an inspiration for one of the characters in the story and who was the one to keep pushing me to write more; and to all the others who lived through some of those stories with me. Finally, to all three people who read it before publication. You know who you are. Readers are welcome to send their feedback to AuthorThomasGoose@gmail.com. If you enjoyed this book, please help me reach more readers!

[Subject: AltAr quarterly update]
[Date: April 1st, 2015]
[Posted by: GM_Kaivax]

Dear Players of AltAr! From the server administration staff, we thank you for your continued interest in our project. We have some exciting news to share with you down below. We had to lock GM_BBungyeol in her room to prevent her from spilling the beans too soon. Keep reading for the summary of upcoming events, a report on server's health, and changes going live on next restart (4 Apr 06:00).

NEW UPCOMING FEATURE

This one is my favourite, and it has been my secret project for a month. Now that I know it is doable, it is time for a reveal.

Through playing with the back-end code of the Music Box set of toys and adding some of my own, I am working on a utility that will allow players with a bit of musical theory knowledge and simple programming skills to create completely new music tracks that will be audible in the game, note by note. Honestly, it is quite simple to do and all the building blocks are in the server files. They even include recorded music notes of multiple instruments. Perhaps it was a semi-completed feature to be expanded later, but it never happened. Anyway, this means that it may even be possible to add some sort of music instruments to the game, which you will be able to use to port any song you want to the game world.

Stay tuned for more updates on this project!

EVENTS

You know it's coming, so let's not delay. Continuing our tradition of announcing major events three months in advance, it is our pleasure to hereby inform you all that this year's Summer Event begins on July 1st and will end on August 31st. This year, the festival returns to Hellesvyand, so get your swimwear ready! For those of you who don't have any or want to have more, don't worry -- rewards will include COMPLETELY new trunks and swimsuits, courtesy of GM_BBungyeol who spent weeks designing, scaling, and texturing them to look great on your characters. If you're excited, please make sure to respond to this thread with "Thank you Ms. Yeol". She will be pleased to read it once she realises the door has been unlocked since this morning. A special donation drive will be opened for everyone who wishes to tip her for her hard, voluntary work; out of all event rewards, those are created from scratch, only for AltAr players!

The event will follow the usual logic. Participate in summer activities, earn tickets, exchange tickets for rewards. Yes, it is possible to obtain them all with no RNG involved!

Activities will include:
-Returning from last year: watergun fights!
-Evening bonfires, also from last year!
-GM_Eldarecht is wrapping up his brand new storyline quest!
-Your colleagues from <Immorality Police> guild will once again host a fashion competition (date TBA)!
-A number of NPC gift boxes will be hidden all over the game world, in all kinds of zones. Damage them to open, top damage gets everything! We will publish a gift-finding leaderboard when all gifts are found or the event ends, whichever comes first. Be warned though, as some Gift Boxes will fight back!
-We're accepting submissions for new custom loading screens!

-We're accepting submissions for other player-driven activities that we will advertise for you! Contact us at events@altar.org with your event idea, who hosts it, what assistance is required, etc.

-As for PvPer... [continue reading]

SERVER HEALTH

If you thought all the good news were limited to the events, it is our pleasure to surprise you once more.

Server pop: the server's playerbase has increased for the third consecutive quarter (up by 11%) and our all-time highest online player count has been beaten on February 14 (what have you been up to, people?) and is now 1144 (including multiboxers, traders, etc).

Server finances: our server's primary expense, hosting, is covered for another 12 months. According to AltAr's Donation Policy [link] 50% of the surplus funds will be paid to the Administration staff as a tip, and the other 50% saved for unexpected server upkeep costs or urgent migrations.

As always, Q1 financial report is available at [link].

CHANGES

Follow this [link] for a detailed changelog.

COMMENTS (191)

[Diki] first B)

[PeepoSweepo] first!

[Dolj] thank you Ms. Yeol

[PeepoSweepo] rip

[-Zoe-] peak online on valentine's day XD Hellesvyand people are at it again [ashalynYa] thank you Ms. Yeol and the entire admin team! <3

[raphanti] @Zoe can confirm, even the ceilings were sticky (͠° ͜ʖ ͠°)

[KARS] thank you ms. yeol

[GM_BBungyeol] thank you Ms. Yeol

[Prast] the new feature is dope. Hope it works

[OmO] meh, my loading screen didn't get featured 2 times in a row, gonna pass this time

[Sapphire] nice

[marino_1919] thank you ms. yeol

[PSP99] time to restock on energy dri... [continue reading]

* * *

[23:35] **[Friend]** Pvro: yo

[23:35] **[Friend]** Pvro: can you come to the inn?

[23:36] **[To: Pvro]**: sure, one sec

Sl4y stood up, summoned his mount, and made his way to the usual inn where his guild, Havoc, kept their spawn point during guild operations. He was calm but curious; he was friends with Pvro for over a year now, but even for him to be called aside at such an hour was not normal. What is it about, he wondered?

The sign above the door read The Far Horizon. There was nobody inside as he walked in, save the NPCs. He assumed Pvro must be upstairs, and sure enough, he found him in one of the suites. But as he walked into the living room of one of them, he found others too. Trillex wiggled around, an MMORPG's universal sign of impatience, but sat down then Sl4y walked in. Venetia the Warlock, stood beside Pvro who sat by a table. Sl4y immediately recognized his situation: he had been invited to a private meeting of Havoc's leadership in the form of Pvro, pronounced "pooro," and Trillex. Venetia was present as a close friend of both of them, but not an officer himself.

This was an upstairs inn room like pretty much every other such room in the city. Designing unique interiors for each building in a city is not something game developers would do; why do the work from scratch every time you need another building? Nevertheless, Sl4y knew it for a fact that just like each city's architectural style was characteristic to it, so was their unique interior style. Even if copied, the room was not poorly done by any means, and it was not a lazy copy either. It was lit by a few magic orbs glowing faintly with white light as they hovered below the ceiling, and by two windows open wide letting in bright moonlight. The floorboards were bare wood and they would play a creaking sound when walked on as if they were real.

The tables and chairs were the same as elsewhere in Argentia, but someone took the effort to at least move them around a bit. A few paintings of local streets and a map of Insal Kingdom decorated the plastered walls painted white. The room was simple overall, but not dilapidated by any means. A side door led to a bedroom.

'hi,' typed Sl4y to the room.

'Yo :),' returned Pvro, and Trillex /waved his hand. Sl4y knew Trillex and Venetia as non-chatty people, especially the latter. Venetia was a god of the game, but his English was not good. So maybe they were chatty, just not in English.

'Should I join voicecoms?' asked Sl4y.

'No, no, we're not on it. Trillex just put his son to sleep. Anyway, we had a little discussion, Sl4y. It's late so let me just drop it. Listen: Trillex has to step down as the Officer.'

Sl4y was not surprised, but couldn't help but wonder why he was being told this in such a way, in this semi-private meeting instead of just sending it by guild chat. He got a little tense.

'Why?' he asked, although he probably knew the answer.

'Same reason. He's a daddy now, and he can't spend as much time in-game as he used to.'

'And I have another little bugger on the way,' said Trillex.

'Nice,' said Sl4y, not really thinking so.

'We need an Officer, now more than ever,' continued Pvro. 'We lost Nyrah last month. You know we're not doing too well recently, our progress sucks, people complain, so we gotta do something. Blah blah, here's the gist of it: you take Tril's place. How's that?'

Sl4y suspected this might be the topic of this meeting from the moment he walked in, but at best he expected to be asked to propose a new officer. But to be himself nominated instead?

'Why me?' he asked.

'Because you can be trusted to do the job. You're active, you don't dodge responsibility, even if you don't like it. You've been here long enough, people know you, and you played the game for years. The boys agree. You ask us "why me?" but I ask you: who else?'

'Slam1go, Beli, Lonecow, Doublehead?'

'Beli I can understand, but she has beef with too many people. But Slam1go? He speaks before he thinks and is a jerk all around. Lonecow is even worse. Don't tell him I said that.'

'And Doublehead?'

'Playing some other game lately.'

'Hmm… I don't know, man. Hey, since when is being a jerk a career blocker around here?'

'Well, I really considered Slam1go, but he can't hold his tongue when it's needed. We can't let him publically speak with guild's authority and shit. So to answer your question: since now, I guess.'

'That rules me out, then.'

'Hehe, nope. I know what you are.'

'Let me ask you instead,' suddenly said Trillex. 'Why not? What stops you?'

'Seems unfair,' said Sl4y, uncertainly. 'I feel others are more qualified. Some have been members for years and have never been Officers.'

'You have been a member long enough,' Pvro pointed out.

'I was way less confident or qualified being an Officer than you are now. Seriously, stop overthinking this. It's just a game after all. A RPG even. Play the role.'

'An RPG.' Sl4y corrected.

'Fuck off.'

In truth, Sl4y had no counter to Trillex's point and he mulled over the thought, watching his buddies' characters as he did. Only now did he notice Trillex wearing, quite literally, beach clothes: a flower shirt, almost unbuttoned, shorts, sandals – no, flip-flops! - and a straw hat. That was a man who said "I'm going on vacation" without really saying it, which must have been an ironic joke at his own expense given his present situation.

Pvro, who mained a Rogue build for Assassin, wore what looked like a hotch-potch of gear sets, although Sl4y knew Pvro would not put style above performance. So his gear, now barely visible as he sat behind the table, looked somewhat like that of a naval captain (or pirate captain?) with that dark-green cloak with high collar, draped over his shoulders but kept together with a golden chain no less. But he was also like a street thug with the less fancy leathers underneath the cloak. Even if appearing to be mismatched and unkempt, it was top-notch PvP gear. Somewhere underneath his cloak was sheathed a pair of short swords and other tools of a roguish person's trade. Poisons, blinding dusts, lockpicks, and probably some less ethical accessories. A bottle of drinkable but also very flammable alcohol? A crushed brick in a sock for knocking targets unconscious? You never know with those players.

As for Venetia's grim presence…

Nevermind that. Sly's thoughts returned to the situation. Indeed, why not? Why not take it? It was true he felt undeserving. Havoc was a guild with over six years of history, and he was in it for one and a half. He did not feel he should be elevated over some other members who have seen it being created.

But that was not all. This was not the first time he was offered leadership or co-leadership of a guild. Twice before his smaller guilds collapsed not long after he took over, and in a third case, it even broke apart on the same day. After the last time he vowed to himself to stay away from the management and just be a simple peon in a larger, well-organised guild.

But Pvro knew this, and still offered him the job. Why?

Pvro jumped up from his seat – it's faster to hit the spacebar than to right-click the chair – and theatrically approached and performed a /slap emote on Sl4y.

'OK look. I've always thought people who don't want to lead are those who should lead. It's my IRL observation. So, are you gonna waste our time much longer? I want to go to bed, gotta get up early tomorrow :v'

Sl4y was about to respond, when Pvro spoke again:

'In fact, you know what? Fuck you, enjoy :D'

[23:51] [Guild] Sl4y has been promoted to Rank 2 <Officers>.

[23:51] **[Guild]** Pvro: grats!

[23:51] **[Guild]** Pvro: good night o/

[23:51] **<Friend>** Pvro has logged out.

Well, fuck.

* * *

Sl4y returned to his usual sitting spot in Argentia. It was an elevated terrace of a two-storey merchant house just off the main road leading through the city from the trade district in the west and the large square with a fountain, a popular meeting place, to the north. The road curved northwards as it went, and had dozens of side streets leading to and away from it. The terrace was furnished with just a few tables and seats, and it overlooked the busy road offering a very good view on everyone passing by.

Argentia was not the main city of ARIS if there even was one, but it was the one where Havoc made their base. Still it was one of the larger towns, and there always were players going back and forth in Sl4y's view. It was the capital city of the Insal kingdom, and the geography was kind to the town. Lore-wise, freshwater was carried from mountains just twenty-five kilometres to the north by two impressive aqueducts raised by kings now long dead, their work outliving them by centuries. The aqueducts were not many, but their capacity was great, easily satisfying the needs of half a million people who called the city their home. The warm climate was good for harvests, but was also said to be somewhat *too warm* at times, as if players could even feel it. Fortunately, the residents could find refuge from summer heat while ensuring their hygiene thanks to a network of public baths akin to that of ancient Rome. A surprisingly ancient sewage system carried away waste to Insalama river that flowed through the town. *You can know the truth of a city by looking at its sewage system*, said someone to Sl4y once. Or was that a quote from another game?

He had a habit of hovering his mouse pointer over people to see who's coming and going, but not really memorising or analysing. Lost looking. This time he ignored them all, having other things on his mind.

Let's take stock of the situation I guess, he thought. Promotion to the highest non-GL rank in the guild opened new options and views in the guild window:

activity logs, MOTD, news dashboard, guild skillpoint allocation, member profile modification. He flicked through them, looking for anything standing out. He was familiar with the Guild UI, having played ARIS for a few years he even had a private guild for his alt characters, not to mention those other few guilds he was in.

Bank! He stood up, cast a spell, and teleported to the city's entry point. He could have walked those fifty metres ingame, but teleporting saved him about ten seconds. From here it was closer to the bank building in Argentia, and inside it, the Guild Vault where new tabs should be visible to him now. The bank and trading area were always the activity hubs of any city in any game, and this was no different. Seeing the game well populated was a source of joy for Sl4y, especially in a game no longer developed, hosted privately by volunteers, and supported by donations. *And at such a late hour*, Sl4y remarked, seeing it was well half past midnight on a Thursday. He had made a small break to prepare some food and brought it to his desk in the meantime, anticipating a longer gaming session that night. The food was already gone.

'All right. What do we have here?' he said, opening the Guild Vault, but the darkness in his room did not deign to respond. He had an idea what he would see, after all he had participated in all the raids and events that dropped some of the loot that goes straight to restricted tabs. He looked past the crafting materials, from the mundane to legendary. It was now part of his job to hand them to those who need them – and who meet the conditions of course. A rule in Havoc was that you can have the Guild's rare components if you show you've collected everything else apart from them. *What else?* Some mediocre reusable gear, useful for mid-level characters. Some commemorative event items that can't be sold, kept for sentimental value, such as the original guild creation receipt from a guild office, dated to one day after the current server iteration was launched. *Pity I missed that moment*, thought Sl4y, but those relics were heartwarming to see regardless. There were also stockpiles of consumables, a cash account, equipment crafting materials from raids of various rarity, and construction materials. And a few other things he did not expect to see. He briefly smiled at them, closed the window, and left the bank returning to his idling spot.

[00:41] **<Friend>** Sapphire has logged in.

A slim figure logged in a flash of light a few steps away, stood still for a few seconds while her game loaded the area, then for another few while she spinned the camera around herself. Having noticed Sl4y, she /waved to Sl4y when she noticed him, and casually sat next to him, shoulder to shoulder. 'Princess Luna, I presume?' asked Sl4y in a private chat.

'xd,' was Sapphire's response. 'I see they put a new hat on you.'

'Yep,' said the Priest with bare head.

'Well, well. It was about time tbh.'

'?'

'Tril clearly was no longer with us even if he logged in. I could tell.'

'Ah.'

'Pvro also asked me if you'd accept it. Not sure why me. But I told him he'd be an idiot not to try.'

'TBH I didn't even accept it, he just dropped it on me.'

'Why didn't you?' she asked.

'You know why.

'Nope.'

'D: remember Nightcrawlers and Wolfcall?'

'What about them?'

'Duh. I get rank 2, guild falls apart. See a pattern here?'

'And it was your fault?'

'It's what the evidence shows,' he said /shrugging.

'Now you're just talking out of your ass.'

'Why?'

'Those guilds were already in decline when you stepped in. I don't know about NC but Hetka promoted you because she thought you'd save Wolfcall.'

'And I didn't. How do you know it, anyway?'

'Girl spy network. I am saying that maybe you are the guy they call to fix shit.'

'She never said that to me,' he typed. Sl4y had no other response to that for a moment. Sapphire tried to show him a different way to look at things, but he was sceptical. It was only her opinion and conjecture after all. He wanted to ask how come she had not told him before about his old guildmaster's, Hetka's, motivations for passing the guild over to him back in the day.

'Well, let's hope it's not what happens this time too,' Sl4y said. 'Things look OK, despite Trilex. So, you said you set me up for this?'

'Of course. All me (:'

'Nice. Thanks a lot. I won't forget the moment you ended my carefree existence.'

'Hey, I had good reasons for it, such as my personal gain. You will get me nice stuff now, right?'

'Yes, honey :('

'xd.'

She must have noticed she had logged out in her combat gear the previous day and still wore it when she logged in, because in an eyeblink her outfit changed to a set of casual clothes. Sl4y knew the inexplicably revealing female Minstrel gear was something Sapphire could tolerate in action, but outside combat situations she would not. She only put up with it due to the class' gameplay being convenient to her.

'By the way,' she said. 'You still on at this hour?'

'Hey, that's my line.' Sl4y /frowned theatrically. 'Just orienting myself in the situation. But I should be going soon tbh. I just wanted to see a few things first, and to respond to some people.'

'Mhm.'

'By the way, I see you finally got the scarf. Looks good on you.'

'Right?' She rose and did a little spin, the engine even animating a little sway of her unbound, long, straight chestnut hair. She was wearing a scarf of a delicate, thin fabric in a striped pattern of green and ocean-blue. It matched her current outfit of ripped denim trousers, a beige sweater, and good old low-cut black-and-white sneakers. She always wore sneakers, in game and out of game, winter or summer, just like she never wore dresses or skirts. ARIS allowed players to freely choose eye and hair colour from an RGB slider, and Sapphire, true to her name, gifted her character with sapphire-blue eyes.

Sl4y knew about fashion and style as much as the next guy, which is not much, but he had always known Sapphire as someone who only follows one style and respects one opinion: her own.

'Autumn outfit eh? Matches your colour palette too. All these years I've never known you for a fashion model.'

'Give me a break,' she typed, and sat back. 'I've never been into that shit, but I tried it once, and now I'm gonna fuck up my exams because of that. If you see me again gathering another nine hundred of something, do me a favour and get my account banned or something.'

'Not a chance. You're an obsessive collector of junk and would wither without it.'

'Well xd.'

'By the way, Maris was on a few hours ago, she asked me to give you this.'

Sl4y opened inventory, flicked through tabs, found the two +4 DEX rings, opened a trade window with Sapphire, and dragged them there.

'Thx. I was wondering where I put them -_-'

'So anyway,' Sapphire added after few moments of silence. 'Congrats. Once again, you're a server VIP. I wonder how Aura would react to this. What would she say.'

'We will never know.' Sl4y signed heavily to his room.

'>:'

Unwilling to dwell on that memory, he sought something else to focus on. A stream of people kept flowing below, having lost much of its volume by this hour, but the trade chat kept scrolling up filled with nonsense talk and even a few genuine trade offers. Logout notifications from friends kept coming every few minutes. NPCs kept walking along their pre-programmed routes. Background symphonic music of Argentia kept playing. Sapphire probably chatted to someone else in the meantime, but sat here with him. Sl4y lived through hundreds of such evenings, and he still enjoyed them. He felt a certain connection, maybe even a bond, with those people who like him were now sitting by their computers and exploring this world, grinding items or levels, doing quests, or just hanging around and chatting with their friends for hours. Even with the unwashed rabble from the rival guilds Execute and the Bulwark alliance, but he would not tell them so.

He looked at the clock and grimaced. He might be a Priest now, but in the morning he would be a facility manager for an IT corporation, and the facility would not manage itself.

'I'll be going to bed now. Good night.'

'Nightt.'

'Ah, just one more thing.'

'?'

'Might as well immediately exploit my new power to fulfill my own wild and twisted desires at the cost of others,' he said before logging out.

[01:12] **[Guild]** <MOTD>: Push-to-talk is now mandatory during guild ops. -Sl4y

* * *

Meanwhile in another guild.

[01:01] **[Guild]** Eggsecute: I heard they have a new commander in Havoc?

[01:01] **[Guild]** Diki: bro that's old news, where have you been

[01:01] **[Guild]** Eggsecute: wtf it happened just hours ago

[01:01] **[Guild]** Diki: yeah that's old news

[01:02] **[Guild]** Sodjong: anyone for leveling 80+?

[01:02] **[Guild]** Eggsecute: XD

[01:02] **[Guild]** Eggsecute: lmao

[01:02] **[Guild]** NA_is_salty_xD: me, inv

[01:02] **[Guild]** NA_is_salty_xD: but give me 3 mins, bio

[01:02] **[Guild]** RapiDfirE: that's good news tho, I always like fights with them

[01:02] **[Guild]** AdFontes: Tril still there?

[01:02] **[Guild]** AdFontes: also who's the new dood then

[01:02] **[Guild]** Diki: Sl4y, plays a priest

[01:02] **[Guild]** AdFontes: what, he wasn't an officer all this time?

[01:02] **[Guild]** Eggsecute: can't say I remember him

[01:02] **[Guild]** Eggsecute: what kind of a priest name is that lul

[01:03] **[Guild]** Diki: you should

[01:03] **[Guild]** Diki: he was badass in the day, a fighter build is named after him even

[01:03] **[Guild]** Diki: he rerolled because they nerfed his build lol

[01:03] **[Guild]** Eggsecute: meh

[01:03] **[Guild]** Eggsecute: he's no Venetia thats for sure

[01:03] **[Guild]** RapiDfirE: who cares about priests =]

[01:03] **[Guild]** Praystation: :[

[01:03] **[Guild]** Praystation: people who want heals maybe? :>

[01:03] **[Guild]** RapiDfirE: its not like I get em anyway lol
[01:03] **[Guild]** Praystation: that's such a hunter thing to say
[01:03] **[Guild]** RapiDfirE: j/k
[01:03] **[Guild]** RapiDfirE: dont add me to shit list pls

* * *

'Vene, you're not saying anything.'

Venetia was listening to the conversation in the voice channel with diminishing attention. He had been gathering materials from elementals in Forsynt Crater. Lore-wise, this was a site of the Forsynt Calamity, where a massive magical explosion from millenia ago had left a hole so vast a city could fit into it. Players leveling in the area learned about those events from local quests, but they offered only dry fragments of the story. The best parts were subtly and implicitly told by the environment. A strange statue here, a curiously well-preserved corpse there, a shadow of an npc appearing in one place, whispering a few strange lines, then fading out again. The site was also a never-exhausting battlefield of various elementals that raged against each other since that explosion, as if nature itself was driven mad by the reality-breaking magics unleashed. Colossal magma giants strode the scorched plains among geysers and fissures spewing things stranger than molten rock from beneath the surface. Raging blaze spirits flickered as they gained or lost stability to the whims of aetheric currents, or were stamped out by the uncaring giants passing overhead. Arcane constructs coalesced into existence where mana tides were particularly strong, and through reasons yet not understood by scholars gained enough sentience to know their lives, such as they were, depended on access to such fissures; they lashed at anyone and anything that came to claim them or just happened to pass by. Or so the game lore said.

As if the place was not hostile enough, a walking mountain of an earth-magma elemental world boss stalked the wastes. It was surprising how something so huge and noisy had a tendency to come up behind players not paying attention to their surroundings, too absorbed by extracting value from the place.

And an excellent farming spot it indeed was. Among other things, potent elemental embers dropped here, required for brewing of the best potions and elixirs, and Venetia needed to restock his supplies. Players frequently battled for control over the valuable grinding spot against everyone who was not with them. A few even tried to come at Venetia, but the smarter ones saw who stood before them and wisely went the other way. The rest got smarter, eventually.

The conversation he was half-ignoring he had heard before in one way or another, and Dereky, Beli, Lonecow and Bokkie were just repeating the same points as previously. But the difference this time was that Trillex had now made a decision. Dereky's mention of his nickname drew Venetia's attention back to the discussion, and he responded with the same response that he had formulated some time before.

'What's there to say? You made your point. This isn't a problem to solve, it's just life. We move on.'

'You are surprisingly calm about this,' pointed out Bokkie but without Lonecow's upset tone.

'Why *surprisingly*?'

'You put more into this game and guild than anyone.'

'The game and guild is not going anywhere,' countered Venetia. 'And it was Pvro who started it, remember?'

'That Pvro is not even here kinda speaks,' interjected Belixner.

'Actually, I didn't invite him to this conversation. I wanted to talk with the few of you specifically, and with Sarevoc and Doublehead but they were busy,' Trillex had to clarify.

'Anyway,' continued Venetia. 'Lonecow, I still don't know what you want from me. Tril has to take care of his family. I understand that, I have my own. What, did you expect everything to always be the same? Forever?'

'No.'

'Then why are you so pissed?' asked Belixner.

'I'm not pissed though?'

'Yeah obviously you aren't LOL,' she mocked.

'I'm disappointed. Trill talked me into trying this game and I stayed, and as far as I know, you too. And it was grand, we kicked arse together, but now we are left with whot? Pvro half-assing it and some randoms running the show while he's gone.'

'Sl4y is a random to you?' objected Trillex.

'Aye he fookin is' said Lonecow. 'I've been on his raids. That dude can't lead for shite. You gotta be a special case of moron to fail so hard, with all the guides you wrote on the forums for them'

'If I recall correctly, you haven't joined any of his events in like half a year,' pointed out Trillex.

'Yeh, because he sucks and pisses me off. The randoms will run this guild into the fookin ground, you will see. Fookin Sl4y, Slam1go, Intervene, and a bunch of kids, randoms, and noobs now too apparently.'

'We were kids and noobs when we started it.'

'Would you do a better job as officer then?' asked Venetia.

'No, because I can't deal with kids and noobs.'

'To be fair,' Zoe jumped in, 'Sl4y has his own ideas and that is a good thing. And Pvro trusts him.'

Trilex sighed. 'Look. I called you all here to ask you to stay and play along nicely. I would hate for this guild to fall apart. We've been in it for over six years. That's six years of history. It shouldn't break up just because I'm quitting the game.'

'It's just not the same without you though,' said Dereky, the Alchemist-Witch Doctor.

[17:39] **[To: Belixner]:** why is he so mad now

'So what will you do?' Trillex asked.

'I was going to take a break anyway. Now's a good time, I think,' said Belixner.

'Fuck knows what I'll do,' complained Lonecow.

[17:40] **[From: Belixner]**: I think he just hates slay for some reason

'I'll stay around, see how it goes.' Zoe's voice carried mostly indifference. She has always had a healthy relationship with gaming.

'Vene?' pushed Trillex when Venetia did not respond.

'What? I'm good, thanks.'

'I will be moving to another house next month, I don't know when I will have a connection there, but a gaming station is already planned, haha,' answered Dereky. 'Also, Sarevoc is on vacation, he will be back on Tuesday.' After that, the conversation fell silent.

Venetia meant what he said. Indeed it was Trillex, his real-life friend, who introduced him to the game, and the rest of the group of "Greeks," as they had been nicknamed in Havoc, in the early days of AltAr. They, together with the Assassin player Pvro from Norway and his few buddies, formed Havoc and with just ten solid members dominated Battlegrounds for a while. Soon afterwards other guilds rose up and overwhelmed Havoc with sheer numbers of players. With no other choice, the guild reluctantly opened itself to new members – who met certain conditions – but the core always remained strong. *Until now, that is.* Things were changing now, Venetia knew.

They were not all Greeks, but Trillex, Dereky, Arastina, Pjj, and Belixner were. So was Venetia, despite his nickname. A standing joke was that Sarevoc was Greek too, just because he was associated with them for such a long time, and he was tired of clarifying it. Furthermore the fact that he was Macedonian only made him more exasperated and frustrated. 'Wow, he's upset like a real Greek,' they would tease him.

Pvro's Nordic gang was smaller, and likewise used to be called Norwegians but that meme was short-lived and now even those who had coined it already forgot it. In addition, only Pvro and Morwrath were from Norway, but calling Pvro a Swede never failed to provoke a response from him. From this group only Pvro now remained, but he was the first and current Guild Leader.

Venetia mulled over those thoughts and memories as he cast Crippling Pain on a level 80 Hunter player so that he could not escape. The soon-to-be victim had foolishly tagged a few mobs that Venetia was targeting, making them not lootable for the Warlock player, and Venetia did not like that at all. He began casting Malefic Curse when all of the sudden, the Hunter spoke:

[17:49] Ârchėr: sorry!

[17:49] Ârchėr: didn't see you :)

Venetia canceled the cast seeing that the Hunter was already leaving the area, though still slowed by Crippling Pain.

[17:49] Venetia: ok np

Venetia never enjoyed going after players who minded their business and who were twenty levels below maximum. He was not like BATS or Ò_Ó, but with his reputation on AltAr people could hardly accept that. He knew that if he stomped everyone into the ground they would leave, and there would be no more people to play with. So when his targets showed respect or manners, or were simply noob enough to be beneath his notice, he spared them. It was important to have people to frag tomorrow.

Unless they met in Battlegrounds or GvG, then things ended differently.

* * *

Sl4y died. That happened frequently, but this time it was *not fine*.

It was a Sunday evening. He and the other fifty or so Havoc members had been defending the last gate in Sal-born Keep, a fortification overlooking the lengthy road from Vir Estia to Argentia, for the last thirty-five minutes. Before that, they had managed to retake the castle from Execute who had taken it from them last Thursday.

Three times a week, on Thursdays, Sundays and Tuesdays, the Guild vs Guild event opened automatically, following a pre-determined schedule known to all players. It was a territory-control wargame, a battle for domination of the Sal-born Keep and the Nordheimburg, although everyone referred to them as just "castles". As per the design principle of ARIS, as much as possible was made to be open-world, that is not isolated from the rest of the world in a separate instance; dungeons, raids, and PvP zones such as GvG battlegrounds. Whichever guild found itself defending the place had to face all the other guilds attacking their gates. The defenders enjoyed a variety of privileges such as secret passages and excellent firing positions, as well as the fact that the attackers often fought against each other as much as against the defenders. It was down to the leadership skills of each Guild Leader or another commander to hold their people in check, and to work towards the goal instead of dedicating themselves to good old slaughter.

Ironically, it was the same motivation that made players both cooperative and disobedient. Dungeons, raids, outdoor PvP, GvG, it was all only a stepping stone to the real end-game content and the highest award a gamer can win: online forum PvP, and bragging rights.

Nevertheless, there were some more tangible benefits to holding a castle. Every week it generated a small amount of gold and some rare item enchantments and other consumable accessories, but nothing that was un-available elsewhere.

On that Sunday Execute was on the defence in Sal-born Keep, but Havoc managed to evict the defenders after only fifteen minutes. Pvro and his guild have been holding it since that moment, but they were being pushed back mercilessly and were down to the last barricade before the command room, which is where Sl4y fell to a stun and a few lucky critical strikes from the enemy.

In retrospection he felt he died like an idiot and he should have avoided that.

Nevertheless, he found himself back in town exactly when his presence at the gate was critical. Needless to say, he was upset. Were it against some other opponent, he would shrug it off, but to die like that to Diki's minions of all people? And in such a moment?

'I'm dead, I'm dead! Prast, Money, heal the gate!' called out Sl4y in the voice chat, hoping Ihealformoney the Paladin would hear him among other voices discussing the frantic moments and keep the gate alive long enough for Sl4y to return.

'But I can barely hold the raid?!' said Prast with annoyance.

[20:52] Sl4y: warp

[20:52] Sl4y: warp

[20:52] Sl4y: warpppppp

Sl4y urged, typing to few other people who were with him in the Far Horizon inn, their designated spawn point in Argentia. In the game's world it was seventy kilometres from the Keep, and like every other guild, they used portals to join the battle from whatever place they chose as their base. Guilds could request for the GMs to set up a portal NPC in a location of guild's choice, but those charged a fee and also required a dialogue interaction from a player, which cost them *seconds*. Gamers are busy people who do not have this kind of time.

Sl4y had already healed everyone around him to full and blessed them too. *What's taking them so long?!*

'Nobody fucking step outside this room unless I specifically tell you to!' Pvro reprimanded his guild sharply. 'SERIOUSLY, how many times do I have to say this? NOT ONE FUCKING STEP BEYOND THIS LINE.' Despite his efforts, there was always someone thinking the rules do not apply to them and dying promptly as a result of it. That was the usual battleground chaos. Some people did not hear or understand the commands from the Guild Leader. Some just did not care, putting their own gaming enjoyment over the good of the many. Controlling fifty individuals in a video game was not a simple task at all, and there were times Havoc fielded up to eighty players.

'I need buffs,' said Vizovia.

'Same,' said Belixner.

'Blinky, start laying traps in the left corridor. Prast, buff Four-Fifteen, he came late.' Pvro's voice was intense in those last minutes of the battle.

'Can't, I'm dead,' responded Blinky.

'Someone's at the door, BRB.' That was Makzine.

'Great timing,' commented Slam1go.

[20:52] **[Raid]** BATS: Execute grouping at the lib, NFP and RezPlease behind them, they not fighting for now

BATS' report from behind enemy lines was worrying but not entirely surprising. Sl4y hoped whoever came across BATS was having a bad time right now. Neither him nor Pvro tried anymore to control the most uncontrollable player of their guild and convince him to return to the defensive line. By now, it was an accepted fact that BATS goes where he pleases. The problem with it was that it created a precedent, and other people thought they can be the exception too.

'Start precasting meteo…' Pvro began when someone unintelligible cut him off.

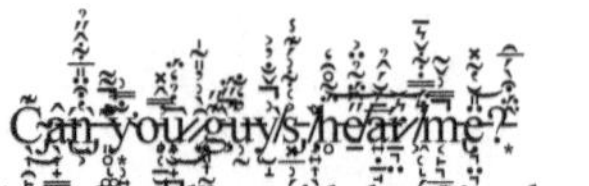

'Argh, who said that?' asked Azarus.

'Fix your mic dude,' helpfully advised Slam1go.

'Oof, my ears,' said Intervene.

'Oops, sorry.'

Meanwhile, Sl4y pushed a fresh recruit as the situation unfolded without him.

[20:52] Sl4y: ZOVIA WARP NOW

As any Mage she could cast portals to places she had visited, GvG castles being high in demand on that list. She must have died about the same time Sl4y did, and she appeared slightly confused.

Sl4y threw a few heals at her hoping this would hasten her movements somehow or catch her attention. Vizovia said nothing but began casting the portal spell after a few seconds that felt like eternity to Sl4y. The moment he saw the vague shape of a portal in the room, he clicked it with ferocity.

Then he regretted it and cursed his stupidity for a second time within just as many moments. He should have read the portal tooltip before clicking it. The place he and few other guildmates found themselves in was not the expected castle outskirts at all. It was an outdoor area somewhere on the southern continent. Vizovia gave them the wrong portal. At least Eightblades at his side was amused.

[20:52] Eightblades: lul

[20:52] Eightblades: xd

'Oh fuck me!' Sl4y cursed at himself. He knew he was partially to blame, having pressured the rookie who probably was already stressed enough in the unfamiliar circumstances. This did not calm him at all, on the contrary, he was even more angry. He unleashed his frustration on a low-level, feline beast Jungle Stalker that just happened to pass them by. Him being a healer did not help the animal at all, the relatively weak Smite still one-shot the target fifty levels below his own, and a few items of very questionable value fell to the ground. A broken claw, a patch of fur, and a rare but still useless Rank 3 Lightning Bolt Scroll.

Sl4y sighed with irritation.

[20:52] Sl4y: back to save, GO

He typed to his unlucky company as if they needed to be told. He picked up the loot – habits die hard – and cast a spell that yanked him back to the spawn point.

One loading screen later he was back in Far Horizon. Vizovia was still the only mage around, which was good news because if more were here, then fewer would be defending the castle. She hadnot taken her wrong warp so she was in the inn all that time and the correct portal was already waiting for them. He hovered his mouse pointer over it to display the tooltip, read it, and took the warp.

As the map loaded again he quietly blessed the SSD technology for quick loading times and listened to the chatter from his headset. Execute was now pushing the barricade, trying to pick off key Havoc defenders while also dishing out damage onto the barricade itself. Since the defenders have been on their toes for over half an hour, their reserves were almost spent.

Sl4y paused outside the Keep for another ten seconds, grouping up with the few allies still emerging from the teleportation. It was better to enter the castle as a group. They had means to join the defenders safely from the back using side entrances open only to the Guid defending the Keep, but those means were sometimes guarded by the attackers to deny the reinforcements.

Not this time, as it turned out. Perhaps attackers threw everything into offense, or maybe someone had already wiped this rearguard. There were player skeletons here, but he could not tell how old they were. Either way, Sl4y, Eightblades, Blinky, and few others went through and reinforced their Guild with the gate still standing.

Sl4y assessed the situation.

About forty of Havoc still stood in varying stages of each one's crisis management in a chamber large enough to easily contain a hundred people. It was in fact a massive staircase. The attackers, coming from the inner courtyard and the library area, would face the defenders in an elevated position and with two flights of stairs to the right and left leading up. There were two other doors on the lower level, but they were decorative only, creating the illusion of this Keep being a real, well-designed structure. Behind Havoc's backs was the final corridor and the thing they had to hold for a few more minutes: the command room, and in the middle of it, a massive crystal pillar pulsing red like an aorta, connecting the spanning the floor and ceiling. Break it with damage, and the castle is yours and the former owners are teleported away.

The Keep served a military function but it testified to the truth of the European middle ages, after which the classic fantasy setting was styled. It was by no means cold, dull, and utilitarian. The inner walls were whitewashed and in many places painted over with images of knights, monsters, past owners, animals, flowers, or had texts written on them in red or gold, or had vibrant heraldic shields and banners hung upon them. The deeper into the structure, the finer the interiors. Most windows were just holes in the walls, but living quarters and inner sanctum had windows with glass, albeit greyish and somewhat opaque. The corridor floors were of neatly cut rectangular light-gray stone slabs that were reminiscent of bathroom tiles but larger and thicker. Here and there an old set of armour stood racked against a wall, wooden benches and large ceramics between them. There were no windows in this particular room as far as Sl4y could see, but it was lit by chandeliers overhead, but not many players ever turned their cameras upwards to look at them. If they had, they would also notice the wooden cross-beams holding the flat, white ceiling that was also adorned with frescoes. Those were the same as in other castles in the game though, just one of the compromises between the artistic vision and game design limitations.

Attackers, be it Execute or any of the other six or seven guilds large and organised enough to pose a threat to Havoc, have just broken down the large barricade of masonry and woodwork. The wall, where it once stood, was as wide as twelve people lined up shoulder-to-shoulder, and tall enough to accommodate a Siege Golem. But those were gone now, fallen to the damage of players attacking. The barricades, just like they can be damaged by every offensive ability in the game, could also be healed and repaired by construction materials, but no guild fielded enough healers to outheal the incoming damage. The necessity to prepare repair materials also put an economic burden on the Guilds holding the castles which worked as a mechanism preventing a Guild from holding it forever, unless they were willing to grind harder and harder each week. Sometimes it was a strategic decision to just let a castle fall.

While the barricade stood, those defenders who hit from distance could venture to the balconies and murder holes overlooking the courtyard and harass the invaders, or even kill them all. This was risky though, as the attackers could hit them back, which is how Sl4y died. With the defensive layer gone, Pvro pulled everyone back and had them concentrate area attacks on the threshold, daring anyone to walk into the downpour of Meteor Strikes, Blizzards, Volatile Concoctions, Malefic Upheaval, Hunter traps, and other pre-casted spells. Now that the end of the battle was only minutes away, people pressed their buttons eagerly.

Sl4y could see 415, Ò_Ó, -Zoe-, Kaitzuuu, Doomcaster, Venetia, Bokkie, and others doing their pre-casting part, now Vizovia joining them too. Sapphire, Rjukan, and Raphanti zoomed back and forth playing cast speed, mana consumption, and cooldown improvement songs. The melees, Intervene, Faystus, ^_Miko_^, Belixner, Gaav, BATS, Pvro himself trying to control chaos, and a dozen and a half others bereft of anything else to do at the moment, waited impatiently on either side of the way in, with blades sharpened, poisons applied, battle shouts refreshed every few seconds despite their far longer duration. Their job begins when magic inevitably fails to hold the line.

As if right on cue, Magic Nullification announced the arrival of visitors. This Scholar ability disrupted all magic in a small area and bought the attackers a few seconds of reprieve from magic damage, and they rolled in like a tide. This was ranged physical damage dealer's time to shine, like that of Kaitzuuu's lone Alchemist-Witch Doctor throwing explosive bottles of acid at high value targets she knew very well, or Doublehead shooting his bolt-action rifle into the crowd, one bullet at a time.

'Honey, go easy with those bombs! You're throwing hours of my life at them!' pleaded Azarus to his partner Kaitzuuu on voice chat, despite sitting next to her by his own gaming station. Witch Doctor's spells were destructive, but the charges needed to be crafted. Of course she would not do it herself.

'No,' she replied. 'Not the time for saving.'

Magic Nullification lasted ten seconds and prevented attackers from using magic, but this favoured Execute. By sheer accident, their guild strangely had many Hunters while Havoc was known for its strong Warlock representation. Hunters were particularly effective when not taking any damage, and Nullification when used irresponsibly had the potential to ruin the caster and his own party, so good Scholars were highly valued. And so due to having just that, the rivals of Havoc returned fire into one of Havoc mages who had to frantically save himself with an expensive healing potion and quick reflexes.

Nullification faded, and the battle erupted in full. Sl4y could see familiar characters stumbling into the chamber. Praystation, RapiDfirE, AdFontes, Diki himself, Proskillver, Mar3k, K_vanad, Quane55, Alice. Wherever Execute displayed discipline and nuked together a single target, there was not much Havoc healers could do. If they reacted immediately, they could buy a few more seconds of the victim's life. Instead, they spread healing across the raid frames on their screens, effectively counteracting the incoming Area of

Effect, or AoE, spells. Of course, they knew which targets ware particularly valuable for the enemy, and those were shielded, warded, and topped off. In ARIS, like in most games of that type, damage is better prevented than healed.

The clock ticking down the last moments before the end of the session at 21:00 made everyone be in a hurry, but to Sl4y the invaders seemed even more hasty than usual after he targeted a few of them and noticed some missing buffs. The explanation presented itself shortly after, but it was not him who noticed it, as he was already fully occupied in trying to keep his raid group, and himself, alive. The effort of resisting player raids that knew what they were doing was so much greater than beating any dungeon raid or the most powerful monster.

'Check-check!' Xyrolol called out the pre-agreed phrase to cut through the chattering voices and deliver his report from outside the battleground, a position he was assigned due to his broken hand. He could still be very useful just by sitting outside and watching the entrance. 'NFP and RezPlease are entering the castle!'

'Thanks Xyro,' said Pvro. 'Well that fucking sucks. Might as well do it now. All right everyone, Recall in fifteen seconds! Be ready!'

AdFontes pushed forward. He and the rest of Execute around him needed no command from Diki to know it was the moment to ignore everything and run forward. Proskillver the Paladin and Retaliator the Warrior were ahead of him trying to clear the path through what few enemy players remained in the penultimate chamber, trying to deal a little bit more damage to their old rivals or at least waste a moment of their time before they too vanished like the rest of their raid did a few seconds ago.

'There's probably a few assassins stealthed around. Rapid, Cass: find them,' Diki ordered two Hunters as the classes best suited for detecting hidden targets due to their Tracking ability among others. 'Everyone else, push, push, push!

Don't stop for them! We have like three minutes to break the pillar, if we do it, nobody will be back in time to take it from us! GO!'

'Yeah, we'll set traps in the corridor behind us if we don't find anyone,' offered CassNL.

'Good, do that.' Diki approved of another player's own initiative. Once again they found a way to exploit their roster imbalance in their favour.

'Need heals,' called a voice.

'Guys in the front, wait five seconds, we're stretched too much!' someone in the back of the raid group insisted.

'No, keep going!' Diki clarified. 'Use potions if you still have them! There won't be another moment for them. Also, Syed, what the fuck are you doing?' he asked, noticing one of his own crouching by a fallen Paladin from Havoc.

[20:58] **[Raid]** 5yed: :)

[20:58] **[Raid]** 5yed: making tea

AdFontes checked the raid frames and saw the status they were in. From the sixty-seven or so who made it to the ante-chamber, over twenty died within those thirty seconds of fighting. There would be more dead if Havoc had not pulled back before the battle was decided. The rest of Execute was still a large group but some were dragging behind, while those closer were low on HP, but healers could at least partially deal with that on the run. This could still end in a spectacular failure, AdFontes remarked, and the server forum will not have mercy commenting on Execute's collective suicide two minutes before the gong. Nevertheless, NFP and RezPlease left them no choice: attack and win, or be crushed between two very unfriendly raids.

Just moments ago, the defenders of Havoc started vanishing from the room one by one, and then the remaining few. GvG arenas did not allow teleportation, but it allowed Town Recall, meaning they returned to base in a desperate gambit. Noone near AdFontes believed for a second Havoc just got up and left the castle to other guilds. No, never that. Havoc were proud and stubborn, and they valued their bragging rights. They were now healing and restocking on consumables before their Guild Leader, Pvro, activated Emergency Recall in the command room, yanking them all back to the battleground. This meant Execute had a golden opportunity to strike in the worst possible moment for the defenders: just a second or two after the Recall went off.

Come in too early, and the dozen or so defenders who stayed on the battle-ground will throw everything they have at the players madly rushing forward, ignoring caution and defensive play. Come in too late, and see the completely refreshed and reinforced raid group in optimal formation and defensive po-sition as the last thing before you die. But come in just when the Recall goes off or within a few seconds afterwards, and you catch their entire raid present in the room, stacked on a very small area, but still seeing loading screens on their monitors and thus being defenceless like a bunch of level one Bambi deer, just with much more hit points.

And since Execute had no means to look inside the command room to know the precise timing, they could only hope to be lucky.

In general, Emergency Recall was a powerful ability but it came with a certain risk, and even more importantly, it was not free to use nor was it available frequently. It cost the Guild a hefty amount of resources – another mechanism of forcing castle ownership change – and once used was unavail-able for 7 days.

'We're gonna be late,' complained someone.

'No no, it's fine, this is good, this is good, just look!' came the response.

They were not lucky as it turned out, but it was not disastrous either. AdFontes could see from a distance the crimson light of the pillar reaching all the way to the roof and the tail end of the group teleportation animation around the pillar. They were just getting into positions, while the few players with slower computers were still immobile. Few of the quicker ones were al-ready spreading over the room, ready to accept the visitors. Execute was less than eighty metres from being in range to attack the objective, a number that meant nothing in the world of pixels but it was just under twice the distance of average ranged attack.

AdFontes was the chief Scholar of his guild, a position he did not get by connections but by his skill. That Magic Nullification moments ago was his doing and it allowed them to cross the downpour of damage from all the Mages and Warlocks and other weird casters, but now it was time to disable as many defenders as possible for as long as possible. Stunning, paralysing, freezing, and otherwise incapacitating – CCing – was now far more preferable to killing them. Killed enemies can come back to the command room very rapidly, but disabled can not bounce to town and back or even log out due to recent combat participation. Furthermore, killing takes more time than neutralising.

And Scholars had a few tricks to do just that. Scholars were practitioners of magic just like Warlocks or Mages, but while those sought aetheric power, Scholars valued understanding. Their ability kit and skill tree was bountiful in disruption and manipulation of magical energies, leaving very little space to the crude practice of casting mindless fireballs. No, Scholars were above that. True, their offense was rather limited, but they could be untouchable when they really needed to.

'Now! CC the hell out of them, and hit the pillar with everything you got! Healers don't forget to hit it too!' called out Diki.

Havoc were defending on the crystal pillar itself now, the column of smooth dark-red mineral dominating the vast chamber. Pvro must have told his minions to let Execute just close enough to have to choose between smashing the Keep control mechanism or eliminating the defenders. *Clever.* The war's objective looked as if it had grown from the middle of the chamber like a peculiar tree, rather than having been placed there; a jagged, irregular stalagnate dozens of metres high, and it seemed to have a pulse like a living being. Tall windows with stained glass mosaics let through the tinted rays of the setting sun. The far end of the chamber was adorned with a large banner displaying the heraldry of the current lords of the Keep, the same banner that was flown in every capital city as long as the guild controls the objective. Along the side walls grew thick columns, and behind one of those columns AdFontes spotted a problem.

The signature Warlock stack of Havoc was really doing the work for them, Pjj, Arastina, Stoencold, Doomcaster, and of course Venetia making their presence felt. At least four Execute members have been affected by Fear at any given time, effectively removing them from combat as they ran around in random directions. AdFontes was sure the Warlocks would have loved to prioritize healers with their CC, but they had to survive the pesky melees swarming them first.

The problem and new goal for AdFontes was a Priest who had positioned himself between two of the columns, making himself very difficult to target for ranged attackers while having excellent line of sight on the most important healing target on the battleground: the pillar. Healing could hardly outweigh the incoming damage if it was focused on a single target, such was the game design. But when every second counted, a tiny bit of healing or shielding could decide the outcome of this evening's GvG. So there was no doubt: the Priest had to be taken out, one way or another, and it had to be from close range. And yet, that player had been shielded by a Force Field from some Mage, which would buy him some time against Assassins, Fighters, Warriors and other melees.

The Priest was performing an ungrateful function. While others enjoyed the game to the fullest, engaged in proper Player vs Player combat and raked in kills or assist credits (very important for "marketing" purposes), he was clicking his heart out in the backlines, unnoticed by almost everyone, spamming Prayers, Devoted Pleas, and Healing Rites and other such blessings on an inanimate NPC who would never thank him.

Diki must have noticed the issue as well, because much like that healer's, his role demanded a broader view.

'Fontes, CC that healer on the right!'

'Already on it!' he said, pushed the glasses on his nose, and sat closer to the screen.

AdFontes managed to click the troublemaker even though only a tiny bit of his model stuck out from cover, and locked target on that Priest. He put Mana Shield and Dissipation Aura on himself, and ran at him. The showdown raged around him and the raid frames on the left of his display were turning increasingly red, but he managed to get through the frontline unharmed. They were already in each other's spell range of forty metres, but the columns broke line of sight, so AdFontes had to get close himself. An enemy profile and health appeared on the side of his screen, and read "Sl4y, Havoc, level 100 Priest". *Ah, it's him,* thought AdFontes. His plan was simple: approach and cast Petrification on unexpecting Sl4y. If he doesn't move, he will be paralyzed for thirty seconds and unable to heal and dispel negative effects from the crystal pillar. If he moves backwards he will lose line of sight to his target, and if he moves forward he will expose himself to more damage, which will also be good.

Sl4y had made one mistake or he had taken a big risk, one that AdFontes intended to exploit fully. By positioning himself like that, he was all on his own. If he would become incapacitated, another support would have to reposition quite far before they could cast a dispel.

As the two-second cast bar appeared on his screen AdFontes congratulated himself on the job well done. Priests had nothing in their spellbook that would save them from this form of CC, and once disabled, they could not cast spells or move anyway. They could just watch and wait to be either dispelled by an ally, or damaged by an enemy – and usually killed too. AdFontes wondered what Sl4y thought at the moment, being outplayed so easily, having seen his assailant come at him unhindered.

Then a weird thing happened and in such a short time AdFontes barely understood what happened. Sl4y stepped forward, changed target to someone from AdFontes' raid group for a split second, too short for the Scholar to read the name, but he managed to notice most of the buffs on his target's target were blue indicating it was a Mage, and that the player was a friendly. In that split second, of all things, a Lightning Bolt shot out from the Priest, who, last AdFontes checked, could not cast elemental magic. Stranger still, the bolt went off without any cast time. The bolt hit some target beyond AdFontes' vision, somewhere behind him, and then returned to strike Sl4y an eyeblink later.

Just after the Petrification cast had completed.

The paralysis effect immediately faded from the Priest, who paused for a second, and returned to healing the crystal with renewed ferocity.

'What…' said AdFontes to his monitor. 'What did he just…?'

Sl4y was laughing.

He wondered what AdFontes thought at the moment, and it made Sl4y laugh even harder. He had just pulled off a trick of the year, one that he once thought about but never considered actually trying to do.

He had noticed the Scholar approaching him, and Sl4y knew what the latter would do once he got close. Sl4y had put himself at an utterly hopeless position: unable to prevent the upcoming CC, and out of sight of Prast or Ihealformoney who could break the negative status on him. Petrification was a good spell, but it had a short range, a cast time, and damage broke the effect on the target. If Sl4y stood in the thick of the fighting, it would do nothing to him except losing control of his actions for just a server tick which is pretty much nothing.

The situation had been dire, and he was scared the Keep would fall without every bit of healing on the crystal that was already taking all kinds of damage from Execute attacks. The problem was that the crystal pillar's health was hidden for everyone, so nobody knew how close it was to breaking.

'Someone help me kill that Shadow Prest, for fuck's sake!' cried Slam1go. 'She's gonna melt the pillar!'

'No, stop breaking my CC!' replied -Zoe-. 'I'm trying to ice her!'

'I kursed her, I kursed her,' came Doomcaster with a third option, increasing the target's casting times by 25% for thirteen seconds with Curse of Aphasia. A more correct term for the spell would be Curse of *Dysarthria* and it even used to be named thus, but it was problematic to pronounce so ARIS creators renamed it to *Aphasia* in a patch.

Sl4y barely registered the conversation, so focused he had been on his own situation. *I should run,* he thought. Except the Scholar could root him in place from mid-range. *I can't run, I can't pre-cast a dispel, I can't cleanse it with elixirs, I can interrupt him maybe once but not twice. I can't cast Mindflayer in this build.* He looked around his screen in desperation for anything that would save him from the upcoming Petrification, but found nothing in his bars or spells. He even opened the bags to see if he had anyth-

A Lightning Bolt scroll, rank 3.

An idea had formed in his head. It was stupid. He had to time it perfectly, and there would be only one shot at it. He dragged the scroll to an easily clickable slot.

He stepped forward, looked around the battlefield for any enemy Mage with a very distinct after-image graphical effect on them. He found one, and put his mouse pointer over him. When AdFontes came at him and in the very moment Sl4y saw a cast bar over his adversary, he clicked the Mage and then followed as soon as his hand allowed with right-clicking the scroll on the bar, thankfully not misclicking it. The Lightning Bolt immediately went off, reflected from the Mage under the effect of Spell Reflect, and hit Sl4y back for trivial damage just after Petrification sank in, immediately canceling the disabling effect.

Sl4y saw the Scholar pause for a second, not doing anything, and realised the other player was wondering what just happened.

Sl4y was laughing.

He was still grinning in the darkness of his room lit only by his monitors when the gong hit and the GvG event ended with the crystal pillar in Sal-born Keep still standing.

Sl4y sat in his Argentia spot, winding down from the stress of the last few minutes and inwardly celebrating the trick he had pulled off. He wondered if anyone saw him be *so cool. Maybe Slam1go recorded it by accident, somewhere in the background?*

Sapphire came over and sat next to him.

[21:00] Sapphire: sheesh that was something

[21:00] Sapphire: afk

And just like that, she was gone for what will probably be several hours.

As was typical for Havoc, the post-guild-op conversation moved to Guild chat so everyone could join. After all, not every guild member attended GvG.

[21:00] **[Guild]** Pvro: yo that was fucking awesome:DD

[21:00] **[Guild]** 415: ez

[21:00] **[Guild]** Doublehead: I was down to 30 bullets lol

[21:00] **[Guild]** Prast: didnt even break a sweat

[21:00] **[Guild]** Doomcaster:))

[21:00] **[Guild]** Doomcaster: ty gn

[21:00] **[Guild]** Xyrolol: gg wp

[21:00] **[Guild]** Pvro: SIGN UP FOR NEXT ONE

[21:00] **[Guild]** Arastina: GG, I will be off next week

[21:00] [Whisper] AdFontes: that was a pretty cool trick

Sl4y barely noticed the private message among the guild chat rolling up in the chatbox.

[21:00] **[Guild]** Belixner: the gong saved me and Intervene from Proskill-ver lol

[21:00] **[Guild]** Intervene: truth

[21:00] **[Guild]** Intervene: that man is fucking insane, when will they nerf him

[21:00] [To: AdFontes]: ty:D

[21:00] [Whisper] AdFontes: too bad nobody will ever know :)))

[21:00] [To: AdFontes]: :(

[21:00] [To: AdFontes]: mean

[21:00] **[Guild]** -Zoe-: much better than thursday at least

[21:00] **[Guild]** Ma_Ris: what happened on thursday?

[21:00] **[Guild]** slowah: oh dang I missed GvG?

[21:00] **[Guild]** Sl4y: yes xD

[21:00] **[Guild]** slowah: fuck me I thought it was 20 my time again ><

[21:00] **[Guild]** Pvro: lmao

[21:00] **[Guild]** -Zoe-: @Mama nothing, we sat on our asses for 1 hour and nobody came

[21:00] **[Guild]** Raphanti: speak for yourself Z :>

[21:00] **[Guild]** Ma_Ris: oh ok

[21:00] **[Guild]** Pvro: hey at least it was cheap

[21:00] **[Guild]** Kaitzuuu: that's what he said.

[21:00] **[Guild]** Kaitzuuu: no really, Azarus said that!

[21:00] **[Guild]** Pvro: which reminds me, today we lost a recall, three gates and a ton of alchemy. So, no recall for next war

[21:01] **[Guild]** Pvro: btw return unused drinks to bank, I'll sort it later (i.e. Sl4y will)

[21:01] **[Guild]** Pvro: and start donating stuff for next week

[21:01] **[Guild]** Pvro: so yeah, Slam1go this heroic victory better be worth it and use it well:D

[21:01] **[Guild]** Slam1go: bruh

[21:01] **[Guild]** Slam1go: I started shitposting minutes before the gongXD

[21:01] **[Guild]** Sl4y: now there's a man dedicated to his job:D

[21:02] **[Guild]** Vizovia: um, I'm very sorry for the wrong warp T_T

[21:02] **[Guild]** Vizovia: everything was happening so fast

[21:02] **[Guild]** -Zoe-: don't worry about it

[21:02] **[Guild]** Vizovia: I made Sl4y late for the gate

[21:02] **[Guild]** Sl4y: it's fine

[21:02] **[Guild]** Slam1go-: yes, it's fine, he shouldn't have died like a tool in the first place XD

[21:02] **[Guild]** slowah: true!

[21:02] **[Guild]** Sl4y: HEY :[

[21:02] **[Guild]** Sl4y: you weren't even there slowah you fucker!

[21:02] **[Guild]** Prast: we didn't need sl4y anyway :-)

[21:02] **[Guild]** -Zoe-: did he yell at you?

[21:02] **[Guild]** Sl4y: only a little!

[21:02] **[Guild]** Vizovia: he did!:p

[21:02] **[Guild]** Slam1go: wow sl4y

[21:02] **[Guild]** Slam1go: didn't I tell you to stop abusing poor rookies? they have feelings you know

[21:02] **[Guild]** Sl4y: WTF you're the one to talk

[21:02] **[Guild]** Sl4y: fuck you guys:D

[Thread: GvG, Sunday 12 Apr]
[Posted by: Slam1go, 14 Apr 2015, 20:58:02]
Good game (˘ ³˘) Congratulations to Execute for almost winning once again! I will never forget the moment when nothing happened ¯_(ツ)_/¯ Maybe try to come back with three legendaries next time?

Also how was Nordheimburg this evening?

[Posted by: Proskillver, 14 Apr 2015, 21:04:04]
Indeed. The excellence that Havoc demonstrated by using basic game mechanics was too much for us. So inspiring!

[Posted by: Oioioibruv, 14 Apr 2015, 21:05:33]
Something needs to be done about Bulwark-ATR alliance. They've been bunkered in Nordheim for three weeks straight now with 120 people defending. this can't be good for the game or fun for anyone to just sit on an objective and make it impossible for other guilds to challenge?

also lmao @ Slam1go shitposting while the game was still on, what a chad :D

[Posted by: DuckIRL, 14 Apr 2015, 21:06:19]
@up Looks OK to me ┬┬┴ ⌐ﾛ°)

[Posted by: CassNL, 14 Apr 2015, 21:07:59]
Balance aside it's amazing Bulwark & ATR manage to hold those numbers for several weeks, given that they must be bored out of their fucking minds kek. I mean, how do they convince people to log in and sit on a spot for an hour? It can't be fun, even if it's "winning".

I say let them rot there until their numbers start to drop and the game balances itself as always.

[Posted by: Stoencold, 14 Apr 2015, 21:09:36]
Cass must be right. After all, Execute are experts in "winning" (⌐ﾗ°)

* * *

'GZ Intervene. Next: Nucia's Silver Locket. That's a… a necklace with intellect and CDR. My favourite flavor. X up in the chat for mainspec, Z for offspec,' Sl4y spoke to his microphone.

Two Xs went up immediately.

[21:42] **[Raid]** Ò_Ó: x

[21:42] **[Raid]** Doomcaster: ч

[21:42] **[Raid]** Doomcaster: sry)

[21:42] **[Raid]** Doomcaster: x

Sl4y gave it another few moments to allow slower members to x up, noting down the previous loot winner in an online spreadsheet. Happy chats continued all around. Nucia was a profitable boss, but not the one they came to Azure Halls for. Better loot and harder fights awaited them down below, provided another group had not already cleared it. Chances were good – if Nucia was up, then probably so was Master Tryfon. People don't skip her on the way down. Nevertheless, he cut into the voice comms.

'Check-check, Gaav, can you go ahead and scout for Tryfon?'

[21:43] **[Raid]** Gaav: k

'Thanks.'

Gaav could be trusted to sneak past hostile mobs, stay unseen by any party already there, and live to report on it back to the group. And to delete their healer or something to wipe them in the right moment while he's there. Meanwhile, nobody else seemed to want the item, so now it was to decide which of the two guys gets it.

Sl4y opened his inventory and checked the item's properties. Yep, that's a good caster necklace, he thought. He scrolled up the chat to find who it was again that X'ed up for it. Ò_Ó and Doomcaster, Mage and Warlock. Both good dudes, both with enough credit to claim it. He inspected them both to see their current slot. It was an upgrade for both of them, but only minor. The ongoing conversations on voice chat were a little distracting, making the decision harder to make. He looked at the raid frames to see again who was in the group. His eyes stopped on another Mage who did not speak up, and a solution came to him. *Here's a person too shy to speak up for herself.*

'Vizovia,' Sl4y addressed her. 'Don't you need it?'

[21:44] **[Raid]** Vizovia: yes

'Uh, yes you do, or yes you don't?'

[21:44] **[Raid]** Vizovia: I need it ^^

'So you have it, trade me.'

[21:44] **[Raid]** Vizovia: Thanks!!! :D

'Oi, grats!' said Ò_Ó.

Ò_Ó, or Eyes, seemed genuinely happy with the outcome even if he lost, Sl4y remarked. Eyes was Havoc's top Mage, and Vizovia was their newest recruit, also a Mage. *Hopefully the two will find an understanding or some kind of a master-student relationship. It'll also reinforce her participation, the neck is a massive upgrade for her after all.*

'OK, we move down. Intervene main tank now, Agnelei offtank. Gaav, is Tryfon up?' asked Sl4y.

[21:45] **[Raid]** Gaav: yes

[21:45] **[Raid]** Gaav: nobody here

The raid followed the path through the corridor maze of Azure Halls, killing trash mobs when they aggroed. The loot was unprofitable so no one went out of their way to tag more crazed partisans. The distance was not long if one knew the way to go, so before long they reached the Courtyard and found Gaav waiting for them on top of two player skeletons.

'You said nobody is here.'

[21:59] **[Raid]** Gaav: not anymore:)

'Right. Five minutes' break, then I explain the tactics. Make it six. Be back five past ten, we need to be quick.'

[21:59] **[Raid]** 415: in general, where is Arastina, Pjj, Dereky, and the others?

[21:59] **[Raid]** 415: or Prast

[21:59] **[Raid]** 415: our damage is too low

[21:59] **[Raid]** 415: and can you 2-healer it? maybe I will go respec

'Uuuh, Four-Fifteen, I don't know. Dereky, Beli, and… Zoe? were signed up yesterday when I looked, but unsigned later,' Sl4y explained. 'Don't respec. We'll manage.'

Sl4y spoke with confidence, but he was not feeling as confident as he sounded and he knew the 415, ever the cynic, would not buy it. Sl4y had been an officer only for a short time now and it did not buy him any particular respect among people who played with him for over a year now. Presently he also led a guild boss hunting raid in absence of Pvro who was supposed to be doing it, or, in the case of his absence, Slam1go was to take over. But it fell to Sl4y, so he handled it without preparation but the raid signup trends were worrying. That was only the second raid without the Greeks involved, but they have been a rare sight for weeks now. Pretty much from the moment Trillex retired, in fact. He resolved to ask Pvro to talk to them.

So far it went fine – after all Sl4y has been playing the game for ages – but he felt, no, he *knew* commanding the group was biting into his own performance as a healer, and by extension, his overall enjoyment. But someone had to do it.

The break time was over, and Sl4y performed a quick ready-check. Everyone except Doomcaster was back, but he already knew the fight well enough.

'OK, is anyone new here? Be honest, it's important.'

[22:06] **[Raid]** Vizovia: me

'I've been here but - NOT NOW - sorryboutthat, no never killed it,' said Faystus.

'Is it the one with dancing back and forth? I need a reminder,' admitted Eightblades. He was a returning player, who has been away from it for about two years, but knew his basics well.

Three out of fifteen is not bad, thought Sl4y. He was glad that almost everyone in his group was experienced with Tryfon. He rated his leadership qualities rather low, nowhere near the old masters he looked up to when he was a teenager himself. But with people who know their job well there is less to worry about. Fortunately, what he was unable to improvise he could prepare ahead of time.

It may have seemed to be a waste of precious time to spend several minutes explaining the strategy to kill a boss when only a fifth of the group needs it, while the others have to wait, but for a boss such as Tryfon there was no way around it. They stood in a corridor leading outside to Master Tryfon's training grounds, run by the armsmaster of the cult dwelling in Azure Halls. The place was reminiscent of a castle courtyard, but adapted into an arena. The cobbled floor in the middle was large enough for dozens of men to practise cuts and thrusts without hurting others, and rows of benches were arranged outside around it. There was only a single way in – the corridor they stood in – and one exit deeper into the dungeon, that would only open on Tryfon's death. Tryfon himself was an imposing giant of a man, fully a head taller than the tallest player in the group, Intervene, and was dressed in beige linen pants that flowed around his legs with every move, barefoot, and bare-chested. He walked along his programmed route, from a training dummy to another, demonstrating his oversized sword slashes to the dozens of weaker NPCs gathered around him.

'OK, so listen. It's a single-target fight. The fight is not complicated, but you must not forget to move while also doing your absolutely best DPS. It is not very long either, but you must pay attention at all times. First we quickly kill the trash, let Agne tank it first. Then we split into two groups, number one starts in front, number two starts back. I've already sorted us during the break, check the raid window for your number. Tryfon will cleave the nearest seven players for a percentage of your max HP every twenty to thirty seconds, starting from twenty-five percent. Each following cleave hits harder, and leaves a flat damage bleeding dot. So we will alternate soaking it. First group gets hit, moves back, second group steps in, repeat. What follows is that we all stand pretty close to him and make only small steps. Simple as that, just make sure you don't mix with the other group. Tanks will move in and out too, but Intervene and Agnelei know it. Melees obviously too. Ihealformoney and me are the group anchors, follow us. If we don't kill him fast enough, he will bleed us to death. Use your foods, elixirs, scrolls etc. All in on damage.'

[22:07] **[Raid]** Doomcaster: back

'Can we move away from the cleave and not get hit?' asked Faystus.

'You can outrange it, but someone else will get hit twice because we all stand close,' answered Ò_Ó.

[22:07] **[Raid]** 415: but if you dodge as assassin then it counts as hit for 0 dmg

'Um,' began the other healer, Ihealformoney, a Paladin. 'The backpacks will not live to the 10th cleave.' Referring to party members below average level or undergeared as "backpacks" was Havoc's meme.

'Yes. Lowest HP is Vizovia, Blinky, and Eightblades, but Eightblades can dodge it sometimes. Use your active dodging skill every third cleave, but not on first. I will bubble Blinky because he's in my group, you put Protection on Zovia.' Sl4y explained. Eightblades could dodge all attacks for a few seconds with cooldown of thirty seconds and had to time it right to be targeted by the cleave, but not be hit. With luck, his passive dodge can also prevent being hit. Protection was a Paladin ability that shared the caster's DEF statistic with a friendly target. It wouldn't work on the cleave, but it worked on bleeds for some reason.

'Aaaaaalso, Agne, your Fortification Aura is off, … ok, thanks.'

'I know. Suppression Aura was better in the corridors.' When Agnelei spoke, everyone listened. His voice as deep as an ocean rumbled in voicechat, oozing confidence and manhood. The guild legend had it that whenever Agnelei spoke, all men who heard it grew a millimeter of facial hair instantly. It was even better considering Agnelei played a slim, blond-haired female Paladin. 'That only gives him more,' -Zoe- had said once, but did not specify what.

'Are we ready to go, then?' asked Intervene.

'...choo!' interrupted a muffled sneeze from Faystus, not for the first time that evening 'Sorry.'

'...nnnno. Four-Fifteen was right. We need more damage. We lack in numbers, gear, and individual skill here and there. Let's try to make it up with teamplay. Eyes and Vizovia, you will throw your Thaumic Acceleration on Four-Fifteen. His single-target is best. How long does it last, and what's the CD?'

'Fifteen seconds duration, two-min CD,' offered Ò_Ó after a moment.

'So we have one, maybe two rounds per fight. Four-Fifteen, how long do you ramp up?'

[22:09] **[Raid]** 415: 18 sec ish

[22:09] **[Raid]** 415: if nobody fucks up

'OK. When trash is dead, Ò_Ó counts to twenty and gives his buff to Four-Fifteen. Zovia, you cast it on Four-Fifteen after third cleave, OK?'

[22:09] **[Raid]** Vizovia: I'll try

'Intervene will reduce some armour on Tryfon after first cleave. Melees and Blinky, keep your CDs until then. Gaav will also do Lethal Intent. All right, I'm getting tired of talking: kill trash, form two groups, rotate in and back out every cleave. OK, that's enough, let's do it. Agne, countdown from fifteen please,' declared Sl4y finally. He hoped all this talk didn't take too long. For one reason, the seasoned raiders hated delays, for another, the newbies tend to forget most of the theory after hearing it. Therefore, shorter is usually better.

PowerOverwhelming heard the strat planning, but he listened for different things than his less experienced buddy Eightblades. He knew the fight. He was here many times so he needed no explanation. What he was really interested in was how Sl4y managed the raid group. As a guild member he had the regular level respect for the Officer, but for a Fighter player who was around during AltAr's first edition, there was much more for him to look up to.

[22:07] **[Friend]** Eightblades: so what do you think

[22:07] **[Friend]** Eightblades: last I was here, we needed at least 24 people to kill tryfon

[22:07] **[To: Eightblades]**: average gear got better since then

[22:07] **[Friend]** Eightblades: 415 seems not optimistic

[22:07] **[To: Eightblades]**: he's always like that

[22:07] **[To: Eightblades]**: but yes, this is going to be hard

[22:07] **[Friend]** Eightblades: btw, what is sl4y wearing? I've never seen that thing

[22:08] **[To: Eightblades]**: it's a unique item for server

[22:08] **[To: Eightblades]**: ie nobody else can have it and yes its fucking rad

[22:08] **[Friend]** Eightblades: fkn cool

[22:08] **[Friend]** Eightblades: dude has been around

'Yes-sir. Attention raiders, this is your offtank speaking. Pull your pants up and follow my lead in fifteen.'

[22:08] **[To: Eightblades]**: I'll tell you about it after the raid

'Three. Two. One. Pulling.'

Being an experienced tank, Agnelei started moving before he finished counting down, knowing how trigger-happy damage dealers, especially those playing a ranged class, can be. It was fairly normal for them to throw their first attacks when the tank says "one" rather than waiting another two or three seconds for the tank to build aggro.

[22:08] Master Tryfon says: Infidel filth? In my domain?! Slay them all!

The Paladin bolted into the mass of supplicants attending Master Tryfon, a heater shield in one hand and a shestoper, a six-feather sceptre-mace, in another. First he activated Contempt, reducing incoming physical damage. Then he blasted them all with Smite to build some aggro on every target near him, and triggered Compulsion to taunt all targets in a radius around him. In the meantime the steel-bound armoured frame of Intervene charged Tryfon himself, slamming his massive tower shield into the boss, then pulled him away from the Paladin to prevent an accidental taunt from Agnelei on the primary target. This arrangement was basic tanking knowledge and was well practised between the two of them, playing to the general strengths of their classes. Warrior tanks excelled at mitigating physical damage from individual targets, while Paladins were best at handling groups of enemies. They could also kite better, since some of their spells were magic-based and thus had some range, allowing the Paladin to maintain threat from distance. One other class that could tank was the Scholar, which had the tools to manage powerful enemy magic users better than anyone, though their aggro holding capability had to be reinforced by other classes. The above rules were flexible, and much depended on skill tree choices and equipment.

PowerOverwhelming followed the plan, and made sure to resist the temptation to blow his cooldowns on the pack of mobs attending the boss. A desire shared by all damage dealers, whether they admit it or not, was to see themselves produce the highest damage numbers possible. Packs of mobs that don't die too easily are the perfect opportunity. Nevertheless, PowerOverwhelming was beyond such selfish behaviour. He was, as he considered himself, one of the old guard. He was there when ARIS was launched, and he was there when

AltAr started, over seven years ago. The legendary past, the new frontier, the exploration of the unknown – he remembered it with excitement he rarely felt these days. He was seventeen at the time, and the game played a huge part in shaping him. He played it for three years or so until the server was wiped clean and restarted, thus ending AltAr's so-called First Edition. On that day, PowerOverwhelming decided to focus on his education instead. But he came back ten months ago, and when he met Eightblades at work – they were both junior airline maintenance engineers – he brought in the older colleague to AltAr. As it turned out, Eightblades had tried the game before the purge and knew the basics.

So having cleared the trash they were now positioning themselves behind the boss as Intervene tanked him near the far wall of the arena positioning him to be hit by ranged players on his right side.

'Intervene, can you call out the cleaves?' said Sl4y.

'Aye. First cleave in… six seconds.'

'Group one melees, stack on your healer now.'

'Cleave!'

A weapon swipe by Master Tryfon afflicted nearest raiders with a respectable amount of damage and a bleeding effect, then he returned to attacking Intervene with ferocious melee attacks. Were he hot tanked, he would two-shot everyone in the group and the fight would be very quick. PowerOverwhelming in group two dutifully jumped back from Tryfon to stack with his group just a few steps away. His HP dropped to seventy-five percent from just one attack, and the bleeding debuff ticked away further chonks of his life bar.

'Move! Group one and two, switch positions, melees back on target, now BURST!' called out the Officer of Havoc.

PowerOverwhelming had no special roles during this fight, he could just focus on waltzing in and out, and executing his ability rotations properly. *Palm Push, Crushing Blow, Wind-up that activates on next autoattack, followed by three autos, Breathing Techni– cancel that, run! Observe the boss. The damned cleaving strike has a distinct animation that signals the timing.* PowerOverwhelming cast Harden Body when he saw the clue he was waiting for. This reduced his incoming damage by fifty percent for six seconds and should save some healer mana. *Okay, now go back.* The inflicted damage numbers flowed nicely on his screen, especially the critical strikes that happened to land on Crushing Blows. One hit for nine thousand which was pretty cool, although he suspected the likes of Doomcasater probably saw numbers five times as high when his Cataclysmic Bolt landed. He thought back again to the times when builds and optimal rotations were not as available online as they were at present. To the times when people discovered builds themselves, and from time to time, someone struck gold.

Someone such as Sl4y himself. The guy who authored the Slayer build for Fighters, a modified version of which PowerOverwhelming was playing that evening.

A lapse in his attention broke his routine, and he had to start from the beginning and suffer a damage output loss. He sighed with irritation, and shook off the distraction, focusing on his play again.

The fight was now going for three minutes and everyone was still alive. He was never good at assessing the group's performance as a whole. His overall awareness of the raid simply sucked. He could not imagine himself calling the shots during guild ops. But everyone was still alive, which was always a good sign legible even to him.

'Three, two, one.' Intervene kept calling.

'Swap positions, swap swap swap! Move!'

[22:11] **[Raid]** Faystus died.

[22:11] Master Tryfon says: Hah!I have target dummies tougher than you!

'Oops,' Faystus said. 'Sorry.'

'Money, pick him up!' Sl4y called out immediately.

The call came when Ihealformoney was casting a long-cast raid-wide heal, but he ceased and began the ten-second cast of Redemption on the flattened Fighter. The Paladin had to remain stationary for the duration of both of those casts, as was the case with every casted spell in the game, but Ihealformoney could be trusted to cancel casting and move when needed. Sl4y sacrificed his instant-cast Desperate Prayer that he had been saving for later in the fight to top up the raid's health over the next six seconds. Ihealformoney managed to finish casting Redemption and a beam of light lifted Faystus back to his legs. Unfortunately, Intervene warned a moment before:

'...two, one!'

[22:11] **[Raid]** Faystus died.

'Thank- oh, what?'

'Fuuuck, that was unfair,' complained Sl4y. 'He cast two Cleaves with minimum time gap. Bad RNG.'

There was no time to explain what happened, but the mistake was obvious to PowerOverwhelming once it happened. In-combat resurrection spells bring back a player at twenty percent of their maximum health, while at this moment in the fight, Tryfon hits everyone in range for sixty-five percent of their maximum health *and* still applies the bleeding damage-over-time effect. The mistake was not waiting for the next Cleave and casting Redemption after it, so that the victim could be healed up before the next slash.

'My bad, hold on. We need you alive.' Sl4y probably felt like an idiot. PowerOverwhelming could imagine him shaking his head to his monitor. Now the raid leader had to fix his own mistake as well as Faystus' initial one. Quantity of Resurrection spells in-combat was limited, and are usually best left for the most valuable members of the group, so the decision was a difficult one. Due to Tryfon's mechanics, every living raid member mattered even if only as a damage soaker. Sl4y apparently chose to resurrect the fallen guild member immediately. His Resurrection was a faster cast than Ihealmoney's

Redemption, but also more costly due to Sl4y's talent choices that preferred casting speed over efficiency or power, so mana was the price to pay.

Seconds later Faystus was back in the fight, shielded against some damage by Sl4y for good measure. That little slip-up cost them no more than fifteen seconds' worth of his damage, three precious cooldowns, and a bit of extra mana.

The fight now was in the crucial moment, the repetitive swipes from Tryfon now hit for seventy percent of half the raid's health every twenty to thirty seconds. They couldn't go for much longer, and the boss was still at least sixty seconds away from death.

A hard decision came from Sl4y.

'Everyone, disengage, back to the corridor! This is a failed attempt, we will try again. Reset him. Just run awa–'

'Check, check! Blinky here. Slay, we have a problem!' interrupted someone's voice.

'What is it?'

'I left my alt lying dead in the corridors we came from. I just noticed a bunch of people passing by.'

'**Who are they?**' asked Agnelei.

'Didn't see.'

'I said run!' Sl4y urged everyone.

'Well, fuck.'

'You gotta be shitting me,' said Intervene.

In ARIS, almost every dungeon and raid was open-world, meaning any group could enter at any time and ruin someone else's day if they chose to. A part of the UI was the safety control switch, which allowed players to choose if their damage should affect only monsters or both monsters and players not in the user's party. The switch, however, did not protect from PvP one way or another.

The raiders from Havoc could see the other player group just moments later. There was no doubt, they came for Tryfon with their safeties off, and they stood between Tryfon murdering Havoc and their only route of escape.

The raid fell apart. In the absence of a clear order one way or the other, some tried to desperately finish Tryfon to take the kill credit and the loot, while others were moving to face the enemy raid. PowerOverwhelming was among the latter group. He saw the rival raid group form up in Havoc's exit path, and knowing what end awaited them, PowerOverwhelming switched off his safety locks, picked a target – some Warlock that happened to be standing relatively close – and threw his combo finishing move that he had been building for Tryfon for over eleven thousand damage. It was not enough, and the Warlock still stood. The valiant Fighter was targeted by several enemy players and destroyed where he stood. His screen turned gray, and a window popped up on the top of his screen with a message and two buttons.

You died. [return to town] [close window]

He sighed with resignation and clicked the first option knowing the raid would surely be over at this point, but just before his vision faded out, something with a friendly health above it bar moved over his corpse. It uncloaked in front of the Warlock PowerOverwhelming had softened and it used Assassination, fully utilizing their class' bonus damage on low-health targets and the few raid buffs that were still on him. The Warlock fell to the ground, and to add insult to the injury, his murderer Gaav evaded death by disappearing into thin air before Warlock's friends could react.

'Back in my day, noone dared to attack us like that,' mused Sl4y. It was really an awful way to end an evening's session with the guild. Not only did they put their hearts and time into a strong boss, but also burned some potions, elixirs, and food consumables to maximise their chances. All this only to deliver a nearly dead boss to another guild that claimed it over Havoc's dead bodies.

'BaCk iN mY dAy.'

'HEY who the fuck said that?' asked Sl4y, not without amusement in his own tone. 'Faystus, you little prick?'

'What? No! I would never! I'm pretty sure it was Four-Fifteen,' said Faystus with as much seriousness as he could muster.

[22:31] **[Raid]** 415: wat :o

'No, I don't think he managed to pull out the light bulb from his mouth yet,' said Ò_Ó.

'Have some respect, Faystus,' said PowerOverwhelming.

'Thank yo-' began Sl4y.

'...for the old man,' Power finished.

'Oh fuck you both,' laughed Sl4y. 'OK, we're calling it a day. Thanks everyone for coming, sign up for GvG on Sunday.'

People started saying their goodbyes and goodnights to the sound of voice chat disconnection pings accompanied by raid leave notifications from the game.

[22:32] **[Raid]** Vizovia: thank you again^^

[22:32] **[Raid]** Vizovia: sorry for not doing high dps

[22:32] **[Raid]** Ò_Ó: you did all right

[22:32] **[Raid]** 415: meh

[22:32] **[Raid]** Doomcaster: o/

[22:32] **[Raid]** Blinky: it wasn't so bad, we killed a few bosses today

[22:32] **[Raid]** Intervene: we'll fook them up tomorrow for that lol

Sl4y didn't have a problem with Vizovia. The girl had a tendency to apologise for all kinds of things, and would do well to build some confidence. As for 415, he must have been disappointed. He's been hunting Tryfon for weeks hoping for the caster gloves to drop. That night they didn't even manage to kill it. Sl4y felt bad for the guildmate; he might have been a pain to deal with sometimes, but he was resourceful and always came prepared. People like him are the kind to leave guild early when things start to go bad. Anyway, he was tired and wanted to sleep, but first he had to deposit some raid loot in the guild bank.

From the town's respawn point by the monument of some legendary knight of ancient past, he mounted up and made his way through streets of ashen cobble, beneath arches and overpassing pedestrian bridges, between rows of merchant houses of stone and wood walls painted white and clay roof tiles in various shades of red and amber. He passed dozens of players going about their business as he was, and went by a large plaza used by players as a vending area. The bank was opposite it, and hard to miss, being one of the town's largest buildings. Falling from its roof took away over a half of a player's health. He knew it, he did it all the time.

He came in mounted through the bank's front door that mercifully was large enough and open ajar at all times, knowing the steed would disappear inside – the game forbade mounting up inside buildings so it forcibly dismounted players at the door. It was a Friday evening. Most guilds ended their raids around this time, so the bank chamber was full of people accessing their stocks or depositing new loot. Trade and crafting went on all over the place. Even the cesspool of spam that was Trade Chat actually deserved its name even if for a while. He interacted with the vault door, which could be a tough task with this many people around it, but Sl4y knew camera tricks that solved this problem easily.

Another thing clouded his thoughts. He didn't say it, but he actually felt what Vizovia expressed. He knew Tryfon would go better if his own performance had been better. He made a bad call with Faystus, and he knew he had been overhealing which burned too much of his mana. If it wasn't for the wipe, courtesy of You Never Wipe Alone guild, they would try the encounter again, but it probably would not succeed anyway. Also, he should have woven more damage spells between the heals. Underestimating the difference that weak but consistent damage spells added by healers could make was a rookie mistake. Just ask any player how many times they wiped on a boss with just 1-2% HP remaining.

[22:34] **[Guild]** Eightblades: when is next boss run?

[22:35] **[Guild]** Eightblades: yo, anyone?

[22:35] **[Guild]** Ihealformoney: ^

[22:35] **[Guild]** Sl4y: any time you want, if you start it:)

[22:35] **[Guild]** Sl4y: I'm busy tomorrow, maybe Mr. Agnelei will host something if you ask him nicely? :>

[22:35] **[Guild]** Agnelei: hmm, maybe

[22:35] **[Guild]** Ò_Ó: @Faystus, why the fuck do you still use voice activation. Learn to fucking push-to-talk already

[22:35] **[Guild]** Sl4y: btw

[22:35] **[Guild]** Sl4y: we're still 400 logs and 150 iron short for GvG, and that's just the basics. Don't let poor Azarus do everything himself

[22:35] **[Guild]** Sl4y: whoever donates gets a kiss from Slam1go

[22:35] **[Guild]** Sl4y: k, I'm out

[22:35] **[Guild]** Azarus: hey, wtf?

[22:35] **[Guild]** Azarus: I desire Slam1go's lips too

[22:36] **[Guild]** Kaitzuuu: you what?

[22:36] **[Guild]** Azarus: :-)

[22:36] **[Guild]** Azarus: dont be mad babe :*

[22:36] **[Guild]** Kaitzuuu: I'm not mad

[22:37] **[Guild]** Agnelei: uh-oh :D

Vizovia had fun.

She was only now winding down from the excitement of her first challenging raid ever, although she knew it was one of the less difficult ones in general. It was strange, stressful, but fun. She only played ARIS for a little over a year, and seriously for half of that, but groups larger than ten people were new to her. Even those ten-player groups were leveling parties. But this? This was cool. It was worth losing some sleep over it. Her parents were already sleeping and she did not want to wake them, so she could not speak on voice chat with her new guild. That, and also because she was extremely shy and was scared to speak to fourteen stranger men she never met.

She even got a new piece of equipment. Epic quality, her first. That one thing added extra eighteen Intelligence (and so extra damage and mana), three hundred health points, and one percent increase casting speed. She took a screenshot of her equipment tab to remember it by. She actually had saved several screenshots that evening. The first kill in Azure Halls, the second and the third, the slightly terrifying torture chamber and dungeons, the Tryfon planning, the fancy high-level gear of game veterans and their fancy cosmetics, pets, mounts; and the death at the hands of You Never Wipe Alone, which was also a cool experience in its own way. She did not think this kind of thing happens to guilds such as Havoc.

Back in the day, when she told her friends she would apply to Havoc without knowing anyone inside it, they told her she was naive. When she told them she was accepted, they thought she was joking. Then, two months ago, they saw her new guild tag over her character's head.

'Maybe they won't bully you.'

'#fucksl4y.'

'You'll be back soon.'

'Good luck, you will need it :)'

'Yo that's pretty cool :D you gonna go GvG?'

'Why them? So many cooler guilds out there.'

They said such things, but so far she has not been bullied, and that supposedly meanest person Sl4y gave her the Locket while two other members raised their hands for it and she did not. One of them even being the guy with a weird nickname who whispered her some tips for each fight. *Do they resent me for taking that item*, she wondered? Also, what was up with that guild's weird reputation, where did that come from?

But then she remembered reading a very spicy and strongly-worded guild chat about best attributes for Scholars between Lonecow, Slam1go, and 415, and that at least partially answered her last question, but still not wholly.

She felt bad about her level being only eighty-five out of the maximum hundred. It allowed her to join and enter the endgame raids, but for the actual challenges, she would not be picked. Even in the lower tier of raids, such as Azure Halls, she felt carried like a backpack.

Her buttocks hurt, her hair was a mess, she hadn't showered since coming home, and she felt the call of her bed. She had school to attend in the morning. She groaned and signed out.

* * *

[22:59] **[Friend]** Eightblades: you were going to tell me smth

[22:59] **[To: Eightblades]**: yeah

[22:59] **[To: Eightblades]**: join me in channel e

[22:59] **[To: Eightblades]**: 3

[22:59] **[Friend]** Eightblades: k

'Yo,' Eightblades greeted his friend on guild's voice chat.

'Sup,' responded PowerOverwhelming. 'Where are you?'

'Lestota.'

'Come to Argentia, and accept my party invite.'

''kay.'

'Now come to my location,' said the Fighter player to Assassin. Being in the same party allowed players to precisely pinpoint each other's location on the map. 'This is Sl4y's favourite spot for idling.'

Eightblades travelled to Argentia and once there took left from the main north-south artery, went up a flight of stairs on the outside of a building, and found himself on a little elevated porch overlooking the street below. There was some outdoor furniture here, a locked door leading inside the NPC's house, the regular stone floor texture underneath, and a wooden fence preventing accidental fall down, although that would not stop players from leaping over it to the street below. Players can not spend precious seconds of their lives walking downstairs.

Sl4y was currently in the process of wasting precious seconds of his life on not doing anything at all, it would seem from the two players' perspective. Sitting around was, after all, an important part of an MMORPG game. He was wearing his Priest gear set, and now that PowerOverwhelming thought about it, Sl4y almost never changed appearance or put casual clothes on his character. And that was for a good reason.

Sitting on the floor with him was Sapphire, Havoc's only female Minstrel, who /waved a hello to the two guildmates, who spoke in the proximity chat, also called the "/s chat".

[23:01] Sapphire: visitors? (:

[23:01] Sl4y: what's up?

[23:01] PowerOverwhelming: hey Sapphire, nice scarf

[23:01] Eightblades: hey hey

[23:01] Sapphire: flatterer.

[23:01] PowerOverwhelming: can you unlock your eq inspect for a second?

He stood in front of the Priest, which was enough of an indication to know whose equipment he meant.

[23:01] Sl4y: ok

'Check out the costume slot, the cape's in it,' the Assassin heard. 'It has the *unique* tag and is signed by him. He can't trade it away, and a duplicate can't be obtained.'

'Yep, I see that,' Eightblades confirmed. Indeed, the item's name was *Sl4y's Devout Cape (Gilded)*.

[23:01] PowerOverwhelming: k

[23:01] PowerOverwhelming: I was about to tell this noob the story behind that drape you have

[23:02] Sl4y: don't mind me :p

'Let's stay and chat a little,' said PowerOverwhelming to Eightblades.

'Okay, but then we go arena. I have to make it to 1700 rating before reset.'

[23:02] Sapphire: oh

[23:02] Sapphire: I want to hear it too <:

[23:02] Sl4y: don't you know it yourself?

[23:02] Sl4y: you've been there xd

[23:02] Sapphire: not from him xD

[23:02] Sapphire: go on!

[23:02] PowerOverwhelming: :)

[23:02] PowerOverwhelming: so

[23:02] PowerOverwhelming: in 2007 was a PvP duel tournament event by GMs

[23:02] Sl4y: good times.

[23:02] PowerOverwhelming: Sl4y took first place, and his reward was a random costume box

[23:02] PowerOverwhelming: the cape dropped from the box obviously

[23:02] PowerOverwhelming: before the tourney admin sayd he would have the thing he got even after the server wipes, and he kept his word

[23:02] PowerOverwhelming: but so many people SO jealous lol (and me too though)

[23:02] PowerOverwhelming: eh, they don't do such cool events anymore :/

[23:02] Sapphire: vacation event is soon, sometimes its good

[23:02] Eightblades: I see you are well informed bro

[23:02] PowerOverwhelming: I was there

[23:02] PowerOverwhelming: I lost to him in ro8 :D

[23:02] Sapphire: xD

Sl4y humbly didn't comment, but was smiling to his memory unbeknownst to anyone.

[23:03] PowerOverwhelming: so anyway

[23:03] PowerOverwhelming: it wasn't even close, he wiped the floor with me

[23:03] PowerOverwhelming: and I thought I was good back then

[23:03] Sl4y: you did allright :)

[23:03] PowerOverwhelming: nah

[23:03] PowerOverwhelming: he won that tournament, and got this cosmetic from the box, then admins removed it from loot table

[23:03] PowerOverwhelming: so it cant drop again

[23:03] Sl4y: I felt so fucking amazing back then lol

[23:03] PowerOverwhelming: but, now get this

[23:03] PowerOverwhelming: the next day they nerfed him XD

[23:03] PowerOverwhelming: and I mean "nerfed him" not "nerfed fighter"

[23:03] Sl4y: fuck this

[23:03] Sl4y: I'm still kinda salty about -_-

[23:03] Sl4y: that was such BS

[23:03] Eightblades: wtf, how?

[23:03] Eightblades: and why :D

[23:03] PowerOverwhelming: back then there were no online guides for the game, builds, talent calculators, etc videos like we have now

[23:03] PowerOverwhelming: people discovered stuff ingame on their own

[23:03] PowerOverwhelming: and this madlad here, somehow invented gold

[23:03] PowerOverwhelming: I still don't know how you did it btw

[23:04] Sl4y: :-)

[23:04] PowerOverwhelming: basically, his Fighter could beat anyone in PvP

[23:04] PowerOverwhelming: something about a perfect amount of DEX and AGI and perfect timing allowed new ability combos

[23:04] PowerOverwhelming: it was both his knowledge and mechanics, so people couldn't just copy it

[23:04] PowerOverwhelming: as far as we know, only Sl4y ever pulled it off

[23:04] PowerOverwhelming: lots of people were mad and accused him of cheating, wanted him banned

[23:04] Sl4y: I still have the forum screenshots :-)

[23:04] PowerOverwhelming: the others, myself included, asked and begged him for his secrets

[23:04] PowerOverwhelming: but he told them all: "I figured it out my-self, so you do it too"

[23:04] PowerOverwhelming: and like that, the legend of "Slayer build" and the meme of "fuck Sl4y" was born :)

[23:04] Sapphire: so it wasn't just your charming personality?

[23:04] Sl4y: in a way, it was :D

[23:04] Eightblades: ok ok but what about the nerf

[23:04] PowerOverwhelming: people complained

[23:04] PowerOverwhelming: the day after the tournament they changed something on server to break the build, I don't remember what it was anymore

[23:05] PowerOverwhelming: they I mean the GMs

[23:05] PowerOverwhelming: it was years ago

[23:05] Sl4y: the ridiculous thing is that it was only changed on our server

[23:05] Sl4y: official servers never had a problem with it

Sl4y /sighed, Sapphire /laughed.

[23:05] PowerOverwhelming: but for a few months, he was a legend

[23:05] PowerOverwhelming: all the girls were his B) one even made it, eh?

[23:05] PowerOverwhelming: that's why this kid Faystus kinda pisses me off tbh, no respect for the OGs

[23:05] PowerOverwhelming: annoying little cunt overall

[23:05] Sl4y: well, we can't expect all people to know some ancient his-tory of an unofficial niche game server

[23:05] Sapphire: look at you, so humble now!

[23:05] Sapphire: believe me guys he did not talk like that in 2007 xD

* * *

Whitecliff Harbor was a starting town built into a dip in the otherwise unbroken chain of white cliffs. It lay on an island not far from the shores of the Insal Kingdom though within its sphere of influence, and its relevance was that of a ship-building capital of the continent. The tall ships launched here were not just a commodity; they were a trademark ensuring strong flow of currency to the shipyard operators. The geography worked to its both detriment and advantage; the port and the shipyards had to fight by chisel and hammer for every bit of additional room, but the cliffs the town was unimaginatively named after were an excellent defence against invaders, and the rocky elevations on its either side overlooking the port were a favourable location for a fortress. As if to further solidify the town's name, the white stone was the primary construction material for all kinds of buildings in the town giving it a picturesque aesthetic, while the array of cranes and warehouses down by the waterline testified to its industrial nature.

A new character spawned on a peer in front of a mighty sailing ship that was implied to have brought them here. The massive vessel served no other purpose than to sell an illusion, there wasn't even a way in for players to explore it. Here in the harbour the newcomers were greeted with tutorials and entry-level quests that led them around the town introducing key concepts, NPCs, and offering training in any secondary profession players required; and from here eventually made their way deeper into the continent. It is also here that the server's guilds fished for new members like seagulls for freshly hatched turtles on a beach. The competition was fierce enough that any new character spotted without a guild would have unwanted guild invitations dropped on them without a word beforehand.

This unwanted experience was taken seriously by server staff, and a solution was improvised. Nobody wanted to log in to a game for the first time and have their first sight be cascading windows they did not understand or ask for. Therefore, a workaround solution was to make all first-time loggers invisible and untargetable until they move. What was thought as only a band-aid solution turned out to be working well enough to never be touched again.

This level 1 girl that just emerged into the world of ARIS did not know about that mechanism or even notice it. As she loaded into the game, she turned around to set off straight for the gate out of town; she still remembered which direction it was towards it. But she had to pause after a few steps and she closed all pesky windows, opened settings, blocked incoming guild invitations. Some of the recruiters tried sending her copypasted invitation messages, but she paid them no mind.

She did not hate it. In fact Lyonni was pleased to find everything just as she remembered it and to find the good old AltAr server still existing, with a vibrant community on it no less.

* * *

'Okay, I'm back,' said Vizovia to her companions, ^_Miko_^ and Ma_Ris, in a private chatroom on Chatterbox as she sat back by her laptop in her room upstairs. Their characters sat by a table in Vir Estia. The three girls were talking in a password-protected voice channel. Were it a physical room in a guild's building, the sign on the door would read "girls only." Their current spot was by the town's main street, a place they chose often for their meetups.

While Argentia, the inland kingdom capital on the river Insalama, held the title for the most practical city to be in and thus players favoured it for their base of operations, Vir Estia was *the* harbour city of the game world, and housed the masters of many crafts, arts, and professions. It was like the Venice of ARIS built on solid ground rather than on a lagoon. It had its large population of players at all times, and it was particularly popular among role-players, but not the Hellesvyand kind of RPers.

'Finished cleaning?' asked Ma_Ris. ^_Miko_^ still seemed to be Away From Keyboard since her Assassin stared blankly into the distance. *She's been AFK a lot recently,* Vizovia remarked.

'Uhm, mom and dad went out so I'm free. Is Mimi still away?'

'Nice! I have you both all to myself today!' said Ma_Ris with genuine happiness in her voice. 'Yes, she must be really busy, but won't log out to keep us some sort of company. Such a sweet girl, isn't she?'

'Yes, yes. I suppose she's a good kid.'

'Aw, you're both kids to me,' Ma_Ris giggled.

'Are we doing anything together today?'

'I've arranged for another kid to come join us so you can make a friend.'

'Ha, ha.'

'He should be here in a moment.' Ma_Ris sounded completely serious.

'What? He?'

'Yup! I'll let him join our channel. Don't worry, he doesn't bite. In fact I think you two would make a cute couple!'

'Don't you think you should ask me or Miko about it first? This was supposed to be a girls' club!' Vizovia liked what she heard less and less with every moment.

'Miko said she's okay with that.'

'Really?' Vizovia sighed audibly. 'What are we going to be doing, then?'

'Oh I don't know yet.'

'So what did you tell him? And who is that person anyway?'

'I told him I have two fantastic girls here who would be happy to meet him, and they're both single!' At that, Vizovia's cheeks flushed red and she was glad to not be seen. She was about to open her mouth to speak in protest, when the Priestess continued. 'He's cute, shy, and naive just like you!'

'That sounds very… HEY!!'

Ma_Ris went into full belly laughter. 'Oh my… sides …I can't!' she was grasping for breath.

'Come on, it wasn't *that* funny…'

When Ma_Ris was able to talk again, she said: 'I'm sorry… I just love to tease you so much. I wish I could pinch your cheeks right now! Oof, my makeup is a mess, I should have washed it off after work…'

'I'll try to remember to never take anything you say seriously now.'

'You would take away so much joy from my life?'

'Sigh…' Vizovia vowed to herself to be less naive. Again. 'At least Miko didn't witness my embarrassment.'

'You're not mad at me, are you?' Ma_Ris asked.

'No… but I'll get back at you one day!'

'Oooh! I can't wait!'

'So anyway,' Vizovia wanted to change the subject as soon as possible. 'It was a good idea to start this channel.'

'Yes. Wait, you thought this was my idea? It was not.'

'No? Whose then?'

'Take a guess.'

'Um…' the Mage was at a loss, but the list of people could not be too long. She considered a few options.

'Sapphire?'

'No, but nice first guess.'

'Zoe or Belixner then?'

'No and no. They are very comfortable with the boys. For some time I thought Beli was one herself.'

'Whoa. Ok, then Trillex or Pvro…?' Vizovia was giving up.

'Nope!'

'Okay, who then?'

'Sl4y. Oh, speaking of which, he just logged in.'

'Him? Really?' asked Vizovia.

'Yes, really. Why is that surprising?'

'It's not something I would suspect him of.'

'What do you mean?' the older girl questioned.

'Just that I didn't think he thinks about us in general.' Vizovia shrugged. 'We never talked.'

'Ah. Sometimes I forget what kind of reputation he has. He's more chill than you think, certainly not scary. To me, anyway. Not after all the embarrassing stories Sapphire told me about him!' Vizovia could *hear* the *smug* in Ma_Ris' voice and imagined a wry grin on her friend's face. Her own face lit up.

'Ooh? Tell me something!'

'I can't.'

'Come on, please?'

'Nooo, sorry! I really can't. I promised Sapphire not to. She does not forgive easily.'

'Fine,' Vizovia capitulated. 'Does he know that you know?'

'Of course not! Are you crazy? After all, Sapphire promised him not to tell anyone.' Both women giggled.

Back when Vizovia joined the guild and had her first contact with Ma_Ris, she was taken aback by how that Priestess behaved. She was like an older sister to all the women in the Guild, even to Sapphire who was older than Ma_Ris. She even gave them all her private phone number, but wisely forbade sharing it further. She was always full of warmth and called all her friends "sweetheart" and "honey" from the very beginning. And as far as Vizovia could tell, all the men in the guild had a soft spot for her, from the top ranks to bottom, which made it even weirder given what everyone on the outside thought of core Havoc guys: try-hard, ruthless elitists. But she was everyone's beautiful ray of sunshine. Whatever she asked for she would get, but had modesty and integrity and rarely asked for anything, which only made her even more liked. *How did such a person end up here in the game and in Havoc of all places?* Vizovia wondered.

By now, Vizovia was accustomed to the affection Ma_Ris showed her so casually. She had plenty to spare for everyone. Ma_Ris was in her mid-twenties, Vizovia remembered, about five or six years older than herself. All she knew about the elder girl was that she worked at a bookstore in a mall.

Vizovia looked at her friend's elegant Priestess – *when did I start calling her a friend?* – and wondered what Ma_Ris was like in real life. Was she as motherly? As friendly and cheerful? What did she look like? Maybe Sapphire knew. Vizovia's own Mage was not much like her real body so she knew the real woman behind the Priestess sitting opposite her did not have to be as tall, especially when wearing those pearl and silver pumps that Vizovia would die for in real life. Maybe the real Ma_Ris was not as elegantly dressed regardless of the occasion (*Oh, I must know how she got that sunday hat!*). Maybe she would not slightly alter the shade of her blond hair from time to time.

Maybe she hated wearing sundresses. Maybe her cheeks did not always look so cheerfully pinchable. Maybe she was not really as curvy. *For real, she must have pushed the sliders to the limit.* Even Vizovia herself could not resist the urge to zoom in a little. *Surely it must have been affecting men around them, even if only as a game avatar, and even if they did not even know it. And then there's her voice too...ah.*

But ^_Miko_^ was nothing like Ma_Ris or Vizovia herself. Where Ma_Ris was the soul of every company, ^_Miko_^ was quite shy towards pretty much everyone and would not speak much; maybe it was because of her quiet, gentle voice, and in that at least she was similar to Vizovia. She was smart enough to have started speaking early and often to everyone soon after joining the crew, because otherwise all the boys would tease her for being shy and keep asking her to speak up which is how Vizovia ended up. Miko did not get overly friendly with people she just met. But at the same time, she joined every party, raid, or event she could, and did a good job there too. She was everywhere, and everyone invited her to everything. Or, at least she used to be everywhere. She seemed to be somewhat less active these last two weeks or so. Nevertheless, to Vizovia the most unique quality of the teenager lay elsewhere. While Vizovia or Ma_Ris thought of and talked about things such as the guild, the game, obtaining new pets or cosmetic items for their collections, or their real-life affairs, Miko thought and talked about obtaining new knives and poisons for her Assassin or how she changed her stat attributes to get a slight performance improvement. In that she was more like the shield-maiden Belixner than like any other female in the guild. In fact, that little devil gave both Vizovia and Ma_Ris tips on playing the game, never having played a Mage or Priest herself, and having played ARIS for a much shorter time. 'You should do fakecasting a useless spell to bait interrupts from people and mobs, noobs fall for it every time,' she once advised Vizovia. *Why did I not think about this myself? It was so obvious!*

'How do you do it?' Vizovia spoke the question just as it popped up in her head. 'How are you always so cheerful?'

'Am I?'

'I think you are.'

'How do you know?'

'That's the feeling I get from you.'

'Hmm. Well...' Ma_Ris seemed to get somewhat more serious momentarily. 'There may be many sides of that, but let me share a little secret with you. You ready?'

'I'm all ears.'

'Good mood is not something that just happens to you. It's a skill you practise.'

Silence was Vizovia's response for a moment. 'What… how can you practise something like that?'

'You can't just flip a switch when you have a bad day to make it not-bad. You have to commit to feeling great long-term, no matter what's going on. I know it sounds like life-coaching bullshit, pardon my language, but it works. As I said, it's a matter of practice, not luck.'

'But you can't practise having a good day.'

'That's the trick. You can, but it takes time.'

'Doesn't make sense to me.'

'But is that not motivating, though? If I am right, then how you feel on a given day depends more on you, on something you can influence, than on coincidence which you can't. It gives you control.'

'Huh.' Vizovia wished the conversation was in game chat so that she could save and re-read it later, but for the time being she had to try to commit that strange idea to memory and examine it like a specimen of unknown species.

Around them life kept going on. Among the throng of people trogging the streets in every direction, Vizovia noticed that she had seen a particular character many times that day.

'Hmm, he's still at it?'

'Who, what?' Ma_Ris asked. 'You ask random questions today, love.'

'Our guildie, the Minstrel. Uh, Ramanti? Raphantiiii…? Let me check in guild, one sec… Yes, Raphanti. He's zooming between the bank, the market, the harbor, crafting something. I noticed him going back and forth before I went AFK. I think he's been at it for like four hours since he said "hi" to me and Miko in the morning. I wonder what he's doing.'

'I can't see him. Where's he now?'

'He just entered the bank building.'

'I see. He's probably just-'

[14:21] **[Guild]** Sl4y: WHO SPAMMED THE GUILD BANK WITH TRASH FOOD

[14:21] **[Guild]** Sl4y: XD

[14:21] **[Guild]** Sl4y: speak up and I won't kill you. maybe.

'Oh wow, do you think we have our answer? Hahaha!' laughed Ma_Ris.

'Haha, should we tell him?'

'No! Let him work it out and see what happens!'

[14:22] **[Guild]** Ò_Ó: I'd tell you who did it but I ain't no snitch

[14:22] **[Guild]** Pvro: ayyy that's kinda fishy

[14:23] **[Guild]** Ò_Ó: but I would break his stupid banjo guitar if I was you :)))

[14:23] **[Guild]** _Raphanti: hey wtf man

[14:23] **[Guild]** Sl4y: why would you do such a thing

[14:23] **[Guild]** _Raphanti: I'm upskilling fishing and cooking on this char

[14:23] **[Guild]** _Raphanti: Im not even done yet :)

[14:23] **[Guild]** Sl4y: but why did you split them into stacks of 5 when they stack up to 20

[14:23] **[Guild]** Sl4y: clean it up -_-

[14:23] **[Guild]** Sl4y: we only have 4 free slots now

[14:23] **[Guild]** _Raphanti: wait what

[14:23] **[Guild]** _Raphanti: I didn't do it

[14:23] **[Guild]** _Raphanti: I'm being framed!

[14:23] **[Guild]** _Raphanti: check the logs!

[14:23] **[Guild]** Ò_Ó: riiiight

[14:23] **[Guild]** Ò_Ó: we totally believe you, right guys?

[14:23] **[Guild]** _Raphanti: o_o you cunt, I'm sure it was you

[14:23] **[Guild]** _Raphanti: anyway I thought the guild could use free stuff

[14:23] **[Guild]** _Raphanti: it's like 800 units of various level consumables

[14:23] **[Guild]** _Raphanti: @everyone all-u-can-eat buffet with buffs in gb right now, free for everyone, courtesy of yours truly! First come, first serve!

[14:24] **[Guild]** Vizovia: :D

[14:24] **[Guild]** Vizovia: I was wondering what you were doing there

[14:24] **[Guild]** Sl4y: TIL bank log only tracks withdraws and deposits but not stack splits, the more you know >_>

[14:24] **[Guild]** Ò_Ó: who would know such things!

[14:25] **[Guild]** -Zoe-: he's like the guy from math questions in elementary school

[14:25] **[Guild]** -Zoe-: Bob buys 60 watermelons something something

[14:25] **[Guild]** _Raphanti: yeah I wish I was back in elementary school

[14:25] **[Guild]** -Zoe-: lol why? it sucked

[14:25] **[Guild]** _Raphanti: so I could talk with you as equal

[14:25] **[Guild]** -Zoe-: XD

[14:25] **[Guild]** Sl4y: wow :D

[14:25] **[Guild]** Ò_Ó: rekt

[14:25] **[Guild]** Pvro: hahaha

[14:25] **[Guild]** Bokkie-: GOTTEM

[14:26] **[Guild]** -Zoe-: go fuck yourself gay bard:D

[14:26] **[Guild]** _Raphanti: fuck me yourself, you coward:>

[14:26] **[Guild]** -Zoe-: ok let me get my strapon brb

[14:26] **[Guild]** _Raphanti: I'm ready

[14:26] **[Guild]** Vizovia: :D

[14:26] **[Guild]** Ma_Ris: I'm glad Miko is afk :D

[14:26] **[Guild]** -Zoe-: honestly is this some kind of law that every guild must have one pervy bard?

[14:26] **[Guild]** Bokkie-: says the one with a strapon!

[14:26] **[Guild]** slowah: I was about to point that out Bokk haha

[14:26] **[Guild]** -Zoe-: it's like it's guaranteed when you join a guild, and it has a bard, he's a damn Pepe le Pew

[14:27] **[Guild]** _Raphanti: of course it's not true

[14:27] **[Guild]** _Raphanti: because we have two!

[14:28] **[Guild]** Rjukan: you rang?

* * *

[21:49] **[Friend]** slowah: ey

[21:49] **[Friend]** slowah: bro

[21:49] **[Friend]** slowah: there's a job:>

[21:49] **[To: slowah]**: suuup

[21:49] **[Friend]** slowah: come to helle, I'll tell you

[21:50] **[To: slowah]**: k

While Sl4y usually hung out in Argentia, slowah preferred something less frequented by masses of players. Not because he disliked company, on the contrary, the opposite was true. So, Hellesvyand it was. The two cities were connected by a convenient ship departing every five minutes, and Sl4y was fortunate to have to wait less than one. A gamer's time is precious. It's not like he had just spent 20 minutes with his feet on his desk, listening to old music, dozing off. Shortly afterwards he arrived at a tropical beach town known in-universe for its beautiful vistas, exotic birds, palm trees, and for being an overall pain to navigate around for mounted players due to the omnipresent narrow planked gangways, jetties, and traps. It was part a shanty town, and part a tropical resort. Outside the universe, it was known as a roleplaying hub for people to show off their hard-earned cosmetic items somewhere, to just hang out together, and to do *the other things* roleplayers did. It was set on a picturesque coastline going south-north, with the in-town beaches frequented by socializing players, and the outskirts being a decent leveling spot for level 30s.

[21:55] **[To: slowah]**: k, where now/

[21:55] **[To: slowah]**: ?

[[slowah] invites you to a Group.][accept][reject]

Sl4y accepted the invitation which allowed him to find the only other party member, slowah himself, on the map of the area. slowah was waiting for him in some seemingly complete random area, between placeholder buildings that didn't even serve any function in the game. In fact, the developers hadn't even blessed them with a doorway, as Sl4y just noticed for the first time ever.

slowah played a Scholar, with a niche supporting build. That was not to say he was a healer; if anything he helped enemy players die, but his kit also featured a couple of nice defensive and utility tools. His avatar now stood before Sl4y, his outfit currently hiding his pretty high-quality raid items and instead displaying a blue floral unbuttoned shirt, and white linen shorts. His neck and wrists were adorned with simple ethnic jewelry. His character's face was handsome, clean-shaven as was Sl4y's, with unruly locks of golden hair and blue eyes behind sunglasses. His look would be incomplete without the cheapest-looking flip-flops he could find in the game, but that was a style choice.

Sl4y used a /slap emote on slowah to say hello to his best friend as was their tradition, and switched to Party chat.

'So? :>'

'OK, so, listen. I need your help to find out something. I met a girl here last week, she's really cool. I even got her pic. But I remember her being with that dick Windsinger =.='

Sl4y didn't know who Windsinger was, but he wasn't going to ask. Instead, he said:

'Hold up. Weren't you with Himika?'

'Not anymore :(‘

'Why, what happened?'

'Doesn't matter.'

Sl4y didn't press for details. This sort of revelation wasn't exactly new with slowah, who continued:

'I don't know if they're still together, but I know she is online and here somewhere :P'

'Wait what? Oh, you mean the new girl.'

'She only told me someone was waiting for her here. I want to know who that is. But I can't show myself or ask her, that would be creepy. Also I have to do some stuff in a moment IRL.'

'Right,' confirmed Sl4y. 'We certainly want to avoid doing creepy things, right?'

':>'

'...right?'

'Duh, obviously. So you will spy on her for me :D'

'D:'

'She knows my characters and she will recognize me. Also it would be suspicious if I just happened to appear where she hangs out around here.'

'And I won't look suspicious, you think? :D'

'You will log in to your assassin alt and approach invisible :)'

'Also wtf dude! xD'

'I know xD'

'What are you, sixteen again?'

'Come on broooooo.'

Sl4y couldn't help but grin to the monitor and shake his head in disbelief.

'Fine, I'll do it xD'

'I love you <3'

'Where are they?'

'Southern beach I think, unless they moved. Online tracker still says she's in the town anyway.'

'K. brb, relog.'

Sl4y logged out to character selection menu, and then immediately logged back in to his priest and asked:

'Uh, what's her name? xD'

The "mission" was not difficult, but it had to be the dumbest thing he ever did for or with slowah, and that said much. They have known each other for years, and were the closest friend to each other despite never having met IRL and being very different in many aspects. Did the current voyeurism quest feel weird? Yes. Was it fun? Strangely, also yes. Who knew or intended for an MMORPG game to allow such experiences? *It's fine as long as nobody finds out*, thought Sl4y. *Unless one day I publish a compilation of all the funny and stupid shit I did online. Anyway, in the end it's all right. We're all anonymous here. It's only a game, is it not?*

Cloaked characters have a movement speed penalty which made the search somewhat tedious. To go around unmounted like some sort of a caveman was already bad enough for Sl4y, but also go slower than normal walking speed? *Ugh.* It took him several minutes and he was close to concluding that either the "intel" was bad, or that the "target" had moved, but eventually he found the player character matching description. Arabesque of the NFP guild. A hunter, level 80, wearing a white, knee-length summer dress and a marigold yellow sun hat with an almost comically oversized brim. The accessories were somewhat lacking in Sl4y's opinion. Long blond hair, bound in a single thick braid; amber eyes, average female height, barefoot. And notably, the feminine body attribute slider pushed quite deep during character creation. Bless whoever designed this in the game's development, thought Sl4y. She looked great all things considered. This *character* looked great, he corrected himself quickly. slowah was confident she was a female IRL, but as far as Sl4y knew, it could be anyone on the other side. A small lime green bird alternated between perching on her shoulder, her head, and flying around on low altitude. It was an easily available summonable pet from an NPC store in Vir Estia. A Tantavosi Chirper? Sl4y was sure he had it somewhere in his collection.

Her companion was a female too, putting slowah's reasons for jealousy to rest at least for now. He paid the non-target little attention. They both sat in the shade of a palm tree, although the server was already in night mode and changed the environment accordingly. The whole game world was engulfed in not exactly the darkness of a night, but more like an eight-hour twilight until daylight returned at 6:00.

Sl4y parked his character close enough to see and hear them, should they do anything that makes sound, and just observed. Should they also speak in a public channel, he would see it in his chatbox and their speech bubbles.

Nothing of note was happening. Arabesque looked as if she was AFK, but her companion – some low-level Paladin, of all classes – gave herself away as not-AFK by left-clicking various NPCs within her range from time to time, which in combat would be equivalent to targeting them. TheRedLady, because what was her name, belonged to NFP as well.

The whole situation reminded Sl4y of older days, when he would very well be in slowah's shoes. The days of working his rear side off to impress someone thinking this would build him some kind of relationship. Nevertheless, Sl4y spared a thought of envy of his friend's rich social life, even if it was only digital, though Sl4y would not admit that out loud. Himself, he barely remembered when anyone sincerely did something as basic as asking him "how are you?".

As for the suspects, that was about it. The two must have been talking either by voice chat, or by private messages because nothing was leaking out to their surroundings. Sl4y's thoughts drifted in boredom. If one of them suddenly stood up and for no reason used an ability that nullifies invisibility in the area thus revealing him, what would he say for himself? What would he do? An unlikely scenario, fortunately, but an extremely embarrassing one. Just in case, he made sure the home teleportation scroll was bound to F1 so that he could panic-button it. For good measure, he also bound it to F2 through F4 as well, in case he missclicked F1. He still felt silly to do all this, but his friend had asked, so he would do it. Furthermore, maybe it was silly, but it was something he never thought about doing in an MMORPG game. The experience was worth having. Maybe one day when they are both older he would tease slowah about this moment.

The two used no emotes, had no visitors, and logged out after – Sl4y checked the time – nineteen minutes of observation. He tried whisping to slowah to see if the jerk was still online, but an error message told him he was not. He made sure to move away from the observation spot to a more public area before logging out, in case he later logged on to this character and got noticed in someone else's hang-out location before he could cloak.

The next day was a non-GvG day, and Sl4y had some time to spend in the evening. One look into the guild window and friendlist told him there was no chance for a proper group activity. slowah has been offline since the previous evening. *Solo grinding it is, then. The bread-and-butter of ARIS and MMORPGs in general.* But Sl4y was curious if Arabesque was online. He opened AltAr's website on his second monitor and clicked his way to the online users' list. A ctrl+f search told him she was online and in Hellesvyand again.

Truth be told, he did not feel like spending another twenty minutes or more sitting back and twiddling his thumbs, but he thought he could at least take a look, see what was up. He hopped into his Assassin and started the search. She was not in her previous location, so he resolved to search for her. He went through the usually popular areas, the streets, a few inns and taverns. Nothing. He was about to give up after as much as three minutes, when he spotted her on the road leading out of the town northwards. He almost failed to recognize her and missed her, as she was now wearing combat gear. He followed uncloaked to not lose her. Out here in the streets he was as good as anonymous anyway.

He found her again outside town attacking a Birgo, a spider-like creature wearing a hard chitinous carapace, designed after real world's coconut crabs.

The game designers even programmed them to imitate a behaviour the coconut crabs sometimes displayed: lifting small objects from the ground and carrying them away to eat elsewhere. In the game, they did that with any item left on the ground by the adventuring players. Except eating it, that is. Arabesque was not "adventuring" since she outleveled the mobs massively, so Sl4y concluded she was grinding them for some purpose. Several dead specimens already dotted the area. He pretended to attack a few of the mobs himself just to act normal, and then headed back into town. That she was grinding things on her own was a good sign. In a grindy game such as this, it was fairly standard for girls to have guys grind for them, although truth be told, many guys did it eagerly and unasked, thinking this will earn them sympathy points. Sl4y bitterly remembered that he used to think like that too. That rarely works as the guys expect. Sometimes they end up being used, and sometimes they assume that they have "earned" a reward from a girl. Those are valuable learning experiences for boys. Still, it was good to see Arabesque working for her own stuff. That was an information slowah would be happy to hear.

On the way to the town gate to the right, in the eastern direction and away from the coastline there was a path. Several hundred metres away, between palm trees and above the thick undergrowth swaying gently in the warm land breeze, an observer could just barely spot the beginning of said dirt path leading up, to the hills surrounding the north-eastern part of the town of Hellesvyand. It was easily missed, it disappeared quickly in the foliage, and it led to no particularly useful or important place game-wise. Sl4y pretended not to see it and continued on his own path south.

Al-Ghabla was both a massive landmass southwest of the Insal Kingdom and the name of an Empire dominating its surface. It was a land of opposites existing side by side: the harsh regime of the Empress ruling from Ghabat--Safi and the settlements living outside its reach; the twin, parallel rivers parting the seemingly infinite stretches of deserts and creating possibly the best farmland in the known world; the barren stretches of land where nothing ever happens and the sites of some of the worst calamities to ever befall the world; the monumental structures of enigmatic purpose left behind by ancient peoples and the primitive canvas tents of nomadic clans making a living at their feet.

One such odd place was west of Ghabat-Safi, a complex of tall sandstone structures now apparently partially submerged in ocean water, although that description is not exactly accurate. It was built on the coast as most structures tend to be, but it was built just slightly below sea level, with all its walkways, floors, and brightly-tiled and then flooded on purpose to ankle-height as if the ancient creators really loved splashing water as they walked. How the perfectly even elevation across the entirety of the complex of structures was achieved, how the salt in the water did not erode or crystallise on any structure, how and why all this was made, and if people lived here then how they had fresh water access, could be anyone's guess. One thing everyone knew and agreed on though, was that its name was Or Anash Qnag, translated to Sixteen Did Not Work, because that's what was written on every outer wall. Perhaps it was some sort of an ancient pun that Imperial College lacked cultural context to understand, but almost all researchers were almost certain their translation was almost correct. The game community joked that in truth it probably meant "future archaeologists will have no idea" or "bob was here".

Lyonni found the place enchanting and having seen it years ago for the first time dearly wished such a place existed in the real world. It did not, but one can dream.

She had business with the nagas that came out of the sea and claimed the place as their own. The vile but intelligent creatures served malignant forces from the world's blackest depths, so removing them with prejudice was high on the priority list of whoever owned the land. She reckoned she could handle them at level 49 with her agile Katar build if she took them one at a time and avoided the Tidal Vanguard Naga, because their Trident Throws and scandalous DEF were a pain to deal with without a proper critical hit chance. She usually got around it with poisons, but Nagas were resistant to it. They were susceptible to lightning damage, but she had no way to do it. She would also have to be careful not to get swarmed - she remembered dying frequently to patrols in that area, but this time she came as a slippery Assassin. If it went well, she could probably stay there until level 59 at least.

Wishing she was at level 60 and that she had a 60% speed increase mount instead of 30% she exited Ghabat-Safi by the north gate and made her way through grasslands along the road flanked on each side by date trees. A desert continent it might have been, but the twin river deltas of Douirat and Afeggu flowing through the Imperial City, some waterway engineering, and coastal winds carrying moisture inland created favourable conditions for life to bloom.

Just outside the city she saw a group of six players idling on the road at the foot of a massive stone obelisk. A variety of classes, she noticed, and all near her level. They were somewhat static for a group of this many people, a few <AFK> tags by their nicknames explaining why it was so. She rode past them not paying them any mind, but she turned around and approached them. There was at least one Priest in the group and at least one Paladin, and a few buffs would make her grind easier even if for less than a half of an hour.

[15:14] Lyonni: hi, buffs please? :)

Nobody in the group moved or said anything, except that one Priestess who said:

[15:14] Anzu_: they're afk :D

[15:14] Lyonni: can you give inspiration then? :)

[15:14] Anzu_: sorry, dark build

[15:14] Lyonni: oh

[15:14] Anzu_: it means I cant cast supporting spells

[15:14] Lyonni: yeah I know

[15:14] Lyonni: thanks anyway, bye :)

Lyonni went back her way towards Or Anash Qnag. It was not far, maybe a minute worth of riding along the road. Less than that for players at level 100 who can go offroad and not be dismounted by roaming animals and monsters. Halfway there she received a private message.

[15:16] [From: Anzu_]: hey, are you going to Qnag? :)

[15:16] [To: Anzu_]: yes

Anzu_ was silent for a moment.

[15:17] [From: Anzu_]: want to join our party as mobber?

[15:17] [From: Anzu_]: our pala had to leave, no other melee in gorup

[15:17] [From: Anzu_]: group*

[15:17] [To: Anzu_]: hmmm

Lyonni was happy to join a group that was going to do the same thing as her anyway, and leveling up faster was really right up her alley, but she considered if she could fulfill that role. She had plenty of dodge rating, an emergency invisibility to save her skin, and a reposition-behind-target ability that can be used to move around quickly. She only lacked one thing, a tool for rapid tagging of monsters from range. She opened her spellbook and spent one of two unspent skill points on Throw Knife. She had been considering where to put them. *Two problems solved*, she thought.

[15:18] [From: Anzu_]: you'd be pulling everything and leading to us
for aoe

[15:18] [To: Anzu_]: yeah I know what it means :P sure let's do it

[[Anzu_] invites you to a Group.][accept][reject]

[15:18] [From: Anzu_]: okie :) we're coming your way

Overall it was going well, but it was hardly a cause for celebration for
her - it was not really difficult once she got familiar with respawn timers and
locations, the patrols, and her own abilities. The group, that she now knew
was full of alts from a guild called Execute, quickly told her to bring larger
amounts of mobs to them.

She did exactly that. She would go down one way, pull everything in the
area either by tagging Nagas with knife throws or just by her proximity, and
run away back to the group while avoiding taking damage so they would crush
the mobs all at the same time. Then they would loot the corpses and repeat
the process. While near her party she made sure to get buffed and walk within
Bard's song range to refresh the movement speed increase. Every slithering
snake-like humanoid enemy in this area was of the aggressive-chaser type and
needed no encouragement to stay on her tail once pulled, so the extra speed
was really good to have. This was the most efficient environment for mobbing large groups, but a mistake could cost her dearly. One lucky blow could
stagger her and allow the rest to dogpile on her. The Vanguards did just that
a few times, but she kept Vanish available for those moments.

It was boring. She'd rather be killing things herself, but the nice EXP in-
come made up for this little sacrifice on her part. It was a good arrangement,
in the end. The group did their job as expected.

The group was apparently led by an Alchemist-build Witch Doctor Xemx,
which she found out only when he called for a ten-minute break after forty minutes of grind. The cynic in her thought: *figures. Witch Doctors create parties*

because nobody invites them because they are useless until level 70ish. Overall, he managed the group well, noticed stragglers quickly, observed everyone's mana, etc. She found the group likeable overall. They seemed to know each other quite well and called each other by names different from current characters' names. It was also during that break that she noticed half the characters were guildless, but the rest were all from the same guild.

[16:00] [Group] XII: I can't get my head around hunter controls. how do I cancel casting without losing target lock?

[16:00] [Group] XII: normally as caster I just make a tiny step but hunters can cast on the move

A few people took the opportunity to stretch or do biological things. Lyonni did not take the break, instead she was considering how to distribute her new attribute and skills points. The question asked in the group chat caught her attention. Since nobody was responding, she decided to help a little.

[16:01] [Group] Lyonni: there are 3 ways

[16:01] [Group] Lyonni: there is a "stop attack" command in your spell book, looks like a normal spell, you can put it in the hotbar

[16:01] [Group] Lyonni: or you can quickly turn your back on the target as the cast goes off. just dont do it with keyboard cuz its lame

[16:02] [Group] Lyonni: or if you want to be pro, have another weapon with you and swap to it with hotbar and swap back again. uses two bar slots tho

[16:02] [Group] XII: hmm how is option 3 better than 1?

[16:02] [Group] Lyonni: it skips animation so its faster by half a second:)

[16:02] [Group] Xemx: wtf this is some 300 IQ minmaxing shit

[16:02] [Group] Lyonni: I used to play a ranger hunter a lot and learned a few things:)

[16:02] [Group] XII: nice. I'll test it later

Anzu_ returned in the meantime and spoke up.

[16:03] [Group] Anzu_: Ranger build is hardcore :o

[16:03] [Group] Lyonni: if you say so, I haven't played it in a while

[16:03] [Group] Xemx: why hardcore?

[16:03] [Group] Anzu_: normally you put skill points to max out some abilities in the tree and ignore others

[16:03] [Group] Anzu_: Ranger takes a bit of everything but on low rank, its complicated

[16:03] [Group] Anzu_: and weird

[16:03] [Group] Anzu_: but you have answers to everything in pvp

[16:03] [Group] Lyonni: more or less, yes

[16:03] [Group] Anzu_: our GL mains Ranger, and also leads raids or gvgs while doing it

[16:03] [Group] Lyonni: impressive :) Diki, right?

[16:03] [Group] Anzu_: yes, you know him?

[16:04] [Group] Lyonni: nope. Now I need to AFK, brb

She typed /afk before leaving to grab a drink.

They wrapped up the grind less than thirty minutes later. Lyonni came out of it with level 54, which she thought she would be at in one or two days later if she had been going at her pace, which was not very fast. The amount of time she dedicated to gaming was not great, but she used it well.

[16:31] [Group] Lyonni: thanks for the party :)

[16:31] [Group] Lyonni: I think it went pretty well

[16:31] [Group] Lyonni: call me again when you need me but I'd rather do some dmg next time

[16:31] [Group] Xemx: yes, pretty good, we even nailed a few rare spawns :) Anzu will send you you share when we sell it

[16:31] [Group] Anzu_: yes

[16:31] [Group] Anzu_: I'll poke you from another char in a sec

[16:31] Anzu_ has left the group.

[16:31] [Group] Lyonni: I'll leave now too, thanks again!

[16:31] You left the group.

Lyonni, knowing the online etiquette, left the group before anyone had to awkwardly ask her to leave. If those people were friends or otherwise familiar with each other, they would not want a stranger present after their cooperation ended.

Her inventory was brimming with low-value drops and she was close to capacity limit, so the first thing she did after returning to town was to dump everything in the stash. She would sort out the usable from absolute trash later when she better remembered which is which. For the most part, her storage was empty. What few things she had in it were a few pretty rare account-bound things, most of them cosmetic or commemorative otherwise. True to her word, Anzu contacted her a moment later, but it was not a trade invitation that came first.

[[Anzu] wants to register you as a friend. Accept / Reject]

Lyonni looked up Anzu's name out of curiosity with a shift-click.

Name: Anzu, level: 100, Class: Paladin, Location: Bridgefort, Guild: <Execute>.

As the continent and the empire that controlled shared the same name, so did a small island of Anabar bear the same name as a sandstone fortress built, or more accurately, carved into it. It was raised centuries ago to guard the only way in or out from the Bay of Ghabat Safi, the primary city of Al-Ghabla Empire. Every ship to pass into the bay did so under the vigilant eye of the watchmen manning the crenellated walls above the sea waves crashing into the rocks beneath. Where there was trade there was wealth, and where there was wealth there were those seeking to take it.

Chambers and corridors were chiselled into the rock, as well as firing slits for brass cannons in the outer walls facing in every direction. There were no towers, and the whole structure was flat, vast, and deep enough for sea moisture to seep into the lowest levels, suitable only to host a few prison cells. More were not needed - Anabar was not a prison structure.

A seagull flying over the island would see, if it had the brains to know such things, Anabar's small harbour facing the mainland, living quarters, courtyards, inner walls, shooting range, armoury, kitchens, gunpowder storage, and finally: the keep. The walls and roofs were nearly indistinguishable from one another, the sandstone's texture on every surface deceiving the eye of an onlooker. Every structure bore a similar, simple appearance as an additional tactical benefit. It was not without its aesthetic, but perhaps it was of the military sort, not for every beholder to appreciate. The passages were narrow and the structures tall enough to protect the personnel from scorching sun, and windows were barred even high above ground or rocky cliffs.

The keep interior told a slightly different story, one of greater opulence and convenience, as it was where the garrison's commander operated from. More importantly though, a tradition of the Imperial dynasties ruling from Ghabat Safi dictated that the heir to the throne must serve a year in the boots of an island watcher, and thus the heart of the fortress at times surprised visitors by its carpets, stained windows, heating, baths, and even a garden. The tradition was intended to expose the highborn youth with the reality of life outside the Imperial Palace, but it seems a certain degree of splendour always found its way even to places where nobility went, even if only for a while. Tapestries and regiment banners adorned the walls, and the dark-grey imported marbles, polished to reflective properties, were a permanent feature of the keep.

What was not a permanent feature were the corpses of Havoc guild hitting the floor in unison as they rolled into a wall of defenders like a wave into the fortress' waterline. As the rotation of Guild-on-Guild wars' warzones would have it, it was one of the two active ones on that evening. Sadly, the players defeated a few times by its defenders - the Bulwark guild and its allies - had not much appreciation at all for the aesthetics the game designers had worked to implement.

The castles hosting GvG events were all more or less linear in the approach to the final chamber, so it was easy for the defenders to reinforce choke points both by their own formations and by in-game mechanics such as erecting barricades or assembling Siege Golems to occupy and distract the attackers. It was one such choke point, one of many really, that Havoc was unable to break through despite several attempts. There were a few minor victories earlier that evening that resulted in Octav and his force of over seventy bodies falling back deeper into the keep and setting new defences there, but real victory was in sight for neither Havoc nor the marauders from minor guilds getting in their way.

The Havoc players, having been sent to the respawn point they had set in the Far Horizons inn in Argentia, discussed their situation.

'Okay but what's the matter, huh? I killed at least three of them this time before I died! If we all could kill only two each, it should be easy!' complained Faystus.

'Wow, you must be really good,' said Ihealformoney. 'Now lower your voice. My head hurts from hearing you.'

'Pfft.'

'How many do they even have there?' asked someone.

'At least eighty in total.'

'Okay but what I want to know is when the fuck did they get so good? They've always been a pushover for us since always. This pisses me off,' wondered Blinky.

'You've been here for like 3 months, dude,' said Makzine.

'**They still suck,**' Agnelei commented on the situation, preparing himself to go in again. '**They're just exploiting their numbers, as always. Zerg on offence, Zerg on defence. We've just never had to attack them before, not for real.**'

'Speaking of wargame metaphors,' Sarevoc stepped in, 'they have no real tactics, just logistics. We're not going fast enough, and they reinforce too fast. And even if we break through them, Octav will just emergency recall them further back. He hasn't used it today or this week. Im not complaining, by the way, just stating the fact.'

'Sounds like complaining to me,' Belixner said. 'I also killed a few this time, like, every time. If we all did this, it would be a piece of cake, but it isn't. Who's not doing their part here? Can Assassins start assassinating people yet?'

'Easy for you to say, we have to close the gap through the magic spam to do anything.'

'Less qq, more pew-pew,' said Ò_Ó, a magic spammer.

'So what now?' asked someone.

'Oof!' exclaimed Ihealformoney. 'I shouldn't have complained about Faystus. I'm sorry.'

'Hah,' said Faystus triumphantly.

'Good to know Mr. Brokenmic is still with us.' Sl4y's sarcasm was immense. 'And I've finally noticed who this was. You're banned from speaking on this server until I undo it, OmO.'

'So what are we doing, Sl4y?' asked PowerOverwhelming. 'We try again?'

'I don't know. Sit tight, don't go anywhere.'

'What's the point?' asked Faystus. 'It's a waste of time.'

'We're discussing it now, give us a sec,' Sl4y reiterated his point.

[20:30] **[Raid]** ^_Miko_^: sorry, I have to go ^^' good luck!!

'Let's try again on Saturday,' Makzine said.

'Why, you wanna go back to your Shadow Raid of Champions or something?' asked PowerOverwhelming.

'Yes, if you must know, but I'll stay if we're trying again.'

'All right everyone, I've heard enough of this,' Slam1go interrupted the conversation. 'Put your pants back up and give me your *full* attention. You're tired of bashing our heads? Then we're going to try something weird and stupid. If it works, we will be cool and awesome, but also they will call us cheaters and losers. If they do that, then fuck them and their opinion, but we're not going to cheat… technically. If we fail, we'll look pathetic, in which case, fuck them too.'

A few snickers answered him, some of them nervous, but nobody spoke, letting him finish.

'We never did anything like this, but let's do it this one time. I talked with Pvro about it once, and he said it's a hilarious idea. I think he thought I was joking. I wasn't!'

This time his words were met with complete silence.

'Just to be clear,' stepped in Sl4y. 'I'm on board with this idea. I'm glad someone steps forward with something for once,' he added, and the sentence sounded like an accusation.

'Okay, then I will tell you the plan. It will be so simple even a Bulwark's Hunter player would understand. Do what I say, exactly how I say, even if you see me doing something else,' he paused, so that the instructions would sink in. 'It is half past eight. I want everyone, and I mean *everyone*, back to base. If you're in the castle, TP out now. Prepare yourselves for a strong attack, be repaired, buffed, healed et cetera. Then log out. Yes, when you're ready to go, log out from the game, but stay here in voice chat. We will log back in at 20:50 ON THE DOT, I will do a countdown too. When we log back, we hop into portals and rush. So you can go have a little break for now, except Eyes and Gaav, you will have a special job in the meantime.'

'Uuuh…' began Ò_Ó, but did not continue, confused, but not the only one.

[20:32] **[Raid]** Gaav: ok

[20:32] **[Raid]** 415: wtf is this plan D:

'This sounds interesting but yes, weird,' said Eightblades.

'God protect us from Slam1go's ideas,' joked Intervene. 'But I've had enough bashing me head against the wall, I'm ready for a trainwreck!'

'Technically not-cheating, eh?' Raphanti asked with amusement. 'I'm starting the recording now. Should be a good video.'

'Do we close the game or just log out…?' asked -Zoe-.

'Just log out, stay in character selection,' Slam1go advised. 'And don't worry, I'll be recording it too.'

'Okie-dokie, then I'll be back in a few, I need a break,' she said and muted herself in Chatterbox as a sign of being AFK.

'Okay, let's do it I guess…' Makzine trailed off, and signed out.

'I hope this is good,' Sarevoc muttered.

'Who needs repairs?' asked Azarus.

'Potions? Elixirs?' followed his girlfriend, Kaitzuuu.

The guild busied itself with combat preparations for a minute, constantly reminded by Slam1go to log out as soon as possible, all that while commenting how unusual the request is. The densely packed hall in the Far Horizons inn in Argentia was getting less crowded by the moment as the fifty-something players gradually vanished until only a few characters were left online.

'We've come here to play the game, and we're logging out during the actual goal of the game, this makes no sense,' complained Xyrolol.

'Hey, let's see where this goes. We've tried and failed to attack properly, and without Pvro we can't do recall. I'm sick of pointless dying, at least in Battlegrounds you get participation rewards,' said Ihealformoney.

'Sl4y, what do you think?' asked Prast.

'I still hear QQ,' said Ò_Ó.

'If you really have to know, then I don't like it, but I agreed to it and I won't complain,' Sl4y replied. 'If it's either fun or successful, I will be happy.'

'LUL at Sl4y being happy,' said someone whose voice grated Sl4y.

Slam1go ignored the conversation, and instead said: 'Okay, Gaav, Eyes, come join me in channel below, I will explain your mission. Everyone else, stay here and wait.'

Ò_Ó was on a mission. He had only eleven minutes or so to travel to some remote location where unrestrained PvP was allowed, then to Geixan city where Bulwark had set their respawn point, but the first place could not be near the second one. A challenging timetable for anyone who was not a Mage. He had a teleportation waypoint saved in a small outpost far to the south, which was a common meeting point for groups taking on Hope's End or Three Trials of Exiled. A quick ride east, a turn left on the crossroads, and he was in the Cursed Woods. He casted a Teleportation Waypoint spell from his spellbook (*no point putting that on the action bars*) then he immediately teleported directly to Geixan, where he remembered to delete someone from his friendlist just in case so he did that quickly too. *Almost got compromised,* he thought.

'I'm ready,' he said on the voice chat, and went straight to the inn where the Bulwark guild was based. He did not enter though, that would have to wait a little. Instead, he met with Gaav in a side alley, finding him stealthed in the middle of it. Without a word from either of them, Ò_Ó parked himself near the Assassin, and waited.

It was 20:49 on the clock. Only Sl4y, Slam1go, Gaav, himself, and a few other guild members who were not participating in GvG were online. It was nearly the time to do perhaps the dumbest, but most daring play he ever attempted.

Meanwhile, Octav was disappointed. With over twenty minutes left to go, he and his guild and the allied ATR guild were dismayed to find that their only attackers of that evening, since Execute and a bunch of other guilds were busy with each other in Nordheimburg, had apparently given up. The corridors between Anabar's entrance and his current defensive line were empty with the exception of a bunch of random PvPers looking for any fight they could get, not really interested in capturing the objective. The said objective required either extreme luck exploited in the middle of a battle for the last room, or an organised effort by dozens of players. The random rabble always showed up, looking to score a frag on a member of the top guilds even if just for the heck of it, or to have even the smallest effect on the war's outcome.

'Yep, they're gone. Even the smaller groups aren't coming if they can't hide behind Havoc,' reported draac, who had been stalking the corridors and reporting activity, or lack thereof, to Octav.

'It seems they even logged out. Completely hopeless,' added Halbdenial. He had a couple of Havoc members in friendlist, being one of the oldest characters on the AltAr servers. He had even been a member of Havoc for some time once, years ago.

The report from draac had come ten minutes before, and a few of Bulwark's members have also logged out since then, expecting no more fun to be had that evening. Some others were probably away from their computers, or doing something else in the background. He could not really blame them.

'So, we gonna invest in this castle now?' asked SINka, repeating the same question she asked three days ago when they won their current territory.

'I think so,' Octav replied honestly. 'At this point, it would be stupid not to take this chance. It seems we can hold it for some time.'

'Nice,' she replied back. 'All this guild tax has to go somewhere.'

'I think I will build defences first, though,' Octav mused.

'Booooring,' said DuckIRL. 'Just what we expect from you, Octav.'

'Hey, it's pragmatic, not boring,' Octav defended himself.

'Boring,' said DuckIRL again.

'We will invest in treasure after next GvG, okay?' asked Octav. In truth, he was impatient to do it himself, but he was a creature of duty, in life and in game. *Business before pleasure* was a rule he lived by.

'Hey, that's weird,' said Halbdenial suddenly. 'Did the server just have a hiccup? I got a pile of login notifications all at once…'

'Seems fine to me, no,' replied UhOhTrouble, and a few others.

'Nothing on my side either.'

'Hm… nevermind, the-'

'Uhh, check-check! Activity spike, Havoc is back!' alarmed draac. 'They're rushing us, and… fuck they got me. I could swear I was stealthed but their warlocks-'

'Okay okay, we heard you,' Octav interrupted. 'Everyone, wake up, we have some more fighting to do.'

This raised the morale of over sixty remaining players grouped in an open-sky courtyard, the long rays of setting sun painting the clouds overhead crimson. A fountain in the middle was, to some, a pretty feature, but it made it difficult for Octav to see the entirety of the large "chamber" and a part of his raid members were always hidden from sight because of it. Still, the place was worth defending. Beyond this point the corridors leading to the GvG crystal pillar forked making defence more problematic. So here they would stand, for now.

He could already see the Havoc characters and the red nametags over their heads coming from the pathways below, now climbing the stairs and soon to walk face-first into the pre-casted area spells his casters maintained. Continuous casting of spells at empty space was a tedious task but effective at revealing sneaky cloakers, and the news of incoming enemies always livened up the involved people to hit that one button with more vigour.

'Eyes, you're up!' said Slam1go.

Ò_Ó was prepared and ready. When the word was given, he casted Invisibility and made his way inside Bulwark's NPC inn-turned-base camp, a place called Xin Tea House. There was nobody in it, except himself, an afking Priest, and Gaav stealthily following the Mage, wordlessly as ever. He found the exact spot on the floor where players killed in GvG areas would spawn. Resurrecting players in GvG was not allowed by game mechanics, so whoever died could only return here. Had to.

Still invisible, he hovered his mouse pointer over the Open Portal spell, and waited, eyes glued to his monitor in the sunset light of his bedroom.

'Here they come!' called Halbdenial, when a few dozen hostile characters rolled into view around the corner. They were going fast, as if followed and pushed by another guild from the back. A common occurrence in such events, and a terrible position to find oneself in: one guild forming a wall in front, another guild attacking in the back. *Poor Havoc can't catch a break,* thought Octav.

Attackers were now inside the maelstrom of meteors, volley shots, blizzards, and other explosions casted by the defenders. It seemed their Scholar was not online that evening, so their best hope was to dash through the danger, taking all the damage, hoping to make it far enough to disrupt the defending casters from unleashing even more pain, and to get restored by their healers. Only a few of them would live long enough to get those heals. It was a foolhardy attempt. In fact, it was odd that Havoc would do something so amateurish. *This is sad to see,* thought Octav. *They're as good as dead.*

But strangely, that's not what happened. Havoc took a sharp turn to the left, exactly towards the position Octav himself was holding. As a Warrior, he had been positioned in the front ranks. It was a nice gift from them, making it easier for him to swing his own sword a little before the end of the evening. He charged at the nearest enemy, a Paladin named Makzine with a radiant two-handed warhammer and a gold-trimmed silver helmet with a scarlet tassel fixed to its back, and a lowered visor with thin, vertical slits masking his face.

'We should be fine,' he stated with confidence. There was no way his team would be dislodged from that position. 'Clean them up, and keep the pre-casting up, another guild could be right behind them. Refresh the buffs and stuff.'

Then he realised that pretty much all of the attackers who still lived were targeting him and only him. His own healers had no hope of keeping him alive even a second longer. In the maelstrom of the dirty, personal, close-quarter fight, he did not at all notice his health crashing down hard. The loading screen that replaced his character's vision told him he had died, which then gave way to the familiar, oriental interior of Xin Tea House. Somehow, Havoc managed to break through the maelstrom and get him specifically. *That's so petty.*

'I'm dead!' he informed his guild. 'Port me back!' There was usually some casual player helping the guild by casting portals from the inn, or someone's alt-character opened in another game client. Before he finished speaking, a familiar swirl of blue-ish and green-ish ether manifested itself in front of him, ready to take him to his destination: back to the island stronghold of Anabar, to take the quick-return passages available only to the defenders. He clicked the portal in a heartbeat, pleased how quickly his request was handled by whoever was at the inn. In his wake the portal that should last well over a minute lingered only for two seconds longer, then vanished into thin air as if it was never there.

For a second time within a minute, a loading screen gave him an unexpected revelation. It was the wrong loading screen, he realised; this particular image was for the Cold, Bitter Darkness expansion to ARIS, instead of the baseline illustration from the first release of the game, where Anabar was already featured.

'Hey, who did that?' he demanded.

Silence fell.

'Did what?' asked draac, after nobody replied to the Guild Leader's question.

'Someone gave me the wrong portal. I thought we talked about this last week?'

Indeed, he found himself in the Cursed Woods, the domain of a Lich dwelling in the dilapidated tower to the east, deeper into the dark, twisted forest where only mist seemed to be alive. A murky meadow was his current whereabouts, some distance from the nearest road. He opened the spellbook to immediately return to his save point.

But suddenly he was a small, green frog.

What- the thought formed in his head, before he realised he was not alone and that he was strangely small. A character with a red nameplate over their head flanked him, and a debuff icon on Octav's UI told him he would remain a frog for another sixteen seconds unless damaged. In the involuntary frog form he could not use abilities or items, but he could still move around with a speed penalty or even jump if he wanted to, but importantly, no effect in the game prevented chatting.

[20:52] Octav: You've got to be shitting me.

He sent the message, while speaking the same to his microphone. He struggled to find the right words to describe what was happening to him, for the situation was bizarre. 'Guys, they... I clicked the wrong portal, now I can't move.'

As he spoke, the Havoc Mage, the one with weird angry emoticon face for a nickname, stared back at him but did nothing. His health was full, meaning he was probably not a part of the latest attack in Anabar. He did not pre-cast the next spell, he did not attempt to pull distance from the Warrior, or escape in any way. The enemy just stood in front of somewhat enraged Octav.

'What do you mean?' voiced Halbdenial from half a world away in response to Octav's question. 'They're dead, only you died, nobody came behind them. Why can't you move?'

Octav prepared himself to fight like hell, punishing the Mage for the terrible mistake of not getting away from a high-end-geared Warrior in melee range even with the health disadvantage. The Polymorph status would wear off in a few seconds. Six... five... four... three...

The effect wore off. He assumed his normal form again, made a step towards Ò_Ó with murderous intent, knowing he would probably not be able to recall to base while the Mage was here and alive. But a step was all he got before a dreaded sound effect of an unstealthing Assassin came from behind his character, and he already knew why the Mage was content just staring at the Guild Leader of Bulwark.

Two seconds later, Octav's Warrior was swaying on his legs, stunned for eight seconds. He took a little bit of damage in the process, and was now at twenty-eight percent of life, having respawned in Xin Tea House with a quarter of life and regenerated a few naturally. He did not bother to eat or wait to get healed before returning to what he thought was the Anabar island. So now, he was being held in place by a Mage and an Assassin, half a world away from his guild, with neither of the captors even trying to kill Octav. *They want to hold me here as long as possible,* he realised.

'I- they- they won't let me move or recall or die. Havoc are here, in the Cursed Woods, and I can't come back!' Octav's voice carried frustration and incredulity.

'They can't be there, because they're coming back at us!' reported draac, probably from his position outside the defensive lines, providing early warning of incoming attackers. 'The full group, dozens of them, coming in quick!'

'Hold that position, don't go out to meet them!' commanded Octav. He switched to chatting with nearby players again:

[20:52] Octav: That's a dick move, really.

[20:52] Octav: Pvro lets you do that?

[20:52] Octav: Unbelievable.

'Now, now! Stop for a few seconds before the last corner, buff up, Mages do Spell Reflect, Hunters load Concussive Round and shit!' urged out Slam1go, rushing together with the rest of Havoc raid group through outdoor colonnades, wide staircases, and windowless corridors leading into the heart of Anabar "castle". 'We don't have slowah today, so maximum CC, then fuck them up! We want to kill as many as possible before, then we regroup faster, then we try to rush the crystal! Also don't click the wrong portal in our base,' he added, and audible laughs answered him.

'Uh, we have a problem,' said Ò_Ó, one of the two captors of Octav who could do that, since Gaav would never speak on voicecomms. 'He's undressing. He will take extra damage from Gaav. I can't chain-poly him, Gaav can't stun without damage. TLDR we have less time.'

'K, whatever,' acknowledged Slam1go.

'This is not going to work,' Bokkie complained.

'Yeah… how the fuck are we going to win? Just because Octav is not there doesn't mean they'll just collapse or-' asked Belixner.

'Hush or get out,' Slam1go snapped to cut the discussion short as he stepped around the corner to take a look at their goal and to lead the way. Beyond the overlapping animations of area-denial magic, he saw a small part of the crowd opposing him. 'Three, two, one, GO! CC on contact, then maximum damage! If you still have some big items or cooldowns, now is the time!' He popped up Harden Body, and his middle finger pushed W into the keyboard hard, ready to press 5 with his index finger where his expensive Full Restoration Potion was. For the best efficiency it should be used at the last possible moment, but he would not take the risk and hit it at thirty percent or so.

The camera following his Fighter from the back captured only a part of the seventy or so enemies some ninety metres ahead of them at the end of a corridor carved in sandstone, and a few of Havoc members sprinting in his wake: Xyrolol, 415, Blinky, some guy called Curran, and Vizovia. As for the rest, a quick glance at the minimap told him the bulk of friendly green dots were on the move behind him, with an exception of a few stragglers. *There are always a few,* he thought, *but no time to manage them now.* He shrugged that fact away.

'Zovia, where is your Spell Reflect?' Slam1go asked, still running.

She stopped in her tracks to bring up the 0.5 second cast and apply the effect that Slam1go specifically told Mages to apply, then resumed the dash.

The two forces collided.

[Thread: KOTH GvG, Sunday 17 Jun]
[Posted by: Octav, 17 Jun 2015, 21:16:07]
I thought initially what Havoc did was a complete degeneracy and a far cry from fair play. However, having cooled down a little, and considering their subterfuge did not work in the end, I now think it was rather amusing. Thanks for the laughs, Pvro. I'll be more careful what I click next time.

-Octav

[Posted by: Sl4y, 17 Jun 2015, 21:18:01]
For the record, Pvro was not on today. Don't tell him we're being naughty when he's not looking :)

[Posted by: K_vanad, 17 Jun 2015, 21:19:56]

@Octav eh? Come on bro, don't drop hints like that without the full story. What did Havoc do? >__>

[Posted by: Halbdenial, 17 Jun 2015, 21:20:25]
Yeah I want to know too! I was there and I still don't know what really happened lol.

[Posted by: Octav, 17 Jun 2015, 21:25:26]
I'll give you the summary because I have to check on my kids and go to bed.

Basically, Havoc sniped me in Anabar, then gave me a fake portal to Cursed Woods, and chain-CCed me there so that I couldn't return to town or castle. Then they kept attacking us and trying to catch us reinforcing the courtyard (the one with fountain), but I told everyone to go to the Crystal room if they die. I managed to return two minutes before the end and didn't even need to do the emergency recall.

[Posted by: Slam1go, 17 Jun 2015, 21:28:44]
Good GvG :-)
I hope a few butthurt people we have here on the inside read Octav's comment. Hi Bokkie, Beli, Sarevoc, and whoever else?
In the end, what matters is that we all have fun and we should remember it's just a game, right? :-)

[Posted by: PowahOverwhelming, 17 Jun 2015, 21:29:59]
After today's battles, I never want to go against Slam1go or be a GL, too stressful xD

[Posted by: Proskillver, 17 Jun 2015, 21:31:01]
I need to quit drugs. I hallucinated about Slam1go speaking of fun and having distance to the game. I'm glad that never happened (✿ᵕ‿ᵕ)

Or did it? (⊙_⊙;)

[Posted by: Slam1go, 17 Jun 2015, 21:33:31]
@up actually I was going to ask if your doctor gave you new meds, because you've been really coherent lately! :-)
Till next time, girls :-)

*** *

[17:43] [Whisper] ^_Miko_^: hey ^^

Sl4y noticed the message only after a few moments, having been focused on a video he was watching on his second monitor. He paused it and alt-tabbed back to the game window. It was from ^_Miko_^. He hasn't been seeing her much online recently, so it piqued his interest. Sl4y could not recall ever having talked to her one on one before.

[17:45] [To: ^_Miko_^]: I was afk, sorry

[17:45] [To: ^_Miko_^]: what's up?

She took her time responding, perhaps being distracted herself. Meanwhile Intervene whisped him too.

[17:47] **[Friend]** Intervene: you ready for arenas in 5min?

[17:47] **[To: Intervene]:** give me a moment, Miko is on and wants something

[17:47] **[Friend]** Intervene: k

[17:47] [Whisper] ^_Miko_^: so ummmmmmmmmmm

I better encourage her a bit or this may take the whole day.

[17:48] [To: ^_Miko_^]: go on, I'm listening

[17:48] [Whisper] ^_Miko_^: ok i need ur help^^

[17:49] [Whisper] ^_Miko_^: i couldnt come to last few raids and fights v_v sorry

[17:49] [Whisper] ^_Miko_^: not my fault

[17:49] [Whisper] ^_Miko_^: my parents forbid me bcos school and stuff :/

[17:49] [Whisper] ^_Miko_^: had a big argument and i got grounded

[17:49] [Whisper] ^_Miko_^: buuuuuuut! I talked with my dad this morning

[17:49] [Whisper] ^_Miko_^: and apparentl I'm not grounded because just school

The messages stopped coming for a moment.

[17:52] [Whisper] ^_Miko_^: ok so he says he needs to talk to u...

[17:52] [To: ^_Miko_^]: what

[17:52] [To: ^_Miko_^]: why? D:

[17:52] [Whisper] ^_Miko_^: i dont know

[17:53] [Whisper] ^_Miko_^: its weird

[17:53] [Whisper] ^_Miko_^: but that's what he says

[17:53] [Whisper] ^_Miko_^: so can u help? ^^

[17:53] [To: ^_Miko_^]: why me?

[17:53] [Whisper] ^_Miko_^: he said the 'clan leader' but I dunno what that is lol

[17:53] [Whisper] ^_Miko_^: pvro is offline

[17:53] [To: ^_Miko_^]: ok I guess

[17:53] [To: ^_Miko_^]: what do I do?

[17:53] [Whisper] ^_Miko_^: he said to get your phone number and he will call you

[17:53] [To: ^_Miko_^]: wow D:

[17:54] [To: ^_Miko_^]: ok then

Sl4y typed the digits in the private chat and sent it.

[17:55] [Whisper] ^_Miko_^: thanks! ^^

[17:55] [Whisper] ^_Miko_^: u're not scary after all

[17:55] [To: ^_Miko_^]: D:

[17:55] [Whisper] ^_Miko_^: I'll go talk to him now, hang on

[17:56] **[To: Intervene]:** this will take a while longer but stand by

What's up with this situation? Sl4y never thought he would be helping a guildmate in such a way, it felt weird. He looked at his phone nervously; he never liked talking over the phone with anyone, and that was unlikely to ever change. And he was about to talk not only to a stranger, but to a parent of a girl he does not really know and never met. *What am I now, a school teacher?*

A trip caretaker? He prepared himself mentally for what will probably be a conversation with a non-technical boomer, involving explanations such as "no sir, online games can't be paused". He knew the type. He has been hearing it from his parents for years now. "Go outside". "Why do you keep sitting in front of that box?". "You're hurting yourself, son." But also "help me with the computer, I clicked something."

The phone rang a moment later, an unknown number displayed on the screen. Sl4y took off his headset, sighed loudly – he *really* did not want this conversation – and answered the call.

'Um. Hello?' he said, not knowing how he should introduce himself.

'Hello, is this Mr. Sl4y?' said the male voice from the phone, but without even a slightest hint of discomfort from pronouncing something as ridiculous as "Mister Slay." *Had they gotten the wrong number it would be such a wacky thing to happen for them.* The voice spoke with an accent from somewhere in the British Isles, but he could not place it more accurately.

'Um, yes.'

'Well then. Good afternoon. I'm Luisa's dad. Daughter tells me she spoke to you already. I know you must be confused, so let me just get it out of the way. My wife and I think she spends too much time online.'

Aaand there it is. This was already going the usual way. *Maybe it is for the better, I've had this conversation too many times myself with my own parents.* He had plenty of arguments and counter-points that he gathered over the years to use on his own family. Not that it ever changed anything.

'However, before you get the wrong idea,' Sl4y heard from the phone. 'I may be a dad, but I'm not that out of touch, I hope. You know, when I was her age, we had a clan, and we were good. What's that...? Ah, apparently you don't call them "clans" anymore. Anyway, Luisa is fifteen. I know games are fun, but school comes first, which is why we had to ground her without games. Summer term is almost over, and her grades are kind of shoddy.'

'I see,' said Sl4y. Sl4y knew ^_Miko_^ was quite young, but did not know how young. If she lived somewhere in the Isles, that explained her good English for someone at fifteen. He was sure he would not survive in an MMORPG using only his second language at that age. *Hold up, did she lie in the guild application about her age? I can't remember how she joined. Check later.*

^_Miko_^'s – or rather Luisa's – father continued. 'Which brings me to why I'm calling. There's another reason. Look, I know what the internet can be like, so I'm also concerned about what kind of contacts she makes, what kind of people she hangs out with. I used to sneak out without my parents knowing to meet strangers from the internet and play team games against them in an internet caf- (What? Don't give me that look… but unlike you, I wasn't a young lass, so that's that).' He stressed that last part. 'She says her clan is cool, but she's young and naive (no, yes, you are, don't argue), so I'd rather hear someone's voice. Apparently you lead that group or something?'

This was an unexpected course of the conversation, and while Sl4y had thought it would be awkward, he was amused instead. Was ^_Miko_^ discovering a completely new side of her dad just now?

'Uh, not exactly, but close enough, I suppose.'

'Good. May I ask your age?'

'Twenty-six.'

'Where're you from?'

'I live in Denmark at the moment,' he said truthfully, but not exhaustively.

'All right. Then I will ask you for a favour. Call me old-fashioned if you want, but I believe that hearing someone's voice, knowing there's a real human on the other side, has meaning. I will trust you.'

'Uh?' said Sl4y, and cringed at his own stupid response.

'I will ask you to keep creeps and weirdos away from her. If you promise me that, we'll let her come back to the game.'

'Hmm. I understand, although I don't know how much I can do. You realise I can't follow her around, control anything she does, or filter private messages to her, or…'

'I know, I know. But you must have *some* influence in that *guild* you have?'

'Well… some, maybe? You know what, okay, I'll do what I can, but you know I can't guarantee anything.'

'Obviously. I am not dropping all responsibility on you. I am only asking you to help me.'

'Understood. Then I promise to do my best, as I said.'

'Excellent. I hope you don't mind if I keep your number, just in case?'

'Not a problem.' Sl4y himself was surprised to say this, but he was getting to like that man.

'Very well. Luisa remains grounded for now, until she catches up with school and shows some good grades.'

'I understand.'

'All right then. Thank you for the talk, have a nice day.'

'Thank you too, bye.'

The conversation ended, and Sl4y added the number to the contact book before putting the phone down. "Miko's dad", he named it, and saved it. He returned to his desk - when had he even gotten up? - and checked in the guild window if Miko was still online. She was, and she even wrote to him first.

[18:01] [Whisper] ^_Miko_^: how was it

[18:01] [Whisper] ^_Miko_^: TELL ME

[18:03] [To: ^_Miko_^]: I regret to say your dad is…

Sl4y deliberately responded slowly and made a pause. For some reason, he felt like teasing her a little.

[18:03] [Whisper] ^_Miko_^: ???

[18:03] [To: ^_Miko_^]: he's pretty cool actually

[18:03] [To: ^_Miko_^]: fix the school shit and come back to us

[18:04] [Whisper] ^_Miko_^: :DD

[18:03] [To: ^_Miko_^]: school stuff* I mean.

[18:04][Whisper] ^_Miko_^: k!

[18:04] [To: ^_Miko_^]: …Luisa ;)

[18:04] [Whisper] ^_Miko_^: if you tell someone about this

[18:04] [Whisper] ^_Miko_^: I'll kill you :)

[18:04] [Whisper] ^_Miko_^: but thanks ^_^

A dot on his interface told him there was a new notification in the social panel.

[^_Miko_^ wants to register you as a friend. Accept / Reject]

'I'm getting so popular lately,' he said to no one in particular before accepting. Also, before letting Intervene know he was ready to rumble, he decided to address the latest task immediately. Business before pleasure was a rule he abided by in his life. Outstanding tasks always detracted from his fun. As far as he could tell, everyone was already quite protective of Miko and he should have mentioned this to her dad but he forgot. But still… there are dozens of people in Havoc, some of whom he knew nothing about or never talked with, and there will be newcomers in the future. *Must prevent plausible deniability for starters.* He opened the guild window, found the guild description box that anyone could read but only he (and Pvro) could modify, and added another line to the "guild rules" section.

Flirting with Miko is strictly forbidden and punishable by death and expulsion, in that order.

[18:05] **[Guild]** <MOTD>: New guild rule :-) -Sl4y

Sl4y was fully aware that a rule such as this is probably going to achieve the opposite effect of what he wanted, but it was funny to him, and they had made him an Officer against his will so he might as well have some fun. He could deal with problems as they arose, and it should be fun to observe some mild guild drama that may come out of this.

[18:05] **[To: Intervene]:** ok, inv

[18:42] **[Guild]** MALDING: YO ENDBRINGER IS UP

[18:42] **[Guild]** MALDING: I think I found him first, just spawned

[18:42] **[Guild]** Chaug: !

[18:42] **[Guild]** Vizix: which one?

[18:42] **[Guild]** MALDING: albrecht

[18:43] **[Guild]** Oioioibruv: the worst.

[18:43] **[Guild]** Maes: the best you mean

[18:43] **[Guild]** Oioioibruv: it suuuuuucks

[18:43] **[Guild]** Oioioibruv: the imps can spawn in stupid places and glitch out

[18:43] **[Guild]** Maes: ye but other gk's are worse

[18:43] **[Guild]** MALDING: ayo we doing it or not? I see 19 people online, not too many at this hour tbh but maybe maybe?

[18:43] **[Guild]** i_ex: log your mains girls, I brb too

[18:43] **[Guild]** Chaug: I will give tardy a call

[18:43] **[Guild]** Chaug: x in chat for invs and start moving to eoh

[18:43] **[Guild]** Chaug: also join me on vc

X's started showing on the You Never Wipe Alone guild's chat, and Chaug responded to each with a raid invite. As soon as the Paladin Dolj joined he designated him a Main Tank and a Raid Assistant, giving him all the raid management rights that Chaug himself had as the owner.

A soft *plink* played from the headset on his neck telling him the first member joined him on the channel, but Chaug was still on the phone with his tardy, the guild leader of ATR. They worked together sometimes as two guilds of similar sizes, and now was one such time.

'What's up, cunt?' greeted him yOydu, one of the senior members. Reliable, active, skilled, but also selfish. A good fit for Chaug's guild. A few more *plinks* followed soon.

'Oi!' said Oioioibruv, the newest member. Chaug was not sure who and when invited him. Apparently, he was versed in the game well enough but new to AltAr. 'Guid day mukkers,' he added. His personality and accent seemed to change depending on whether he was typing or speaking and on his mood.

'Hey, I'm on my way,' informed Maes. 'I'm nearby so I'll be there in five. Maldy you still have eyes on him?'

'He's not here yet. Hey guys, by the way,' Chaug responded only now.

Plink.

'Hiii…' said MALDING, yawning. 'Ya'll remember I called dibs on the legs, right?' he asked.

'Never heard a word of it,' assured Maes.

'Same,' confirmed Chaug.

'Nope, doesn't ring a bell.'

'Don't fuck with me, I said it like four ti- oh I see now. Fuck you guys!'

'Are you watching the boss Maldy?' asked Maes again.

'No, I'm hiding near the choke point. I'll see if someone goes in there.'

Another few *plinks.* There were now thirteen of them. Chaug, MALDING, Maes, Vizix, yOydu, Dolj, Oioioibruv, MorteM, 3stan, and more still joining, each raid member a tiny dot on Chaug's world map, all moving to an area on the southern tip of the gameworld. Their destination could only be reached by ground from the nearest flypoint which was not that close. Mages could open portals to that place if they spent a slot for that, but not many did.

'ATR coming or not?'

'Yeah they're coming, we should have about 20 guys and a witch,' clarified Chaug, to which Vizix snorted audibly.

'Threestan you're balanced six-eight-six now?' asked Vizix.

'Yep,' said 3stan. 'I'm bored of Pyro. I want to be a generic one-two-three tapping monkey now. And it's *Tristan.*'

'Oh, like in the legend? Got it.'

'It's also my real name.'

'Really? Neat.'

'Big mistake!' jumped in MorteM. 'You gave your personal information to internet strangers. Prepare to be hacked, noob!'

'Oh noes. Whatever shall I do?'

'Quickly, change your name!' advised Dolj.

[18:51] **[Friend]** tardy: ok inv

[18:51] tardy has joined the raid group.

Another *plink* told Chaug tardy joined their voice channel too.

''sup everyone,' he said. 'Gimme assist, I will invite my guys.'

'Done,' confirmed Chaug. 'I'm almost there. I see two people waiting already. By the way tardy don't tell me you've only now started moving?'

'Nah, we're on the way. In fact I think I see you in the distance.' tardy invited his guild's few members who decided to join this raid. Representing Along The Road beside tardy himself, there was an Inquisition Priest JimL, a former Game Master of AltAr; a Scholar PSP99 who would be a very welcome sight for Vizix and her immensely mana-consuming Arcanist Mage; an Assassin ChainsyIce, ever experimenting with builds and never having the same combination of traits and attributes two days in a row. *Who knows what he brought today?* There was also a full-support Paladin TheSame, and Sunny, a Minstrel who seemed to be AFK most of the time but somehow always did the expected task in a raid, no more and no less. Finally, Storkk the Hunter, about whom Chaug only remembered that he always fiddled with trap placement during GvG, endlessly correcting them as if trying to achieve some kind of personal enlightenment through perfect trap placement. tardy himself usually played a tanky, utility-oriented Fighter for GvG purposes but for this occasion he brought his *other* character, also a Fighter, but built for a massive combo finisher with maximum damage. They all hopped on the voice comms as well, some with muted microphones, and the big gathering also drew a few guild members doing other things to just sit back and listen.

Chaug caught up with MALDING waiting near the entrance to the canyon that led to End of Hope, an aptly named battlefield and a resting place of several armies that rose to face the malignant invaders from the world's depths and beyond.

Maes was already waiting too, and true to his word, tardy came right behind Chaug. The three of them stood on crossroads, mounted on their steeds of choice - an armoured, saddled black warhorse for Chaug, a deceptively slow turtle for MALDING that he just stood on top of, and a flightless bird with oversized beak and feathers in all shades of blue for Maes.

Within minutes they were all assembled and ready to go. MALDING had assured Chaug nobody passed by them since he spotted the boss, so there was a good chance nobody else knew about it yet. Not only was it an open-world rare boss, but he was also placed in an area without any PvP restrictions. Chaug's raid adopted a "not blue - kill it" stance, where "blue" were people in the same raid group.

'All right,' began Chaug. 'Looks like I was almost right on the money. We have nineteen guys, an almost-certainly-a-girl, and a French.'

'Wha-' began Maes.

'A sorry band of misfits. Not what you'd call a proper raid, but since we found him early, he should still be weakened. It will take a few moments longer, but we can do it. Hopefully nobody's AFK now? No? Okay. All right, you've all been here before, you know the plan. Let's go clear the trash. Dolj, pull everything.'

'Ah, nothing quite like genocide with friends,' said yOydu.

'Who said we're friends?' asked MALDING.

'Hear, hear!' said Chaug.

Two others snickered.

'Hey now! Drop your tsundere act, allright?' yOydu asked. 'I see right through you! Deep inside, you cherish those moments we spend together. The memories we make now, you will recall fondly in the future as some of your finest moments!'

'I really hope there are finer moments ahead…' mused Vizix.

'Also, is it genocide if we're killing demons?' asked Dolj, charging into the ranks of grotesque figures of various forms and sizes that stood between them and the end of the valley, all of them equally disposable. He made sure to capture aggro on as many as possible before backing out into the rain of damage his group delivered, then repeated the process.

'Or is it genocide if they're coming to invade *us*?' JimL offered another question.

Nobody seemed to be interested in trying to answer the questions posed, but the ranks of mortally-challenged henchmen blocking their path to End of Hope were laid low all the same, opening the way into a broad valley with a massive vault door at its end. But between that portal and the player group stretched a vast area littered with remains of ancient armies. Broken frames of siege machines littered the landscape, thousands of spears and swords impaled the ground where a knight had fallen, tattered banners swayed from broken poles, torn patches of textile hung from frames that once had been tents. Broken supply wagons, dried bones, and grotesque skulls of inhumans silently greeted Chaug's raid. Spectral apparitions of long-gone men and women manifested randomly out of thin air, attending to a task only they could perceive or engaging in combat against other shades, and then vanished again like water into the soil. The cloudy, blue skies over their heads changed hue to bloody red with coils of thick smoke rolling over it as they set foot in End of Hope. Ash swirled around them in wailing winds.

Such an apocalyptic setting fit well with the figurehead of subterranean armies, the Endbringer, a surprisingly human-looking General of hellish armies.

<Knight Champion Albrecht, Humanoid, Level ??>, read its tooltip. But this was a deception, an act that came to demons as naturally as breathing to mortals, and while it was a force of habit to refer to this entity as *he*, it was an *it*. It was the animated and possessed body of a once-great Knight Champion Albrecht, one who had slain hideous beasts by the dozen before he met his end. Now his broken but still large form stood shakily on a patch of beaten ground, the Champion's bloodied white surcoat hanging over an intricately engraved chest-plate, other pieces of plate strapped to its limbs, a layer of chainmail and leather padding underneath completing his once-knightly appearance. His sword had broken diagonally three-quarters down its length, but still *it* clutched the hilt.

Behind it in the distance lay the massive basalt-wrought gateway, now closed, to whatever place the twisted amalgamations of forms called home. It was speculated that one day this would be an entrance to a raid-size dungeon, and Enbringers were its gatekeepers and heralds of what was to come.

It was a rare encounter. The respawn timer for Endbringers was randomised between three days and a week, and it could spawn as one of several variants, each with different abilities and loot. And loot made it worthwhile to go out of one's way, travel all the way down south to the valley of End of Hope, and check if the foe is up for grabs, or even sit around waiting for it. Guaranteed drop of Molecule of Chaos or Speck of Ether; up to three Bars of Immaculate Steel, all highly sought-after for crafting and improving equipment; a box of rank 7 health and mana restoration potions; a 5% chance for one of the seven Blessed Weapons of Atinnoch; several bags of gems to exchange for currency at an NPC vendor; and, most importantly, a 0.5% chance for a legendary-tier item drop. A local NPC faction also recognizes every participant of a successful takedown as an ally, granting permission to purchase a unique mount.

'Ah, good! He's fresh. We can burst it down to like ninety percent before it transforms,' assessed yOydu.

'Yeah yeah,' agreed Chaug. 'We burn the fuck out of it on pull, use your damage pots and shit. Blow everything, you will have your CDs back before it's at ten percent, easily. PSP, feed mana to Vizix during the bursts, otherwise save it for healers. Divine Inspiration on Vizix too. Hunters watch our backs. Everyone should know what to do. Ready?'

A few nods came his way, which to Chaug was good enough.

'OK, here we go. Dolj do a countdown and pull.'

Arcanist Mage was a weird and unpopular build; tough to play, needed a pocket scholar to really shine, and specialised in single-target damage. Too slow and too vulnerable to status effects for PvP. Almost every talent granted new ability to use that had to be used in synergy with each other, but that meant using baseline Mage abilities was a loss of precious Damage Per Second. Even if executed flawlessly, a regular Elementalist ape was nearly as good but with half the effort and attention required. The fully-charged Matter Destabilisation Ray was simply awesome though, everyone's favourite sight to behold. In terms of raw damage output though, no class bar the few individuals who owned a Legendary item came close to Witch Doctors who were laughably easy to play, but required greater dedication to preparation than any other. In a way, Witch Doctors such as MorteM fought by money and time spent farming rather than by weapon or spell. Nevertheless, during a short window in the start of the fight she expected to leave everyone behind in damage numbers.

'...three, two,' counted Dolj. She started casting Thaumic Acceleration on herself at *two*. 'One, go,' finished the tank.

In the very same moment a buff appeared in her status bar, the Divine Inspiration from JimL, reducing her mana costs by half, and a debuff appeared on the boss, Accusation, increasing damage taken from all magic by a few percent, also from JimL. Truly, the Inquisition Priest was a friend of all casters, and its debuffs was only a part of what it brought to the raid, next to minimal mana restoration, minimal but constant healing, and not irrelevant damage. Aside from JimL's buff, she got her TA too. It was time to go all-in. Spells started flying from all around her, and melees rushed to unload everything they had from up close. Particles filled her screen.

[19:09] Champion Albrecht: <rambles incoherently>

A few spammable Elm Fires, as a filler and resource build-up. Thaumburst every three Elms. Disruption Bolt when her ring effect triggers for shorter cast. She watched her buffs as Discharge stacks increased passively with every Arcanist-specific spell she used. For now she did not hit for much, but with Thaumic Acceleration she could squeeze a dozen spells in a few seconds and build up the stacks.

[19:09] Champion Albrecht: …friends of yours, "Champion"?

Ten seconds into the fight. Improved Trance, to make her casts uninterruptable by damage and movement for nine seconds, though significantly slowing said movement. Multicasting, giving her a twenty-five percent chance to duplicate every spell she casts at decreased effectiveness. Now was the time. Her final Arcanist talent from level 100. One that was only good when the stars aligned.

Matter Destabilisation Ray entered the stage. It was as if her character had let loose a neutron star at the enemy. A thick ray of silver light shot out from her, ticking damage several times per second, with each tick having a chance to proc the Multicasting. Each proc thickened the beam, each with its own chance for a critical hit, and each added Discharge stacks passively up to a hundred. Damage numbers started filling her vision and she smiled from ear to ear seeing the flood of digits she could not even read anymore, so dense it was. As long as they were four-digit numbers, it was awesome enough.

'Nice!' said 3stan.

'UNLIMITED POWE-'

'Shut up, Maldy,' said Chaug. 'PSP you're up'

'I know, I know,' said PSP99 with irritation. He knew his role well and needed no micro-management.

The Ray had no duration limit, it went on as long as she had mana to sustain it, and its cost increased with every second. PSP99 transferred his mana to her when she was at twenty percent, allowing her a dozen more seconds of channelling. Then came the tricky part. She had to cancel the Ray with just enough mana left to follow it with Discharge at maximum stacks. In fact, many stacks were lost during the Matter Destabilisation Ray because she reached the upper limit, but that was unavoidable. Had she cancelled it too soon, she would have lost some Ray DPS, if too late, Discharge would not go off due to empty mana pool. There was no systematic way to do it, only practised instinct. She played it safe and broke off the channelling with more than enough mana for Discharge. The stack consumer spell triggered a massive arc explosion of static on the boss, but unluckily, it did not crit or Multicast. Still, hitting it for over forty thousand was one of the hardest single blows an ARIS player can do. Now that her hard-hitter was burned, she would spend the next minute or two recovering and regaining some mana while throwing cheap filler spells at the Endbringer.

Their Minstrel, Sunny, zipped back and forth from the melee group to the rangeds scattered around, switching songs he played on his instruments depending on who was near him. While everyone's buffs were fresh enough, he joined the damage-dealing effort with his rifle, even if only for a few seconds.

The Endbringer wearing the flesh of Champion Albrecht just stood there and soaked the hurt a paltry group of twenty mortals could throw at him; even the healers had nothing else to do than cast offensive spells. This was scripted behaviour. But at ninety percent of remaining health, the fight changed.

[19:09] Champion Albrecht: …ah… you wish to enter Master's domain. You may not.

Its voice rasped and resonated with an unnatural echo that should not be in a vast open space such as this. It was as if two voices spoke from one body.

In a swirl of red miasma and what looked like black lightning, the Endbringer grew from the mortal shell of Albrecht like a snake shedding its old skin, but grew six-fold as if the vessel it had parasited upon kept the Endbringer's infernal might contained. It still maintained a vague humanoid body plan as if Champion Albrecht's physical form had imprinted on the Endbringer's essence. Pieces of armour and cloth hung from him haphazardly, but he hardly needed those anymore.

The creature stretched to its full height, tall as a siege tower, stretched the wings that grew from his back and beat once as if to test them, then walked a few paces on its backward-bending hoofed limbs and picked up a pair of over-sized axes scattered among the battlefield remains, likely cast aside by some other ancient fiend from the world's depths. Only then the beast turned to face adversaries who had been pounding it all this time. It began attacking the tank with weapons while also occasionally setting parts of the large arena on fire or summoning impish familiars to shoot feeble but numerous darkfire bolt volleys at the players. Nothing the group could not handle, but that was only the start.

The fight progressed nicely, the mechanics were not too difficult yet, and they used the pre-transformation window really well. They shaved off more than 10% of the creature's health. To Chaug, this was acceptable, but the pressure was rising. The longer they fought it, the greater the chances of-

MorteM's health rapidly dropped, catching the healers totally unprepared for it. A few unexpected debuff icons briefly flashed on his status bar in raid frames, then he simply dropped dead.

'Hey what-' he began.

Both Chaug and Dolj were in melee, raining physical blows on the Endbringer, the former behind the boss and the latter with his back to the raid group, so neither saw what happened to the bomb-throwing Witch Doctor.

'Gank!' called out MALDING.

Vizix and a few of her co-raiders turned to face a group of players with red nameplates on them, already engaging their casters in melee range. Others in her group were doing the opposite - moving around the boss, away from what turned out to be Havoc members attacking them, but really uncertain what to do, their damage rotations breaking apart. Unless Chaug or someone else acted fast, the group risked collapse just out of the distraction created by gankers, let alone the killing of MorteM.

'Dolj, stay on it, TheSame with Dolj, everyone else fight back! Don't let the boss disengage,' he spoke confidently, but had no idea if this was the right call. Nevertheless, he adhered to a principle that a bad decision executed quickly was better than no decision. He broke into a run, closing the forty-fifty metre distance between Endbringer and his group's backline that now became the frontline with tardy and ChainsyIce in tow behind him. In the span of two seconds he assessed the situation: his Witch Doctor already dead, 3stan now evading death just by the grace of Mage's panic button and a quick absorption shield from JimL. Force Field would buy him a few seconds of life, but no more.

They were being attacked by two Warriors, a Mage, a Priest, and a Warlock. A very small group compared to his own, but he had to keep the Endbringer engaged in combat lest he regenerates outside it and their effort goes to waste. He recognized Sl4y from distance, his unique item setting him apart from others and, Chaug remarked, making him a giant target.

Without waiting for Chaug's orders, Maes took over the initiative. 'CC Sl4y, kill the Mage first, on the left, the one with short name! Someone peel the Warriors off yOydu!'

Chaug charged at a Warrior wearing elite PvP plate gear in dull brass-metal grey tint from head to heels including a set of spiked shoulderpads and gauntlets and an oversized two-handed sword who was kicking up a bladestorm on yOydu. Red droplets splattering around from the blade betrayed the expensive

Bloodbath enchantment. The charge briefly stunned Belixner, but Chaug immediately switched his target to the other Warrior, Intervene, the one with twin weapons. All he wanted was to just do a Maim on him, giving yOydu even as little as two seconds to stabilise and scuttle away a few steps. Vizix remembered Belixner as pretty ferocious. Very aggressive, relentless, knowing the profession through and through from maining it for years. A Havoc old guard, together with Ò_Ó the Mage.

It seemed Ò_Ó was doing an impressive job at staying alive and shaking off his enemies by cleverly using terrain features, breaking line of sight while slowing pursuers with frost spells, but by doing so he also lost the sight of Sl4y and ended up not getting a crucial heal, dropping to the ground eventually. For some reason Sl4y was not CCed as Maes commanded but that was beside the point; the little ganking group was already getting crushed by the four-to-one advantage. Vizix saw the two Warriors had refused to be shaken off from yOydu, so she did what Mages usually would not do, but then again, she played Arcanist, so perhaps she was crazy after all. She teleported herself right on top of yOydu and his assailants and cast a Force Push, knocking the two angry swirls of spikes and blades a dozen metres away. This little damage ended up killing one of them in the process, but she could still pay for this with her life in a moment, unless-

'There's one on my healer!' called Dolj.

An Assassin had exploited the attention of everyone being elsewhere and uncloaked behind TheSame who was holding Dolj all by himself. Dolj in the meantime wisely burned his damage reduction abilities and would hold out fine for a few moments. The same could not be said about the healer, who was already pretty much dead. Chaug must have noticed the whole situation too late to react, and could only watch as the black-clad form with a red scarf trailing behind it vanished again, probably seeking another victim that was not a tank.

'Jim, pick him up! Vizix, stack on Yo and do a Force Field. Protect our Paladin from the Assassin. 3stan, yOydu, Maes, Maldy, Storkk, get back on the boss already.'

Vizix was already stacked on yOydu now frantically healing himself and Sunny the Minstrel. It seemed the Havoc people targeted the supports, an obvious choice that she would also make. She pressed the FF hotkey and a telekinetic barrier surrounded a tiny area around them. She would have to sustain it for its full duration of six seconds, but others were already handling the threat.

Of the small invading party only Sl4y, Doomcaster, and Belixner were still standing, plus the Assassin hiding somewhere. Intervene was in the process of falling to his face. They would all get disposed of quickly, so Chaug must have decided to go back on the boss in case the Assassin shows up again.

'Dolj, pop a defensive if you have one. Sunny, casting speed song, now. yOydu, rez the pally, give him a chance to die again. TheSame, stack with melees when you're back. Their 'sin got away, might still be here. MorteM, I'll pick you up in a moment, try not to trip over this time.'

'Haha, okay.'

[19:14] [Raid] TheSame: ok

In the end only MorteM was a casualty of the attack, and only a temporary one. A few precious cooldowns were lost too, but that was what they were designed for. The group stabilised soon enough and was back to nuking the boss and dodging his own mechanics. Mana for healing should not be a problem either, with an Inquisition Priest and a Scholar that tardy brought with him.

'Who was that Assassin anyway?' asked yOydu after a moment.

'I didn't see,' admitted Chaug. 'Who died to him again, one of pallies?'

[19:15] [Raid] TheSame: it was GAav

'Hmm,' said Chaug.

'He's a good one,' offered a new voice, ChainsyIce, Gaav's fellow Assassin.

'Yeah, yeah, I know. But not even he can pop up and do anything before we blow him up.'

'True.'

Another twenty percent of boss health was torn down over a few minutes. They continued to dance around the frontal attacks, round up summoned imps and AoE them down, or reposition completely when fire and black lightning rained from the sky. They even managed to disengage a healer from the fight to let him drink up to full mana. This may not be possible again, as with the Endbringer's decreasing health, his damage from melee swings increased, putting a steadily-increasing strain on healers.

'They might be coming back soon,' advised MALDING.

'Aye,' agreed Oioioibruv. 'We shoulda seen them coming last toim, but now we stand higher so we can't miss them, can we.'

'You know what, just in case, let's keep a tighter spread,' Chaug decided. 'Vizix, Maes, Hunters, everyone ranged stack on yOydu. Move together. I'll put a star mark over his head.'

After another fifteen percent down they were roughly halfway done.

[19:17] **[Guild]** Frostalot: hey I see you guys in hope edn

[19:17] **[Guild]** Frostalot: care for more dps?

[19:17] **[Guild]** Unk: I can come too

[19:17] **[Guild]** MALDING: where have you guys been 20 mins ago

[19:17] **[Guild]** Unk: we were testing something funny :) will explain later

Chaug had to wait for a calmer moment between Endbringer's mechanics to respond in guild chat. He also had to pause doing damage for a moment, but he was used to it as a frequent raid leader.

[19:18] **[Guild]** Chaug: come if you can, but we're at 50% already

[19:18] **[Guild]** Frostalot: ok we're coming

'Hey, what's he doing?' suddenly asked Sunny.

'Hmm? What's who doing, where?' said Chaug, distracted.

'Just right over there to the left and above. It's this Gaav guy climbing on a broken siege tower or something.'

'Hmm,' said Chaug again. He turned his camera to see the spot Sunny mentioned, while his character still faced the boss so he could continue to Open Wounds here or Overhead Smash there at the press of his buttons.

Chaug found Havoc's elusive Assassin thirty or fourty metres away, aligning himself for a jump from one broken piece of a wooden siege tower to another. Its inner staircase was shattered at the bottom so it was inaccessible from the ground, but he had managed to somehow mount up to gain movement speed, jump from a nearby rock, and land on some invisible piece of geometry on the tower's outer wall. From that spot, he hopped to another micro-ledge, then made his way inside a hole blown in its side. It was at that moment when he was spotted. He took a few seconds to orient himself and judge the distance to the shattered staircase inside the once-mobile structure and made the jump and landed on the lowest stair. Then he just trudged up the rest of the way to stand atop.

'He's targeting our boss. I mean the demon, not you, boss,' said Maes.

'Wait, don't tell me he's... oh no, MOVE THE BOSS!' said yOydu.

'To where?' Dolj was confused. He was focused on the movements and abilities the Endbringer cycled through and on responding to them.

'Right! No, my right, your left!' urged yOydu.

It was too late. The lone figure standing on top of a tower was outside the range and direct line of sight of the raiders on the ground, but he had the raid boss in his. A tiny object shot from his hand, a dagger or a shuriken, or maybe even just a stone. Then another, then another, all impacting the infernal beast, which suddenly ceased attacking, spread its wings, beat them once as if to warm them up, and lifted off the ground with a powerful upward leap.

'What the fuck?' asked a few people at once.

'It's relocating…?' said Chaug. 'Chase it and taunt A-SAP! It's gonna regen out of combat!'

'Right!' confirmed the tank.

'Everyone follow Dolj,' commanded Chaug, as the Endbringer demon landed some hundred and twenty metres away, more than twice the length of a typical offensive spell.

'Um, so what just happened?' asked 3stan. 'Why did it fly away?'

'I think I know. He forced our boss to break from the fight and fly elsewhere in the area,' explained yOydu. 'Boss AI is coded to evade when attacked from outside game bounds. It's an anti-exploit mechanic. Gaav puzzle-jumped onto a spot where boss can't follow, so it counts as out of bounds. Just my guess though.'

'WTF, that's a dick move,' said 3stan.

'Aye, we should remember that,' said Oioioibruv. 'A lil' PvP never killed anyone, but this? Fook me.'

Maes, like the rest of the squad, was pleased to see that the new area the winged beast chose randomly was bereft of structures, ruins, and notable terrain features. It was a shallow dip but large in diameter, big enough to contain four raids such as theirs. No way for a pesky knife thrower to mess with them around here.

An arrow on the edge of his minimap told him one of their raiders was not with the group.

'Storkk, what are you still doing there?' he asked.

'~~Laying traps,~~' the Hunter explained. *Must be one of those people with bad mic*, Maes thought. They annoyed him. '~~I'm coming already.~~'

'Why did you do that? I didn't ask you to,' asked Chaug.

'~~I thought it's a good idea, the sin has only one way down and I trapped it.~~'

That happened regularly in and around You Never Wipe Alone guild. Members and allies by convenience rather than by discipline or loyalty, and with a single rule: don't take anything seriously, including the game and the guild. This was Chaug's vision, but such a policy came at a cost: cultivating individualism and levity meant someone always did whatever they wanted, whenever they wanted, consequences be damned. This stood in contrast to the very idea of forming a guild, but somehow it worked. Even YNWA members needed someone to talk to, or do group content. Storkk was not of his guild, but apparently he operated as if he was.

'Get your ass back here,' Chaug demanded and began to add: 'He's going to own you if-'

'Oh shit...' said Storkk, his voice quality getting even worse with the louder, more emotional outburst, and Maes already knew what the reaction meant.

The Hunter became the prey. Raid frames told Maes Storkk's health bar, greyed out die to distance, was dropping and a few status effects were on him too. An Assassin's effects, of course. He tapped the M key and quickly looked at the distance between the group's current position and where the siege tower was. Too far.

'Everyone, stay on the boss, don't get distracted,' said Chaug, apparently arriving at the same conclusion. 'Dude will be dead before you reach him.'

'Sorry, I don't know how he got down here so fast.'

'Imps, imps!' called out JimL, as a dozen fiery imps spawned in a pack nearby.

'I see them,' confirmed 3stan, and turned to cast Meteor Strikes and Chain Lightnings as their location. Vizix had already put a Chronostasis under their feet, slowing their movements and casting speed. It was a cooldown that would be very useful against the next PvP incident should it come to pass, but then again, sitting on an unused cooldown was a waste too. Meanwhile, the true form of the demonic Endbringer continued to pummel down Dolj, occasionally stomp with its plated hooves stunning melee fighters, and throw ranged attacks at the more distant players.

'Brassknight patrol coming from the left, we're in their way,' signalled someone.

'We circle right around the boss. Everyone keep anchoring on yOydu. Move.'

'Storkk is not dead yet. Hmm,' observed Maes.

'~~Help?~~'

'No. Save your breath and don't do that again,' said tardy, reprimanding his own guild member. 'If you can, disengage and get back here, if not, try to die quickly.'

'Or, maybe, try to live as long as you can to keep him busy?' offered MALDING.

'~~He can't kill me but won't let go~~...'

After another ten seconds or so Storkk was still alive at a third of his health but roughly in the same position, according to the map. Then, suddenly, his health dropped to zero.

'~~He got me.~~'

'Yeah, no shit?' said MALDING, laughing.

'That was weird though. He could have killed him any time he wanted. I wonder if he was keeping our Hunter pinned down to lower our DPS?' asked Vizix.

'Killing him immediately would achieve the same result,' pointed out ChainsyIce.

'That's because he wanted one of our healers to break away and go save him,' JimL stated, sparking a chorus of *oooh*'s from the listeners.

'Clever bastard,' Maes had to admit.

Chaug snipped the conversation.

'Enough chit-chat, pull your pants back up and kill this thing.'

Havoc was on the run. As expected by Chaug, they had come back for round two, but unfortunately for them, YNWA and ATR had received reinforcements just minutes before. Frostalot, Unk, Teeg, Shioya and a few others shaved off a few minutes from the time needed to deplete the Endbringer's health bar. The lower he got, the more it thrashed and harder it hit, but with an extra healer it was manageable. Dolj withstood the fight, and Chaug once again had to inwardly praise his tank for his good positioning, timing, and overall performance. To praise him publicly risked pumping the tank's ego, which was best avoided.

The Endbringer, as if sensing its imminent end, began manifesting its true form of an otherworldly, eldritch being. Body parts shimmered in and out of existence, suggesting rather than actually assuming the form of something very non-human, as if a pyramid of flesh; its howls seemed to be coming from every direction at once, making it difficult to grasp what or where it actually was. It thrashed wildly in its final moments, swatting a few players like flies as a farewell gift. This was one of the darker motifs of the game and came with a dramatic piece of music and graphic visuals, but it was difficult to feel the immersion after experiencing it dozens of times.

Inevitably, the infernal creature was beaten and its place spawned a large, brass-bound chest, an odd flesh-coloured oily light seeping through the cracks in the shell. It took eight seconds to open it and multiple people could attempt it simultaneously, even opportunist ninjas. Taking any damage or moving during the opening interrupted the attempt. For this reason it was not enough for a guild or a group to defeat a boss, they also needed to defend the loot from vultures, i.e. other players. Some players subscribed to some code of ethics and would never lay a hand on another group's loot. Some players did not, such as Chaug and his guild themselves.

None came to challenge them, and the loot was picked up and split by Chaug as agreed with tardy beforehand: Speck of Ether, one Bar of Immaculate

Steel, and two bags of jewels for his guild, the rest, whatever it would be, would be kept by You Never Wipe Alone. Chaug thanked everyone for participation and called the raid. People started taking portals or teleporting to home point by their own means.

It was at that moment when Havoc came back for round two, only to discover they came late and YNWA were wrapping things up. YNWA stopped what they were doing. For an awkward moment, the two groups eyed each other from a distance, waiting to see what the other group would do. Their numbers were more even now, although Havoc still was at a disadvantage. An uneven fight by any measure, but that would never stop Chaug.

He summoned his armoured skeletal warhorse, faint red mist billowing within its ribcage and from its nostrils.

'Fucking get them,' he said, and others mounted their steeds as well. They dashed straight for Havoc's position up a delicate slope overlooking them. Seeing this unfold, Havoc turned around and fled towards the exit from End of Hope, as if to spite the very name of the cursed valley. Chaug quickly checked who was on pursuit with him, and found nine members total. Oioioibruv was there, as was Maes, 3stan, Dolj, Frostalot, Unk, and tardy with his healer, TheSame.

'They're running?' asked Dolj.

'Yes, but keep chasing. They can't escape!' urged Maes.

'Why? They run as fast as we do.'

'See for yourself.'

Indeed, Havoc was trapped. They ran into the bottleneck and found that dozens of hostile mobs had already respawned within it. They posed no threat by themselves, but riding through them would certainly dismount them all and swarm them, and they would be forced to fight not only the monsters but also You Never Wipe Alone. A certain death, an embarrassing one at that. So Havoc did the only thing they could in this situation - they stopped outside the range of the shambling undead and demonic knights of ages past, and turned around once again, this time to face the incoming group of Chaug and his allies as a last stand. Chaug was pleased to see it. The rival guild wasted his time that evening with their guerilla attacks, hoping to wipe his raid either by their own hand or that of the boss. He was really looking forward to killing them for it.

Havoc's Mage, the one with the weird nickname, put a Blizzard between them and the incoming YNWA party so that the raining ice shards would dismount and slow their charge. For the first time that day he was able to take a look at them all. There were six of them - *six that I can see,* he corrected himself - but his Guild Leader counterpart, Pvro, did not seem to be around. But there was the huge warrior dude Belixner, Doomcaster, Gaav hiding somewhere, a Fighter called PowerOverwhelming, and a combat Paladin, Makzine. Behind them all, that old codger Sl4y.

Chaug made no effort to micro-manage the engagement by calling out priority targets or coordinating crowd-controls. He just wanted to enjoy the PvP combat against people who wanted the same thing, and hoped his side would just win. And even if they were to lose somehow, then so what? He only made sure his followers were grouped up nicely and then he did just the bare minimum of informing his team that he was all-in and encouraging them to follow.

'Aight, let's go, gogogogo! No stopping!'

The two parties connected by colourful rays of magic and ranged attacks and by close and personal bladework. The battle seemed to be going in his favour, with enemy Warlock punished quickly for standing just a little bit too far in the front and the Fighter quickly dropping in health. For their part, Gaav ambushed one of YNWA's healers, TheSame, for the second time that evening, perhaps seeking to exploit a weakness he had found earlier. This time the Paladin would not die easily thanks to the efforts of yOydu. Chaug would have broken away to peel the Assassin off, but he himself got caught in a hell of stunlocks and slows from Makzine's massive, two-handed battlemace.

Suddenly, Dolj exploded in the process of beating down on PowerOverwhelming. Green and purple particles of malefic magic shot out from Dolj's body towards his still-living allies as it collapsed to the ground to the sound of a dying human's whimper.

'What was th-' began someone.

'Up on the cliff! Silence him!' called someone else. 'How did he even get there?!'

Up above on a ledge overlooking them stood a robed male figure bathed in a purple haze of Desperate Call to Power, an ability of Warlocks. The caster's position offered him protection from melee attacks as he unleashed long casts on Maes' allies below with impunity, not that Chaug's group had any melees in it other than himself. While casters such as Warlocks usually have to carefully pick their casting windows lest they be caught by an interruption spell or forced to reposition, this one exploited the opportunity to unleash even an eight-second cast of Mark of Chaos, an ability rarely seen in PvP due to its cumbersome mechanic.

Players don't recognize each other by each other's character face or other things too small on their monitor displays, but this unexpected threat could be identified by his gear even without reading the nameplate over his head. The crimson-red robe with black trims from Throne of Carrion; the staff Malevolence, so aptly named; the hood shadowing the character's face almost utterly. A black sash bound his waist, adorned with multiple pouches and satchels for carrying reagents for spells of very questionable ethics. The hand clutching the staff was entirely skeletal, which was the unique effect of the Hollowed Handwraps, one of the two copies of this item existing on the server. Unlike Sl4y's asymmetrical cloak, this was a legendary item that combined both unique looks and combat utility. Strangely though, the other existing copy of this item did not seem to be used by anyone, thus magnifying the Warlock's uniqueness. Perhaps the other copy was bound to an account whose owner had quit the game for good. Overall, this Warlock fully embraced the class fantasy and had a matching outfit to go with it, and the resulting imposing look was only bolstered by the difficulties the Warlock had gone through to acquire his gear, as well as by the grim reputation he had made for himself.

'Who is this being of purest edge?!' asked Oioioibruv.

'It's fucking *Venetia*,' said Maes to his group, groaning. Venetia, the Warlock player everyone who was someone had to know by reputation. The lifetime PvP kill participation leaderboard king. The gap between him and the runner-up was large enough that it would take more than a year to catch up, provided that Venetia would somehow embrace pacifism for such a long time. Venetia had put a few curses and dots on Dolj but the real pain was still to come. Maes saw Venetia exploit his nearly untouchable high ground position and activate his Dark Bargain, sacrificing seventy percent of his health in exchange for extra fifty percent of spell damage. He followed it with a cast Mark of Chaos on the Paladin Dolj, a beefy target who would live just long enough to be the host of the unrolling combo. Next came Expulsion, executing a spell sequence that Warlock players fantasise about in hectic PvP conditions. Expulsion, nicknamed "Dotonation" by the playerbase, was limited to one use per 30 minutes and caused the Mark of Chaos to explode, doing damage scaled with the amount of Warlock's effects on the target, and then also spreading a copy of those effects randomly among their nearby allies.

Venetia had managed to put several dots and effects on the Paladin at fifty percent of his health remaining so the execution spell floored the target where he stood, the ailments now spread across their small party. He was also free to continue shooting the fish in the barrel. Chaug and the rest of YNWA guild could only curse in frustration of being demolished in such a fashion.

Maes had noticed the incoming nuclear strike and put enough distance between himself and Dolj. He would warn his team about it, but there was not enough time to articulate the thought, and the voice comms were bustling with combat chatter anyway. As his team started to fall apart, he disengaged, mounted up, and fled back deeper into End of Hope, avoiding all the patrolling regular and elite monsters serving whatever lord that commanded them. With the ancient battlefield littered with broken siege engines, craters left by explosions, ditches, torn tents and makeshift barricades, it was fairly easy to find a spot out of sight, and cast a Return Home.

'Sorry guys, I couldn't help you,' he said to the team. Casting bar on his screen progressed slowly.

'That's fine, raid is called anyway,' said Chaug. 'We did alright today, I think.'

'Yeah,' said a couple of voices.

Maes opened his inventory to check the equipment damage to be repaired, and the consumables he used up. As he looked, a message in chat drew his attention.

Then his heart jumped up to his throat when a speech bubble from someone just next to him popped up, and his Return Home spell never completed.

[19:31] BATS: q:)

* * *

[21:51] **[Guild]** Vizovia: um, I have a question

[21:51] **[Guild]** Vizovia: how can I get a [Molecule of Chaos]?

Vizovia had hit level 91 on her mage earlier in the afternoon which allowed her to finally equip The Ocular, a pretty good one-handed magic rod. For a level 91 Mage only three other one-handed weapons were better depending on the build, but the differences were small. Arcanist Mage favoured flat Intellect bonus while Elementalist pulled ahead with extra critical hit rating. The Ocular was better than the previous two-handed staff she used, even despite the fact her other weapon slot, the off-hand, was rather poor in quality for the time being. Still, just the bonus intellect stat conferred by Ocular was an improvement of more than eight percent. She was unlikely to get her hands on another weapon of this quality in the near future – probably not before she hits level 96 – so now it was time to utilise it to the maximum. And that meant socketing and enchanting it, which in turn meant obtaining runes and Enchanting materials, and therefore, expenses and effort. Dusts and Motes were relatively easy and cheap to get, whereas Sigils were quite expensive considering she needed twelve of them. It would drain her pocket almost completely, but it was necessary and worth the investment. Ò_Ó told her so, a week ago when Ocular had dropped and Slam1go awarded it to her as he was serving as the group leader at the time. *This is what gold is for*, someone else added.

But the last reagent, a Molecule of Chaos, was a problem.

[21:51] **[Guild]** 415: 90+ raid trash drop with small chance

[21:51] **[Guild]** Azarus: or market

[21:51] **[Guild]** Azarus: but it ain't cheap

[21:51] **[Guild]** slowah: it's ez, just be Azarus and grind money all day

[21:51] **[Guild]** slowah: then buy whatever you need

[21:51] **[Guild]** slowah: =]

[21:51] **[Guild]** Azarus: can confirm, it works

[21:51] **[Guild]** Azarus: even better when you dont feed tons of mats to your wife every week

[21:51] **[Guild]** Vizovia: xD

[21:51] **[Guild]** slowah: pray for this man

[21:51] **[Guild]** Vizovia: well I am 91 and poor

[21:51] **[Guild]** Sl4y: no problem, I'll assign you a husband who will work himself to death for you

[21:51] **[Guild]** Vizovia: um, what xD

[21:51] **[Guild]** Azarus: can confirm, it works :/

[21:52] **[Guild]** Sl4y: ok but seriously, I have a better idea

[21:52] **[Guild]** Sl4y: come find me in Argentia

[[Sl4y] invites you to a Group.][accept][reject]

Sl4y sat by a wooden table in a gallery overlooking the great fountain in Argentia, which just like the decorative railing owed its brightness to the red-veined marble the Kingdom was known for. Major city arteries coming from east, south, and north met here, while a cobbled alley to the west led to the Dresdver Palace, the seat of the Kingdom's royal court according to the game lore. This was not Sl4y's usual spot, but it was one Sapphire liked. The building was just one of the merchant houses, open to players at all times, but the gallery was accessible from the outside. It offered a good view on the large square where the main roads met, and where two tall flag poles on either side of the fountain displayed the current owners of GvG castles for all to see: Havoc's somewhat simplistic design of an inverted trinity symbol in white over pitch-black background and with an etched golden trim; and a more elaborate design for Bulwark, a bassinet-type helmet with the vertical--slitted visor down, over a white-and-red checker pattern background. There was meaning behind Bulwark's heraldry. The founder, Octav, apparently was a big chunk of a man who practised bohurt, a niche contact sport imitating medieval combat, with armours, sword, shields, et cetera. The chequered background stood for his homeland, Croatia. Along The Road Guild, the allies of Bulwark, was not represented since only the actual owner was ever displayed despite the allied contributions.

Sl4y's eye sniped Vizovia approaching across the large square. A bare-headed, sky blue-haired Mage dismounted outside from a feathered lime-green raptor mount and entered the gallery by the staircase from the street, waving a gloved hand at the people expecting her. She was thin-bodied and of average female height, and she came wearing her Mage gear. A gossamer-thin white mantle enveloped her shoulders, its folds held together on her chest by a clasp. The mantle gently billowed behind her as she walked, and the underlying buttoned tunic was thigh-length, revealing her bare knees. The tunic was sleeveless but her gloves covered her forearms almost up to her elbows. Her large, fuschia-pink eyes complemented her colours nicely. Overall, she looked pretty good. In fact, she looked *too good* for a level 91 character who was still leveling. Was she deliberately wearing sub-optimal but pretty gear? Sl4y made a mental note to inspect her before the next party to make sure she did not confuse a raid for a fashion show. Still, he had to admit whoever she was in real life, she had style.

Sl4y was not sitting alone, and something in her awkward pause told Sl4y that Vizovia was taken by surprise when she came upstairs.

[21:58] Vizovia: um, sorry to spoil your moment ^^

[21:58] Sapphire: what moment?

[21:58] Sapphire: ahh!

Sapphire was the other mature girl of the guild but one that would grimace if called "big sis" or something of the sort. Funnily enough, nobody seemed to know her real age precisely, probably except for Sl4y who would not tell. Even if Vizovia had not seen the nickname over the Minstrel's head, she would identify her by chestnut hair and narrow eyes observing her from underneath a fringe. To Vizovia's perception she projected an aura of silent confidence and quiet judgement. They never talked one-on-one; she seemed to often log in around the time Vizovia usually goes to bed or just minutes before the GvG.

[21:58] Sapphire: don't mind me, just enjoying my evening with Patrick :)

Sl4y was surprised for a very short moment and wondered who this Patrick may be, but then it hit him.

[21:58] Sl4y: it's fine V, I invited you here myself didn't I

[21:58] Sl4y: is this what you need?

Sl4y said, opening a trade window with the younger Mage, and dragged the item she needed from his inventory into it, but has not confirmed the deal yet. He had been in the Bank building when the /guild conversation started. *I'm pretty sure we had a few Molecules in here somewhere*, he had thought as he moved from his own storage to that of Havoc. He would give her one of his own, but he did not have any himself. But his intuition was correct and he picked up one of them from Havoc's restricted storage and moved it to his bags, then he opened the transaction log, and wrote "for Vizovia" underneath the latest entry. It was unlikely anyone would even read the log, as only those lamentable few of Veteran rank and above could even open it, much less make a fuss out of it. Certainly, people like Venetia, Belixner, or Sarevoc had at least a few of their own in stash and had nothing to do with them. Then he returned to the gallery where Sapphire waited for him, which was also where Vizovia found them a few moments later.

[21:58] Vizovia: yes!

[21:58] Vizovia: how much?

[21:58] Sl4y: 0

[21:58] Vizovia: :o

[21:58] Sl4y: a gift from the guild :p

[21:58] Sl4y: but first - what do you need it for?

[21:58] Vizovia: Avalanche ench

[21:58] Sl4y: isn't thaumic torrent better?

[21:58] Vizovia: I thought it is, but o_o says no

[21:58] Sl4y: I have no idea why, but I won't argue with his mage wisdom I guess

[21:58] Sl4y: here you go :)

Sl4y confirmed the trade.

[21:58] Vizovia: thank you :3

[21:58] Vizovia: do we have some sort of procedure for requesting gbank stuff?

[21:58] Sl4y: no, but maybe we should

[21:58] Sl4y: take it before I write it:D

[21:58] Vizovia: ok haha

[21:59] Vizovia: I'll leave you two alone now then ^^'

[21:59] Vizovia: thanks again!

[Vizovia cheers]

[Vizovia waves at you]

[Vizovia waves at Sapphire]

[21:59] Sapphire: cya (:

Vizovia then casually jumped over the railing down onto the cobbled street to save the few seconds she would otherwise lose taking the stairs. Gamers are busy people who do not have this kind of time. Sl4y got an impression she was embarrassed or something, and wondered if she felt the need to vanish as soon as possible. At the same time he wondered if she was doing a little celebratory dance as she turned the corner. Not that the game allowed this kind of celebration, but it is the thought that counts. He typed a message.

[22:00] **[To: Sapphire]**: really? PATRICK? XD

[22:00] **[Friend]** Sapphire: XD

[22:00] **[Friend]** Sapphire: the first name that came to me

[22:00] **[Friend]** Sapphire: should we tell her?

[22:00] **[To: Sapphire]**: no xD

[22:00] **[To: Sapphire]**: well it's up to you tbh, I don't mind

[22:00] **[Friend]** Sapphire: then dont

[22:00] **[Friend]** Sapphire: that hasn't happened in a while

[22:00] **[To: Sapphire]**: yeah

[22:00] **[To: Sapphire]**: it takes me back:D

[22:01] **[Friend]** Sapphire: not since the honeymoon island incident xD

[22:01] **[Friend]** Sapphire: dont know if you noticed, but I forgot to change outfits again

[22:01] **[Friend]** Sapphire: I was in slut uniform all this time

[22:01] **[To: Sapphire]**: I might have noticed this very revealing costume, yes.

[22:01] **[Friend]** Sapphire: why did they even make them this way? its supposed to protect me. so unrealistic

[22:01] **[Friend]** Sapphire: horny game devs smh =_=

[22:01] **[To: Sapphire]**: unrealistic?

[22:01] **[To: Sapphire]**: I'm a Priest dripping with gold. Looks very realistic to me =]

Vizovia had easily acquired the Molecule, the item she thought would be most problematic to get and therefore would be the last to be collected. But now it was in her inventory while the most basic stuff was not. Fortunately she knew where to find it herself.She pranced giddily through the town. Not only did she now carry a new weapon, but also now held an epic-quality reagent in her inventory, that she would otherwise have to spend several hours getting. *Guilds can be pretty great!*

[Friend] Ò_Ó has logged in.

She was about to check if Ò_Ó is online; she needed to talk to him when he just happened to log in. She waited a few minutes before she whisped him through the friendlist.

'Hey, got a moment? Two questions only,' She sent to him.

'Sure, what's up?' The answer came immediately.

'You sure it's Avalanche not something else?'

'Ofc.'

'OK then. I'll get the rest of the dusts and motes now ^^'

'You got the molecule already?' asked Ò_Ó.

'Yes, just now. Sl4y gave me one! :D'

'Good, I should have told you to check with him first, I forgot. Is he still on?'

'He's hanging out with Sapphire now. I didn't know they were so close.'

'Are they?' said Ò_Ó.

'What?'

'Nothing. You said you wanted to ask something else?'

'Yes, I have the last nine levels to get, where do I put the last stats and skills?'

'It doesn't matter, you are still leveling so you will reset stats and skills at 100 anyway. Then you will fine-tune your build for whatever you want to do :p'

'Hm, ok.'

'Just put it stats in INT and skills in area spells, Meteor Strike or Freezing Gust, or even Chain Lightning. Don't invest in raid buffs. When in doubt, take damage :)'

'Ok, thank you ^^'

'Now, I need you for something. Got a few moments?' he asked.

'Yes.'

'Great. Come find me :)'

He opened a portal and brought her to Fulgrad, a minor town in the southern continent. It was a nearly insignificant place, except for being a safe refuge among maps flagged for player versus player combat, and a home to a few vendors of goods sold nowhere else, such as tiny rainbow-scaled lizard pets and firecrackers. But the town's most important business was gems and jewellery. Players come to Fulgrad from all over the world of ARIS to buy the finest wedding rings from NPC vendors. From here a bridge took players across the river to a dungeon, the Fulgradorn Mines, and the local area was bountiful in high-experience mobs such as fire-breathing Salamanders the size of a passenger car, stalking the foothills of a volcano fuming to the south. They were slow, but very, very patient. Why chase prey, when you can just roast it by setting the area on fire? It's not like it moves afterwards.

'Stay dismounted. Cast Invisibility when I do,' he typed to her.

Vizovia and Ò_Ó left the town by the west gate and entered a forest of amazingly tall trees spreading their crowns wide and forming a canopy overhead akin to sequoias. The underside of leaves viewed from down below looked silvery or blue-ish giving the whole place an eerie feeling. The ground level's foliage was unsurprisingly modest, since the trees overhead absorbed almost all of the daylight, leaving very little for plants growing underfoot. A tall yellow-and-blue grass was reminiscent of a savannah, and massive branches strewn the forest floor as they dropped dry or broken from the tree tops high above, creating an excellent home for all kinds of insects as they rot and decompose on the ground.

Ò_Ó had led her along the road at first, but soon they went offroad. To Vizovia it seemed like her companion did not really know where they were going. They were taking turns left or right in apparently random places.

'Are you looking for something?' She asked him.

'No. Looking for someone, and trying to not be looked at while we're at it. Ah, there we go! See that guy?' asked Ò_Ó. Slightly uphill from them was a Witch Doctor player mobbing and AoE-ing Skantids; insect-like creatures living in large colonies, their thick chitinous plating indicating their high DEF attributes. Their behaviour seemed to be modelled on ants or bees. Fire worked best against them, but not every class had access to elemental attacks. One also had to be careful to engage them carefully and individually, for when attacked, Skantids were programmed to summon other nearby drones to assist them. A careless player could get rapidly swarmed, but this Witch Doctor was doing a good job preventing that. *How unfortunate for him*, thought Ò_Ó.

'Yes,' said Vizovia at his side.

'Great! Now kill him.'

'What?'

'You heard me. Fold him.'

'I thought you needed my help. Why not do it yourself?'

'Because you must do it :)'

'Why?'

'Because I'm telling you to :D'

'...'

'Come on. He's getting away.'

'But he's just doing a quest or something!'

'Yeah. I know. But this is a PvP zone, he knows the risks. Go in there and gank him.'

'But why?!'

'Why, why... so many questions. Consider it therapy.'

'Therapy for what? Speak sense please.'

'For being a noob and a doormat. Like that time you passed on boots in Azure Halls because Doom rolled for it. Yeah I noticed that. Or the time you got camped outside Hardline and didn't ask on /g for help. Were it me, I wouldn't call for help either, but that is because I am stubborn and I have pride and you don't, you were just shy.'

'How do you know about that? :/' She was not enjoying this conversation.

'Because it was my sister's party who camped you, that's how :D'

'OMG what's wrong with you people :/ what are you, a family of bullies?'

'You should meet our eldest bro. Now, go kill this dude.'

'He is 6 levels above me!'

'Then we're in luck he's low.'

'Are you enjoying this?'

'Yes :D but Sl4y also asked me to babysit you.'

'He didn't. You know I'm an adult, right?' Vizovia asked.

'Did I say babysit? Of course I meant "mentor you".'

'That sounds bet-'

'But you are a baby.'

Vizovia sighed with irritation loudly enough that her cat woke up. The good mood she had after obtaining the Molecule of Chaos was leaving the party.

'But he's weak now, won't that be super lame to attack him now?' she asked.

'True. I'll tell him you want to duel him at full strength.'

'No!'

'Then off you go! :D Fold his ass! While we're at it, I'll check your technique. What would you open with in this situation? CC or burst?'

'Sigh. If he sees me first then-' Vizovia began but was interrupted.

'Don't tell me, show me. Wreck him and assert dominance! Then spit on him!'

'Ugh, but you asked -_- Fine, I'll try, then leave me alone, geez -_- '

A moment later an Witch Doctor by the name of Numeu5 lay on the ground defeated, but still inside his body. It was a short struggle. He was at forty percent HP and a few skills on cooldown when the Pyroclasm hit him, and it critted too. Before he knew what hit him, Ice Shackle rooted him in place. He could only turn his camera towards the source of the damage: a female

Mage from Havoc no less, one that he recognized somehow, casting some lightning-school spell at him from about 30 metres away and the direction he came from. That was just a few metres outside his range, but her Shackle prevented him from moving. She even had put a Force Field on herself just in case he could close the gap somehow. She played it well, meaning he could only watch his death.

She came over to where he lay among the still corpses of broken insectoids and stood over him. What she said next was not "haha ez" or something in this vein that he expected from Havoc people. Instead, what followed was:

[22:25] Vizovia: hello! And I'm sorry ^^'

[22:25] Vizovia: I just really needed to kill you

[22:25] Vizovia: I hope you don't mind :3

He now recognized a few details about her. Numeus himself was a member of Execute, the chief among the rival guilds of Havoc, and several members of both sides regularly exchanged insults and provocations on server's forums. His current character, Numeu5 was his third character on the server and he did not even bother to have it join the guild. Nevertheless, he now recalled seeing a new Mage in Havoc during the regular battles. He might have even killed her himself a few times when he was on his Hunter, Numeus. She was either new, or someone's alt. If she even was a *she*.

But somehow, his death did not feel entirely negative. Her character looked gorgeous, but she was ruthless enough to surprise-attack him, skilled enough to not screw up this simple gank, but also oddly nice. Since when Havoc had people like that?

[22:25] Numeu5: you're awfully polite for someone stabbing someone else in the back

[22:25] Vizovia: sorry, I really had to^^'

He was about to type his response, when another Mage emerged from thin air next to Vizovia and downed Numeus's, and Numeus knew it was

Invisibility that had concealed the newcomer. So there were two of them, but only one attacked. It was that dude with a weird name, Ò_Ó, whom Numeus knew well. Not personally of course, they just killed each other hundreds of times over the years of AltAr.

[22:26] Ò_Ó: hello sir! You have been folded by the feminine hands of Vizovia. How would you rate your ganking experience this day?

[22:26] Numeu5: D:

[22:26] Numeu5: it was awful, not recommended

[22:26] Numeu5: but I give it all 4 points out of 10 just because I've never been ganked by an angel before

He said then released his body. Vizovia and Ò_Ó now stood over an empty player skeleton.

'So, how was it? :D' asked Ò_Ó.

'I thought he would be pissed off, but you managed to turn it into a joke somehow.'

'Yes, and you have a new fan now too :D'

'I won't comment on that,' said Vizovia bashfully.

'By the way, this guy you killed is a veteran from Execute, I'm sure he won't remember you or hold a grudge or anything. But you better get that lvl 100 soon.'

'I'll kill you xD'

'You promise? If you do, do it properly, I'd hate to die from a lame gank (like he did xD). Next time try to have a few extra steps of distance between you and them, you were too close. Mages outrange alchemy attacks. Had he been more prepared, he could have some bombs to drop on you. And if you open with Pyroclasm, cast TA first.'

'TA?'

'[Thaumic Acceleration]' Ò_Ó linked the spell in chat.

'Ah.'

'But following with a root and pre-casting FF on yourself was a good idea. Anyway he was low so it was EZ this time. Not much to learn from that.'

'Mhm.'

'Now let's go make you some more enemies!'

Vizovia groaned inwardly.

* * *

[11:15] [Whisper] Ma_Ris: hello hello!

[11:15] [Whisper] Ma_Ris: /gchat told me I can find you here ^^

[11:15] [To: Ma_Ris]: hey

[11:15] [To: Ma_Ris]: yep this is my alt for farming

[11:15] [To: Ma_Ris]: what's up?

[11:15] [Whisper] Ma_Ris: I need Pvro or you, but I can't catch him, so…

[11:15] [To: Ma_Ris]: yeah I noticed that too :F

[11:15] [Whisper] Ma_Ris: can you log in Sl4y and meet me in Whitecliff?

[11:16] [To: Ma_Ris]: yeah sure, give me a few moments

Truth be told, Sl4y was busy collecting the rare Motive Spark and he did not abandon it eagerly. The Spark, said to be the force animating all kinds of elementals, dropped from Silicate Golem at eight percent chance and fetched a good price that would cover his weekly expenses in one go. Earlier that day he had noticed, by pure accident, another player defeating the rare Silicate Golem here in the foothills of Mount Sarun. He knew the creature spawns after three hours with a variance of thirty minutes, and he had been camping its respawn area on his Hunter, Sl3y, for three hours and twenty minutes, meaning he was less than ten minutes away from spawnkilling it. He knew it precisely, because he noted down its previous time of death. But it was Ma_Ris who asked for his help. *One does not say "no" to Ma_Ris.* He logged out immediately and switched to his Priest.

Not for the first time he examined his own eagerness to attend to Ma_Ris and to do so without delay, which was something he noticed in other guys in the guild too. Even the cynics extraordinaire like Lonecow, Slam1go, and 415 seemed to be affected by her aura one way or another. The effect was powerful enough to affect even the hot-tempered Belixner, a woman herself. *Let us hope Ma_Ris never uses her powers for evil,* Sl4y thought. It was still a gap in his knowledge as to how a person like her found herself in this pretty tryhard guild. She did not exactly fit the profile, and he made a mental note to ask about it later.

There was also that little repressed problem nagging at the back of his thoughts. Havoc was an old guild and it had a long-time reputation for winning. There have always been members who are in just for socialisation - friends and family of members - but the proportions of socials to soldiers has been skewed as of late. The likes of 415, Bokkie, or Lonecow sneered at it. *Come to think of it, when have I last seen Lonecow online?*

Within minutes he was in a starting zone for new players, having taken a transportation service in the form of a sailing ship coursing to and from Vir Estia and Whitecliff Harbor. Effectively, it was an instantaneous teleportation from the mainland harbour to the smaller harbour on the Kneep island off the coast of Insal Kingdom, but to create an illusion of a ship taking time to travel from one port to another, the service was on a five-minute timer. Come too early or too late and be stuck waiting, but at least have the opportunity to behold the aesthetics of a majestic three-mast frigate gracefully approaching the quay with its white sails neatly handed, or temporarily stowed. It was a pet peeve of Sl4y that games frequently depicted tall ships entering port or docked in full sail, but once again creators of ARIS have proven they did their research.

She had not told him where exactly in Whitecliff Harbor to meet her, so he invited her to a group through the Guild interface.

[11:22] This player is already in a group.

[11:22] [To: Ma_Ris]: where now?

[11:22] [Whisper] Ma_Ris: the boat :)

He made his way along the waterline to the pier where new players who chose Insal as the starting location began their adventure in the world of ARIS, the other two locations being the exotic Fal-Rashida and the frontier bastion of Hardline in the cold north. From here they set off on quests and would be allowed to travel off the island at level ten.

He accepted the request though he already knew where he would find Ma_Ris, and sure enough, he spotted the tall woman in green-tinted garb of a Priestess clutching a silver-tipped staff in one hand and a heavy tome in another, and wearing an arctic blue headband hopelessly losing the battle to keep her golden armpit-length hair in one place on the wind. She was never difficult to miss.

But she did not stand there alone, for a fresh level one Warrior girl orbited her like an electron; if it was not for the group frames to the left of his display telling him there were two other people in the party, Sl4y would have thought this was some pet or an annoying noob bothering Ma_Ris.

Sl4y switched to group chat and greeted both ladies.

'Here I am, what's up?'

'Hi! How did you get here so fast?' asked Ma_Ris.

'I'm always fast :)'

'Mhm. Well, I'd like to introduce to you my little sister ^^ Madie, say hi to uncle!'

'Uncle?'

Sl4y looked closely at the novice who now stood still and noticed she had created her character with very clear facial and hair similarity to Ma_Ris. She made herself slightly shorter and while the big sister had her hair parting on the left, the little one had it on the right. She stood still for a few moments.

'Hi,' she sent after a moment.

'Isn't she cute? :D It's her first time playing ARIS.'

'Yes, very cute :) Welcome to the game, Madie :)'

'I need to find her glasses to wear,' Ma_Ris said. 'So she looks more like herself.'

'I have glasses somewhere, you can have them.'

'Oh, which ones?'

'Uh… I don't know. Does it matter?'

'Duh, of course!'

'Stay here, I will fetch them,' he turned around, summoned his avian mount, and rode off towards the local Bank to access his global storage. Being called an 'uncle' to Ma_Ris' little sister kindled a little warm feeling in his chest. *I don't even know the words to describe glasses. Do they have names for the frame types or something?* Meanwhile he continued to chat.

'So, can we add her?' Ma_Ris asked.

'To what?'

'To the guild, duh! You're slow today :D'

'I'm always slow :) You said little sis. How little?'

'She's 9 :)'

'I see,' he paused. 'Hold up. You sure about this? Our gchat isn't very family-friendly, you know.'

'She doesn't know English yet, but hmm… do we have a rank for someone like her? ^^'

'Not really…' he said, predicting the next thing she would say.

'Can we create it so everyone knows?'

And there it is, he sighed inwardly. It was not that he was unwilling to help, quite the opposite, but there was a complication he could not even tell Ma_Ris about. Once again it came back to the conflicting opinions and expectations of what Havoc should be. Historically it has been the winners' guild and for many it still was, despite some mixed results within the last weeks. It was true that it was created by real-life friends, but they were also very dedicated to the game. *But now to bring little children to the guild?* He was not even sure if he himself was OK with it, but he had a lethal certainty there would be reactions such as "the fuck is Sl4y doing, he's turning the guild into a kindergarten now too?" from a couple of people, and the bulk of them being members for years. Their opinion should matter, Sl4y believed. He could just tell Ma_Ris all of this, but to say something like "sorry, we're too hardcore for such casuals" felt like something for which he would *actually* deserve the "fucking Sl4y" greeting from people.

But then again, they've been removing themselves from the guild already, little by little. What weight is there in the opinions of those who do not contribute much anymore? Also, am I not chosen by Pvro and Trillex to make decisions? And here was Ma_Ris, personally contributing to the livelihood of the community, making things happen, bringing topics to talk about.

The choice is simple after all.

'Sure,' he said. 'I don't see why not :) I'm omw,' he said, grabbing the glasses from his storage. He did not even know when and how he got this cosmetic item, like so many in his stash. *It sucks a kid already has to wear glasses at nine,* he thought as he went. Whitecliff Harbor was not a large town, so he was back with the girls in less than thirty seconds and opened a trade with Ma_Ris. The little one had run off somewhere by then. *Or maybe she dropped off the pier into the seawater.*

'They're different :(But do you mind if I borrow them anyway?' Ma_Ris asked.

'Just take it. I'm afraid there aren't too many types in the game. Are you two in one room now?'

'Yes :) Thank you ^^'

'OK, here goes inv.'

Sl4y opened the Guild control window, fixed something in the Rank system, then clicked <Add Member> and typed Ma_Delyn.

[11:25] Guild invitation sent.

[11:25] Ma_Delyn accepted the invitation.

[11:25] **[Guild]** Ma_Delyn has joined the guild.

[11:25] **[Guild]** Ma_Delyn has been promoted to Rank 7 <Underage Socials>.

'Welcome aboard Madie :)' said Sl4y, wondering if the young one would even notice the message. She did not react as far as he could tell from the chat.

Oh right, Ma said she can't read English, Sl4y slapped his forehead.

'Thanks! :D' sent Ma_Ris in her stead.

'No problem. I think it's pretty cool you bring her here :) Is her name Madeline?'

'No, it's closer to Magdalene, but she liked Ma_Delyn ^_^ we call her Madie at home'

[11:26] **[Guild]** Raphanti: ooh who's that?

[11:26] **[Guild]** Sl4y: someone you will stay away from :)

[11:26] **[Guild]** Raphanti: hmph

[11:26] **[Guild]** Raphanti: prohibitions only expand demands!

'Right, uncle is going back to my alt then, maybe my rare is still there. Good luck:p' Sl4y said, quit the party, logged out, and switched back to Sl3y.

[11:26] **[Guild]** Ma_Ris: everyone please say hi to my little sister ^^

[11:26] **[Guild]** slowah: o/

[11:26] **[Guild]** Doomcaster: hi

[11:26] **[Guild]** Arastina: awwww welcome!

[11:26] **[Guild]** -Zoe-: we have a new rank for babies? cool! now put Raphanti in it!

[11:26] **[Guild]** Azarus: hey kiddo

[11:26] **[Guild]** Vizovia: Maris has a little sister? this is too adorable to be true :D

[11:26] **[Guild]** Slam1go: hi kid, GvG is tomorrow, be ready, thanks

[11:27] **[Guild]** Maxitaur: a warrior? you sure about this?

[11:27] **[Guild]** Ma_Ris: she wanted it Maxi:)

[11:27] **[Guild]** Prast: hello hello

[11:27] **[Guild]** Ma_Ris: she says "hi everyone" :)

[11:27] **[Guild]** Eightblades: Maris outsources farming for the summer event starting tomorrow. smart!

[11:27] **[Guild]** Eightblades: I should train my nephew too… why didn't I think of this before?

[11:27] **[Guild]** Azarus: shit it's tomorrow?

[11:27] **[Guild]** Azarus: sorry, I mean: oh dang! :p

[11:27] **[Guild]** Ma_Ris: don't worry, she can't see the gchat ^^

[11:27] **[Guild]** Ma_Ris: or read it…

* * *

The first day of June brought rainfall going on from dawn well into noon with no signs of stopping, a relief from the scorching heat of the past few days. Having woken up that morning after nine, she slipped out of her summer pyjamas, looked with satisfaction at her school clothes still lying in a corner where she had thrown them two days before, and put on worn-out, comfy shorts and a formerly white, stretched tanktop. Wearing anything else was not an option, just like brushing her hair. She knew she should have something done about its length again, but until then, tying it quickly behind her head was good enough.

'Vacation! Now I can study 14 hours a day uninterrupted =.=' She had seen Sapphire say that in guild chat once. Vizovia shuddered at such intensity of education. She had passed all her school exams to an acceptable (to her) degree and there would be no more school until September. Mom made her breakfast after which Vizovia retreated immediately to her room to catch up with the anime backlog, and then it was gaming time. Being left alone to do her own things was a blessing she made sure to appreciate while it lasted.

She opened the game, typed her password, selected her Mage, and entered the world.

Welcome to AltAr! Remember to never share your password. No new messages.

[12:36] **[Guild]** <MOTD>: Rank 4 and above: send me a message if you're leaving for vacation. -Sl4y

It was the long-awaited Summer Event launch day. There were a few things that Vizovia had been looking forward to doing, or more accurately, things she looked forward to having. There was much grind to be had as always, but there were some group objectives too. She had read the patch notes the day before and had a vague idea of what she wanted. First off the list: a fancy swimsuit costume for her Mage. There were GM-designed quests that could only be completed when wearing a swimsuit and sandals or flip-flops. Other items on her list were a sunday hat like Ma_Ris wore that one time, free character re-customization tickets, and a coloured nickname for 30 days…

She checked her friendlist to see who was available to group up. Aside from ^_Miko_^, she noticed two of her friends from the previous guild with whom she was on good terms but they were both below level 80. They were also an in-game couple so she decided not to bother them. But there was also Ma_Ris.

[12:37] **[To: Ma_Ris]**: hey hey!

[12:37] **[Friend]** Ma_Ris: hi<3

[12:37] **[To: Ma_Ris]**: I want some event rewards

[12:37] **[To: Ma_Ris]**: wanna go for something?

[12:37] **[Friend]** Ma_Ris: aw, not now, dear

[12:37] **[Friend]** Ma_Ris: I'm babysitting Madie near WCH

[12:37] **[Friend]** Ma_Ris: we're almost level 10 :)

[12:37] **[To: Ma_Ris]**: aw that's so sweet :D I wish I had a sibling

[12:37] **[To: Ma_Ris]**: need a hand?

[12:37] **[Friend]** Ma_Ris: we're good, thank you

[12:38] **[Friend]** Ma_Ris: do you know what is really cool?

[12:38] **[To: Ma_Ris]**: nope

[12:38] **[Friend]** Ma_Ris: I noticed it a long time ago, but recently I didn't see it happen much anymore because I rarely go out with this char

[12:38] **[Friend]** Ma_Ris: random people pass us by and give us buffs or kill things for us

[12:38] **[Friend]** Ma_Ris: or /cheer or /clap at us both

[12:38] **[Friend]** Ma_Ris: all total strangers to me

[12:38] **[To: Ma_Ris]**: you have that effect on people :)

[12:38] **[Friend]** Ma_Ris: no no, it's not that

[12:38] **[Friend]** Ma_Ris: it doesn't happen when I'm on alts

[12:38] **[Friend]** Ma_Ris: I think it's the guild tag

[12:38] **[Friend]** Ma_Ris: strangers help us because they see Havoc under our names

[12:38] **[To: Ma_Ris]**: uhhh

[12:38] **[To: Ma_Ris]**: if you step out into PvP zones, you will change your mind xD

[12:38] **[To: Ma_Ris]**: some people REALLY hate us

[12:38] **[Friend]** Ma_Ris: why?

[12:38] **[To: Ma_Ris]**: you tell me, you've been here longer

[12:38] **[Friend]** Ma_Ris: only by a few months

Vizovia opened the Guild window to see who else was online. She continued to feel like a newcomer and was embarrassed to ask for groups and attention lest anyone thinks she's too awful at the game to solve her own problems or needs babysitting. *I mean, even more babysitting* she thought, recalling the episode with Ò_Ó.

Name	Class	Rank	Location	Level
Intervene	Warrior	Member	Arena	100
Ma_Ris	Priest	Social	Kneep	97
Gaav <AFK>	Assassin	Veteran	Ghabat Safi	100
Venetia	Warlock	Veteran	Battlegrounds	100
Reptilla	Hunter	Alts	Maggiura	44
Sl4y	Priest	Officer	Argentia	100
^_Miko_^ <DND>	Assassin	Member	Kalama Beach	100
Ma_Delyn	Warrior	Underage S…	Kneep	9
Bokkiesmom	Minstrel	Alt	Hardline	39
BATS <DND>	Assassin	Member	Kalama Beach	100
Kaitzuuu <AFK>	Witch Doctor	Member	Vir Estia	100
PowerOverwhelming	Fighter	Member	Salt Mines	99
Vizovia	Mage	Member	Argentia	92
415 <AFK>	Mage	NERD	Argentia	100

She read the table top to bottom and it looked like pretty much everyone was doing something already. She was happy to see ^_Miko_^ online, she had been coming online rather rarely for the last month or so, and currently seemed to be doing the Summer Event grind on the beach already. Gaav was AFK as always, the Greeks never joined anything, and Sl4y never seemed to leave Argentia. When did he even do other things to stay in the game?

She was close to his spot, so she decided to go up there to say hello if nothing else. He helped her out a few times already while she could do nothing for him, but she could at least visit him from time to time (and check out that sick cape!).

Sure enough, he was where he always was, but sitting on the marble floor with his back to Vizovia. It was not a strange or rare sight at all. After several minutes of inactivity, player characters would sit down and an Away From Keyboard (AFK) tag would appear over their heads. Sitting position varied by class, and his was more of a crouch than a sit. She took this opportunity to take a look at him closely, pushing the mousewheel with her finger to zoom closer. Sl4y's character was quite tall but rather slender in terms of physique. His short, black hair was loose, just one of baseline haircuts available in the character creation. If he had ever unlocked additional styles, he did not use them. His head was bare which was a rarity in a game allowing people to compete in fashion, so to have a slot for one of many fancy headgear costumes and not use it was a radical statement. Simply put, his character model was just *plain*. She got closer and circled around to see him from the front and finally noticed a hint of extravagance other than the unique asymmetrical cloak he was already known for: his eyes swirled with the shades of amber and gold. She never noticed that before. A tiny detail visible only from up close, and definitely not a baseline customization option. She did not even know where he could possibly have obtained that.

'Can I help you? :P' he said suddenly without standing up, startling her a little.

'Just came to say hi ^^'

'Ah :) Are you doing anything now?'

'Nope, was thinking to find a group for an event boss or something.'

'Hmm. Say, do you have a preq for Hidden Cove? :)'

'I don't think so :('

'If you go do it now, you can join me and Intervene for a dungeon.'

That made her giddy, her little problem basically solved itself before she even thought about it. *Again.*

Meanwhile a flash of light and a characteristic whooshing sound announced the login of another player next to them.

'How long will this take?' asked Vizovia.

'About 30 mins and done.'

'Excuse me girl, what are you doing?' asked Sapphire who just showed up and caught only the tail end of the conversation. 'This guy is mine to use. Find your own husbando (:'

Sl4y rose and turned to Sapphire.

'Hey now, there's no need to be jealous. We're not doing anything weird. It's just sex.' He said and approached Vizovia's character extremely close. 'It's 500 gold an hour, right?'

'WHAT XD'

'Are you fucking serious?' demanded Sapphire. 'You only pay me 400.'

'She's younger,' Sl4y calmly explained.

'Um xD'

'I'm sorry Zovia, I'll sort this out. Go prepare yourself, we will wait :)' said Sl4y.

'OK I guess xD,' said Vizovia and left.

Sl4y and Sapphire waited a moment to make sure the Mage was far enough to not pick up their chat.

'XD I'm dying,' said Sapphire. 'My stomach hurts'

'Your timing was perfect, literally couldn't get better xDD I'm screen-shotting this.'

'Guess I don't need my morning coffee now:D'

'But it's well past noon :P You just got up?'

'Nope. Yesterday they moved my today's class from 16 to this morning >< I slept 4 hours. I got up at 7, hit snooze, fell asleep again. I arrived at 9 aaaaaand I walked into a surprise exam, with only 10 minutes left.'

'lmao.'

'So I'm like: fine! Hold my beer! I sit down, take the test, solve 4/5 problems like a boss. The lady checks the sheets and says "which one of you is <my surname>?"''

'And?'

'I say it's me and I mentally prepare for her rant about that one problem I didn't even try doing because it was open-ended and I didn't have the time. But no, she points at my another answer and asks how come I know the thing that was not covered yet. I'm like: shit °_° Now that she knows I'm ahead of others, she won't leave me alone -_-'

'That could only happen to you, seriously'

'Conclusion: fuck morning classes, keep sleeping =.='

'So I see you're not only a weeb, but a geek too'

'I'm also cute af'

'Nice. Marry me?' he even emoted a /kneel in front of her.

'Where's the ring?'

'Didn't bring one'

'Then fuck off.'

Intervene was, next to slowah and Sapphire, one of Sl4y's good friends and the oldest one at that. Which was to say, Sl4y hated his guts and wished he would die horribly.

'There's no need to be upset,' said Intervene innocently. 'We're alive.'

'That's odd, I could swear everyone but me is dead,' Sl4y retorted.

'Should have healed us then, eh?'

'There's no cure for what you have.'

Their Hidden Cove party consisted of Sl4y healing, Intervene tanking, and Vizovia plus another Fighter and Hunter doing damage. The latter two were pick-ups that Intervene had invited since nobody they knew wanted to join, meaning they were total strangers to the former three. For this reason the party communicated on both voice comms and in-game Group chat. Vizovia was with them on Chatterbox, but her microphone was disabled.

In contrast to other dungeons in the game, Hidden Cove was a custom invention of AltAr staff for the recurring Summer Events, so it was already known to players who played it for more than a year. Strangely though, it was instanced rather than open-world like other dungeons. The administration must have decided that this was the only technically-feasible option, or that it was better for some reason. Sl4y suspected this was explained somewhere in the forums, but he did not care enough to read it.

The dungeon was an outdoor area, a narrow bay surrounded by rocky cliffs on either side, accessible through a short system of tunnels where the previous two bosses and packs of pirates had been. The final boss, Pirate Captain Torrent (*ha-ha, very clever, AltAr*) stood on the shore near a wooden jetty leading to his pirate ship, his large hat clearly broadcasting to everyone "I am important here" while a wicked cutlass and a black powder pistol tucked behind his many belts spoke of his problem-solving skills. Sl4y thought pirates were boring and that the game could always use more non-human enemies, but at least humanoids could be given clever dialogue lines.

'What the hell is with this bloke's name?' asked Intervene rhetorically, referring to the Hunter that had tagged along with them. 'Vituvi… helta… m-something? Bloody hell, it's a headache to read.'

'Yeah. But you know, maybe we shouldn't complain. We have guys like Ò_Ó and 415. Hey, know what? This gives me an idea. Let's make new characters with the least pronounceable names possible and form an arena team, will make target calling harder for the enemy.'

Sl4y finished resurrecting fallen party members one by one which depleted his mana so he sat down to consume a restoration drink, questioning his life choices that led him to be in that group. He had told Vizovia this would be a thirty-minute trip, but they had been in it for longer than that, and the last boss, the one they had actually come to defeat, was still alive. Overall it was not going well, and the communication barrier they discovered they had was not making anything easier. They had failed three times already, and Sl4y managed to survive the last attempt only because he noticed the failure early, allowing himself to stop healing and instead squeeze the seven-second cast of Providence on himself and deliberately walk into his death. Providence brought him back to life instantly, but the boss despawned once the server registered all players as dead.

The peg-legged, grog-infused maritime salvage expert and redistributor of abandoned goods was not particularly hard-hitting himself and was optimised for players at level 80, but ignoring his mechanics spelled swift demise to anyone. Between the cannonball strikes from the ship setting the ground on fire and the nasty bleeding effect caused by his pistol shots, made for a deceptively simple encounter.

'Ready to go?'

'Wait. I'll try talking sense into those morons again.'

[13:42] [Group] Sl4y: ok, I'll explain one more time -_-

[13:42] [Group] Sl4y: big X under your feet = cannons target you = run away

[13:42] [Group] Sl4y: cannonball makes fire on the ground

[13:42] [Group] Sl4y: dont stand in fire

[13:42] [Group] Tuui: just go

[13:42] [Group] Sl4y: dont stand between boss and pistol shot target

[13:42] [Group] Sl4y: it is that simple

[13:42] [Group] Vitunviheltämäjänkä: ?

[13:42] [Group] Sl4y: understood?

[13:42] [Group] Tuui: go go

'Sigh. I don't think they understood,' complained Sl4y. 'Also, Zovia, I know this is difficult for casters, but I really need you to move faster too. Use shorter cast spells if you have to, high dps does not matter that much here. Okay?'

[13:43] [Group] Vizovia: ok

'Ready?' asked the tank.

'Wait a sec, let me refresh buff-'

[13:59] Pirate Captain Torrent: What's that? Arr you trying to shut down ol' Torrent?

'Oh for fuck's sake! Really? Could not wait a few seconds?'

'You can refresh buffs while we're starting, yes? Nothing is happening for a moment,' said Intervene lightly, having already engaged Torrent.

'I'm starting with ninety percent mana. If we wipe 'cause of oom, that's on you.'

'If we get to oom, then we've already failed, yes?'

The moment Pirate Captain Torrent took any damage was when dozens of rank-and-file invulnerable pirate NPCs surrounded the fight creating an arena with limited space. The pick-up Fighter, Tuui, was already delivering fist and knee combos onto the Captain's back, Intervene was blocking and parrying the cutlas swings and keeping the boss focused, while Vizovia and a hunter with an unpronounceable name cycled throwing damaging abilities from afar, be it bow shots or bolts of fire and lightning. Sl4y positioned himself to be within casting range to all his friendly targets.

At sixty seconds in without a major failure, Sl4y allowed himself to be cautiously optimistic. *It's going well so far.*

It's not going well.

'Aaaargh!' Sl4y vented his frustration as he assessed the situation while frantically pressing 123QERTFG and other shift-key combinations, trying to keep the party alive. Prayer on Intervene. Reposition to get the Hunter in range and cast Desparate Prayer on him. Healing Rites on everyone. Step aside to not get hit by the pistol shot. Absolve on Vizovia. Healing Rites again.

Patches of fire littered the ground, covering approximately forty percent of the arena and would burn until the fight's end - a side effect of the cannonball explosions. He had to step into the fire a few times and take damage himself to catch Vizovia or the Hunter and top them off. *At least the melees don't run around.* The last pistol shot, an attack that pierces all enemies until it hits its target, hit both Tuui and Sl4y, because the former did not move out of the way. Intervene could have moved the boss to prevent this, but he had no way to know the Fighter would not react himself. The shot left behind a damage over time effect that would drain their health until fully healed.

[14:00] [Group] Tuui: HEAL MAYBE?

'What a cunt. I'm gonna fucking choke him myself. That's more mana down the drain, what a fucking clown this guy is,' said Sl4y.

'I tell you what mate, for someone who chose to play a healer, you sure do hate healing,' said Intervene.

'Can't outheal stupidity,' Sl4y muttered under the pressure. He wanted to say more but had no time for it. At least Vizovia dodged that last shot, but had to step into the fire to do so. It became increasingly difficult to move with all the fire underneath. But Vizovia made mistakes too. He saw her waste some good spells with long cooldowns by using them just before the cannon barrage and having to move.

Suddenly, Tuui the Fighter just died.

'Huh? What happened to him?' asked Sl4y.

'Oops, the boss slapped him. What a terrible loss!'

'How?'

'I might have been spamming damage instead of aggro for a while.'

'Nice job, fuckface. He's gonna rant in three.. two...'

[14:00] [Group] Tuui: fck tank aggo???

'And there we have it,' agreed Intervene. 'Rez him?'

Sl4y was about to respond with a positive, but then he got targeted by Captain's pistol, a thin red line connecting the barrel and Sl4y himself.

'You know what?' he asked. 'This gives me an idea. Fuck that guy, and fuck the other guy too. I'm fucking done. Watch this!' Sl4y said as he started making his way around patches of fire to where the V-guy, the Hunter, stood. The debuff on his display told him exactly when the bullet would be fired, and just a second before that moment he stepped up behind the Hunter. Then he healed himself to full instantly with Desperate Prayer and the bleeding debuff faded from him instantly. 'Hey Zovia, listen up, go stand near the boss, over there to the right, no, no, your right, and hold that position and don't make a step. Yes, stop, there! Go all in, burn it!' He did not register if she typed any response.

Sl4y had removed the debuff only from himself. He watched with satisfaction as his so-called teammate's health rapidly dropped to zero, tick after tick, from the grevious wound Pirate Captain Torrent had inflicted upon him. No doubt he was frothing in front of his computer right now.

[14:01] [Group] Vitunviheltämäjänkä: Mitä vittua nuo tyypit tekevät??? Minä aion erota tästä porukasta

[14:01] [Group] Tuui: -_-

'Wipe it?' asked Intervene.

'No, keep going!' urged Sl4y, looking at the party frames. It was down to himself at thirty percent mana, Vizovia blasting away, and Intervene not even having to move all fight long, just hacking away with his hand axe and bashing Torrent with his tower shield, and Torrent himself still at over twenty percent of his health after a few minutes. A factor complicating the situation was that at fifteen percent health, Torrent would double the intensity of his abilities. Sl4y could not spare the attention to do the math in his head, and besides, he was not capable of such calculation anyway. But he could look at the remaining area which was the real death clock, the pace at which they damaged Torrent, and his own capabilities, and conclude: *this looks doable.*

He turned around and quickly positioned himself on the edge of the arena carefully avoiding the fire patches and soon enough Torrent's dialogue line told Sl4y he would soon have lead raining down on his location.

[14:02] Pirate Captain Torrent: you'll never sink us!

He stepped over to the nearest patch of fire, careful not to tread on it even by a pixel. As the shots came down he tip-toed sideways, along the wall of pirate NPCs making up the outer wall of the arena, and the explosion radius of each round overlapped greatly with another already existing patch, effectively covering extremely little ground with each barrage. This bombardment lasted for a short time. Sl4y stopped, refreshed short-duration casting speed and damage resistance buffs on Vizovia and Intervene, and-

[14:02] Pirate Captain Torrent: you wouldn't download a galleon!

He had to move again, step by step, circumventing older flame patches and sometimes getting hit despite his best efforts. In the corner of his eye he noticed Vizovia having the pistol shot debuff and threw a Desperate Prayer at her. He had noticed it too late and it did not heal her fully. *She has to survive somehow on her own for a moment. Just a few more steps.*

'Hey, did you suddenly remember how to use mitigations?' asked Sl4y, noticing a familiar buff fade away from Intervene as he looked at the tank's health bar. Maybe Torrent was not a hard-hitter, but he still did enough to keep a healer busy if not desperate.

'No, I just stopped trusting you bruv,' replied the tank. 'I'm a strong, independent Warrior who needs no healer. Save the princess instead, aight?'

'Next time use them when they're useful, cunt,' said Sl4y, finding a small stack of Mana Potions in his inventory to drag it to the action bar and clicking it, then targeting Vizovia with a Plea and Suppression, the former healing over time for a decent chunk of health and the latter preventing all damage for a moment. 'What's the point of a cooldown you never use?'

'The point is to get Sl4y tilted, it's boring otherwise.'

'Nice job. Why do I even group with you, fuckface?'

'Hei, miten he muka voittavat tämän pelin?'

[14:04] [Group] Vizovia: guys stop that pls

Since he was now the most distant target at all times Torrent would choose him to be followed by the big red X underneath his feet, meaning Sl4y now had total control over placements of the no-go spots. He would lead the shots around the arena, laying down those patches as tightly as possible. The barrages lasted slightly longer than before, and would now trigger slightly more frequently, forcing him to move even more.

[14:04] [Group] Tuui: REZ ME

Sl4y's fingers danced on his keyboard, his attention divided between single-handedly handling a boss mechanic, frantically healing himself and two others, and profusely throwing curses that would impress a Warlock, but he decided it was important to stop for a second and provide a response to a valued team member.

[14:04] [Group] Sl4y: nah

[14:04] [Group] Sl4y: you stay dead

[14:04] [Group] Sl4y: it's better this way

[14:07] Tuui has left the group.
[14:07] Vitunviheltämäjänkä has left the group.
'Well, goodbye then,' Intervene commented on their departure. Neither the pick-ups nor the Havoc members said anything to the other part of the group since they finally defeated Torrent. Sl4y had graciously brought everyone back to life, including Vizovia who died at one percent of Torrent's health. But it was not by her mistake. She died, because Sl4y had not removed Captain's bleed effect from her to conserve his last, precious droplets of mana. It was a difficult decision, and Sl4y was by no means confident in it, but in the end they succeeded. He was disappointed it came to this, though. He had wanted to "accidentally" let Intervene die just before Torrent did so that the Warrior would have to spend a few extra silvers on gear repairs, but without Intervene Torrent had a chance to wreck both Vizovia and Sl4y on the spot. In the end, Sl4y and Intervene (mostly Intervene, Sl4y had to admit) dealt enough damage to end the fight. All five group members picked up their share of loot, after which Sl4y just kicked out the randoms from the group without ceremony.

[14:07] [Group] Vizovia: that was pretty awesome!:D

[14:07] [Group] Vizovia: I thought we're dead but then we killed it

[14:07] [Group] Vizovia: somehow

'Pfft, I never doubted,' said Intervene.

'Not even when you popped Indomitable?' teased Sl4y, 'Anyway, grats Zovia! You and I did a good job.'

[14:08] [Group] Vizovia: how did you even do all that @_@

'Eh, it's really nothing special. This was, uh, used to be the proper way to do a boss like that back in the day, yes?' said Intervene.

'Yeah. Nobody does mechanics like that anymore because everyone out-levels and outgears everything. I miss the days when we actually struggled

to kill non-raid stuff, and even some raids are too easy now.' After a moment
Sl4y added: 'Anyway, it's nice to have a good tank.'

'Oh my gosh, thank-'

'Unfortunately, we only had you.'

Vizovia heard them both explode into laughter.

'Well screw you, I'm off to get some dinner. Arenas later?'

'Sure,' Sl4y agreed.

Boys are weird, she thought.

* * *

An ocean gulf, roughly as distant from Hellesvyand on the southern reaches of Insal Kingdom as it was from Fal-Rashida in Al-Ghabla Empire, was dotted with tropical islands of various sizes. Its geographical position blessed the archipelago with warm currents, nearly infinite summer, sandy beaches, a coral reef between itself and Hellesvyand to the east, a plenitude of both terrestrial and marine wildlife, of vibrant flora, and of shipwrecks.

It was the place for an enthusiast of wooden huts with thatched roofs, of buried treasures, of obnoxiously loud birds, of pirates, of a high demand for rum, of hidden coves, of dense jungles, and of being eaten by huge beasts.

There were also crabs, which is why Warrior Xx_WojownikPL_xX was merely curious, rather than suspicious, as to why a peculiar crab had been following him for a few moments now.

He had been distributing daggers to crabs in the shallow water of Turquoise Bay as a daily quest for the Summer Event. Thus armed crabs would gratefully march away into the salty waters to join The Great Crustacean War that was rumoured to take place away from the prying eyes of annoying terrestrial bipedal mammals. But when the mammal targeted this one crab and used the Bundle of Daggers at him, he only got an error message: *invalid target.*

That's weird, he thought.

Perhaps it was the long hours of gaming and late nighttime that took toll on his brain. Only after a moment did he have the presence of mind to actually read the tooltip displayed when he hovered his mouse over his strange follower.

Amber Shallows Crab

Companion Pet

It was not one of the natural Amber Shallows Crab mobs, but a summonable pet animal that followed its owner around. *I don't remember summoning any pets.* He went to the Collections tab, found his Crab as one of the first on the list of the Companion Pets he owned, and double-clicked it to unsummon. To his surprise, now two crabs stood by his feet instead of zero.

What the... what a weird bug. Maybe one is not mine? But I do not see anyon-

'Ohfuckohfuckohfuck!' he said aloud, panic rising in his voice, as he unsheathed his two-handed swo-

His character groaned in pain with an ear-grating "oof!" as Xx_WojownikPL_xX's heart pounded. As if sensing the best moment to strike, or perhaps noticing the unsheathing animation, an Assassin Backstabbed Xx_WojownikPL_xX from stealth for increased damage, revealing himself in the process. An audio effect told him he was critically hit, and two sickly green debuff icons told him he had been poisoned, and had been stunned for three seconds too. His involuntary impulse was to fight back as hard as possible, knowing Warriors were the natural counters of Assassins and planning to use it to his full advantage. When the initial stun effect faded, he turned around to face the Assassin with an attack sequence ready at his fingertips, but somehow the enemy was behind him again, continuously raining blows from the back. Xx_WojownikPL_xX used Backhand, an ability specifically designed to counter enemies such as this, but somehow it hit only empty air. The opponent had vanished, only to reappear two seconds later and Backstab him again. Groaning in frustration, the Warrior player slammed his fingers on his keyboard hoping yet to squeeze enough damage on the roguish bastard to prevail. Lunge and Open Wounds connected, Counterstrike even critted which was great, but Pommel Blow missed which was terrible; he really needed that stun to land.

Before he died from the stabs, blinds, poisons and the train of stuns unleashed on him, he noticed two things.

First thing was the identity of the attacker.

BATS, Level 100 Assassin

<Havoc>

Second thing was that his attacks against the Assassin did much more damage than they should. As his character hit the ground, he saw the bastard wearing only a dagger and a mace in each hand, and swimming trunks. Nothing else.

He's not even wearing his gear, Xx_WojownikPL_xX realised, and gritted his teeth in anger as he clicked to respawn in the nearby town.

Before his screen faded, he heard the dreaded Assassin stealthing again into complete invisibility and a clatter of tiny crab legs departing from his corpse.

He respawned in Flat Booty, a town of improvised infrastructure, criss-crossing gangways, and consciously-challenged sailors located on one of the largest islands in the archipelago. Embracing a desire to never meet that guy again and suppressing his anger at being schooled so hard, he turned away from the eastern exit out of town that he had taken last time and instead went the opposite direction. Sandy beaches stretched for kilometres all around the island, but only a few areas spawned crabs in the shallows. He mounted on his armoured warhorse and rode west, avoiding the road, wading through foliage and occasional tigers pouncing on him.

Before leaving the safety and cover of the trees and bushes he waited a minute observing the direction he came from, towards Flat Booty town, but saw nobody following him so he decided it was time to resume questing.

A clatter of crab legs suddenly came from behind him and the empty space beside him spoke with a chat bubble.

[03:35] BATS: q:)

This time Xx_WojownikPL_xX was not going to go down easily. His enemy made a mistake: he gave away his presence instead of opening the fight, and had a pet out which gave away his position. If he, a Warrior, could land the first blow on the fragile rogue, he would have a massive advantage. Time was short. He popped Indomitable, Blademaster's Focus, and Unchecked

Anger all at once, while also reaching to a sidebar to consume a potion for a temporary Strength boost. He swung his weapon around wildly, landing a blow on the Assassin who *stood right there just a second ago* and applying a bleed-

Except he did not land any attacks on any target. No tiny crab was visible anywhere either. And then, after a few seconds of thrashing around, he came to a realisation. He watched all of his precious long-cooldown abilities fade away, abilities that he had recklessly used all at once.

[03:36] BATS: q:)

A Backstab and a stun shattered Xx_WojownikPL_xX's hopes of running away.

* * *

A direct ray of sunlight right in her face told Sapphire it was time to get up from bed, which would be an entirely normal thing to happen to anyone if it was not for the fact that her bedroom's window was in the western wall of her apartment. She rolled on her side to reach for her mobile phone and checked the time: 19:02. "New email" icon was lit up, but it could wait. So could the missed phone call from her ex-boyfriend.

She would still be sleeping had she remembered to roll down the blinders before she went to bed. Still lying she considered her options: if she got up and blocked the pleasantly warm but insufferably bright beam of electromagnetism then went back to bed, there was a non-trivial chance she would fall asleep again. Or, she could roll on her other side and face away from the window but that would not solve this existential problem either, as the room was simply too bright. With a titanic effort she rolled off from the bed and began her "day," but she rolled down the blinds anyway. She had work to do.

Having changed her clothes, watered the plants, then watered herself, she made a few sandwiches for herself which she brought to the desk where her computer was, starting the machine with a press of her toe. Biology notes and books needed to be deported from the desk to the now-free bed. One bite of a sandwich was enough for now, so she pushed the plate away. Once the system loaded, she pressed "play" on some random playlist and logged into ARIS. While it loaded she gathered up her hair and began brushing it, which would take quite a while; her straight brown hair was long enough for her to sit on, which sometimes she did unwittingly to her unpleasant surprises, such as when she tried to bend forward or turn her head. It was an exercise in patience to wash it and brush it, it was heavy to carry, and it felt hot on summer days such as this one; overall it was a pain. But not even once did she consider having it cut. It has always been her most distinguishing feature, *her thing,* and that was that.

[19:23] **[Guild]** <MOTD>: Imperial Catacombs all boss run & farm | 20:00 GMT+1 | meetup @GS | Leader: Ò_Ó

Oh, an IC raid? I could use that, she thought, though her plans for the evening were different. She had logged onto her Minstrel just to see what everyone was up to, planning to jump to her level 95 Hunter, the build of which she had changed two days before to be custom-fit for a singular purpose.

[19:23] **[Guild]** Sapphire: good morning ._.

[19:23] **[Guild]** Eightblades: morning? =]

[19:23] **[Guild]** DagoN: hi

[19:23] **[Guild]** Blinky: hello

[19:23] **[Guild]** Agnelei: hey

[19:23] **[Guild]** Vizovia: good evening senpai ^.^

[19:23] **[Guild]** Rjukan: right on time lol

[19:23] **[Guild]** Ò_Ó: Saph IC at 8? we need you

[19:24] **[Guild]** Sapphire: idk

[19:24] **[Guild]** Ò_Ó: ok, you're going :P

[19:24] **[Guild]** Sapphire: xd.

She accepted the raid group invite and saw there were only seven other people in it, and according to the MOTD the planned start was over half an hour away. She still had time to do a few things around her apartment. In the meantime she travelled to Ghabat Safi, the desert metropolis on the southern continent.

A desert city it might be, but its water wells and fountains kept both the populace and vegetation alive, and the tall architecture casted cool shadows onto the streets built narrowly by design to minimise sun exposure. Clever feats of urban planning made it a surprisingly livable place, and a good-looking too if one had a liking for Middle-Eastern themes. Sapphire was not very enthusiastic about such a setting, but she knew Sl4y was especially fond of mosaics since he had visited Morocco once. The elaborate tile patterns were used here generously as both floor and wall decoration around Ghabat Safi. The locally abundant sandstone was the primary building material as would be expected, and windows often had no glass panes but had wooden shutters. It gave the feeling of an Aladdin setting, or that of Prince of Persia.

She rarely visited this city and she was often surprised that players "lived" in other places than Hellesvyand, Vir Estia, and Argentia. In fact, it was like discovering a new game, since there were so many people hanging out in this place that she normally did not see elsewhere. This desert metropolis teemed with life and bustled with activity. Designated trading areas were full of players vending their goods due to a lack of centralised trading system in ARIS. It was a controversial feature, a relic from older days of game design which some saw as archaic and detrimental to player experience, while others saw as crucial for maintaining the core of MMORPGS - player interactions. Characters sat around in shaded alleys, alcoves, or rode past her to and fro on mounts of all shapes and sizes: ordinary steeds such as horses, or wolves; exotic birds and tusked beasts; or mounts on the funny side such as goblins carrying a player on their backs or barrels to roll on. And then there always was also that one player mounted on the largest beast they could find, and having used toys or potions made themselves even bigger and parked on top of an important NPC effectively blocking it from view. Older players knew camera tricks to counter such behaviour, but for newbies it was a pain to deal with and reports and complaints would usually follow. As a response to the problem and as a manifestation of the lead Game Master's sense of humour, a nearby NPC was programmed to call a player "son of a camel" whenever it detected this happening.

It was not a rule that each class had a "class city" by any means, although Hellesvyand was such a place for Minstrels and Vir Estia for Witch Doctors. Ghabat-Safi, very fittingly with the aesthetic, was the site for most of the quests available only to Assassin class. GS was what an appropriator of misplaced items, a scholar of applied toxicology, and a knife enthusiast called home. They were tolerated by the Palace and the Imperial Court residing there. More than that, they were cultivated and taxed, and oftentimes commissioned as problem-solvers. As long as nobody rocked the boat too much, the odd truce between daytime peacekeepers and the plain-sight underworld would continue. In addition, a popular activity in Ghabat-Safi involved finding a house with roof access and then traversing the city by rooftops only, jumping from one to another. The architecture was perfect for it.

Ò_Ó invited her to a raid group and she accepted. Seeing everyone was still scattered all over the place, few people among them not even on the same continent as the meeting place, she knew she could go AFK for a while no problem. It was well before eight o'clock anyway. She rode her sea turtle mount (*It should be called a tortoise, it literally can't swim!*) past narrow streets with locals drinking coffee sitting by tiny tables, small traders selling spices and tobacco, and an elderly man in a turban feeding stray cats, and parked her character in the Grand Vault of Three Vizirs which was a fancy local name for what was pretty much just a Bank for players. Aside from a few dozen of players of all kinds of levels, affiliations, and classes, there was a tiny water fountain to the side, a large circular blue-and-white mosaic on the floor with inscriptions in a language she could not read, and chairs and cushions for visitors to sit in in the side naves.

She came back a few minutes later just in time to see a local resident clad in grey so dark it seemed black and with a Havoc guild tag over his head enter the place through the front door. He went hooded but one could see his purple hair dropping down on his face blocking much of his vision, which only in a game world was a reasonable choice for anyone regularly partaking in combat. A long, tattered, purple scarf covered the bottom half of his face and trailed behind him as he walked, reminding Sapphire of what they wore in that one Dune adaptation. Tall, leather boots protecting ankles from unnatural bending befitted someone in a profession in which occasional drops from rooftops were to be expected. His Katars were sheathed underneath a piece of clothing Sapphire could not really name; it was a thin, loose cloth skirt, but unlike a typical women's skirt hanging from hips, this thing hung from his belt and covered his legs from the sides and the back. It was tattered and torn like the scarf, and dyed dark-grey like most of his outfit, and when he moved it flapped revealing an inner layer of red cloth. Leather straps across his waist and chest held his tools of the trade. No flappy cloth scraps on his arms though, those were bound-skin tight in cloth and fastened with thin leather straps, which was probably more for the rule of cool than an actually good design. Such a character was right at home in the desert setting of Al-Ghabla. The outfit's last element were fingerless gloves, one of which was now waving a hello to Sapphire.

[19:29] **[Friend]** Gaav: he's afk?

[19:29] **[To: Gaav]**: what, who? xd

[19:29] **[Friend]** Gaav: him

[19:29] Gaav points at Sl4y.

Just now Sapphire noticed a familiar Priest staring blankly into a wall nearby with a big <AFK> next to his name overhead.

[19:29] **[To: Gaav]**: I didn't even know he was there xD

[19:29] **[Friend]** Gaav: ok

[19:30] **[Friend]** Gaav: since you're here, check this out

A trade request from Gaav popped up on her screen and she accepted it. On the right side of the window, where the items proposed for exchange by the other player were listed, she now saw a sealed scroll icon that made her heart jump a little just by looking at its colour. It was the orange of Legendary items, the rarest possible tier of items, and had a name written in orange to match: Eldritch Gift. She right-clicked it to read the description:

Enchantment: Eldritch Gift
Consumable (1)
Class: Any
Slot: Head
Description: accept a dark bargain and embrace Demon-
hood.
Enchanted item cannot be dropped or traded.

[19:30] **[To: Gaav]**: D:

[19:30] **[To: Gaav]**: amazing!! I wonder what it does.

Gaav cancelled the trade.

[19:30] **[Friend]** Gaav: a bunch of things

[19:30] **[Friend]** Gaav: system flags you as a demon instead of human. You're immune to buffs and heals from priests and paladins and you receive double holy damage xd

[19:30] **[Friend]** Gaav: in return, you see invisible and stealthed enemies near you and you're immune to bleeds and polymorph, also extra fire resistance

[19:30] **[To: Gaav]**: o_0

[19:30] **[To: Gaav]**: it doesn't sound good to me

[19:30] **[To: Gaav]**: Sl4y is back btw

Gaav approached Sl4y without a word to either her or Sl4y, and Sapphire presumed the Assassin did exactly the same thing to Sl4y, talking to the Priest by direct message.

[19:31] Sl4y: oh fuck me!

[19:31] Sl4y: :O

[19:31] Sl4y: how did you get that?

[19:31] Sl4y: nice. Should we go get you something for this?

[19:32] Sl4y: ...you sure about this?

[19:32] Sl4y: okay, your choice

[19:32] Sl4y: who else knows?

[19:32] Sl4y: ok, keep it this way, I'll sort it out

[19:32] **[Friend]** Sl4y: tell nobody about this!

[19:32] **[Friend]** Sl4y: it could be some time before anyone uses it

[19:33] **[To: Sl4y]**: I'm not stupid xd

[19:33] **[Friend]** Sl4y: better safe than sorry

[19:33] **[Friend]** Sl4y: but I'm hyped af

[19:33] **[To: Sl4y]**: you must be, you almost gave it away on gen chat

[19:33] **[Friend]** Sl4y: nah, I wouldn't

[19:33] **[Friend]** Sl4y: but it's fucking cool D: 0.5% drop from a rare world mini-boss and he even killed it all by himself so nobody saw it

[19:33] **[To: Sl4y]**: sounds like Gaav, yes (:

[19:33] **[To: Sl4y]**: where did he get it?

[19:33] **[Friend]** Sl4y: dimensional rift in shatterspine

[19:34] **[Friend]** Sl4y: you're going IC with us?

[19:34] **[To: Sl4y]**: yep. but I hope for a quick clear, then I go back to my thing

[19:34] **[To: Sl4y]**: I won't lose to her ><

[19:34] **[Friend]** Sl4y: wut

[19:34] **[Friend]** Sl4y: lose what to whom now?

[19:34] **[To: Sl4y]**: I didn't tell you?

[19:34] **[To: Sl4y]**: Anzu challenged me again

[19:34] **[Friend]** Sl4y: oh no

[19:34] **[To: Sl4y]**: <:

[19:34] **[Friend]** Sl4y: oh no

[19:34] **[Friend]** Sl4y: what has she done

[19:35] **[Friend]** Sl4y: what's at stake?

[19:35] **[To: Sl4y]**: winning? xD

[19:35] **[Friend]** Sl4y: …I should have known:p

[19:35] **[Friend]** Sl4y: so that's what you've been up to

[19:35] **[To: Sl4y]**: yep

[19:35] **[Friend]** Sl4y: wow _^_

[19:36] **[Friend]** Sl4y: what's your plan?

[19:36] **[To: Sl4y]**: crypt raiding, tamer hunterrr

[19:36] **[To: Sl4y]**: she's doing arti somewhere, I see her online even now >_>

[19:36] **[Friend]** Sl4y: maybe she's afking outside just to mess with your head xD

[19:36] **[To: Sl4y]**: maybe. I check now and then, she's rarely in towns

[19:36] **[Friend]** Sl4y: ok then. isn't there too much competition in crypts nowadays?

[19:36] **[To: Sl4y]**: kind of, but its fine

[19:36] **[Friend]** Sl4y: hell no, the enemy must be beaten

[19:36] **[Friend]** Sl4y: you know what, I have a better spot in mind

[19:36] **[Friend]** Sl4y: it's an old trick but almost nobody knows about it, I think

[19:36] **[Friend]** Sl4y: you have a paladin on 80+ now right?

[19:36] **[To: Sl4y]**: yeah

[19:36] **[To: Sl4y]**: but I like my spot ._.

[19:36] **[Friend]** Sl4y: you will like mine too

[19:36] **[To: Sl4y]**: ok, tell me more after IC

* * *

BATS was, perhaps, the most hated player on AltAr. He did not think it was unfair or undeserved. Neither was it an accident; it was hard work. If anything, he was disappointed by people who thought him simply a loser without a life who only preyed upon people weaker than himself. *Uncultured fools,* he thought about them all. He was an artist, a master of the craft, and the common rabble was unable to appreciate him. Nevertheless, he was known, and he did prey on people weaker than him. He loved receiving letters from his fans, such as the private message he had just received:

[19:19] [Whisper] fuzzi0: you motherfucker

[19:19] [Whisper] fuzzi0: I hope you and your entirefamily get cancer

[19:19] [Whisper] fuzzi0: fuck you noob

[19:19] [Whisper] fuzzi0: learn to play

It went on for a while. BATS saved screenshots.

This one worked out even better than he expected. The opponent was good and BATS almost lost that fight, having survived with only a sliver of health. For almost everyone, to lose a fight by such a narrow margin was the most infuriating feeling. BATS had not planned this - one would have to be a five-dimensional 200 IQ genius to predict the outcome of an unexpected duel with a multitude of variables.

[19:21] [To: fuzzi0]: q:)

BATS opened a notepad application in the background, scrolled to the bottom, and added another name to the list. He would make sure to do something extra for this fan next time they met.

Such "feedback" from people came in various ways: private messages, street talk, forum posts, voice chats. There were even petitions to ban him for griefing but AltAr administration did not see any breach of Code of Conduct in the evidence presented against him. BATS expected this outcome, as he knew exactly what the Code of Conduct allowed.

The archipelago around Flat Booty port was still a hot zone of player activity, but BATS was getting bored of it and roamed around Forsynth Crater for a while. The nice thing about this place was that he could extract maximum salt from people here by not doing much. Sometimes all he needed to trip a careless player was to stab him once in the worst possible moment for them, and let the elementals the victim had tagged do the rest while BATS vanished again. *Sometimes the very threat of an invisible enemy is enough to kill them.* But his favourite moments were those when he simply uncloaked next to someone and just stood there watching the panicked player react to the new sudden threat next to them by turning their backs on the monsters, and paying the blood price for it.

This time though, he had made his way north to one of the areas neighbouring the Crater to check a few ol' reliable spots. Between the Crater and the mountains even further north rose dozens of massive pillars of rock, known simply as the Pillars, jutting up from the ground as if a titanic hedgehog was buried underneath, each spike dozens of metres in diameter at minimum. This created a peculiar stone forest, but underneath it was a regular soil so all kinds of typical, continental vegetation lived here: grasses, ferns, trees, flowers. Among those pillars a magic research base-camp was erected for the purposes of Elemental study, the Pillar Watchpost, and it was connected to the quick-travel system by NPC Mages maintaining it. Though the place was far enough from Forsynth to not be utterly shattered by the calamity unleashed there, the pillars' facades were visibly blackened on the sides facing the Crater. By in-game terms, the camp was less than two minutes of mounted ride from the Crater's rim, but was only one of the few quick-travel points from which it could be accessed.

BATS' mount choice of the day was, appropriately, a tiny mountain "giant", a bipedal humanoid clump of mossy pebbles carrying the player on its shoulders. It even had a loincloth for modesty. The Assassin rode the dirt paths twisting in the shadows of rocky spires and leafy trees, and soon came to the northern edge of the Pillars where the feet of tall cliffs denoted the border of Alxis Mountains. There he dismounted and stealthed immediately. This was not a particularly populous location since it was tucked in the corner of the map and was a dead end, but a few rare monsters spawned here either in their caves or patrolled the area, and there was almost always someone camping their spawns. Sometimes the campers fought each other for the territory, sometimes they just AFKed here unaware of each other hidden behind a tree, on a tree, or even on the bottom of a pond with water-breathing potion enabled. Sometimes an unlucky herbalist was mistaken for a competitor and killed mercilessly. Needless to say, a place such as this was a blessing for BATS. Nothing tilted people quite as well as ganking them just before a long-awaited rare monster spawned ahead.

The player whose name he had just put on his list of people to be tormented with extra effort was one such person, laying stealthed in wait near a cave where a special white tiger Shanhao spawned several times a day, making it significantly less rare than many other enemies in the game considered rare. BATS reckoned this one dropped a white tiger cub as a pet or something like that. Anyway, the victim had been an Assassin like himself who probably felt safe being stealthed, but that was little protection from BATS. Like a submarine searching for another submarine, he sniffed nearby looking carefully for an air blur betraying a stealthed player, found a target, and pounced on his back immediately. The Assassin resisted quite well, but in Assassin duels whoever struck first usually came out alive given their low health but high damage.

Satisfied with himself and having screenshotted the angry messages he had received to be savoured later, he set off to find another victim, and soon his lucky star blessed him again. Someone was attempting the bane of all

RPGs: an escort quest. A female Hunter, by the looks of it, from a guild he did not recognize by name so it was probably not important. It was an escort of a wounded local militia man who was captured and locked in a cage by harpies from their nesting grounds to the west of white tiger's cave.

Fuck yes, he thought excitedly. *Now to just wait at the very end of the escort route and pwn her. Or him.*

He was still quite far away. Being not only on foot but also stealthed meant he moved with a significant speed penalty, but he'd rather stay this way and slowly catch up. He had enough time, the destination was still somewhat far away. Once he got closer he would rush the final gap and attack immediately. Of all classes in the game, Hunters detected hidden enemies with the greatest ease, sometimes even by accident. What worked for him though was that there were no aggressive enemies between the harpy nests and the safety of Pillar Watchpost, so she likely was not very vigilant for attacks here.

The enchanted mobile suits of empty armour, guardians of the mages at the Post, were already seen in the distance when he got in Sprint range. Soon enough it was time to strike. In another minute or so her quest would be completed as the frustratingly slow NPC shuffled his stupid feet, and BATS still needed some time to actually floor the target before that time to make sure her quest fails. He used Sprint, still invisible, and charged at the enemy with his daggers poisoned and both weapons bared. But then the unexpected happened and he stopped in his tracks.

Someone had pounced at his target first, another Assassin being the only explanation. BATS stood and enjoyed the show, waiting to see who would win the fight and whom he would kill afterwards. However, when he moused over the new Assassin, he realised he may not get to frag any of them, for the Assassin who was likely to win was from a guild no other than his own.

^_Miko_^ wore, of all things, an incomplete, mismatched, and low-tiered set of solo-arena PvP gear: deep-crimson skin-tight leathers such as Combatant

Bodysuit, Legwraps too by the looks of it but it could be the Rival Legwraps (*they look almost the same!*); the gloves he could not see well enough to identify, and the rest of accessories were not visible at all. The tattered cloak, a signature visual of the class she dyed black but the model was almost always the same for all Assassins, with notable exception for a few legendaries which this was certainly not one of. She used a twin dagger backstabbing style similar but not identical to his own, although judging from the debuffs on the Hunter, ^_Miko_^ from a variety of poisons available to Assassins chose the flat damage ones. *Not what I would do,* he thought. What customization was visible to him from the distance was that her right arm was bare from shoulder to wrist, and that a medium-length brown ponytail flowed behind her bare head.

The Hunter was just below max level at 98, and wore what looked to BATS in the distance to be a collage of leveling and dungeon gear, certainly not with attributes suitable for PvP. The recurve bow was good, he noticed, a drop from the final boss of Peaks of Korobros, a massive Roc inspired by Middle-Eastern folklore. She was likely to be using it for quite some time after dinging 100. Nevertheless, the emerald-green of her hood and cloak was an ugly contrast to the chestpiece of crimson-red leather, white gloves, and other crimes against consistency. *A leveling gear in its full glory,* summed up BATS. *No need to look twice at it.*

^_Miko_^ handled the Hunter pretty well, BATS had to admit. The ambush worked greatly in her favour making the victim unable to benefit from a Hunter's greatest assets, pre-positioned traps and range, but still ^_Miko_^ displayed good execution. To do a simple thing right when it matters is a skill too, he knew.

The dead Hunter lay on the ground for a few moments before releasing the body, after which BATS spoke in general chat next to her.

[19:28] BATS: nice job :D

[19:28] BATS: Though you kinda stole her from me =/

She froze, perhaps surprised by the sudden company so close to her, but unable to see or attack it. After a moment, she must have realised it was her guildie and she was not in danger from him.

[19:29] ^_Miko_^: sorry! ^^

[19:29] BATS: nah we're good bro q:)

[19:29] ^_Miko_^: sis* ^^

[19:29] BATS: what?

[19:29] ^_Miko_^: I'm a girl XD

[19:29] BATS: hah. Nice try, FBI

[19:29] ^_Miko_^: what??

[19:29] BATS: nevermind, it's an older meme… you must be like 10 :-/

[19:29] ^_Miko_^: PFFF! Almost 16!

[19:29] BATS: why so young? =/

[19:30] ^_Miko_^: ? XD

[19:30] BATS: Nvm. Why did you kill her?

[19:30] ^_Miko_^: cuz I hate hunters:D and she blocked my escort q.

[19:30] BATS: hunters give you trouble on arenas?

[19:30] ^_Miko_^: mhm :(and warriors :(

[19:30] BATS: I could give you a few tips later if you wan

BATS said, and then guild chat drew his attention.

[19:30] **[Guild]** Ò_Ó: HAHA

[19:30] **[Guild]** Ò_Ó: which one of you just ganked my sister

[19:30] **[Guild]** Ò_Ó: @BATS?

[19:30] **[Guild]** BATS: sorry, I thought she's single q:)

[19:30] **[Guild]** Ò_Ó: lmao

[19:30] **[Guild]** BATS: tbh that wasn't me q:)

[19:30] **[Guild]** Ò_Ó: she's whining from her room about Havoc again

[19:30] **[Guild]** Ò_Ó: who then? she was on her hunter, notPuca or smth like that

[19:30] **[Guild]** BATS: dunno, probably Miko or something

[19:30] **[Guild]** Ò_Ó: mhm riiiiiight

[19:31] **[Guild]** ^_Miko_^: actually, it was me XD

[19:31] **[Guild]** Ò_Ó: lol what

[19:31] **[Guild]** Ò_Ó: little Miko is a bad girl?

[19:31] **[Guild]** Ò_Ó: @Vizovia why can't you be like her ;_;

[19:31] **[Guild]** Vizovia: _^_

[19:31] **[Guild]** Vizovia: our Miko is special <3

[19:31] **[Guild]** ^_Miko_^: I'm not bad v_v

[19:31] **[Guild]** ^_Miko_^: but she took the quest I wanted, so…

[19:31] **[Guild]** BATS: you'll all refer to her by her street name now, Lil' M.

[19:31] **[Guild]** Vizovia: xD

[19:31] **[Guild]** Ò_Ó: lmao

[19:31] **[Guild]** Slam1go: I don't know what's weirder here, this scenario or that Butts discovered how to use guild chat : D

[19:32] ^_Miko_^: later! I'll go do that q before harpies respawn ^^

The empty space replied as she summoned and mounted up on a grey Worg the size of a small car and departed.

[19:32] BATS: ok q:)

BATS moved off the road so that a passer-by would not detect him by accident. There he stood immobile, waiting, led by a hunch.

'Ha,' he muttered to himself a moment later. That same Hunter, notPuca indeed, was now leaving the camp on a floating cloud mount, following the road towards the harpy nesting grounds. *That is not a newbie mount,* he remarked. *Wait… is she the Paladin Pukka from my list? Same person? Gotta be.*

He did not move an inch when she went past him, following ^_Miko_^'s steps from a few moments before. Now he started to move, still invisible, until the target disappeared behind a few turns and obstacles. He did not need to tail her, he knew where she was going. He scrolled up the chat, clicked the other Assassin's name and sent to her:

[19:33] [To: ^_Miko_^]: heads up, she's coming for u

[19:33] [Whisper] ^_Miko_^: oh shucks

[19:33] [To: ^_Miko_^]: dont stand close to the npc

BATS waited a moment, uncloaked, summoned his tiny giant mount, and followed the two women, but did not tell ^_Miko_^ he was doing so. He wanted to see something. He rode only for a moment before he dismounted and became invisible again. He really loved the feeling of invisibility, the thrill of the hunt, choosing the moment to pounce, the finding of creative ways to provoke and confuse people. Their stress and paranoia. He's been playing the game for years and still enjoyed doing what he did as if it was week one.

He looked for an elevated vantage point to see what happens next but found none, so he just went further along the dirt road through the meadows and trees. An observant player close by, if there was one, could notice the tiny movements of grass blades as a blur moved slowly over them. He saw the Hunter a few dozen metres ahead of him reach the same escort NPC that she had failed to protect just minutes before shuffle its feet towards the camp. She dismounted without stopping and launched a flare in the sky before her feet even hit the ground. BATS wondered if ^_Miko_^ took his advice or wrongly stood close enough to be revealed by flare. In fact, he did not even know if she was still in the area at all, but if she was, then she dodged the flare. not-Puca then released a few offensive abilities in random directions, hoping one would just happen to land where a hidden Assassin was, or perhaps bait them to make a wrong move. *Typical moves,* thought BATS, *typical, but they work.*

The Hunter wriggled around, knowing not to face the same direction for longer than a split second to make it impossible for the Assassin to attack her from the back.

Suddenly, ^_Miko_^ revealed herself just a few steps from notPuca, to BATS' surprise. He initially thought: *why show herself like that? She's made it easy for the Hunter. What a blunder.* But immediately he withdrew his judgement, because ^_Miko_^ used Blink Strike, a precious skill with a pretty damn long cooldown of three minutes, meaning she would not have it again in this fight. It teleported her behind her target in the blink of an eye and immediately cast Ankle Kick, thus solving the problem of positioning and of the Hunter moving away. BATS learned long ago to not do that kind of opening with Hunters, and ^_Miko_^ was now discovering why. The nimble ranger was prepared this time, and reacted to ^_Miko_^ 's gap closer with Hunter's gap opener leaping a dozen steps forward, then turned around on the spot and loosed an enchanted arrow at her sneaky assailant. The arrow would prevent afflicted targets from turning invisible for some time.

BATS' colleague now desperately needed to get back to close range if she had any hopes of defeating the opponent again. *Did she pick Improved Vanish at level 70? It could allow her to go invisible while dropping all negative effects and get behind her again. Or she could also try to run away. Unlikely to work, though. Hunters happen to be good at hunting things.* ^_Miko_^ was either aware of this option or too stubborn to turn away, so forward she went, using Evasion for a temporary dodge chance buff and using Sprint for some extra movement speed to catch the Hunter who could now just hold down the sidestep button and shoot at the Assassin sideways. The Ankle Kick that ^_Miko_^ did immediately after Blink Strike really paid for itself, as without it the Hunter could now just run away at full speed instead of shuffling her feet like an escorted NPC.

Nope, she's dead, concluded BATS. He started moving again while the fight lasted, inclined to salvage something out of the situation. As he prowled forward through the tall grass, notPuca made a mistake of her own. Feeling confident perhaps as her health was at comfortable 7409, so about eighty percent compared to the Assassin's fifty percent at 4674, she chose to use Vital Point Shot, an ability with a cast time that could only be done by standing still. Thus she gave ^_Miko_^ an opportunity to return to the fight. A throwing knife flew out from the Assassin's outstretched hand and hit notPuca squarely in the torso, breaking her spellcasting, momentarily staggering her too. *It was really well done*, remarked BATS, *considering Vital Point Shot has only a two-second cast time. Very good reaction time by the kid.* ^_Miko_^ finally managed to get back in melee range, and notPuca seemed to be genuinely concerned.

^_Miko_^'s achievement was short-lived. A bear trap sprung up from the ground and immobilised the girl completely, while BATS found new respect for the Hunter. He did not see her place the trap at all, and now even suspected the casted ability was used as a bait and distraction as well. *Very clever if true.*

In the end, ^_Miko_^ either did not have or did not think to use Improved Vanish to reposition or save her skin. Ten seconds later ^_Miko_^ lay defeated on the ground. notPuca stood over her for a moment, probably typing a message.

[19:35] notPuca: xD what now, bitch

She said, and then performed a /spit emote. This kind of disrespect towards an opponent on the ground made BATS very happy, but it did not change what he was about to do at all. In fact, it made it even better.

[19:35] BATS: me q:)

He spoke from behind her, still stealthed, and immediately Blackjacked her before she thought to do anything. He could crush her instantaneously, but that was not his style. The Blackjack stunned her for four seconds or until she took damage from any source. BATS was careful not to attack, but instead moved to her front, waited the rest of the four-second window, and then he used Pocket Sand to blind her for another two seconds. The Hunter's model swayed in place while the player behind the character frantically attempted to regain control. It was not to be. Something appeared in BATS' hand and he threw it at her feet. The improvised flashbang grenade – a product of alchemy that hardly anyone ever uses since it was heavily nerfed in a patch fourteen months ago that reduced its explosion radius and making it share cooldown with potions again – disoriented her for another three seconds. At this point, he suspected, she must have thought it was her turn to do something. He used Vanish and disappeared from her sight, only to uncloak behind her and deliver a Backstab for critical damage. notPuca's underleveled character yelped briefly and fell to the ground face down.

Perhaps only then did notPuca realise she was finished off by someone she had met in the past several times, for only one player on the server would go around geared like that and get away with it. The rogue wore a cheap mask with the most innocent smile that can possibly be carved, rainbow-coloured wig, naked torso, leather trousers that looked like taken off a level 10 mob somewhere in a starting zone. All this contrasted with a very wicked-looking dagger drenched in black liquid in each hand. What she could not see were very high-end accessories and jewellery equipped on him. She watched as he impaled the ground through her character's corpse with a long stick that turned out to be a flagpole with a "thumb down" emote printed on the banner.

She returned to town without saying a word. BATS glanced at ^_Miko_^ laying on the ground, watching everything that happened. He invited her to party and continued there:

'Wait a minute before you get up, she might be waiting at the camp's exit for you. Make her wait =]' he said. As an Assassin he could not resurrect dead players so the girl's only choice was to return to life at the closest neutral spawn base or camp like the other player.

'I almost had her v_v,' she said.

'You think?'

'She was pretty low.'

'Nope. You lost that fight within the first two seconds =]'

'...'

BATS wondered if the triple dot meant she was upset.

'What are you wearing btw xD' she asked. *Not upset, then.*

'Why, what should I be wearing? :-/'

'Real PvP or raid items?'

'Where's the fun in that :-\'

[19:36] **[Guild]** Ò_Ó: XD

[19:36] **[Guild]** Ò_Ó: WHAT DID YOU DO TO HER, SHE'S FUMING XDDD

[19:36] **[Guild]** Ò_Ó: stormed out of her room, this is so funny I can't

[19:36] **[Guild]** ^_Miko_^: it was batsy this time :D

[19:36] **[Guild]** BATS: I swear it was an accident.

[19:36] **[Guild]** BATS: she tripped and fell on my daggers

[19:36] **[Guild]** BATS: q:)

[19:36] **[Guild]** Vizovia: I'm beginning to see why some people hate us

[19:37] **[Guild]** Ò_Ó: I assure you she hated us already xD which is why she's so pissed rn

BATS replayed both fights in his mind. *Her idea to open with Blink Strike was creative and could be salvaged with better skill tree choices. Wait, no, maybe she has good choices but forgot to use them. The knife throw to interrupt was excellently timed. She did not use Smoke Bomb because it's useless against a Hunter. Also she owned her really quick in that first fight so she must have practised some good combos. She dodged every flare and skillshot before the second fight. She plays solo arenas too! And more importantly though: she was utterly fearless in both duels, the fact she even took the second fight against her hardcounter proves this. And she said she was, what, fifteen? Sixteen? When I was sixteen, I was a keyboard-turner who thought the Ninja build was good. Ugh.*

She's good, he realised, *but she can be damn **scary** if she's... guided.*

'Are you specced for Pocket Sand?' He asked her.

'Specced?'

'Did you pick Pocket Sand at level 50?'

'No, stun length.'

'That's useless if you're not using at least one mace =]'

'But PS does not work from behind and I always want to be behind, no?'

'You will never be behind 100% of the time. Also you can just quickly step forward, cast it sideways, and return, it takes less than a second. Just hold down RMB, tap Q just a little. Even if you're only a pixel in front of her, cast it, and tap E back again. Go change it to PS today,' he advised.

'OK… wait, how did you use Blackjack with daggers?' she asked.

'You can drag a weapon to action bars and quickly switch weapons in combat.'

'Oh… OHHHH!! That opens a lot of possibilities!' BATS was imagining that the young one's mind was being blown at the moment at things that were obvious to him.

'Do you have Improved Vanish at 70?'

'Yes! ^^'

'Then use it sometimes D: It's a wonderful tool for every purpose, especially running away. Remember to always be a backstabbing little bastard, run away and hit again later. It's a strong play but also makes ppl mad AF q:)'

'Ok xD'

'Now get up, and then wanna go see what we can find in the Crater? =]'

Later that evening it was time to hit the bed, but BATS would not sign out from the game. He very rarely did. Instead, he ran over to another area, parked his character in one of several hiding spots he found over the years, and turned Stealth on. Staying stealthed consumed mana, but he had mana regen equipment that was completely useless to an Assassin in any other situation. Each such hiding spot was outdoor, away from any farming areas, quest objectives, and player travelling routes. Some required precise jumping from a structure or a tree to another, or dropping down from a cliff, just barely surviving the fall. Some required diving underwater and finding a pocket of air in a decorative shipwreck or a cave. His location was impossible to determine, but people would know he was still online. Always.

He set an alarm clock for 3 AM and went to bed. It has been a few days since he last woke up at night, killed a few players, and went back to sleep.

Being hated was hard work.

* * *

'Everyone should be in town, if you're still in castle then you're deaf or don't give a shit!' said Pvro. 'Portals please!' Pvro requested of all Mages. 'Only SBK!'

'We should regroup and resu-' someone began.

'No! GOGOGOGO we have a window! Go even if you're not ready!' Pvro urged everyone on the channel. 'We killed a few big ones, maybe we can catch them on the return walk!'

'We're getting attacked by all kinds of randoms on the way. Are they helping Execs?' someone asked.

'No, they just want some action. The usual.'

'Ignore them, just disengage,' Pvro commanded. 'Stun them, root them, turn around, and keep running to the Red Room!'

'God, this is hard to watch, we're running around like headless chickens. Must you chase everything? Faystus? Xyro? BATS you too?' Slam1go was exasperated. He has been giving sub-commands to everyone, micro-managing people who hardly showed signs of wanting to be managed.

[20:49] **[Friend]** Ma_Ris: that doesn't sound too good :(

[20:49] **[Guild]** Makzine: just came home, should I log my pala or hunter?

'Fuck, I forgot to take any potions,' complained Blinky.

'Check check, it seems Bulwark-ATR fucked off somewhere else,' reported Xyrolol. 'They're all gone. YNWA is still ganking here though, as per usual.'

'They must have gone to the other castle for sure.'

'Someone tell Makzine to bring a Hunter, we need trap removal.'

[20:49] **[To: Ma_Ris]**: yes

[20:49] **[To: Ma_Ris]**: how long have you been listening?

'**They will take Nordheimburg in no time**.' Agnelei's voice rumbled.

'Ah damn it, wish we had done that,' said -Zoe-, expressing what many others must have been thinking.

[20:49] **[Friend]** Ma_Ris: maybe 10 mins

'Too late for that now,' Slam1go summarised as if to cut the discussion.

'Is it though? Maybe we can exploit it,' proposed Intervene. 'They break the randoms holding it, they think the day is over, then we roll in before they put up proper defence.'

A heavy Greek accent commented. 'Don't be too sure Bulwark can take it.' That was Venetia.

'We really should have made some kind of deal with Bulwark and ATR to take down Execute today. Octav mentioned it himself on the forums,' said Blinky.

'We did have a deal, but - imagine this - SOMEONE kept attacking their people before I came in, so that's history now, good job.' Pvro did not sound happy.

'Funny how that works.'

'Shush, Slam1go,' I heard enough today.'

Although Vizovia was relatively new to the guild and to ARIS as a game, she eagerly participated in guild wars with Havoc. She was certain she was making many mistakes, died too easily, panicked under stress, and just did not have the speed of hands required to manage skills, movement, and usable items, but she wanted to participate because that's what everyone - *well, almost everyone* - did.

Ma_Ris for example, though she has been playing ARIS for years, never participated in GvGs. She did not find it enjoyable, she said when asked, but she sometimes joined the guild voice channel to listen to everyone's talk. She knew not to disturb the operation so most of the time she remained silent, but during the more boring evenings she would talk to everyone and unknowingly raise morale and prevent people from wandering away from the computer. Both Vizovia and ^_Miko_^ attempted to convince their friend to participate directly, telling her every hand helps even if it's just casting buffs every now and then, but to no effect.

[20:48] [Raid] Poweroverwhelming died.

[20:48] [Raid] Faystus died.

[20:48] [Raid] Blinky died.

'HOW THE FUCK DID YOU MANAGE TO DIE,' Slam1go all but yelled to his microphone. 'I'm fucking losing it. HOLD. POSITION. IN. THE. FUCKING. RED. ROOM. How is this so difficult to do?'

'I just wanted to check inside man, chill,' Faystus said.

'Now you're checking the respawn in town, good job,' commented Slam1go and a few snickers went off in the voice comms.

Pvro was more diplomatic. 'I'm bored of repeating this too. Hold means hold. We're waiting for everyone here.'

This Wednesday evening Havoc was on the offence from the very beginning, and after fifty minutes was yet to take the territory and hold it for more than a few minutes. The mood was tense. Havoc's disappointing failure to end the day session controlling a castle would now be the second time in a row, eroding morale in a guild unaccustomed to losing.

[20:49] **[Friend]** Ma_Ris: what's with Slam1go today?

[20:49] **[Raid]** Sapphire: buff

[20:49] **[Raid]** Makzine: me too

[20:49] **[To: Ma_Ris]**: Pvro came 15 mins late today

[20:49] **[To: Ma_Ris]**: a few people are kinda upset

'Raphanti, song is down, no AFK now please,' reprimanded Pvro.

[20:49] **[Friend]** Ma_Ris: I see

[20:49] **[Raid]** Intervene: where is arastina and pjj?

[20:49] **[Raid]** Stoencold: Vacation.

[20:49] **[Raid]** Intervene: oh right, they said something about that

[20:49] **[Raid]** Xyrolol: Dereky too?

[20:49] **[Raid]** Stoencold: Still moving to another place I think.

The guild was holding position inside Sal-Born Keep, not far from the final barricade where Execute had been successfully defending against all attacks for the past eighteen minutes. Only when everyone made it to the Red Room, were buffed, and healed up after partisan attacks, then Pvro would give the countdown and the call to push forward. Execute knew exactly what was coming and they were prepared for sure.

[20:52] **[To: Ma_Ris]**: I really hate attacking v_v

[20:52] **[Friend]** Ma_Ris: stay strong dear

[20:52] **[Friend]** Ma_Ris: btw good news for you, there's a wedding this evening after GvG

[20:52] **[Friend]** Ma_Ris: I'm invited, you coming with me?

[20:52] **[To: Ma_Ris]**: @_@ yes!

[20:52] **[To: Ma_Ris]**: what time?

[20:52] **[Friend]** Ma_Ris: 9pm

Pvro brought Vizovia's attention back to the situation. 'Okay, ready? On my mark, we rush in. slowah cast null on T minus one. You know what to do. ALL RIGHT, HERE WE GO. Five, four, three, two, one, GOGO-GOGOGO!'

[20:52] **[To: Ma_Ris]**: ok

'Aaaaand I'm dead,' said someone.

'Fuck!' said someone else.

'The fuck is this damage? Hunters are OP.'

'I couldn't even selfpot once.'

'I got through with some people but we lost too many on the way in.'

'One null is not enough.'

'Fuck this, we can't make it.'

[20:53] **[Friend]** Ma_Ris: …that didn't sound too good either

'Where is everyone else? We're like eight core people short today.'

'Vacations?'

'Execute don't have vacations then? They're more numerous than ever.'

[20:53] **[To: Ma_Ris]**: this looks bad…

'Dunno, mate.'

'I never thought we would end a GvG day like this.'

'Are we gonna try again?'

'What for? I don't see the point today.'

'Ye, kinda pointless.'

'Pvro, are we done for tonight?'

'I think tha-' began Pvro.

'I'm sorry, but I missed the moment this became full of WHINY ASS BITCH PUSSY QUITTERS!' All of the sudden, it was now Sl4y who had been speaking above others talking in Chatterbox. Vizovia was not sure if his tone carried genuine anger or it was meant to be humorous. 'You say this is pointless? Well let me tell you what else is pointless, playing video games is fucking pointless, yet here you are. Where else would you rather be, if not running into a meat-grinder with your homies? Now put on your gamer pants back on, and GET YOUR ASSES INTO THE PORTALS, we try one more time. Exec are probably sitting there laughing how easy we are now, and I for one won't suffer their fucking satisfaction SO LET'S GO FUCK THEM. I mean, won't somebody think of poor Slam1go getting shat on on forums later?'

A silence held for a few seconds, then a dozen voices went off more or less in the same instant. A few hearty laughs and gasps too.

'Wow.'

'Uhhh…'

'Haha, okay, putting on my gamer pants back now!'

'Yes sir, fucking them right now sir!'

'Daaaamn.'

'All right, one more try I guess.'

'Could not say it better myself,' said Pvro trying to contain laughter in his tone. 'OK boons, we're doing it. Everyone rush to Red Room, CC any

Execs you see on the way, DO NOT KILL THEM, they help us by not being where they need them to be! Portals pleeeease! Now, thank you!'

The fight was over minutes later. Vizovia disconnected from the GvG channel and removed her headset. Coming back to reality, she realised her legs were shaking a little. She did not even know when GvGs became so emotional for her, but she definitely needed to collect herself.

Ma_Ris had waited until now to chat her up, knowing that Vizovia might have missed her message in the heat of the moment otherwise.

[21:01] **[Friend]** Ma_Ris: that speech from the boys though :D

[21:01] **[Friend]** Ma_Ris: if only the attack worked in the end, what a little legend that would be to remember :)

[21:01] **[To: Ma_Ris]**: sheesh I'm so tired after this

[21:01] **[To: Ma_Ris]**: now that I think about it, I don't know if I heard anything from Sl4y all game long until that moment

[21:01] **[Friend]** Ma_Ris: usually a bad sign, he's silent and sulky when he's angry. He made it sound like a joke, but he was really upset I suspect

[21:01] **[To: Ma_Ris]**: so you know him long enough to know?

[21:01] **[Friend]** Ma_Ris: yes and no^^

[21:02] **[Friend]** Ma_Ris: I knew him for years only by reputation and gossip until he joined us here

[21:02] **[Friend]** Ma_Ris: Sapphire probably knows better

[21:02] **[Friend]** Ma_Ris: anyway I'm waiting for you in girls' room

[21:02] **[To: Ma_Ris]**: give me a moment please, I need a break

[21:02] **[To: Ma_Ris]**: I'll be there in 15

[21:02] **[Friend]** Ma_Ris: sure <3

[21:02] **[Guild]** Raphanti: today sucked not gonna lie

[21:02] **[Guild]** Rjukan: yes.

[21:02] **[Guild]** PowerOverwhelming: you know its bad when raphanti isnt putting it as a joke

[21:02] **[Guild]** Stoencold: With how we do recently I will be shocked if we hold it for 5 minutes on saturday even if we take it.

[21:02] **[Guild]** Azarus: we need changes, agreed. We got lazy

[21:02] **[Guild]** Slam1go: everyone should do homework and improve their play

[21:02] **[Guild]** Slam1go: some things I saw today are a fucking joke guys

[21:02] **[Guild]** Slam1go: and I mean EVERYONE

[21:02] **[Guild]** Stoencold: Truth.

[21:02] **[Guild]** Xyrolol: hey at least we still have building mats. it's called being optimistic, I think

[21:02] **[Guild]** Sl4y: that sounds awful, let's not do that D:

[21:02] **[Guild]** Pvro: all right everyone, I am sorry I was late today

[21:03] **[Guild]** Pvro: but we cannot rely on me so much, I have a life too you know

[21:03] **[Guild]** Pvro: secondly, as I posted on the forums just yesterday: since nobody else volunteered, Slam1go is the official stand-in GvG commander

[21:03] **[Guild]** Pvro: follow his lead as if it was mine

[21:03] **[Guild]** 415: what's this "life" you speak of?

[21:03] **[Guild]** Sl4y: that sounds awful, let's not do that D:

[Thread: KOTH GvG, Wednesday 25 Jun]
[Posted by: Proskillver, 25 Jun 2015, 21:07:54]
Congrats to Havoc for almost winning. Again :)

[Posted by: Slam1go, 25 Jun 2015, 21:11:05]

All right, all right. Today we recognize Execute as the rightful winners of the day. It is only natural that they should own SBK.

I mean, it's even named Salt-Born Keep after them =]

[Posted by: Proskillver, 25 Jun 2015, 21:11:58]
Haha you're still talking, amazing! Most people would shut up
already :)

[Posted by: MALDING, 25 Jun 2015, 21:13:39]
Another day without Havoc on top? This is the beginning of a new
era or something.
Get your shit together guys, I can't take another day looking at the
ugly Execute and BW/ATR flags XD

[Posted by: __draac__, 25 Jun 2015, 21:19:52]
Glad to see Slam1go still talking shit after Havoc taking such a
beating! :D I had to ask Octav to take us to the other castle because it
was such a sorry sight. BTW Slam1go you should get some magic def
man, you melt from shadow dmg like your circle of friends
    ...
oh wait!

[Posted by: Slam1go, 25 Jun 2015, 21:23:16]
@up Keep laughing pal =] shadowpriest nerfs are around the corner,
we'll see how you melt anything then =]

'Hey hey!' said Vizovia as she joined Ma_Ris on voice chat. 'Sorry I took
so long, my mom called, and… eh, nevermind.'

'It's fine, we got plenty of time. Come meet me in Helle.'

'Sure. Is that where this wedding will be?' Vizovia asked, teleporting herself directly and quickly to Hellesvyand. It was really good to play a Mage sometimes.

'Yes, exactly. Let me invite you… there.' Vizovia accepted Ma_Ris' party invitation. 'Come here.'

'On my way. So, who's getting married?'

'You and Eyes,' said Ma_Ris.

Vizovia burst with amusement. 'Ha-ha, very funny.'

'Tee-hee! It's my friend Blau and a guy she met here a few months ago.'

'Ah. I don't know her. Isn't this a little sudden though?'

'It's typical for Blau. She's kinda crazy like that. She told me only 2 hours ago or so.'

'I see. I've never been to a game wedding. What should I know?'

'Nothing really, it's pretty casual normally. It's a simple thing but I remember you said you wanted to see one, so I got you a front-row seat!'

'You're an angel. I only heard they can be expen- hold the phone, are you trying on dresses?' Vizovia gasped.

She had just found her friend by a beach a few hundred metres from the center of town, if a place such as this even existed in a place such as Hellesvyand. The whole place was built along a sandy white beach on the coast of Coral Bay using wood predominantly – some of it curiously covered in barnacles – and ropes and straw for the rest. Some of the largest structures in the town were in fact massive ships dragged out from the sea and bashed together to form a maze of gangways, stairs, ladders, and ropes. Ma_ris was, as Vizovia had just discovered, away from the amalgamation of vessels inside one of the larger circular huts that had a Banker NPC in them, surrounded by both NPC and player-owned vending stalls. Ma_Ris was flicking through her outfits like through a catalogue, Vizovia thought.

'Yes, why?' Ma_Ris spoke matter-of-factly.

'I don't have any. I didn't think I needed a fancy outfit.'

'We don't,' assured Ma_Ris. 'But are we gonna miss an opportunity to dress up a little?' She giggled. 'You'll wear one of mine. Unless you don't want to?'

'If you don't mind lending me one,' Vizovia chuckled. 'By the way, isn't this crazy? I got bothered over wearing the right fake digital clothes over a fake digital character in a video game in front of internet people I will never meet in real life.'

'That's the magic of MMOs for you. I'm not really into video games at all but I keep sitting here. It's crazy, but awesome in a way. Now, try those on!' Ma_Ris said, trading six items to Vizovia. 'Keep one you like, then we'll find some accessory to go with it.'

'Wait, half of them are white. Is that okay with the bride?'

'Yes, traditions don't matter much. Your own gear is white anyway.'

'Well, I do like white.' Vizovia agreed. 'Eh. How nice they all fit us perfectly... I wish it worked like that in real life. Me and my stupid thighs.' She sighed. 'By the way, is little Miko not coming with us?'

'Nope. She said she's doing other things.'

'I see. I'll keep this one I think, here, take the rest. How did you even get all those?'

'Oh, you know... events, quests, crafting, don't know what else. Gifts from guys maybe. It just builds up over the years without you knowing it.'

Vizovia nodded. 'I've always thought I don't want to spend too much time obtaining items that aren't real, but now I want them. Feels weird.'

'I know what you mean. Now let's find something to go with it! By the way, the one you chose is yours now.'

A shrine just outside Hellesvyand was designed specifically to serve as a wedding venue, one of four such places in ARIS. It was meant for those preferring a casual, modest ceremony under naked sky to be shared with a few friends. For those seeking extravagance and all the pomp associated with weddings, there was Argentia Cathedral with its massive capacity, bells ringing high overhead tower, imposing altar artfully carved in marble and finest wood, adorned with finest art. The newlyweds could march down the alley to the sound organ music, trumpets, and company of notable NPC characters from various quests and lore.

Which was ironic, because it was in Hellesvyand where people interested in this kind of thing spend most of their time, and thus the little shrine was often more packed than the grand church in the Insal Kingdom's capital. In fairness, the designers of ARIS could not have known which places in the world would be favoured by which type of players, for what reason, and on which of its many independent servers; some of them international, some local, some officially supported, and some were "unsupported". But they knew something of what players are like everywhere you go, so they wisely locked using any abilities inside the shrine to minimise visual and auditory clutter and griefing.

Maybe forty people could fill the few clickable wooden benches arrayed before a simple wooden dais, behind which stood a human-height flower arch. By human design and planning, a row of palm trees grew on each side, their trunks bending inwards to form a bit of a canopy overhead to provide some refuge from the sun and rain, although most weddings were held late in the evening. For this reason, the canopy was also used to hang lanterns illuminating the scene below with warm candlelight.

Several NPCs stood outside the shrine, one to register couples for time slots so that no two weddings could be scheduled at the same time, one to conduct the ceremony, another to instruct players on the process and requirements. The whole process was automated, but there were communities in AltAr that would, on very rare occasions, plan and arrange a wedding conducted by players in its entirety. Ma_Ris' links with such role-playing communities were never strong so even she only heard about them, never having attended any.

'Whoa… this is magical. I didn't know lighting changes when a wedding is going on here,' Vizovia admitted.

She and Ma_Ris arrived early, giving them the privilege to choose any seat they wanted and observe other invitees arriving. *And judge them,* added Vizovia in the privacy of her head.

'Do we register our attendance somewhere? Will the game not kick us out?' Vizovia had asked before they entered, familiar enough with game mechanics by now to expect this kind of thing.

'No, invitation is only by word-of-mouth, really. Anyone can walk in and stay.'

After another few minutes there were already a dozen other people in the shrine, and Vizovia started seeing a pattern.

'Hey, there's only a few people here but almost everyone is with Bulwark or Along The Road.'

'Yes,' confirmed Ma_Ris. 'Blau is a social in Bulwark.'

'And her groom?'

'I don't know.'

'I see. You know, it's kind of funny,' laughed Vizovia. 'I just spent an hour killing them and dying to them in the castle – okay, mostly dying – and now I'm with them at a wedding, all on the same evening.'

'It gets even weirder, look who's coming,' said Ma_Ris.

Of all the people who would ever attend an RP event, even if it was a basic one, it was no other than Slam1go who entered the shrine. He noticed his two guildmates and sat his character on a bench in the third row, just behind Vizovia and Ma_ris.

[20:47] Slam1go: sup ladies

[20:47] Vizovia: you here? :o

[20:47] Slam1go: yeah =]

[20:47] Vizovia: didn't you just shittalk Bulwark & ATR on forums and guild chat?

[20:47] Slam1go: yeah, so? =]

[20:47] Slam1go: not a problem for me

[20:47] Slam1go: rave invited me and I said sure, I'll come and make sure to remember if you say or do something dumb

[20:47] Ma_Ris: he's the groom?

[20:47] Slam1go: wtf is a groom

[20:48] Ma_Ris: it's the man getting married xD

[20:48] Slam1go: ah =] yes he is then

[20:48] Ma_Ris: so you two are friends?

[20:48] Slam1go: I hope not XD

[20:48] Vizovia: what xD

[20:48] Ma_Ris: male friendships, V _^_ how are you in different guilds?

[20:48] Slam1go: he's a filthy casual pleb=]

[20:48] Slam1go: I need to go AFK, brb

'What a guy,' chuckled Vizovia, not commenting on "casualness" of herself and Ma_Ris who are in Havoc somehow. Ten minutes before the start, the little shrine was halfway to full capacity. Late arrivals would have to take standing places. 'Hm, don't you think guys look kinda plain? Pretty much nobody here put on a suit or some other elegant costume, with one or two exceptions.'

'I've always thought men don't have enough elegant clothing options, and I mean in real life too. We have all kinds of outfits in all kinds of colours and cuts, but men only have suits. At least it's cheaper for them, I guess.' After a moment she added. 'I guess there are ceremonial uniforms too, but those are for military people and they're pretty much suits too. Sometimes it's good to be a woman, online or not.'

'I see. Maybe you're right. I don't know what other things there are in ARIS for them though, but I imagine you know it better than me… but I guess guys just prefer to show off their combat gear anyway.'

'Oh, definitely,' admitted Ma_Ris. 'Good observation, actually. Males compete on their horn size right?' Ma_Ris chuckled. 'Females judge their health and capabilities. Goes to show we're all just animals, doesn't it?'

'Mhm… my family hates to hear such talk.'

'I see,' nodded Ma_Ris. It was not the first time she heard about Vizovia's struggle of living with a… *conservative* family. 'You want to study biology, right?'

'Mhm,' agreed Vizovia.

'Did you know Sapphire is in fourth term marine biology?'

'Yeah, I heard. I think you told me that yourself actually,' Vizovia said with a smile.

'Really? I might have. Anyway I'm glad we're on voice, the chat is getting really hard to read with all those people here.'

'Do you think we overdressed?' Vizovia asked.

'No, never. We make other people underdressed, remember that!' Vizovia could hear the genuine smile behind Ma_Ris' words and it made her own mood better. *It is a nice evening,* she thought.

'Which reminds me,' said Vizovia. 'I just have to ask: how come a bombshell angel like you is unmarried, since you're into that thing?'

'Hah, where did that come from?'

'Just asking. You've been here long, you know everyone, everyone likes you. You *know* how they see you. You could take any guy you wanted.'

'And start a civil war?' Ma_Ris replied.

'Haha. Answer the question!'

'It's not so easy as you make it seem.'

'For you, it should be?' pressed Vizovia.

'I don't really have an answer, my dear.'

'Okay, fine. I won't pry.'

'But if I ever do, I will make sure to invite you. To my wedding, I mean.'

'Aww, thanks.'

'Hey, are you not going to tell me the same thing? Hmph!'

'Yes, yes, sure. I will. I doubt it will happen though, it all feels weird to me so far.'

Vizovia looked at the chatbox just in time to notice Slam1go between all the spam rolling up.

[20:51] Slam1go: hey

[20:51] Slam1go: do you know this girl he's marrying?

'I think this is for you,' said Vizovia.

'What?'

'Slam1go on chat.'

'Oops, I wasn't reading.'

[20:52] Slam1go: ;_; ignored

[20:52] Ma_Ris: sorry! ^^'

[20:52] Ma_Ris: chat is going so fast here :) What did you ask?

[20:52] Slam1go: do you know the girl? :p

[20:52] Ma_Ris: yes

[20:52] Slam1go: you sure she's a woman IRL?:p

[20:52] Ma_Ris: uh

[20:52] Ma_Ris: I never met her IRL but I'm pretty sure

[20:52] Ma_Ris: I think I would know otherwise :)

[20:52] Slam1go: ok if you say so

[20:52] Slam1go: one can never be too careful XD

[20:52] Ma_Ris: what if we two were guys IRL?:>

[20:53] Slam1go: then I would have won that bet with raphanti XD

[20:53] Vizovia: xD

[20:53] Ma_Ris: _^_

Two minutes before the top of the hour, when all the seats were already taken and people were already taking standing spots, the tuxedo-wearing groom rushed into the shrine and went straight for the bench Slam1go was in.

[20:58] rave: ej cwelu wstawaj

[20:58] Slam1go: D:

[20:58] rave: stań tutaj

[20:58] Slam1go: po co

[20:58] rave: no stań

'What do you think they're talking about?' asked Vizovia.

'No clue,' replied Ma_Ris.

rave was bouncing up and down in a spot to the side of the flower arch, the universal sign for "right here" or "hurry up". In this case, it was both. Slam1go rose from the bench, leaped over the front rows, and took the indicated spot.

[20:58] Slam1go: i?

[20:58] rave: i tak stój, to nie potrwa długo

[20:58] Slam1go: co D:

[20:58] rave: pomysł żony =] stój ładnie i nie wierć się

[20:58] Slam1go: D:

With those words, rave left the shrine again.

'Oooh, he's the best man now,' guessed Ma_Ris as she noticed a Minstrel from Along The Road by the name of HatePanda quickly walking down the aisle. 'Some other girl is taking the opposite side.'

'I don't know much about politics here but that looks very awkward lol,' Vizovia said. 'Slam1go must be the most hated person here and he was put front and center.'

'Maybe rave is trolling someone. Slam1go for example,' Ma_Ris laughed.

In the end, the ceremony was nothing special. Vizovia had learned early in her ARIS adventure that player marriages were a thing, but in fairness, when Ma_Ris said she could show her an example one day she also warned it was better to not be hyped too much about it.

Maybe the most interesting feature was the one she already knew about, one that popped up in the chatbox at the top of the hour.

[21:00] [World] A marriage ceremony of Blau and rave will take place in Hellesvyand Shrine.

She has seen those many times, but she never bothered to drop whatever she was doing and crash into a wedding of players she did not know; and even if she did, she would be at least several minutes late anyway. Nevertheless, the global message was a nice touch, and those who did not like to see it could filter it out.

The rest was mostly automated, pre-planned, accordingly scripted in-game, and quite unsophisticated. The ceremony was kept in a secular manner and the town official NPC leading it spoke a few sentences, and asked both players to confirm their intention to marry each other. It was programmed to detect a single "yes" spoken in chat by the registered couple. Vizovia wondered what would happen if either of them said "no" or did not answer quickly enough. They also had to emote /kiss on each other, which she found cute.

Then it posted a few more lines of text, music played, flowers were thrown. There was a throwable flower bouquet sold outside the shrine. Vizovia observed that the normally talkative people had gone silent for the duration like they would during a real wedding, but the moment it ended and the couple walked out, guests started /clapping, /cheering, /dancing, and doing all kinds of other emotes. A variety of noisy spells would probably be spammed too if they were enabled. Slam1go vanished somewhere in the meantime, probably on first opportunity. Some people approached the newlyweds with gifts, but that was their own initiative rather than an expected act or a set point on the agenda.

'Maybe the most interesting element of all this, to me at least, is seeing who marries whom and who attends it,' said Ma_Ris afterwards, as if guessing what Vizovia was thinking.

That checks out, thought Vizovia. *Ma_Ris plays the game for the social interactions more so than for the game itself.* 'It's kind of adorable that a video game allows this kind of thing. Six months ago I had only a vague idea such things existed. I wonder how much further online interactions can go,' she mused.

Ma_Ris had plenty to say on the topic, but said nothing.

* * *

The Streets of Hardline were empty an hour before the summer sunrise when a brand new adventurer stepped into the world. His friends had told him the game can be brutal at times, and that people would find creative ways to kill him. He was not sure if they were pulling his leg, but he was in a habit of very early wake-ups anyway. The fingers of his left hand fell onto the WASD keys automatically, and he looked around with his mouse, pleased the game's controls were like any other proper MMORPG he played. He saw empty bars on the bottom of the screen numbered from one to nine, an assignment he would reconfigure pretty quickly to something more optimal, but not just yet.

No movement in sight and no living soul came across him as he completed the few introductory quests teaching movement, targeting, interactions and such trivial things. He left them behind having decided to explore the starting location a little.

Then a weird thing happened. Suddenly his screen was completely filled by what looked like a wall of brown fur, that seemed to move just right to block his vision. He hovered his pointer over it, and the tooltip informed him he was looking at a player.

Oioioibruv, Level 100 Paladin

<You Never Wipe Alone>

It was a player mounted on a really big woolly mammoth mount, who for some reason decided to spend his time at four in the morning toying with a newbie in a starting location. The newbie tried going around the mammoth, but a mounted player was faster and repositioned quickly.

'What are you doing?' typed the tiny human next to a great, tusked beast. As he waited for a response, he thought he briefly heard sounds of combat and steps of two or three sets of feet. But the impression faded quickly and he paid it no mind. In the end, the Paladin simply left without a word and disappeared around a corner.

The newbie thought something weird just happened to him, and he would try to remember to ask his mates about it later.

Another pair of eyes opened not far and not much later, looking for prey, but instead it found something interesting. *Someone is doing something odd*, the observer realised. The interest was piqued, and the eyes followed the anomaly with curiosity.

* * *

Sl4y woke up and reached for his phone tucked between the mattress and the bed frame. Once his vision returned from being blinded by its brightness, the display told him it was Saturday, August 25th, two minutes after seven. The peak of summer hoisted the sun high up in the sky even at such an early hour, and Sl4y already knew there would be no more sleeping. Not since he already opened his eyes.

Sl4y turned on his computer, then made himself some breakfast and brought it to the desk, where he started ARIS and logged his Priest in the background while he did other things. When he finished them, he noticed that he was dead.

He did not even bother to check who killed him but someone, somewhere, was probably celebrating having killed "fucking Sl4y". He had logged out the day before far north in the wildlands of Runthak between Hardline and Urgill Battlements where he had been gathering herbs for a while before going to sleep. Not thinking much about it, he just released the body and respawned in Hardline.

Then his nice morning got spoiled when he scrolled up and read the first message the system printed in his chatbox after logging in.

[07:29] **[Guild]** <MOTD>: Vacay time, back in two weeks:D /Pvro

The ever-so-cheerful and notorious airhead of a Guild Leader not only popped up just to leave a message overnight that he will be absent even longer, but he also did it by overwriting Sl4y's previous MOTD inviting sign-ups for today's alt-character run through Five Geixan Trials led by Intervene.

There were things Sl4y wanted to discuss with Pvro for weeks now, and he could only do an exasperated sigh over having missed a chance to talk to him. Wherever Pvro had gone, it sounded like he was not planning to show up online for the next two weeks. Sl4y wanted to choke him. *How did a guy like him hold together a guild for so many years? Was it Trillex all along, from the backstage?*

He opened his Friendlist to get more answers, ticking the "display offline" option.

Name	Class	Status
Intervene	Warrior Lv 100	Offline (8h)
slowah	Scholar Lv 100	Offline (1d)
Ethereal	Fighter Lv 98	Offline (2d)
Aura	Warrior Lv 3	Offline (3yrs)
Pvro	Assassin Lv 100	Offline (4h)
Sapphire	Minstrel Lv 100	Offline (3h)
Alvea	Paladin Lv 97	Offline (2d)
Sonran	Scholar Lv 100	Offline (3mo)
Seh	Warrior Lv 100	Online <AFK>
Tycho	Witch Doctor Lv 100	Offline (4mo)
Mage	Priest Lv 100	Online
SINka	Assassin Lv 100	Offline (12h)

[show more]

If Pvro was online at around 3 AM then perhaps Sapphire talked with him, but Sl4y knew he would not hear from her for at least six more hours until she woke up.

[07:30] **[Guild]** Slam1go: I see Pvro was here. Did he do the alliance?

And now Slam1go was chatting him up as well. *Great,*

[07:30] **[Guild]** Sl4y: yes he was but he didn't do shit. Probably didn't even check the inbox

[07:30] **[Guild]** Slam1go: fucking real lifer

[07:30] **[Guild]** Slam1go: -___-

[07:30] **[Guild]** Slam1go: we fucking need that alliance =.=

[07:31] **[Guild]** Sl4y: I know, only he can set it up

Sl4y could already feel he will be having similar conversations over the day. There were a couple of things Pvro was needed for: quarrels to settle, guild bank rights, diplomacy with other guilds…

[07:31] **[Guild]** Slam1go: that's fucking bullshit

[07:31] **[Guild]** Slam1go: I guess I will talk to Chippy and freeze the deal

[07:31] **[Guild]** Slam1go: and the gbank? Still the same problem?

[07:31] **[Guild]** Sl4y: yes, but I promoted you to veteran yesterday. Use it wisely

[07:31] **[Guild]** Slam1go: don't trust me? :-)

[07:31] **[Guild]** Sl4y: as far as treasury goes I trust nobody, even myself :p

That was an evasive answer. The fact was that Sl4y has always had some doubts about Slam1go. It wasn't an intense dislike like he had for two or three other people in the guild and a dozen others outside, it was just… he did not know what. He had never seen Slam1go do or say anything suspicious, but still, there was something. Perhaps it was just a personality conflict. Slam1go certainly knew Sl4y's opinion of him as well, so Sl4y did not need to act nice in front of him.

[07:31] **[Guild]** Slam1go: who watches the watchmen, I wonder

[07:31] **[Guild]** Sl4y: you wouldn't presume I'm taking the guild stuff for myself?

[07:32] **[Guild]** Slam1go: no, I'm saying that if you did, we wouldn't know about it

[07:32] **[Guild]** Sl4y: you know what, that's a fair point. I'll put up a log screenshot somewhere

[07:32] **[Guild]** Slam1go: whatever, dude =]

Sl4y was glad that this conversation seemed to be over, if only for a while, but then it turned out it was not over at all.

[07:34] [Whisper] Slam1go: btw I dont know if you forgot, but pvro gave me the GvG leading job

Slam1go's switch from guild chat to private messages foretold a more sensitive topic to be discussed. Sl4y wanted to get through it as soon as possible and get down to other things.

[07:34] [To: Slam1go]: yeah, so?

[07:34] [Whisper] Slam1go: I will appreciate it if you stop questioning me publicly during war, or do the job yourself, k?

[07:34] [Whisper] Slam1go: what's that called again? second-guessing?

Slam1go's words gave Sl4y pause. He searched his memory of the latest GvG on Wednesday and the few times he pointed out a problem or raised a question, like that time when he said that defending the outermost gate was pointless. In Sl4y's mind, every such instance was in good faith.

[07:35] [To: Slam1go]: I thought I'm helping you -_-

[07:35] [Whisper] Slam1go: you're not, I don't need it.

[07:35] [To: Slam1go]: how are you so confident you're never wrong then?

[07:35] [Whisper] Slam1go: I learned a thing or two from korean servers

[07:35] [Whisper] Slam1go: anyway, just do your things, I will do mine

[07:35] [Whisper] Slam1go: at lest while I'm still here -_-

[07:35] [To: Slam1go]: you planning to leave too?

[07:36] [Whisper] Slam1go: dunno. If I wanted, I'd be gone by now. But we can't keep this forever, we need GL powers or we need some other solution

[07:36] [To: Slam1go]: such as?

[07:36] [Whisper] Slam1go: dunno, you figure it out

[07:36] [To: Slam1go]: why me?

[07:37] [Whisper] Slam1go: cuz you're so smart I guess =]

[07:37] [Whisper] Slam1go: ok, afk

The game was hardcoded to not allow guild members to promote people all the way up to their own rank, which was a weird decision by game designers but it was what it was. As long as a guild had an active Guild Leader, there was no problem. Unfortunately for Havoc, Pvro (and Trillex?) left the bank access' permissions in a messy state. He helped where he could by just using his own permissions and handing things to whoever needed it. Another problem was that a tab in the guild storage was accessible only to Pvro for some reason, and Sl4y did not even know what was in there.

And then there was also the other, worse problem. Havoc could no longer dominate the PvP world of AltAr single-handedly. They needed allies, or at least cease-fires with some other secondary tier guilds. And once again, only Pvro had the right to click that button…

Sl4y was looking forward to trying some 5v5 Arena matches with Intervene, Slowah, PowerOverwhelming, and either little ^_Miko_^ or Eightblades if she does not show up later that day. But for now, he would tend to the guild duties.

Sl4y has been in Hardline town since his untimely demise outside the walls, courtesy of a random stranger, which saved him the trip he would have to make anyway. From the infirmary for wounded soldiers he set off towards the Guild Office, a service available in every capital and a few other major cities in the game world. There he could receive the guild mail, and check his own while he was at it.

Hardline's defensive, military character has rubbed itself on every street and structure: stone towers hosting ballistae on their tops, supply wagons going to and from the garrisons around the city, scant decor, narrow windows, and every civilian NPC carrying some weapon, women included. But the place was not austere; people of Hardline venerated heroes and commanders and honoured them with statues, sculptures, and built them something akin to altars to ancestors rather than deities. Red cloth was particularly common despite the fact that, or perhaps precisely because of it, the characteristic crimson dye was made of secretions of shallow-water rock snails that lived only near the southern continent. Coastal communities of Al-Ghabla owed their existence to that northern demand for the dye, while the crimson banners and robes were paid by gold nuggets carried by local rivers. Gameplay-wise, the area was unique in that it was both a starting location and a gateway to high-level zones, giving newcomers an opportunity to cross paths with level 100 characters and interact with them.

[07:38] [Town] yndo45: someone give me 10g

[07:38] [Town] yndo45: PLZ

Or do that, I guess.

The location of Hardline on the side of a mountain meant large elevation differences between districts. There was a time-saving shortcut he could use by dropping down mounted onto a rooftop taking some damage, and then leaping over to neighbouring roofs a few times. He slid off the edge in front of the Guild Office building, dismounted and approached a mailbox in front of it.

Are you serious? Read a message from Sl4y's favourite guild member. It was short, but Sl4y knew what was behind it - Faystus was upset at Sl4y for demoting him down to the lowest rank as punishment for breaking guild rules, effectively stripping him of guild membership benefits such as paid equipment repair and shared storage withdrawals, and hurting his pride. The youngster broke a guild rule that Sl4y had himself added only recently, true, but a breach of conduct should be addressed lest a bad precedent is established for others to see. Sl4y felt weird doing it and knew it was a weird thing to do in a video game, but he also felt justified by the magnitude of the unforgivable crime that Faystus had committed. Refusing to use push-to-talk in voice comms instead of voice-activation warranted at least a death by firing squad in Sl4y's mind. *That little mouth-breather should be glad he got off easily. If I hear him chewing something one more time while he complains about his needed items not dropping, I swear I will kick him out and tell other guilds to avoid him.* It was a petty thing to do, but Sl4y would not hold back from it.

Also, funny how everything boils down to the same two things most of the time. MMORPGs really are just loot and player interaction. Who knew?

Sl4y put Faystus out of his mind and opened the other mailbox, the one receiving in-game mail addressed to the guild as a whole. That such a thing even existed was not usual, a custom-made feature of AltAr by GM_Kaivax on his own initiative. It was not a popular feature in that not many people used it, but it was harmless, even though Kaivax had to evict a few pointless NPCs from a few places in the game world and replace them with a few of his own to make it happen. Sl4y liked it. The little things are what distinguishes a great, memorable game (or a server) from a bland triple-A soulless, goal-oriented construct, he believed.

Sl4y was among those who did not care about the "guild mail" feature until he got to access it in Havoc, where it became one of his favourite things in the game, and it was thanks to moments like this:

WHY THE FUCK do you tolerate such POS like that little fucker BATS? I've been playing the game for 3 years and I remember when Havoc meant something and it was respectable now you accept people who only grief people for no reason rather than learning to actually PvP. No wonder you can't win GvG and Execute owns you hard lmao :DDD L2p XDD

As far as complaints about BATS went this one was fairly cultured, but it pleased Sl4y that BATS was still in shape. As the sender likely expected, the feedback would be taken seriously, duly processed, and consequences would be drawn immediately. Sl4y copied the message and pasted to in-game mail directly to BATS, making sure to add the sender's name underneath it. BATS appreciated the feedback, Sl4y knew, and the author would be contacted shortly wherever he was. BATS had his ways of finding people.

Truth be told, some of those messages were in breach of AltAr's terms of service and if reported, the sender could receive a temp-ban. The server rules permitted vulgarities and insults, but never threats, and there were a few in the past. Sl4y, or Pvro and Trillex before him, never reported any of it.

For now, business was done. He absent-mindedly walked out into the alleys of Hardline and gravitated towards the Keep where most players hung out. This early in the morning not much was going on since most players were still asleep or otherwise busy, which made it a good time to venture into places where players often committed suicide by walking into the wrong kind of another player, or to check spawns of some rare enemies with unique loot. Sl4y needed to get to Vir Estia first and pick up a weekly boss-slaying quest before relogging to his Hunter. His current home location was, ironically, sent to Hardline rather than in Argentia as usual. He made his way to the Airship Master NPC up a tall, square-based stone tower in Hardline's battlements to the south to use the ferry service. The NPC collected a small fee from every player boarding the airship, an important job in a world where heroes pulled money out of thin air. Players boarded the airship by interacting with the NPC and choosing the correct dialogue option. So Sl4y ran upstairs to the platform on top of the tower, clicked the NPC, and-

Uh...?

The Airship Master was not there.

Sl4y blinked twice and furrowed his brow, thinking the morning sleepiness was still fogging his thoughts and he just went up the wrong tower like an idiot. *No, this is the right place. It should be here. How can it not be here?*

He noticed then there were two other people there with him, one he even knew, likely having the same problem.

[07:42] Sl4y: sup cass, you nerd

[07:42] CassNL: o/ slay, you bastard

[07:42] CassNL: got any new builds I can steal?

[07:42] Sl4y: I wish :(I'm not cool like that anymore

[07:42] Sl4y: anyway, isn't something missing here?

[07:42] CassNL: yes

[07:42] CassNL: something's fucky

It was then that Sl4y started paying attention to the local chat, which he usually ignored because it was full of nonsense, spam, dumb questions, and stale memes. He scrolled up to read through the last few moments, and he didn't have to go far to find some sort of confirmation.

[07:41] [Town] stormssc: it didn't respawn yet

[07:41] [Town] stormssc: I've been waiting for 20m at least -_-

[07:41] [Town] Xx_WojownikPL_xX: this is not her spot though?

[07:41] [Town] kudo: no no, it was right heer yesterday, 100%

[07:41] [Town] yndo45: 20g plz!!!!! anyone?

[07:42] [Town] Iseria: how do I go to arg from here?

He only caught the tail end of the conversation, but he got the idea that something was amiss. A few people were discussing some game issue but none of them were near him. Were they also having a problem with a missing NPC but a completely different one?

[07:43] [Town] Sl4y: are you guys having a missing NPC?

[07:43] [Town] stormssc: ye

[07:43] [Town] Sl4y: which one?

[07:43] [Town] kudo: Lady Redrow, event npc

[07:43] [Town] stormssc: ^

[07:43] [Town] Sl4y: D:

It was weird, but now it's alarming. Lady Redrow was a noble girl living in the Keep of Hardline and was completely unrelated to Airship Master, but according to other players in the town, she was missing as well. *What else is missing? And how can an NPC go missing anyway?!*

Sl4y had been on the top of the airship tower for almost an hour and the Airship Master still had not appeared in that time, while CassNL had long ago disappeared somewhere. Sl4y was mildly amused about the situation knowing that a server restart would solve the problem, but he still followed the topic out of sheer curiosity - it was the most interesting thing to happen in weeks. He wondered what could cause such an incident. *Had an NPC died somehow it would have returned well within one hour. Must be some kind of bug then and it should be reported, but other people probably spammed it a lot by now.* He brought himself more food in the meantime. Soon more of his friends and guildmates would log in and be confused by what they hear all over the place, so Sl4y posted a quick note on Havoc's forums. *Lots of people may be distracted today, you might want to go kill some rares and mini-bosses while they're busy,* he added at the end.

More people have come to Hardline, either by airship from Vir Estia which still operated normally in inbound direction or by magic. Some came already aware of the problem, but curious to see it for themselves. The problem was getting back, as many players were only now finding out. Unless they had their homebound spell ready to go, had a Mage to give them a portal, or took the long trek by ground, they were stuck in the cold north of Fallen Kingdom.

And so the crowd in Hardline grew and found itself unable to go back south through normal means. Sl4y had been AFK for half an hour and when he came back he only saw more of the same: confused random people talking about the issue, and random people talking about random people being confused.

[08:49] [Town] Vizix: Stop the QQ noobs, it only takes 20 minutes to ride to Estia :) if you dont die ofc!

[08:49] [Town] rbDarius: word.

[08:49] [Town] u1867: selling portals @ bank, 10g

[08:49] [Town] JohnH: hey wtf mages profiting from a crisis?

[08:49] [Town] u1867: business is business, kid =]

[08:50] [Town] Byanc: selling portals @ bank, 9g

[08:50] [Town] Woodchuck: where is the airboat npc? I can't return to VE

[08:50] [Town] u1867: HEY

[08:50] [Town] Byanc: =]

[08:50] [Town] yndo45: 50g pls??? some one

[08:50] [Town] NuMa: get a job dude

[08:50] [Town] NuMa: but remember: no profession is shameful, unless you're a mage xd

[08:50] [Town] Grimsha: hey what happened to the chick in the keep, and why is everyone here

[08:50] [Town] N1mko: hey what is going on here??

[08:50] [Town] Angelycas: ffs can you people stop spamming about it already?

[08:50] [Town] Byanc: no =]

[08:50] [Town] Byanc: selling portals @ bank, 9g

[08:50] [Town] Byanc: selling portals @ bank, 9g

[08:50] [Town] Vizix: @Angelycas /leave town, you're welcome

[08:50] [Town] Decimás: O LOOK AT THE TIME

[08:50] [Town] Decimás: 12

[08:50] [Town] Decimás: 11 | 1

[08:50] [Town] Decimás: 10 | 2

[08:50] [Town] Decimás: 9   —----->STFU

[08:50] [Town] Decimás: 8   4

[08:50] [Town] Decimás: 7   5

[08:50] [Town] Decimás: 6

[08:51] [Town] Angelycas: LOL

[08:51] [Town] Grimsha: touche sir I will stfu now

[08:51] [Town] Socialist: very clever lol

[08:51] [Town] Aphrôdite: rofl

[08:51] [Town] Theevilness: LMAO

[08:51] [Town] Kutaro: no offense but that was more annoying

This went on and only the names changed over time. In situations such as this people often created the most resilient memes that would be remembered for years to come, and Sl4y already took a few screenshots of some of the funnier interactions in the chat. In the meantime, he updated guild MOTD to warn about one-way trips to Hardline. Around the same time, he came to understand that people were in a rush to turn in the Summer Event quests to Lady Redrow and obtain the rewards, since less than ten days remained of the event. Maybe someone should post some kind of warning on the Vir Estia side of airship service, but Sl4y suspected the Town chat over there was probably already similar to the epicentre of the issue here in Hardline.

Another twenty minutes went by as he was eating his breakfast when special messages finally popped up in everyone's chat in bold, yellow letters.

[SERVER] Hello people, I'm here (´･･)/(._.`) Go easy on those bug reports now – give me a moment while I look into it. -Kaivax

[SERVER] As a FYI to everyone, there seems to be an NPC or two missing from the game. Will let you know when there's something to know.

[09:22] [Town] Woodchuck: heckin finally

[09:22] [Town] NuMa: nothing to see here, move along

[09:22] [Town] rbDarius: wow big daddy himself showed up

[09:22] [Town] u1867: hurry up people, buy limited edition crisis deluxe mage portals™ while they're available! Only 7g each!

Sl4y had thought Kaivax would restore the services quickly, perhaps with an unscheduled server restart, but what he expected to be five minutes of work for Kaivax became ten, then fifteen, then thirty. Meanwhile people were getting increasingly impatient again, and as people kept waking up and logging into the game in Hardline or arriving at it from the outside, the crowd was growing in size. Sl4y was still observing it all with a mixture of curiosity and mild amusement, and the Airship tower was now packed with player characters of all kinds of levels and classes. It was like an anthill. He felt somewhat detached from the problem, having seen his share of weird things in game since he started playing it on AltAr. It was as if he was an anthropologist studying a culture and its reaction to unusual situations.

Eventually, the kind-of-long-awaited resolution to the problem came as another server-wide announcement from Kaivax.

[SERVER] Attention!

[09:59] [Town] Iseria: here we go!

[09:59] [Town] kudo: took them a while didnt it

[09:59] [Town] Angelycas: finally xd

[SERVER] An update about the reported bug with missing 2 Hardline NPCs is as follows:

[SERVER] There is no bug (˜ ᴶ ˝) So, please do not report those two anymore, thanks.

[SERVER] Have a nice day! -Kaivax

[10:00] [Town] hate_me: WHAT

[10:00] [Town] Alurah: lol what

[10:00] [Town] Vizix: XD

[10:00] [Town] | TankSpank |: really???

Sl4y's eyebrows were raised to the maximum and his lips froze in the act of saying *What?* Like people around him he was perplexed. This was not a resolution he thought was coming at all. This was getting out of hand, and now he himself needed to get to Vir Estia but there was still no Mage online in the guild to help him out with a portal. He would not stomach the humiliation of asking a stranger for one. He decided to take the long ride south through the ruined bridge over Rogadill Strait. None of the zones between Hardline and his destination were designated as PvP zones, but cutting corners could spell untimely demise for impatient players straying off the road. He found himself among two or three dozen of players reaching the same conclusion, leaving Hardline through the southern gate. Or at least this is what amateurs did, because professionals knew leaping down from the walls was half a moment faster. Gamers are busy people who do not have this kind of time.

'Pala immune, switch target!' called out Intervene.

'I silence the Doc, nuke the Brawler!' added Sonran, the third party member playing arenas with Intervene and Sl4y, a Druid build of Witch Doctor. Their voices were raised in the heat of combat, trying to coordinate their fight against an enemy party of equal size made up of a Paladin, a Spiritualist-Witch Doctor, and a Fighter in Brawler setup.

'Get him the fuck off me while you're at it!' complained Sl4y. 'He's training my ass unpunished, you useless fucks, where is the CC?' Sl4y's health was dropping and he ran out of both defensives to protect himself and movement tricks to shake off the rival player by jumping from platform to platform or kiting him to where the opposing healer could not target him. The other damage dealer did not rest either and blew off large chunks of both Intervene's and Sonran's health, which Sl4y needed to heal quickly but the annoying pest kept interrupting his casts. They had almost killed the Paladin before he had burned his Divine Intervention, becoming invulnerable to all attacks but also unable to attack himself.

Sonran surrounded himself with a damaging whirlwind after casting Roots at the feet of the Brawler, buying Sl4y some valuable time to pull away. Meanwhile, Intervene did a Charge at the same target, removing the Roots almost the same instant they triggered but at least stunning the target for half a second.

'Oops,' said Intervene, realising he had undone his teammate's efforts.

'Good job,' said Sonran sarcastically. 'Now kill him, gogogo! Before Pala is healed!'

Positioned behind a thick wooden pillar and out of everyone's sight, Sl4y healed himself to full and even took a risk and allowed himself three seconds of drinking to restore mana now that he was out of combat. The mana recovered this way was a paltry 5% of his total pool, but in case of a protracted fight every bit counted. Then he sprang from behind the column and started casting healing rites at his buddies.

In the meantime, the enemy Doctor and the Paladin were let loose and went for Sl4y, seeking to crush the healer while his teammates were trying to kill the Fighter. Sl4y saw them coming, and said:

'They're coming for me! Finish that guy if you can, now is a chance!' Sl4y would throw everything he had at himself to waste as much opponent's time as possible. Sonran noticed an opportunity:

'I'll push him down, keep the others up here!' he said, referring to the wooden platform they had been standing on. He did what he intended without waiting for any confirmation, and a gust of wind blew the enemy Fighter downstairs to the dirty ground level, then Sonran followed him down with Intervene where they could frag him out of sight of either healer.

'Nice!'

'Nice!' they both yelled after a few moments, clearly indicating their target was dead.

The fight was over less than a minute later. Sl4y managed to heal himself a few times between the attacks of Paladin and his Spiritualist, shield himself once, and shake off the Spiritualist's target lock a few times by breaking his line of sight with obstacles in the arena. Meanwhile, Intervene and Sonran came back up, having killed the Fighter on the floor below. The Wind Gust from Sonran had turned out to be a clutch play. Sl4y was at this point on his last legs and eventually dropped dead to the enemies, but his teammates managed to clean up and seize the victory for the team, bringing their daily score to paltry five wins against five losses.

'Well that was fucking exhausting,' said Intervene. 'Only ten games a week for the weekly quest, but it gets my blood pumping a lot. Maybe I should take a break from that.'

'Old man mode again?' teased slowah, who was with them on the voice channel but kept quiet during the trio's matches.

'Yes,' admitted Intervene. 'Oh well, the Gladiator reputation is a good reward at least. A few weeks more and I will have the mount and the sword upgrade.'

'I'm surprised you didn't get it by now,' commented slowah again. 'As an old man of the guild and all that, you know.'

'Eh, I suppose I never had decent people to do it with, and even today I still have only you good-for-nothing wankers. *Yeh, I'll be ready, love.*' That last bit was spoken beside the microphone.

With their weekly assignment done, the three of them went their separate ways from the front of an Arena Master in Ghabat Safi, which queued player parties for three-versus-three fights in a small arena randomly chosen from a few locations in the game. slowah was not the only person on voice comms with them, as the strange events of that morning had brought a few others to find out what was going on. Doomcaster, Ò_Ó and a few others were online too; Vizovia was in the channel too but had her microphone muted for an hour now; Prast, Makzine, and Agnelei had gone AFK.

'Are you going somewhere, Mike? You're leaving us for a *woman*?!' accused slowah.

'Yeh, can't stand ya sorry wankers for too long. But speaking of wankers and women, how is your new charming little Hunter friend?'

'Eh? I never told you I have a new *Hunter* friend.'

'And yet she tamed you no problem!'

Sl4y, Sonran, Ò_Ó and Intervene laughed, and even the usually silent Doomcaster snickered.

'Really, a *Hunter*?' teased Ò_Ó. 'I thought *even you* have *some* standards!'

'Hahaha, that's so funny, guys! Haven't laughed this much since you got banned for 3 days for harassing a GM, Eyes!' slowah retorted.

'Hey, I have no regrets. Trigger-happy and easily-offended GMs and moderators deserve to be made fun of. And he lost the job afterwards so I won!'

'You really enjoy playing with fire, lol. Anyway, we've just been chatting, actually. She's worried about the NPC thing,' slowah said, referring to his definitely-not-tamer.

Everyone was silent for a few seconds, so Intervene finally asked, perhaps out of sheer politeness.

'Why?'

slowah sighed. 'She got into her head that she would pick up every quest from Redrow and turn in everything at once when completed. She's almost got everything now, but she can't turn in.' He paused. 'I told her it will be fixed no problem soon.'

'Well, a similar thing happened last year when a quest mob didn't spawn for a week and they fixed it and kept the event open for a while to let everyone complete the quest. I feel like I'm the only person to remember that now that people panic so much,' said Sonran.

'I'm not so sure you're right this time. I mean you, slowah,' said Sl4y after a moment.

'Why?' it was slowah's turn to ask.

'I've been thinking about it and-'

'Don't hurt yourself,' the Druid interrupted.

'Shut up. Anyway, this case is *weird.* It was a normal bug, until Kaivax came in and then it got fishy. He came in, investigated, took extra long to do it, and then said there's no problem when very clearly there is one.'

'Yeah, I've been wondering about that myself,' said Ò_Ó. 'If there is no bug, why did he take so long to let everyone know?'

'So, yeah, I see two possibilities. Gigabrain time, okay? One: he's faking it. He said precisely *there is no bug* but he didn't deny the dudes are missing.

Heck, he could even have pretended to log in and investigate. Now that I think about it, Kaivax rarely shows up himself to do that kind of thing.'

'Okay, but why would he do all that?' asked slowah. 'I mean, to pretend to do a thing.'

'This… could be some new content, but I can't imagine what is that supposed to achieve.' Sl4y said. 'I admit this doesn't really make sense. Why design an event with quests and then make it impossible to finish the quests? Why would an Airship guy go *poof* too? Doesn't add up.'

'Hmm,' wisely sounded a few voices, obviously clueless.

'And the second theory: he logged in, found something weird that isn't a bug, so he couldn't fix it but said it's not a bug. He was specific. Maybe it's some game mechanic we never knew about?'

'Hard to imagine there would be such mechanics that we wouldn't know about in such an old game. Is Gaav on? He knows shit nobody else knows,' said Ò_Ó.

'Maybe ask your former GM friend?' joked Sonran.

$$* * *$$

The Old Lands was one of the favourite areas of the game for Sl4y, despite its unimaginative name. A huge landmass to the northwest of Insal Kingdom was separated from it by the treacherous and tumultuous Breach Sea. Two straits were suitable connectors between them, and the eastern one, the Roggadill Strait, even used to be spanned with a massive bridge in the ancient days. Now derelict and broken, the massive ruin served only as a reminder of the greatness of past ages but was still passable on foot. Air travel from Vir Estia was available for players – *until this week,* thought Sl4y – but transportation of heavy goods was nearly impossible without big detours by sea and land.

Named after the once-great but now fallen kingdom by the name of Run-thak Os-Virdânos that nobody bothered to learn, it was both a wilderness and a battlefield. Several remaining bastions of humanity stood their ground against giants, trolls, and goblins behind massive walls on the outside and ironclad re-solve on the inside. It was in its most important fortress, Hardline, that players could choose to begin their journey in ARIS. Those who did were thrown into a frantic wall-top defence scenario as the very first thing, and many players hold this introduction as a test of character, for not every newcomer to the game en-joys being crushed by a giant's tree-trunk of a club when they take the slightest wrong move or detour. In short, this was a realm of danger, risk, excitement, and profit for those who survive it.

Further north from this already far north were lands hardly mapped. The cartographers of human kingdoms to the south, when drawing their maps, would shrug and inscribe the area with something along the lines of "here be dragons." And who knows, perhaps dragons there indeed were. This was more than lore, it was a unique game mechanic too; in the northernmost reaches, the game map quite literally could not be trusted and players had to learn to navigate by landmarks.

A player could only reach level 20-22 in and around Hardline, at which point one had to travel south to warmer lands. The rest of the landmass would welcome them again at level 80, as was the design of ARIS creators. The dangers of Old Land were not for the inexperienced to handle. It was never meant to be a low-level zone, but it worked well for marketing. Sl4y went there fishing.

Rivers west of Hardline were excellent fishing spots for Bluescale Salmon travelling upstream to breed. Find a suitable spot, uninstall the bear that had claimed it first, and enjoy your catch. There was something strangely comforting in this moment, nostalgic even. An early Sunday morning, simple task of casting a line, catching fish, and all that to the sound of one of the game's best musical pieces, heavily featuring the Swedish Nyckelharpa. That morning could be better only if it was snowing outside Sl4y's window, but it was the middle of summer.

Sl4y followed a path weaving through mossy rocks and pine trees, hearing the distinct rumble of a mountain river cascading downstream nearby. Deer and elks foraged for food between patches of snow that dotted the landscape, their peaceful existence somewhat contrasting with the profile of the continent at large. As he finally arrived at the Olevatin river, he noticed someone fishing there already: a low-level Warlock, likely still adventuring in the area. There was no reason for Sl4y to move elsewhere, fishing in ARIS was entirely independent of other players.

But when Sl4y cast his first line, the Warlock by the name of Mørklødet approached him.

'Hi!' he said. 'Nice cloak bro.'

'Thanks :)' said Sl4y

'Can you spare a minute and help me kill the rare bear above this waterfall? I almost solo'd it, but died twice -.-'

'Sure,' Sl4y agreed. 'Invite me. Can you go find it first?'

'I know where it will be,' assured Mørklødet. 'Let's go.'

'K.'

True to his word, the stranger found the prey immediately: Old Baggi, a large, scarred, black bear feasting upon a fat salmon. The animal was at level 30, certainly too strong for a level 20 caster to take alone. *And this guy said he almost solo'd it?*

'This is normally a group quest,' said Mørklødet as if reading Sl4's mind. 'Not many people around here at this hour tho.'

'I didn't even know about it.'

'It's for a cloak with cold resists,' he explained, attacking the target first. It was important to make sure he tagged it before Sl4y would oneshot it with even his weakest spell at level 100.

Mørklødet thanked him, disbanded the party, before he went his way he suddenly opened a trade request with Sl4y, which Sl4y accepted.

'?' Sl4y typed.

'Take it. Been skilling fishing while waiting here for help.' Sixty units of Bluescale Salmon, two dozen of other local fish and even a few 1-2% drop chance ones appeared in the trade interface.

'You sure? Those are kinda valuable.'

'I know, I won't need it for a long time, but you will, I think. Just take it.'

'Cool, thanks :)' said Sl4y, accepting the gift.

Sl4y paused for a second. The player in front of him appeared to be quite knowledgeable at the game for a newbie. Someone's alt, perhaps? He wondered if he had accidentally found a promising recruit, but something prevented him from opening the topic. It's not how it worked in Havoc, Sl4y knew. People usually ask to join Havoc, not the other way around, and the unspoken rule has always been worn by Havoc like a badge.

But then again… this pride was not Sl4y's own, really. It belonged to the old-timer core of the guild. *The same core that now was barely visible during guild operations. GvG? A few still attend. Raids? I haven't seen any Greeks sign up to my last three groups. Are they just avoiding me? I should ask Agnelei and Slam1go if they had more luck getting the likes of Venetia, Stoencold, Arastina, Pjj, Doublehead, etc. to join them.*

Furthermore, they entrusted the only real Officer role in the guild to me. Does that not mean Pvro and Trillex trust my decisions? It's not like they stick around to check on me. For quite some time, Sl4y had a premonition that Havoc will soon need recruits, and here he was, with an opportunity in front of him.

'You new here?' probed Sl4y, before the stranger left.

'To this server, yeah.' Good sign.

'I see. Been playing ARIS long?'

'A few years. I just moved back to Denmark from Singapore, so my pings to the KR servers are terrible now :/'

'Oof,' said Sl4y. 'All this stuff and people left behind.'

'Yeah :/ but what can you do :s I always knew this would happen.'

'Say, wanna join a guild? We're a big one here :)' Sl4y felt awkward asking this, and he winced at his forced politeness. He decided not to read his own message again.

'No,' said Mørklødet, almost immediately, without asking any questions. 'Not a fan of guilds.'

'I think we have a few people like that inside already D: but okay, I understand. Cya then.'

'Yep, bye!' said Mørklødet, departing.

Sl4y went back to casting the hook into the stream on repeat. He thought of many things. Of what he would do next. Of leveling another character to do Tailoring with. Of the Airship Master and Lady Redrow, still missing from Hardline after almost two full days, and of both the rage of players unable to obtain some rewards and of the utter amusement, or even profiteering, from others; and of how the Game Master team strangely refuses to say literally anything on the topic. Of the upcoming GvG and how the guild was no longer almost guaranteed to win it every week.

Sapphire looked at her stash of items, or more appropriately, a hoard of items. Twenty-two hundred and fifteen units of cloth for crafting that she hardly ever used to craft anything. Eleven hundred shiny, cut gems of all sizes and colours (*sapphires are best*) that are not particularly useful for anything other than selling to a vendor for profit, but *they look good in storage so they stay*. She had at least a hundred of each. Three hundred random fortune cards - they do nothing, only generate a random text about your future. The text can be hilarious sometimes, and when she plays with them sometimes and obtains a particularly funny one, she gives it to one of her friends whom it fits. Ninety one speed scrolls, those she actually used often, but disliked going under a hundred in reserve. She made a mental note to go get more later. Seven hundred and ninety three Rank 9 Healing Potions. Over two thousand Mana Potions. *What? They may be needed later.* The list went on.

Were Sapphire a fantasy creature she would be a dragon, the kind that lies on its hoard of treasures and turns knights to ash.

To her it was fun to obtain unholy amounts of an item, or more accurately, to *own* unholy amounts of an item. Opening her stash and seeing a four-digit number next to an item in her inventory, even if complete trash, gave her a sense of satisfaction and of a job well done. She was not rich in terms of huge amounts of cash, but she had tons of assets.

Crimson Sashes she collected as trophies from crazed Supplicants told her how many she had killed since Sl4y told her about that location and how it can be utilised (*exploited*, was the word he had used). Nineteen thousand, four hundred, and nine.

Time to get more.

She repaired her Paladin's equipment paying a fee of fifty-ish gold, the character now at level 98 from all this voluntary labour. Repairs were frequent now since her equipment worked overtime to keep her going. This was a necessary expense, like in business. *Gotta spend money to make money.* The shield was particularly prone to damage with all that blocking all the time. She solved the problem by bringing two to every run, although the secondary shield was a mid-tier item she bought from a player market in Argentia. Still, it improved her gold per hour gains by extending the time spent on site between repairs.

Then it was down the same route she would have burned in her mind for all eternity. Take a fast travel to Urgill Battlements, mount up, leave through the main gate, cross a river, ride into the griffon nesting grounds and head straight for the dungeon entrance hidden inside it. She would pull at least a dozen very upset griffons at level 80 just by passing near them, but she would lose them all when she took the leap over the gaping chasm that this fortress used as a castle would use a moat. There was a stone bridge nearby, but it could not be crossed by a single adventurer without clearing it of enemies, even by a well equipped and max-level one. She could clear it out, but that would cost her precious time. The zealots on the bridge also left a debuff effect that was only mildly annoying in effect but lasting thirty minutes. Unacceptable. Fortunately, Sl4y had shown her a spot where a mounted player can use a cheap speed scroll, make a jump from a dilapidated brick watchtower on one side, and hit the ground on the other side of the ravine, bypassing the bridge guards. She failed the jump the first two times she tried it and fell to her death, and was ready to tell Sl4y where he could shove his "advice" but she was good for the third jump and ever since. *How do people even discover those shortcuts?*

[23:44] **[Guild]** Ò_Ó: so yeah, I paid a PC wizard to fix that and now its fine

[23:44] **[Guild]** slowah: tbh its not that hard to fix, let me know next time it fails to boot and I'll talk you through it

[23:45] **[Guild]** Raphanti: or just do what Zoe does with all her problems

[23:45] **[Guild]** -Zoe-: oh no

[23:45] **[Guild]** slowah: HERE IT COMES

[23:45] **[Guild]** Raphanti: call an adult

[23:45] **[Guild]** -Zoe-: I fucking knew it

[23:45] **[Guild]** Agnelei: gottem:D

[23:45] **[Guild]** Ò_Ó: <grabs popcorn>

Sapphire smiled to herself. The guild chat antics were a welcome distraction from the tediousness. She had a habit of reading everything posted there during her grinding sessions. Those folks and a playlist, that was what made it bearable for her. *Also, can Zoe and Raphanti get a room already?* She wondered if he had seen her picture yet. Sapphire herself had, so she strongly suspected that if he had, he would promptly rethink teasing her for immaturity.

She returned to her earlier thoughts. She was now crossing into an underrated grind spot, using a trick probably almost nobody knew, to grind mobs that were not too simple to efficiently kill either. What a long way she had come from those days ten years before, when she started playing the game to stay in touch with her school friend after her parents moved to France.

This unnamed fortress was an unremarkable questing area with a bunch of forgettable shady cultist NPCs with very nasty abilities. Most people left this place at the end of their quest chain and never looked back. Those who bothered to read the quest descriptions would at least know what the place was about.

It was not that the current villain group of the month found a free evil fortress and claimed ownership of it. It was *the place* that claimed *the occupants.* There was a malicious presence that dwelled in it and beckoned the lost, exiled, and dispossessed, as the lore had it, but nothing ever explained what it was exactly. No demon, no cursed artefact, no terrible prisoner chained underneath would ever be found, because there was none. The very structure itself was *wrong*, it seemed. It was chiselled to a mathematical imperfection. The slightly confusing layout, the airflows designed to produce a barely perceptible hum, the subtle asymmetry in all dimensions, the delicate rumble underfoot that was so much like a thump-thump of a heartbeat, water drops falling from ceilings with irregular frequency. Elements of the puzzle at best, but not the whole puzzle itself.

Gaav once speculated it was a proof of concept for a Lovecraftian-themed dungeon or raid. Perhaps someone on the ARIS design team had attempted to create a place of uncanny discomfort for a player through sheer ambience, using only subtle visual and audio cues. It actually worked on Sapphire the first few times she was here.

She remembered a little conversation she had with Sl4y while they stood inside the structure, back when he was showing her this place.

'Down here,' he had said in a vast staircase leading down into very dimly lit passages.

'Follow you into a dark cellar? I hope I will have all my organs when I get out.'

'Not if I steal your heart,' was his response.

Smooth bastard.

She jumped down that same staircase over the railing because it was faster, and because it helped lose the few hound-beasts hitting her in the back and slowing her down. Taking the stairs in the normal way would take a few extra seconds, and gamers are busy people who do not have this kind of time.

Just one level down was a vast chamber where dozens of level 84 robed, hooded figures of various shapes and sizes knelt with their heads bowed at a distance of several metres from each other. They were some kind of death cult that Sapphire no longer remembered the name of, and all had wicked daggers hidden within their robes. On the far end from the entrance was a primitive stone altar - *a bench, really* - with some book on it, a quest item she could not do anything with anymore.

[23:47] **[Guild]** Prast: Eyes do you ever think about changing your nick-name?

[23:47] **[Guild]** Ò_Ó: why would I

[23:47] **[Guild]** Prast: cuz nobody can type it and we have to call you "Eyes"? D:

[23:47] **[Guild]** Ò_Ó: just do an ò

[23:47] **[Guild]** Ò_Ó: it's easy brò

[23:47] **[Guild]** 415: sòunds reasònable tò me.

Sl4y had explained to her what the trick here was.

'Basically, the attacks of each of those Crimson Supplicants are weak but they have a nasty combo of two abilities: Mark for Death, and Throatseeker or something like that. The first one puts an instant short debuff on you that increases damage taken the next attack you get, like, four times. They are clever enough to stop auto-attacking the target to not consume it and cast the second for damage that almost oneshots you unless you're a tank. Normally they should be taken one at a time, stunned or kited while they cast the Throatseeker and then just killed. Anyway, TLDR don't get hit by Throatseeker.'

She activated Mandate of Heaven giving herself unmounted movement speed increase and immunity to slows and ran into the middle, pulling as many Supplicants as possible, then circled around the chamber to pull all thirty-six. The sheer number of enemies auto-attacking her immediately consumed every Mark for Death; landing a Throatseeker on the Mark was nearly a mathematical impossibility in this situation. Weak though their attacks may be, they would still overwhelm even a tank-character if not played properly. They were quite quick on their feet making kiting difficult - twice the reason to come with a tank.

She rounded them all up in front of her and started slashing them down. Fortification Aura passively increased her physical armour attribute, while Conviction healed her for a small amount each time she took any damage; the two abilities worked wonderfully together. Being the only target meant she needed not to worry about taunting, which freed her skill rotations to deal damage more frequently. Smite was not a strong ability but it hit all targets in a small cone while the bulk of the work was done by spamming Retribution every cooldown, effectively reflecting Supplicants' damage back at them for two seconds. A group stun from a Supreme Authority here and there helped too. Those and few other abilities and attacks allowed her to slowly but inevitably grind down the entire group to death at the cost of less than half of her health.

[23:50] **[Guild]** Slam1go: 56 people online and only 40ish on GvG today

[23:50] **[Guild]** Slam1go: remind me again why we have socials in the guild?

[23:50] **[Guild]** Raphanti: to have girls (⌐■_■)

[23:50] **[Guild]** Sl4y: that is the correct answer

[23:50] **[Guild]** Agnelei: fair.

[23:50] **[Guild]** slowah: truth

[23:50] **[Guild]** Belixner: HOLD UP

[23:50] **[Guild]** Doublehead: makes sense

[23:50] **[Guild]** Slam1go: ok, good point

[23:50] **[Guild]** Venetia: ^

[23:51] **[Guild]** Ma_Ris: that's right. Bow before me, peasants.

[23:51] **[Guild]** Ma_Ris: I mean: yay! I'm glad to be of help! :D

[23:51] **[Guild]** Agnelei: holy shit Doublehead is on. Where have you been, dawg?

[23:51] **[Guild]** Doublehead: I'm mostly playing Omega Online 2 now

[23:51] **[Guild]** Doublehead: but the server is down at the moment xD

[23:51] **[Guild]** Slam1go: eh, I tried it, not as good as OO1 =/

Her favourite part came next: looting. Sapphire had three minutes or so until the first killed one respawned in the same room. Beside the Crimson Sashes she could use as a component for some decorative headgears there were cloth scraps for all kinds of crafting, common daggers good only for selling to an NPC, Forbidden Prayer Tomes (rare), Cultist Tokens (rarer still) and quite a bit of cash. The profits from this farm were pretty good, especially when she finally sells all the Sashes and if she decides to sell the Cloth. So far she generated nearly a quarter million gold out of thin air, and wondered how Anzu was doing. *How do we even decide who won?* she wondered, not for the first time.

After the first day of farming the Supplicants she briefly thought she was dumb to allow herself to be dragged away from working towards the Summer Event rewards. *Or studying, I suppose.* Then she realised she could use money to just buy almost any reward she wants and the rest she could grind out in the meantime. Besides, Lady Redrow was still mysteriously missing so Sapphire could not complete Midsummer Night Bonfire for her. How long has it been, three days? She played the game for a very long time, and has been on AltAr since day one. She even personally met GM_Kaivax once. But she could not recall a situation such as this, and even more so than Sl4y she was very suspicious of the server staff's participation in the affair. But whatever happened to Lady Redrow, the vanishing of Airship Master was both funny and fascinating to see: the wholesomeness of those offering free portals to any city, the avarice of those showing up when the former are not around, and the rage of players over the inactivity of GMs on the matter.

Anyway, how come more people don't come down here? Her thoughts ping-ponged from topic to topic. If this place was so good, there should be more people competing for those stabby crazies. She suspected this was because of the annoying bridge that hardly anyone knew how to bypass, the dangerous skill combo, and the movement speed of the mobs making them hard to kite for single players. Bringing friends was an option, but it divided the profits. Add the fact it was one of the oldest parts of the game that not many people were excited about these days, and you have an excellent niche to exploit. As an added bonus, it was even somewhat fun to kill such groups all by herself.

She could do that five or six more times before her bags were full (those daggers took a slot each) or her equipment came too close to wearing down.

Waiting for the respawns was a good moment to take a small bio break, so she parked her Paladin in an alcove inside the chamber where respawned crazies *should* not aggro on her, took a bite of a bun she brought two hours earlier, removed her headset, and left the room.

Things took her a little longer. She returned to her character being still alive but no longer alone. There was no reason to think this area would be hers forever; after all this was a quest location open to anyone, and over the course of last week she saw a couple of people here. But now Sapphire stayed where she was and observed the newcomer for a while to find out if there would be PvP in the nearest future or not.

She saw a female Assassin brandishing a pair of katar-like claws for weapons finish off a Crimson Supplicant. Several corpses were strewn around her already. She wore decent gear, judging from her damage and health pool, and was only level 86 herself. But what was strange was the fact that this Assassin then pulled not one but six cultists at the same time, no more and no less, unlike the other strangers Sapphire had met here who wisely took one enemy at a time.

And then she noticed another thing: that Assassin made it through the bridge without taking the Heretic Brand effect from the Crimson Zealots, which increased the range at which the affected player aggroed nearby monsters - twice as annoying for an Assassin. Since she was not branded, she either managed to oneshot every enemy on the bridge, which was unlikely, or she lost the effect before descending down to where Sapphire was.

Or she knows the jump too.

Sapphire suspected this girl, or whoever played that character, knew what she was doing, and her hunch was supported by the guild tag above her head.

Execute.

That by itself did not mean trouble, since Sapphire was friends with several people in the rival guild. Not everyone thought like she did; the good, old-fashioned vendetta sometimes meant someone would end up flat on the ground. She did not recognize the player's nickname. Perhaps it was that new person that her friend Anzu mentioned recently. Regardless, Sapphire was currently on her Paladin Alvea, and she never joined Havoc as an alt on this character so she was anonymous.

She took stock of her available cooldowns. *I don't really play this class, but If push comes to shove, I can probably handle all the mobs plus a lowbie 'sin anyway. If not, I will go do something else,* she thought and decided to just ignore the competitor. She tagged all the mobs she could get that were not fixed at the other player, and pulled them aside to kill uninterrupted. The Assassin, having dealt with her own few mobs, seemed to watch Sapphire - or Alvea - at work for a moment, then proceeded to loot the unholy book from the altar, and headed for the exit.

Sapphire went back to her things.

* * *

[22:44] Nervandur: eyyyy!

[Nervandur waves at you.]

[22:45] Nervandur: :\

[Nervandur pokes you]

Vizovia alt-tabbed from the stat- and skill-tree simulators she tinkered with in the background back to the game window, and noticed she was no longer alone. She had stopped randomly on some random street between Vir Estia's market district and the City Watch infirmary she visited to pick up a quest. The buildings on each side were typical trader houses with the ground floor open for whatever business each owner was in, and the upper floor or two were for the trader and their family to live in. It was a shortcut between two broader streets, more like an alley really, and she had stopped there when she thought of a small change to her Mage build and minimised the game to simulate it.

Not only was someone standing in front of her, but this someone also kept talking to her. She did not recognize the character at first glance, but she knew the name.

[22:46] Vizovia: oh hey ^^"

[22:46] Nervandur: long time to see! Got a moment? :)

[22:46] Vizovia: sure

She sat down on the ground, and the purple-cloaked Paladin beside her did the same to her right.

[22:46] Nervandur: yep, I don't think I've seen you at all since you left

[22:46] Vizovia: bad luck I guess, I hang around Estia frequently

[22:46] Nervandur: ah, I see. My base is in hdl now

[22:46] Vizovia: too dark for me

[22:46] Nervandur: close to content though. Anyway, so you're not coming back?

[22:46] Vizovia: is the drama with Bloodberry and Redemptor still going?

[22:47] Nervandur: heh, not anymore, Blood gave up

[22:47] Vizovia: sad.

[22:47] Nervandur: I guess I was wrong when I said you'd be back before we know it

[22:47] Nervandur: I'm still surprised they took you in though

Vizovia /gasped.

[22:47] Vizovia: why?

[22:47] Nervandur: cuz of how they are in Havoc I guess. I tried joining once and they said no, but a dude with lower level and worse gear got taken. Gotta have friends in high places I guess. Or be cute:p

[22:47] Nervandur: its admirable you made it ofcourse!

[22:47] Nervandur: so how is it in Havoc?

[22:47] Vizovia: hmm

[22:47] Vizovia: check my weapon :)

The bold, purple letters of The Ocular still brought a jolt of satisfaction to her. She unlocked her equipment for inspection to demonstrate the rod obtained during one of the raids with Havoc that Agnelei led, enchanted with the most expensive enchant she ever used and socketed with high-end runes. It paled in comparison with what some other people in the guild carried, she knew, but to her this was a big upgrade. By her previous little guild's standards, this was not achievable.

[22:47] Nervandur: fuuck that's not bad

[22:47] Vizovia: and I got it almost for free ^^

[22:47] Nervandur: :O how??

[22:47] Vizovia: other casters in the raid had better stuff so they gave it to me within a week after I joined ^^ I couldn't even use it back then :D

[22:48] Vizovia: then Sl4y gave me a Molecule to craft Avalanche, the rest was easy

[22:48] Nervandur: hold up. Really, Sl4y??

[22:48] Vizovia: ? what do yo u mean

[22:48] Nervandur: nothing, it's just weird to hear you got it from him

[22:48] Vizovia: do you know him?

[22:48] Nervandur: grouped with him a few times long ago, but mostly just heard things

And there it was again. Every now and then she came across people expressing strange sentiments, dislike even, towards Havoc or Sl4y. It was like Ma_Ris' positivity aura, but the opposite. Everyone seemed to adore Ma_Ris, and while Vizovia knew Ma_Ris was a great person she had no idea how the larger community came to have this thing for her. Was this some kind of a thought-virus, a meme in the technical meaning of the word, to also hear "Sl4y" and think "evil" without ever interacting with him? Even more so than with BATS or Slam1go? She decided to investigate just a little.

[22:48] Vizovia: what things? I want some gossip :>

[22:48] Nervandur: hmm

[22:48] Nervandur: I heard he "stole someone's girl" (not my words) and that he copied his famous build from someone else… but apparently it's some super-old stuff and nobody remembers details anymore

Or it's that it never happened, Vizovia thought.

[22:48] Vizovia: any idea who the girl is?

[22:48] Nervandur: nope, but one guy said she doesn't play anymore so I guess it's not important now. You know I can call Blood here, she knows more rumours than me

If that's true, then it can't be Sapphire. That's a very big if *though…* She decided it would be better to not show too much interest. She would later share what she heard with Ma_Ris, but Vizovia suspected all that was old news to *Miss Agent.*

[22:48] Vizovia: anyway, to be fair, he took the Molecule from guild bank, not his own stuff:)

[22:49] Nervandur: still pretty nice to have such things lying around

[22:49] Nervandur: but how do you even stand them? People like BATS, Slam1go or that o_O guy. Must be rough for you

[22:49] Vizovia: not really ^^

[22:49] Vizovia: they're all surprisingly funny for the most part ^^ Slam1go can be really rude but they told me not to worry about him. Also I've hardly ever seen BATS say a word

[22:49] Vizovia: but you know what, they take GvG seriously. I'm getting yelled at sometimes but that's normal here :D they also help when I need it

[22:49] Vizovia: but in general: I have an older girl friend here who constantly pranks me, a Mage tutor who makes me kill people, and a couple that starts acting weird whenever I show up xD Oh and a teenage girl that owns me so hard you wouldn't believe. There are a few women overall.

[22:49] Nervandur: xD where do they find those people

[22:49] Vizovia: oh and there's also Beli… she plays a male character and she's a veteran here. Maybe the only girl to do so lol

[22:49] Nervandur: Belixner is a she!? :O

[22:49] Nervandur: Andre will be devastated. Or excited, idk xD

She excused herself from the conversation. 'I have to go do a few event dailies before I go to sleep ^^,' she had said and stood up. They could chat with each other from any place in the game with the private message utility – Whisper – but her colleague from the previous guild took the hint, thanked for the chat, and went his way. She was honest in that at least, there really were some time-limited rewards to obtain and she wanted them all. Late evening on a weekday was a good time for it since the competition from other players for monsters was lower.

But she also had something to think about. Her first guild, Nightwalkers, was a small social guild with ten to fourteen active members, with no conditions or requirements to join. Everyone was welcome. They did small things together: a hunt for a single rare monster, an item grinding session, or just sitting around in Hellesvyand together and chatting. But she left that guild because of its leadership change, or more precisely, uncertain leadership and direction. Bloodberry was the head at the time when Vizovia joined, until one day someone called Redemptor came in and called himself the rightful Guild Leader. Others informed Vizovia that technically he was in the right as the creator and first GL of Nightwalkers. Some real-life reasons took him away from the game and he made his then-girlfriend, Bloodberry, an interim GL.

Except, when he returned after several months Bloodberry refused to step down, and was supported by a part of the guild. She did a far better job than Red ever did, they said. But a word is a word, said the others. And so the struggle went for a week, and the atmosphere in the guild could be chopped like firewood. Eventually, Vizovia realised she no longer enjoyed her time there and applied to Havoc.

And now that she was in Havoc, she was sensing an unease with leadership again, except it was not a power struggle this time, but rather a power void. Pvro was hardly visible, though he still held the GL title. The raids were led by whoever volunteered – usually by Sl4y, Slam1go, Agnelei, or Intervene – and their focus was tilted towards gear and upgrades for less advanced colleagues, which was odd to see for Vizovia. She expected people caring mostly about their own needs. Meanwhile, the GvGs were led by Slam1go, who fortunately seemed to always have time and the will to show up. But effectively, Sl4y held the reins. *Reluctantly so*, she thought.

It was not even that it felt bad in Havoc. Her tenure was not long, but she still remembered seeing Pvro regularly in April or so, and she sensed something was missing. *Well duh, he was the first and only GL for years, obviously,* she mocked herself.

Vibration of her phone distracted her for a moment. It was from her friend, a real-life one this time, inviting her out. Vizovia typed a response accepting the invitation out of politeness, but not really feeling like going anywhere. Perhaps she would change her mind by Thursday evening. It was a non-GvG day, so it was fine.

She briefly acknowledged how she started planning her life around the game, but dismissed the thought. *I accepted, didn't I?*

She walked on foot across Vir Estia under the starry night sky, rolling the thoughts in her head, not realising she forgot to mount up. Players went by her in every direction on errands of their own, or sat around in small groups embracing a lazy Saturday evening. Vizovia approved that from the comfort of her pyjamas. Some groups talked in public, some others sat or wiggled around silently, likely talking on their voice comms, maybe discussing the raid they just had, a show they watched, or a video game. She saw Diki from Execute being AFK in front of the Bank, and a bunch of random people, mostly newbies, pretend to be just passing by while ogling his endgame Hunter gear and his plated Ursine War Beast mount, the black variant. It even had a flag pole behind the saddle, flying the colours of Execute. The players in the crowd were probably taking screenshots too. *So that's the life of a server's iconic person.* She knew Venetia was one such figure inside her own guild, though she hardly ever saw him in any city. *He's a Warlock. Who's then the iconic Mage of AltAr? Is there one?*

Maybe I will become it.

Haha, no.

She stopped in her tracks when a majestic white beast crossed her path and a pang of envy touched her heart. Here was a player riding a Snowfur Sabertooth Felinid, not the pathetic, reused, nerfed model that almost everyone had, but the real deal, the one with shiny blue eyes and no stupid saddle. She wanted it. It would fit her Mage outfit and her sky-blue hair perfectly, although by the time she obtains it somehow her gear and preferred colour palette may be different. *Hell no, if I get the kitten, I will also get whatever I need to fit it, and that's that.* But obtaining it was "a bit of a challenge" as her dad would say. It could only be looted in the level 80+ Sacred Grove run from the chest at the end of it, a rare reward for completing an in-dungeon event on a timer. It could not be solo'd, because the challenge mechanics required simultaneous clicking of some buttons or orbs of some sort – she forgot what exactly that was – but it required at least four people on the triggers and others to support. And the problem was people did not want to do Sacred Grove anymore, so there were hardly any pick-up groups, ever. And even if she had one, she would have to win the mount too… And as if all that was not enough, the dragon-kin enemies in Sacred Grove had some pretty damn high magic resistance. The obstacles just piled on.

BUT I WANT IT.

She watched the player with the riding beast from her dreams disappear around a corner.

What can I do?

There were some decent drops in the Grove that someone could be interested in. Even if she asked a few friends to try it they would have to execute the mechanics correctly, and even if that worked somehow, the loot fairy could just say "no". No, she needed a consistent, repeatable approach. *But why not try once and see what it looks like in practice?*

An idea formed in her head, one that she would not dare on any other day. It was simply not something a background character like Vizovia would do. Maybe it was the late hour and the sleepiness that suppressed her usual resistance. Maybe Ò_Ó knew what he was doing. Maybe she got "yelled at" by Sl4y and Slam1go just right.

Her fingertips nudged alt+G to open the guild window, switched to Calendar tab, and added a new event for Tuesday at 21:00 server time.

Sacred Grove collectible run - full clear with timed chest! :D

Hosted by: Vizovia | Tuesday, August 25, 21:00 CEST | 0 interested, 0 going | Sign-ups: open

She didn't know why she added the emote. She had deleted it because it looked silly, but then added it back because she liked it there. She sat back in her chair for a moment twisting a strand of her hair, staring critically at what she created in search of any mistake she could have made in the title, and refreshing the window nervously as if it was going to change anything. She realised she should have specified somewhere that she needed people who can manage the challenge of timed run, then realised she would fail her own criteria and demanding it of others was unfair.

To her surprise, something changed almost immediately.

| 0 interested, 1 going |

Only when a zero flicked to one was she hit by the realisation that she would now be expected to organise and lead everything, and there was no turning back. And she would have to *talk* to them… unless she deleted the event *right now,* before more people could see it. She pushed the temptation away, though she quietly hoped one of the veterans would join and lead it for her. A dark piece of her mind had quietly hoped nobody would sign up so that she would avoid having to deal with the whole thing, a thought she did not even know she had until one of the zeros became a one. As it turned out, this was not from one of the veterans, but it was from someone better. She understood what it meant for her perspectives of getting more sign-ups; more would surely follow now. Vizovia wrote her a private message while they were both still online.

[23:19] **[To: Ma_Ris]**: I love you <333

* * *

Lyonni made her way on foot through empty castle corridors, following the path from the dirt courtyard to the carpeted throne room. This PvP zone prohibited all mounts, even outside its business hours. Less than half an hour ago it was packed with players at each other's throats giving it their best so that their colours would end up on top at the end. This evening, fate had it that it was the green banner with white trim adorning the flagpoles at the gate, inside this zone, and in the game's capital cities.

Apparently, it was her new guild's unwritten tradition that should they end a GvG holding a castle, they stay inside it for some time to discuss and celebrate a little. She had not participated in the battles, but soon she would. Nevertheless, every member was welcome at the "party", regardless of rank or level or contribution. The painted, plastered walls of Nordheimburg's interiors gave way to the gilded frames of paintings, stained windows, and floors polished until reflection. The throne room was where the GvG objective would be found, although it was called thus only as a nickname by the playerbase, as there was actually no throne in this chamber or anywhere else for that matter.

Everyone was on voice chat, even those who already left the party or signed out from the game to do other things. She had joined it too for the last few minutes of the GvG hour, and the atmosphere was rather relaxed. From what she understood, there was no fighting in this castle for the last ten minutes or so. Apparently, Bulwark and friends settled for taking Sal-born Keep, Havoc gave up attacking not long before the end, and the various mid- and small-size guilds either attacked Bulwark or each other somewhere down in the courtyard. The small fish easily outnumbered the largest GvG powers, but they were kitchen sinks of PvP and did not have the drive needed to organise themselves to pose a threat. However, in the maelstrom of multi-guild combat a lucky opportunist regularly managed to land the last blow on the crystalline objective in the throne room and claim the territory for their micro-guild, even if for a short, memorable moment.

Inside the massive chamber were less than two dozen players and Lyonni could see a few she had already grouped with before, including her new friend Anzu. She also recognized a few veterans such as the holder of guild's only Legendary item, Proskillver, as well as Retaliator, and CassNL. Another dozen were still on the voice channel. This was the first time Lyonni saw Anzu in her PvP wargear, the thick overlapping plates of her silver Crusader-Paladin armour with heavy pauldrons giving her a bit of bulky outline, but the wearer was still unmistakably female. An elegant exotic weapon sheathed on her back was fashioned after the far-eastern Geixan school of metalwork recognizable by its curved blade, red tassels, and lack of crossguard. In fact the Paladin aesthetic was a strange fit with such a blade, but Paladin's special weapon enchantment, Malleus, gave it a silvery glow making it fit together well enough.

A conversation was ongoing for some time before Lyonni came in and parked her character somewhere.

'What's the point of having battles if the outcome is decided, RapiD?' asked someone called Quane44. Lyonni did not know people by voice yet, but she enabled Chatterbox' in-game overlay to give herself that information on screen.

'You miss my point. I'm not saying it's super-fun right now, I'm saying we should make the best of this period and invest in this base,' replied RapiD-firE. 'Havoc may get their shit back together soon, but the fact is right now they're not a big threat.'

'They better,' mused Diki, from his position on top of a flag pole. *He must know some jumping puzzle in the room by now, he must have been here hundreds of times,* Lyonni observed. *Just like they had fought other guilds in this room hundreds of times over the years.* 'There should always be more rivals than rewards, else it's no fun,' he continued. To Lyonni, it sounded like he was speaking to himself more so than to his guild. And yet, everyone must have heard him because nobody spoke after that, maybe expecting him to continue. Lyonni decided to break the awkward moment of silence and asked:

'So what's wrong with them?'

'We don't know,' admitted Proskillver, a veteran of the guild. His voice carried a thick German accent. 'They're just *meh.*'

'I know a guy who quit Havoc. I didn't ask him for details, but he said he didn't like some new people.' That was Quane44, one of what seemed like dozens of Hunters in the guild. Lyonni could see him in the chamber crafting something in his hands by the dozen. Bandages, maybe.

'WTF I can hardly see them have more people than usual. Less, actually,' said the voice of Xemx. Him Lyonni remembered from that first party near Ghabat Safi weeks before, but he was not in the throne room with them.

'Don't know, that's what I heard,' shrugged Quane44.

'Eh, they'll be fine,' said Proskillver. 'All guilds have ups and downs. Not the first time for them. The pendulum swings their way now. This is nothing new, I tell you.'

'You guys seem concerned about it,' Lyonni pointed out.

'Because our fun depends on them in a way,' suggested Diki. A few voices mumbled assent.

'Bulwark are big and strong and all, but somehow I don't care if I lose to them or beat them. But with Havoc it's personal,' confirmed CassNL. 'There is satisfaction to be had.'

'Yeah, this,' said two voices at the same time.

'Also, poor Slam1go, how is he going to shipost forums now?' joked RapiDfirE, and got a few snorts.

'Do you talk with Pvro, Diki?' asked Anzu.

'I would, if he was online sometimes. My friendlist says he's been offline for two weeks straight. But I think I missed him on GvG longer than that…' he trailed off.

'Mmmm, that sounds bad,' said someone whose name Lyonni didn't catch.

'I have a friend in Havoc. I'll ask her what's up when I see her, but she never mentioned anything odd herself,' said Anzu.

'You have friends in Havoc?' asked 5yed, a Samurai-Warrior, incredulous.

'Duh. Of course, many people do,' said Anzu. 'I have friends in many guilds, some I've known for years. I've been in a rival guild myself before I came here,' she added.

'Oh,' said 5yed.

'So who's calling the shots now for them?' came a question from someone in the audience.

'Sl4y, from what I heard' said Diki. 'The thing is, I've never known him as a combat commander.'

'Did you say Slay leads Havoc?' asked Lyonni.

'Yes. Why, you know him?'

'...everyone knew him when I played the game. Do you?' Lyonni returned the question.

'Of course. We've been both playing here for years. Been in groups together many times. He hasn't been a part of a larger guild until last year or so, however. Anyway,' said Diki, 'to be clear, I'm pretty sure it's actually Slam1go calling the shots for the most part. But I tell you what, guys: Havoc was from the very start a weird blend of tryhards and friends at the same time,' he mused. 'Maybe someone got too tryhard and some relations broke.'

'Or not tryhard enough,' suggested Proskillver.

Lyonni was no longer listening to the conversation.

* * *

'Nope. He hasn't said anything to me. Just popped in, left a note, and fucked right off into the night,' said the latest message in private chat.

'What the fuck -_- this has been going for weeks already, no? If he does not want to play, why not just hand over the reins.'

'I don't understand it myself.'

'I hope he's not doing the Aura Special.'

'Oof... I think it's been about 4 years now as of this month. Time flies.'

'That reminds me,' Sapphire spoke. 'You won't believe what Vizovia asked me some time ago.'

'Hmm?'

'She asked me who's Aura.'

'Uh-oh,' Sl4y replied. 'I wonder where she heard about her. Ma_ris, I suspect?'

'Our little game is over.'

'Why? V didn't say anything suggesting she knows. Or did she?'

'If she still thought we're a couple, she wouldn't bring up your ex to me. She's not stupid, you know.'

'I guess you're right. But on that topic!' Sl4y said. 'Did you know she posted a raid in our calendar on Tuesday? I mean, she posted it before that, but the party happened on a Tuesday.'

'Mhm. I saw it after it was done. How did it go?'

'I don't know,' Sl4y admitted. 'I wasn't there. But! I heard she not only proposed it, but she started the invites herself, and kind of *led* the thing until the end, and they almost did a timed run on their first try. They have another Sacred Grove scheduled next week.'

'Uh? She almost nailed it just like that?'

'Not exactly. It turned out our PowerOverwhelming knows the dungeon inside out from his day, and assisted a lot as they went. She was super nervous, but did okay for her debut. Power said lots of boys signed up curious how a girl leads a party and they want more.'

'I wish them good luck.'

'I, for one, am happy to hear it. It's nice to know that *something* goes right in this guild lately. Did you notice Lonecow and Morwrath /gquit? I have a feeling they're not the last ones.'

'I haven't, but I admit I haven't looked at the roster lately. I kind of don't want to, either.'

'Well it's not going to get better while we're not looking. I will take my optimism shots where I can find them. On that note, I have one more tidbit – did you see Miko and BATS in castle yesterday?'

'You'll be surprised, but no, though that sounds weird,' she was amused again. 'What are you anyway, FBI? Watching everyone and shit?'

'Pfft. Nevermind, then. Your loss!'

'All right, all right. What did you see?'

'Maybe I imagined it, but it looked like Miko was following BATS around a couple of times. You know, he has a habit of going rogue (hehe lol) and it really stands out when two people do it. But it seemed that they would roam stealthed, he would find a target, and they both fold it, then escape and repeat, like a submarine wolfpack.'

Sapphire "sounded" more lively now, as much as that is possible through a written message. 'Heh, that is precious ngl. BATS is the last person in the fucking world I would imagine ever babysitting anyone. How did *that* happen?'

'That's the best part - I have no clue. And I'm not going to ask.'

'I have to see it for myself next time.'

'And little Miko is going up on the table too. I mean the boards. Can you imagine? Her dad asked me to keep dangerous dudes from her (I told you about this). Huh. Turns out she was the danger all this time.' Inwardly, Sl4y remembered he made a promise to her dad and he intended to keep it. He thought about that conversation several times since then, but still was not quite sure what to do about the promise he made. 'Say, what do you know about our BATS IRL?'

* * *

[Thread: We're in your base, stealing your dudes]
[Posted by Chaug, 30 Aug 2015, 23:01:52]

Dear people of AltAr, we bring you good news and bad news.

The good news is that the two somewhat important Non-
-Player Characters that have been reported as missing are not missing at all. Not to the You Never Wipe Alone guild because we know
exactly where they are.

The bad news is that you can't have them back.

Or should we say, you can't have them back just yet. If you
take a look at the attached screenshot, you will find that they are alive
and well, keeping us company in a secret location. They may appear to be punching our friend, but we assure you all it is an illusion,
nothing more.

The smart ones among you will have realised by now that this
is a ransom note. To cut to the chase, we will release the hostages
when all of the following conditions are met:

☐ A sum of 69420 gold is transferred to our agent NonCon-
sensualDonation from any source or a number of sources. We
care not from whence the gold flows, only that it flows.

☐ The GL of each major guild sings us a song on our Chatter-
Box.

☐ Someone draws a pretty birthday card for Vizix and sends it
to ransoms@ynwa.gg. No digital cards, only pictures/scans of
drawings on paper!

To be honest we thought someone would find us by now, but we will admit that you all were not even aware you should have been looking. Nevertheless, we heard one of our guests is particularly desired to return to her usual place before August 31th 23:59, which is about 25 hours from now.

Don't bother calling the authorities. They can't help you.

Please feel free to QQ as much as you want below.
Sincerely,
<You Never Wipe Alone> Guild.

[Posted by: DuckIRL, 30 Aug 2015, 23:03:14]
wat
Edit: also, first!

[Posted by: OmO, 30 Aug 2015, 23:04:19]
this is so random XD

[Posted by: Slam1go, 30 Aug 2015, 23:04:43]
dis thread gonna b gud

[Posted by: Diki, 30 Aug 2015, 23:06:08]
Uhhh this is awkward. BRB transferring GL rank to someone else :-)

[Posted by: Vrbica, 30 Aug 2015, 23:09:22]
You bastards! XD

[Posted by: KARS, 30 Aug 2015, 23:13:57]

So the theory that GMs did not fix the bug because there is no bug was correct, but I guess literally nobody thought NPCs were abducted :D How did you even pull it off?

Also, the black highlight and white letters style is a nice touch, looks proper!

[Posted by: Halbdenial, 30 Aug 2015, 23:18:44]

@Chaug you fucked up with the screenshot my man. There are hints about your location in it. Also this can only be somewhere in the north so it narrows down the possible hideouts by 90% of the game world. Don't bother deleting it, I already have a copy. Enjoy your swift deaths :D

[Posted by: RapiDfirE, 30 Aug 2015, 23:19:10]

I'm gonna make a party and kill you all personally lol, see ya to-morrow =]

Also +1 for the ancient meme in the title, very dank

* * *

On the next day the forum thread was on its way to becoming the most commented thread in years. Words of congratulations for ingenuity. Words of insult for disrupting the game experience. Words of amusement. Some demanded that the large guilds pay the ransom for the good of the community, while others pointed out the kidnappers' demands were intended to be unrealistic. Nobody knew how much, if any gold was transferred. Many swore to track down the kidnappers' hideout and defeat wherever stands in their way, at least communicate it to the rest of the server. Some were certain there would be a leak soon. Indeed, the location was eventually shared. And then it was shared again, but in an area quite distant from the first one. Then someone was certain it was neither of the two, and those who said it's both were speculating at best, and deliberately misinforming the community at worst. Some said the YNWA guild had death squads patrolling the kingdom, others said the cave holding the hostages was almost unprotected.

In a word it was chaos, and You Never Wipe Alone guild thrived in it.

By afternoon of the next day after the ransom note went out into the world both hostages were still held captive, and several large parties, raids even, were forming in Hardline, each one promising to liberate the hostages by force.

[15:14] **[Guild]** Raphanti: wouldn't it be cool if we saved the day?

[15:14] **[Guild]** slowah: what do you mean

[15:14] **[Guild]** Raphanti: it's pretty cool content that YNWA creates right now, it's will be memorable

[15:14] **[Guild]** Slam1go: meh, casual content

[15:14] **[Guild]** Raphanti: wrong, fool

[15:14] **[Guild]** Raphanti: think about it. if we're part of the story, such as by pwning them in the end, we will have extra bragging rights

[15:14] **[Guild]** Slam1go: ok you sonofabitch, I'm in!

[15:14] **[Guild]** -Zoe-: so you do have good ideas sometimes! sign me up!

[15:14] **[Guild]** Raphanti: too bad its a weekday, people are still at work or school :f

[15:14] **[Guild]** Raphanti: I wish Zoe was here tho

[15:14] **[Guild]** -Zoe-: xD

[15:14] **[Guild]** Raphanti: sometimes I still hear her voice :<

[15:14] **[Guild]** slowah: I almost forgot we have unfinished business with YNWA

[15:14] **[Guild]** slowah: fuck it, I'm starting this if you aren't. I'll call Sl4y and Intervene

[15:33] **[Town]** Halbdenial-: LFM EPIC PVP AGAINST SERVER GRIEF-ERS, NEED ALL, WHISP ME WITH X

[15:33] **[Town]** Halbdenial-: LFM EPIC PVP AGAINST SERVER GRIEF-ERS, NEED ALL, WHISP ME WITH X

[15:33] **[Town]** Halbdenial-: LFM EPIC PVP AGAINST SERVER GRIEF-ERS, NEED ALL, WHISP ME WITH X

[15:33] **[Raid]** AlexRed: do we know where they are then?

[15:33] **[Raid]** RapiDfirE: YEAH DONT WORRY I WILL LEAD THE WAY

Lilke_ was not sure if she understood the situation. She was only seventeen and her English was not great, and she was relatively new to the game only at level 34, but she understood something interesting was going on, and she wanted to participate. From reading the chat flood, she surmised a few PvP groups were being created to punish people who made the Airship Master and some other NPC not relevant to her disappear from the server. Not being able to freely travel from Vir Estia to Hardline and back was a pain, and paying even small tips for player portal services was not an option for her if she wanted to buy a 60% bonus speed mount soon. Fortunately for her, there were no requirements to join other than being able to use 30% speed mount, and the master of the raid group, someone called RapiDfirE from a guild called <Execute>, accepted everyone. She joined and hoped she would not be a burden with her low level. The raid ads still flooded the [Town] chat, not only in Hardline but in every major city and hub in the game, telling everyone to move north ASAP by any means to take part in a great hunt before it's over.

Eight people were present on Havoc's voice channel, but the course of action was unclear and the enthusiasm was somewhat throttled down.

'We don't even know where they are,' Sl4y pointed out. 'Only that it is somewhere in the Fallen Kingdom, and in a cave. There are dozens of them.'

'We can narrow it down,' advised Vizovia. 'We also know it's not a quest location, because someone would notice them within the last week.'

'Good point,' Sl4y made sure to give her credit for her input. 'But it's also possible it was noticed by someone who doesn't post on forums or talk to anyone we know.'

'I must say they have good discipline. A week straight, and nobody leaked any info? Not even a little?' Slam1go wondered.

'It's not their first rodeo,' said Raphanti.

'I think their operation must be pretty small. More people means more chances to leak info,' Slam1go continued his dissertation.

'You're only speculating, we won't know until we find them,' said Sl4y.

'Thanks for telling me, Captain Obvious.'

'Too bad it's a Monday, little Miko would have loved this action,' Vizovia said quietly when everyone else fell silent, out of options and ideas.

A glimmer of an idea lit up in Sl4y's mind. On the real side of life, he removed his feet from his desk and pulled his keyboard closer back to its place. There was one person who might have at least noticed something. It was a long shot, but why not try it?

[15:22] **[Guild]** Sl4y: @BATS, do you know where Chaug's chaps hide?

No response came, as Sl4y expected. It's not like BATS had a habit of even reading the guild chat, let alone responding to it, but maybe this time he wou-

[15:23] **[Guild]** BATS: duh ofc I know

[15:23] **[Guild]** BATS: I'm in there with them q:)

'Okay,' said Raphanti. 'Now what?'

'Dunno. My idea was to invite some people and then let Sl4y do all the work,' admitted slowah.

'Ah, the usual then?' Sl4y asked. 'Let's just skip forward to the moment where you all fail to follow my plan, hm?'

Sl4y, slowah, Raphanti, Vizovia, PowerOverwhelming, and two junior members Okus and NDZ_hyte about whom Sl4y knew nothing about, were upstairs in a tannery workshop in Hardline, waiting for the rest of the party to catch up. Intervene was offline, at work. -Zoe- and 415 were on their way, and Sl4y was trying in vain to invite Gaav who was persistently AFK. Venetia was unfortunately offline – Sl4y thought that one guildmate would enjoy this ad-hoc activity a lot. Slam1go was present in "body" as well, but had gone AFK too. They had met elsewhere in the town, but Raphanti suggested they hide lest someone notices a Havoc group forming in Hardline separately from everyone else, as if they were planning something. Little did outsiders know how little Havoc was planning ahead.

'By the way, now if someone notices us walking into this store and not going out, it's going to be even more suspicious. People are now looking weirdly at everything lol,' said Sl4y. 'Ah, -Zoe-, when you arrive do let us know if the Airship Master is back yet. Maybe someone already liberated them?'

'It's still not there, I passed by just minutes ago,' said Vizovia. 'At least the Airship Master isn't.'

'We would know if it was back, the town chat would piss itself,' pointed out slowah. 'Forums too. Everyone is super interested in this story, it's pretty cool I have to say…' He trailed off, then continued. 'Hey, since we don't know what we're really up against or what we're doing, mind if I invite someone while we're waiting?'

'You ask us? It's your party, technically,' said -Zoe-.

'No, if it's anyone's, it's Raphanti's. He came up with the idea.'

'Who, me? Naah. I'm just along for the ride.'

'Okay so who is it?' Sl4y asked.

 Silence fell,

'Who is what…?' asked slowah, confused by Sl4y's question.

'Who's the tank, and What's the Mage,' helpfully offered PowerOverwhelming.

'What are you talking about?'

'Yes.'

'I'm so confused, what the fuck are you t-' Sl4y paused, then something that sounded like a slap on a forehead could be heard. Then a groan. 'Heh. Who's the tank, What's the Mage, Idon'tknow is the Priest…' Sl4y did a hearty chuckle. 'That is so old, dude. Anyway, just invite whoever you want slow, lol.'

'Give me the Assist, dawg,' replied slowah.

'Oh right, you don't have it. Done.'

[16:52] Arabesque has joined the raid.

'Oooooh!' said a few voices, while Sl4y thought *act natural!* to himself. 'Who's that?' asked PowerOverwhelming.

'The slowah tamer,' Raphanti jumped to answer before slowah could open his mouth.

'Funny,' said slowah.

[15:35] **[Raid]** Arabesque: hi :)

[15:35] **[Raid]** Raphanti: WHALECUM

[15:35] **[Raid]** Sl4y: hi

[15:35] **[Raid]** Vizovia: hello! ^^

[15:35] **[Raid]** Okus: hi

'Is she gonna join us in voice?' asked Raphanti.

Sl4y was quick to rain on the Minstrel's parade. 'This server is for guild members only.'

'I know, I know, I will keep her updated,' slowah said. 'Actually it's even OK if she dies as long as she participates a little, hehe,' he added.

'Haha, say no more,' Sl4y assured his understanding as the group's only real healer, since a Minstrel's regeneration buff is only supplementary.

[15:36] **[Raid]** Raphanti: Ara, what does that word mean? Your name?

'Rapher, come on, control yourself dude,' slowah said, but he was amused himself too. 'Let her be!'

'Hey, you invited her to our group so she will be exposed to full Havoc experience!' Raphanti protested. 'Besides, I'm just making friends. What's wrong with that?'

'For once, I agree with him,' -Zoe- stepped in without mentioning Raphanti by name. 'I went through this, so she has too! Right, Zee?'

'Yes,' agreed Vizovia.

Everyone shared a little laugh.

[15:36] **[Raid]** Arabesque: it's a piano song my dad used to play :)

'I have bad news for you, slowah,' Raphanti began with concern in his voice. 'She's too sophisticated for a dork like you.'

Another wave of snickers rolled through the assembled guildmates.

'*Sopiscated*, wHat DOes ThAt mEaN?' slowah asked in a mocking simpleton voice.

'All right, back to the topic at hand,' Sl4y interrupted the banter. 'I have info from BATS, but there's just one problem.' A pause for dramatic effect.

'Batsy is a master troll and baiter. A *masterbaiter even,* hehe get it? Anyway, who's to say he's not working with Chaug to draw us in?'

'What makes you say that?' asked -Zoe-.

'The ransom post and just knowing BATS a little. Chaug wanted Guild Leaders to embarrass themselves by signing them a song or something, so maybe it's a part of trying to have some fun at the big guilds' expense.'

'To be honest I kind of assumed Batsy's intel is just fake and there would be nothing there,' said slowah. 'I didn't consider a trap. He wouldn't do that to us, would he?'

Noone said anything.

'Would he…?'

'He literally named himself after backstabbing,' pointed out Sl4y.

'Wait. WHAT? BATS backwards… I never noticed,' said -Zoe-. 'No, shut the fuck up Raph!'

'I didn't say anything!'

'I heard you thinki-'

'You dumbass.'

'What was that???'

'I didn't say anything!'

'Anyway, so if it *is* a trap, then so what?' shrugged Vizovia, her voice quiet and gentle whereas -Zoe-'s was as if always coming through a grin. 'If we die, then we die, and respawn. At least we will know what killed us, and that it was the right place. They wouldn't be defending the wrong place as a decoy, yes? No?'

'Hmm, that would be weird even by their standards,' admitted Sl4y.

'And if we find nothing we go back here, so nothing will be lost.'

'All right, since you've shattered my efforts to build up tension in this top secret operation with your hard facts and logic, and since Four-Fifteen finally showed up, here's the plan,' Sl4y paused, cleared his throat, and continued:

'We go south-west to the Valley, we walk through the front door, kill them, question marks, profit? Slam1go will catch up with us when he's back. Also, I brought forty Major Invisibility Potions for some reason, I'll distribute them now.'

'Very unsophisticated,' Raphanti acknowledged, taking his share of potions. 'Perfect with slowah in group.'

'OK, we should leave the town one by one and re-group outside,' said slowah, ignoring the jab.

'This secrecy is completely unnecessary and way over the top… so let's do it. We meet outside town, I go first, find me on the map,' Sl4y said before going downstairs to mount up and leave Hardline.

[15:37] **[Raid]** RapiDfirE: OK LAST 7 SPOTS IN THE RAID AND THEN WE MOVE OUT. DONT BE AFK NOW OR YOU ARE LEFT BE-HIND

Lilke_ joined the public raid group when half the slots were still empty. It went from twenty members to thirty-three within a few minutes, and the last seven slots took longer to fill than the first twenty, but in the end there were forty nicknames in the table as expected. People seemed excited, and a lot of questions were asked in chat. RapiDfirE answered only some of them. *Probably busy organising the activity,* she suspected. She was glad someone was doing it so that others can just have fun. What a wholesome game she found!

[15:37] **[Raid]** M3lk0r: do we really need this many people for this? There are like two other raids formed here

[15:37] **[Raid]** Angelycas: brb one sec

[15:37] **[Raid]** RapiDfirE: we want to be first and also they dont know where the target is, but i do, i have a spy

[15:38] **[Raid]** RapiDfirE: SRY LACK OF CAPS

[15:38] **[Raid]** RapiDfirE: ITS ALSO WHY WE NEED TO HURRY UP, CUZ THEY MIGHT FIND THEM FIRST BY ACCIDENT OR SOME-THING LOL

[15:38] **[Raid]** RapiDfirE: I PUT AN X ON ME SO YOU SEE ME BETTER WHEN WE GO

Lilke_ only then managed to see the character of the raid leader when a big red X appeared over RapiDfirE's head. The guy looked well-equipped and he was likewise surrounded by what looked like veterans of the game. *It's a good sign,* she thought. They were in some courtyard in the town, not far from the city gates leading north into the dangerous wilderness, and the place was packed. Apparently more than one raid gathered here while waiting for more players, but the impatience of the crowd was palpable, visible in its spamming of spells, moving back and forth, jumping around, using toys to pass the time. Here and there groups of people were having mounts-offs. Someone had asked before if the high-level mobs won't kill half the raid before it gets to the destination, but someone else assured that with such a big group there should be enough protection. At least, this is what she thought they said.

Two minutes later the raid group was full, although by looking at the world map, Lilke_ could tell a few members were not even on the right con-tinent. *Their loss,* she shrugged.

[15:40] **[Raid]** AlexRed: are we going??

[15:40] **[Raid]** Pieepsh: yeah lets gooooooooooooooooo

[15:40] **[Raid]** RapiDfirE: WAIT, NOBODY LEAVE YET

[15:40] **[Raid]** JungGad: wtf man lets go, why wait?

[15:40] **[Raid]** RapiDfirE: BECAUSE I SAY SO AND MY SPY GIVES ME INFO. WAIT

Now the raid chat was really getting rowdy. Players were impatient and really wanted to get going before the other raids organised themselves. Their group's town chat spam did not relent, indicating they were still looking for members. One minute felt like ten minutes.

[15:41] **[Raid]** RapiDfirE: OK LETS GO, EVERYONE FOLLOW RED X, I WILL STOP FROM TIME TO TIME TO LET YOU CATCH UP IF YOU HAVE NEWBIE MOUNT

[15:41] **[Raid]** RapiDfirE: GOGOGOGOGO

And so almost forty players left the safety of town on a myriad of mounts, trailed by pets, brandishing weapons and glistening with equipment of various quality. They followed the leader who marked himself with a big, red X over his head so everyone could see him in the crowd. As promised, the raid leader stopped every now and then to re-group allowing the slower players to catch up. Behind them in the distance another raid group was leaving Hardline the same way.

[15:43] **[Raid]** Pieepsh: they are following us

[15:43] **[Raid]** RapiDfirE: DONT WORRY THEY HAVE NO IDEA WHERE TO GO. FUCK THEM, WE WILL BE FIRST ANYWAY. ITS NOT FAR FROM HERE

They rolled through snowy plains, following cobbled road twisting between jagged rocks and pine trees. Lilke_ could see rock trolls, giants, wyverns and packs of wolves upwards of level 90 as she clutched the designated path, careful not to stray and aggro anything with her low level's huge aggro radius. At some point she thought she even noticed yet another raid group, the third one by her count and much smaller than her current group, that seemed to be going the same way at first, but then they broke off somewhere into the wilderness.

She was mildly comforted by the fact that there were others in the group with even lower levels than her own. The local area's name colour changed from amber to red when they emerged into a wide snowy valley with sharp mountains on either side, and several paths branching away from the plain.

She also started seeing player skeletons littering the ground here and there, likely victims of that local fauna. Or maybe those were the remains of the players they had come to kill, and the raid came too late?

[15:48] **[Raid]** RapiDfirE: OK WE HAVE TO REGROUP HERE, THIS IS THE LAST STOP

[15:48] **[Raid]** JungGad: we should go, there is no time

[15:48] **[Raid]** Pieepsh: whose corpses are those? who died here?

[15:48] **[Raid]** RapiDfirE: NO, WE NEED EVERYONE, THEY ARE DEFENDING THEIR CAVE HARD

[15:48] **[Raid]** RapiDfirE: ONE MINUTE AND WE GO

Lilke_ and a dozen other slower players reached the regrouping point only a few moments before the second raid group that followed them came close enough to read individual nicknames above their heads. *We are getting delayed because of me and-*

[15:49] **[Raid]** Pieepsh has left the group.

[15:49] **[Raid]** JungGad has left the group.

[15:49] **[Raid]** AlexRed has left the group.

[15:49] **[Raid]** Angelycas has left the group.

[15:49] **[Raid]** BigF has left the group.

[15:49] **[Raid]** Victor9090: ?

[15:49] **[Raid]** Victor9090 has left the group.

Lilke_ had only a second of time to think why people started leaving the group one by one all of the sudden before the raid frames disappeared from her screen as well, and the nameplates of nearly eighty players, mostly above her level and gathered around her, turned from green or blue to angry, flashing red.

[15:49] You have been removed from the group.

The pin dropped in her head. She connected the dots and understood, entirely too late, how she and dozens of other players from both raid groups got played. Fear gripped her heart as gasps of death filled her ears, before she too joined the skeletons on the ground.

'Fuck me sideways, they're really here,' said Slam1go impressed, pointing out the remains of previous players who got too close to the territory Chaug's guild had seized. 'No! Don't move past me, they will see you. Stay behind the ridge line.'

'How many do you think they are?' asked NDZ_hyte of the overall audience.

'I said today that I think they're a small group because they managed to keep the secret for a week. Less than ten, I guess. But who knows?' asked Slam1go rhetorically. 'Also who knows if they called in extra people for the last day?'

'How come we have not a single Assassin in this group? We're literally trying to assassinate some guys, this party is so scuffed, geez,' remarked Sl4y, examining the composition of the group. Himself healing as a Priest; Vizo-via, -Zoe-, and 415 on his alt as Mages; Slam1go and PowerOverwhelming as Fighters; Raphanti supporting as a Minstrel, good to have him with the bulk of their damage coming from Mages; slowah with offensive support as Scholar and his *e-girlfriend* Arabesque on a Hunter. Okus came with an un-healable Dark Priest, and NDZ_hyte brought a Warlock. *You can always rely on having a Warlock in Havoc at least*, Sl4y remarked. Then he realised he forgot about one important thing.

'Scratch that, I'm stupid,' he said, and sent an invite to the last party member.

[15:52] BATS has joined the raid group.

[15:52] **[Raid]** BATS: o/

[15:52] **[Raid]** BATS: took your time didn't you

With him, that made 12 people. Sl4y had talked to him privately before even forming the group. BATS shared the information on the whereabouts of You Never Wipe Alone guild on the condition that he will participate in killing them, but he would do it in his own way and he would stay hidden until "the moment is right". Sl4y did not even try to ask what that meant exactly.

'So what was the plan? I already forgot,' asked Okus, though Sl4y had
to look at the Chatterbox window on his second screen to know who it was.
Funny guy, aren't you?

'We have a plan?' Slam1go was incredulous. 'When did we make it?'

'When you were jacking off to your DPS metrics fifteen minutes ago,' rebuked Sl4y. 'Beyond the ridge to the west – that's left on your maps – there's
a cave network entrance, same layout as anywhere else in the game. There are
some guys hidden inside. We run in and kick ass, but since I already brought
the potions, let's try to make the most of the surprise. Everyone here is above
level 90, right? Good. The distance is about a hundred metres, we go on foot
invisible. Everyone, and I mean *everyone* consume the invi pot on my mark.
slowah, make sure Arabesqua does it too. Then we run forward to get as close
as possible undetected. And then… we will see.'

'They may know we're here already,' pointed out PowerOverwhelming.

'Um,' spoke up Vizovia, 'I have an idea… may I?'

'Sure,' said Sl4y.

'Something killed those few players in front of the cave. There could be
Assassins stealthed there. How about we draw them out first? Otherwise they
may hit us from the back or form up with those inside.'

'How?' asked Sl4y.

'We send Arabesqua first. She's from a different guild and will look like
a random wandering around. If there are Assassins there, they'll pounce on
her. She's also a female, so easy victim, gankers love that.' Hearing that from
her was hilarious to Sl4y, but he suppressed his amusement.

'In other words, use her as bait?' asked slowah.

'Um… yes.'

'Little Zovia, wow did you get such an evil idea?' asked -Zoe-, amused.

[15:54] [**Raid**] 416: assassin paranoia comes with being a caster =]

'Haha, what Four-Fifteen says,' Vizovia agreed.

'I don't mind it, slowah. If she's okay with that, let's do it,' Sl4y said.

'One sec, I'll ask her.'

'Make sure to tell her she might die here and be left behind if we're busy.'

A moment passed while the Scholar talked to the Hunter by private message. Meanwhile, Sl4y took a little peak at the path they were to follow through the trees and ferns, and saw a few skeletons lying there just as Slam1go had reported, but they were all near the dark fissure leading underground. This suggested that the closer one got to the rocks, the deadlier it got.

'She says she will be happy to,' slowah said.

'Hold on,' said -Zoe-. 'The moment they see us, they will warn the people inside we're coming.'

'Yes, so what?' asked Raphanti. 'They must be expecting someone will come eventually, and they can't really call for reinforcements.'

'OK, then the *plan* is almost the same,' Sl4y once again cut the conversation. 'We make it as simple as possible. Now listen…'

Teeg was quite bored.

A glance at the clock told him his shift would be over in little over an hour. To just sit around in front of their hideout twirling thumbs for hours was a mind-numbingly boring way to spend one's last day of vacation, but he had volunteered for this and would not quit. He thought of the squad behind him, back in the cave, and knew they were suffering the boredom too. But the whole kidnapping of Airship Master and Lady Redrow was such a wacky idea, and in its weird way it was so fun too. Nobody did such a thing before, and that was awesome. Some of the conversations they had on voice comms over the last week were pure gold. *But anyway, this is my last watch. I can do it, but then I'm going outside, away from the computer. For real this time.*

A comforting thought was that his misery was shared by a fellow Assassin, Shioya, stealthed and immobile next to him. Their assignment was to gank with extreme prejudice anyone coming within fifty metres of the cave entrance so that no one could even peek inside. Unlike the cave team, they had to pay at least partial attention to the surroundings, and Teeg did exactly that: *partial* attention. The other part was on a coding project on his laptop, but that was boring too. He craved to go outside and dive into the sea, it was still summer after all. Living in Portugal had its perks.

'Someone is coming.' Shioya's voice came from the headset on Teeg's neck. He pulled it up and turned in his chair towards his PC with the game on. Whoever was online in the guild was in the voice channel at all times, a command strongly enforced by Chaug. He only managed to convince a guild of notorious individualists to such discipline on the back of his promise of master-level trolling, and so far, he delivered. Nevertheless, some of the online people were doing their own things in the background. Everyone had been silent for some time before Shioya spoke up.

'I see him,' Teeg confirmed. 'Coming right this way. Another lost noobie,' he added.

A Hunter was coming right towards them on foot, with clear intent to enter the cave - there was nothing else of note in the nearest area, except maybe herbs to pick or map to explore. Had Teeg been a herbalist by secondary profession he would see nearby herbs on the radar, but without it he could only guess.

If she's exploring, she's about to find something all right, he thought.

He right-clicked the target and a katar blade slipped into his right hand while a twin claw sprung from his left wrist. The Qatil specialisation for Assassins lacked crowd control utilities but made up for it with its lethality; it was unparalleled in just *deleting* people, especially in an ambush situation. He did not need to coordinate with Shioya who already had his twin sickle weapons drawn. They were chained to his wrist for throwing and pulling himself to his target when needed. Teeg reluctantly admitted that the Ninja build was interesting and maybe even engaging in gameplay, but Qatil was where the numbers were at.

'Have you killed him yet?' Chaug's voice buzzed in their ears.

'About to,' said Shioya.

Both Assassins held position on either side of the cave entrance and made no move until the intruder was in melee range of both of them. Without ceremony, they attacked; Teeg with Slice and Dice, and Shioya with Mutilation. *Just another easy victim,* he thought, but he nevertheless appreciated the distraction a lot. Within the first three seconds the Hunter from some unimportant no-name guild was at half health and was unable to make even a small step, let alone escape or fight back. Just one Assassin in melee range is a pain to deal with for a Hunter; two is an execution. Teeg hoped he could at least cast one Cross Cut before Shioya finishes him or her.

Then he noticed another red nameplate in the corner of his vision. Before he could spare the attention from killing the Hunter to the newcomer and see who that was, a few more appeared all of the sudden in his immediate vicinity. *I didn't see them approach, they weren't here a second ago! I'm sure of it!*

'Hey, what the-'

'Who are the-,' broke off Shioya. 'Shit!' was all he managed to say before about a dozen figures emerged as if they had teleported to him, and they immediately dropped a world of hurt on the two Assassins. Shioya died where he stood and started saying something to his mic. Teeg was desperately spamming his Vanish hotkey while trying to run into the cave opening. The assailants were already on the move heading straight for the secret hideout, prioritising instant or fast-cast abilities thrown at the two You Never Wipe Alone Assassins. It was a rush tactic, Teeg realised. They were not here by accident.

Teeg managed to make only a few steps inside the tunnel when among a burst of punches, dots, and spells a Brimbolt from a Warlock lethally hit him in the back. The enemy party hurried over his corpse even before the death animation completed.

'They're coming, they're coming!,' he yelled into his headset's microphone, startled and with his heart thumping.

'What? Who? How many?' demanded Chaug.

'Havoc!'

Activity spiked in the cavern. All of the sudden, prone or sitting adventurers jumped to their feet and started frantically buffing themselves and each other, Hunters laid traps, casters aimed and pre-casted spells into the tunnel leading to and out of their large cavern. In all, nine players were preparing to receive the invaders in their lair; six damage dealers and two healers among them. There was also a Warrior tank in the deep end of the cavern who stayed where he was, with two figures hitting with what could as well be wet noodles for all the damage they did.

The place was bisected by a small stream of cold water, and in general was quite wet with water trickling down the walls in several places or dripping from stalactites, coalescing into puddles and trickling further down the cracks. A bunch of thick-furred predator beasts spawned here, but they were not a problem for a level 100 character. They were more of a nuisance than a threat, and had to be killed eight times per hour. Their carcasses lingered on the craggy floor for a time after death. Glowing crystals in the shades of green and blue protruding from the walls and the roof provided lighting. The walls were extremely uneven and jagged as if some tremendous force rammed rocky spikes into them. It was from one such tiny ledge formed by a crystal shard of emerald green, a dozen metres above ground, that BATS observed the bustle below. He had trickjumped onto it a week before, from shelf to shelf, on the same night You Never Wipe Alone brought their hostages here. Getting the right timing of slamming the spacebar while moving forward and landing on the next step was tricky, but still less difficult than he thought it would be. The people below were too busy to search for potential spies on that first day, and although they have been checking for invisible enemies around the cavern from time to time since then, the detection spells only worked horizontally. BATS was too far up to be in range.

He had been curious about what they were doing. Within the last twenty-four hours even someone as detached from forums as BATS heard about the ransom post, and suddenly everything made sense to him. He had not been sitting for a week straight just looking down at YNWA guild's Warrior tanking two NPCs around the clock, with occasional heal being thrown at him by a Paladin who might as well be the same player as the Warrior but on a different multi-boxed account. Instead, BATS logged off quite a lot over the last week leaving his character where it was, promising himself to catch up with his weekly quota of innocent deaths when this is over. That could wait; there were memories to be made here, such as the memory of being scared to touch the keyboard and accidentally moving a step, dropping down from his perch, and revealing himself by taking fall damage. Had Pvro been active lately BATS would have to make sure to be logged off during GvG hours lest an emergency guild summon yanked him from his perch.

The Airship Master and Lady Redrow did almost no damage with their autoattacks, and were not scripted to have any offensive abilities. They were never intended to be in combat at all. They could be tanked for hours by a well-geared tank before they needed any healing. BATS admired the dedication to the elaborate trolling by YNWA. *To spend a week maintaining aggro on two NPCs after dragging them away all the way here from town, while also patrolling the area and killing anyone who got too close to discover them? And do all that for what, for a prank? Incredible.*

The first Havoc player was just around the corner in the tunnel according to BATS' on-screen radar. Seconds later Slam1go was the first to burst into the chamber at top speed with another Fighter in tow, and then a Scholar entered the fray disrupting magic from two YNWA mages directed at the rest of the party following him. The two Fighters threw themselves at some Warrior first, probably because he was the closest, but having taken one look at the situation they switched to yOydu, knowing him to be the main healer of YNWA guild. They became under fire by pretty much everyone in that cavern immediately. Then three Mages, a Priest, and a Warlock came in, all buffed for quicker casting and lesser spell delay by a caster's best friend, a Minstrel playing songs behind them on a string instrument. BATS briefly wondered what the reaction of the kidnappers was when more and more Havoc members just kept coming in.

The moment was right. BATS had been patient, so very patient, but no more. He slid down. The fall unstealthed him, but even if anyone from YNWA noticed him coming from the back it was too late. Blades sang a poisonous song as he sank the daggers into the back of a Priest trying to keep yOydu alive. BATS imagined the surprise and shock in their communications and had only one thing to say to that:

[15:58] BATS: q:)

* * *

Thread: The negotiations were short
[Posted by <u>Chaug</u>, 31 Aug 2015, 19:28:29]
Dear AltAr community,

We thank you for participating in our ad-hoc special event. Of course we all know you did not have a choice to participate or not :-) I assure you that if our party wasn't crashed, we would still be at it.

I'm writing this summary on a direct ~~threat~~ request from Kaivax. Doing it after the party was his condition for allowing it once he found us :D Thanks for being a good lad.

To begin with, it was Unk's idea. He came up with it, tested it privately on some other server or maybe even his own, then told me about it, and I organised it. I also added a few ideas. I did not think this would work, and even so, I believed all NPCs had a disengage mechanism programmed in their behaviour that would kick in after a long fight like a frenzy timer on a boss, but I guess not!

So how did we do it?
South-east of Hellesvyand, on the coast of Navigator's Sea, there's a village of jungle trolls (Masmatra Village), with a rare forest troll shaman spawn. It has garbage loot even for level 40s... BUT! It can do mind control on players lasting ridiculously long: whole 30 seconds or until any damage is taken.

This is where stupid begins! We had a ~~victim~~ volunteer on a priest tag the shaman, and keep casting, cancelling, and recasting again the home return spell to Hardline. But first, this person had to be completely SHITFACED with alcohol. This is important, it wouldn't work without it. So, now just to wait until we're blessed by RNGesus and the troll kindly decides to use MC.

The trick here is that AI can't do cast cancels, so once the MC lands on our dude at ~95% casting of Return, we have a MCed player in Hardline a few seconds later.

This is where alcohol comes in. Drunk players, even MCed, can't target anything beyond a few metres away from them, so they will attack the only target it has within range: our second helper waiting in Hardline ☺

Then we quickly kite the MCed payload all the way to the tower, and park it next to the Airship Master. MCed player recognizes NPCs as allies, and buffs them. And here comes the ~~exploit~~ unintended gameplay mechanic:

An NPC getting buffed by a MCed player enters combat!

So now we have Airship Master in combat with our agent =] All we have to do now is to kite him to the "free candy" van.

Repeat for Lady Redrow for the lulz while we're at it.

A bunch of random facts:

We PRAYED for no server restart during this time lol

We had to make sure our Priest is not specced for Mind Control himself to prevent some weird chain reaction. That would be funny as heck though.

We made sure to not be seen doing it. We observed the area for a couple of days before we started. We noted the least active routes and hours for players. The funniest thing was Oioioibruv using some toys and potions to increase his size and park a mammoth on top of some guy who almost spotted us, so the bloke couldn't see shit on his screen xD

Waking up at 4 AM to steal them and then taking shifts to keep the hostages in combat for a week was fucking killing us IRL but we also had a lot of good laughs. ~~I have the best guild~~ <3

The NPCs do almost no damage, a good tank can hold them solo for a long time and go AFK

Kaivax popped up in our cave on day one, laughed his bum off, said he will allow it this once, and disappeared :) Then he announced to everyone there is no bug, but technically there was, just not the one that people reported - the bug was the MC mechanic

Initially we only planned this for the boat dude, but we decided to rustle more jimmies by fucking with the event =]

So, congrats to Havoc guild for tracking us down and bombing the operation in less than 17 hours from ransom note, on a weekday. You all owe the release of hostages to them and to one ~~guy~~ girl from NFP whom they used as bait XD Fucking Sl4y, classy as always! Also Unk thanks Slam1go for inspiring him with that Octav abduction.

Edit: ALSO ALSO! Special shoutouts to Halbdenial, Octav, RapidFirE, Alghouti,and a bunch of other dudes who organised fake hostage rescues XD This was my idea and I talked to them in secret, but it worked better than I expected lmao. I am looking forward to the videos from the bloodbath!

[Posted by: GM_Kaivax, 31 Aug 2015, 19:29:01]
Just popping here real quick to inform everyone that in recognition of the effort that You Never Wipe Alone guild invested into this

elaborate disruption of other players' experience, <u>the event will not be extended</u>, and that nothing will be reimbursed to players who might have missed any rewards because of this "incident".

YNWA guild will take the full brunt of everyone's frustration and suffer the consequences, because they worked hard to earn it (˘ ³˘).

Also, the Mind Control "trick" they used will not work again as of tomorrow's server maintenance so don't try it.

[Posted by: <u>Vrbica</u>, 31 Aug 2015, 19:32:16]
WHAT XD I just realised I got ganked twice near hardline by Chaug's goons in the middle of nowhere and I was like WTF are they even here?! Turns out I accidentally got to close to the secret project!!

Thanks Havoc for letting me have my epic stuff!

[Posted by: <u>Iseria</u>, 31 Aug 2015, 19:35:24]
WTF?!

I don't get what Kaivax and the admins are thinking. It's their job to maintain smooth experience for everyone. We pay donations to the server and this is the support we get? I'm not gonna donate anymore lol

Griefers should be punished

[Posted by: <u>maka-76</u>, 31 Aug 2015, 19:37:08]
@up +1

[Posted by: <u>Halbdenial</u>, 31 Aug 2015, 19:39:39]
Then punish them :-) You're free to gank them, undercut their auctions, refuse to group with them, or I dunno, call them stinky poopers or something.

Kaivax is a champ for knowing MMORPG should simulate real life including the assholes

[Posted by: CassNL, 31 Aug 2015, 19:39:47]
Well well, Havoc still can do things. Who knew? Thanks from my sister, she really wanted Redrow back.

[Posted by: rapidfire, 31 Aug 2015, 19:43:35]
I will forever remember the 2015 Hostage Rescue Incident XD thanks Chaug for the content it was hilarious!

[Posted by: Slam1go, 31 Aug 2015, 19:46:00]
Stay tuned for the hostage rescue video I'm editing :^) But fuck me, I want the footage from the fake rescue slaughter T_T

[Posted by: Diki, 31 Aug 2015, 19:47:58]
Aww I wanted us to find them first :(

[Posted by: Sl4y, 31 Aug 2015, 19:51:11]
This was so fun even 415 stopped complaining for a second and there's finally another guild to compete for the #1 public enemy title :D
Our party was completely half-assed and our strat was pretty much RUSH B with a minor exception of ABSOLUTE BRILLIANCE from yours truly

BTW, to everyone who says "thank you Havoc", BATS says "come say that to my face q:)"

* * *

Warm summer days were slowly giving way to the autumn cold. September rolled in with tectonic certainty, unstoppable, deaf to pleas and wishes of those enjoying their summer breaks. As was foretold back in April, the Summer Event lasted two full months and came to an end. The 2015 edition would be remembered forever for the Hostage Rescue Massacre with varying degrees of fondness.

What was advertised as a fashion show was, for the most part, exactly that, but with new items on the agenda. The Immorality Police guild was composed of players going to great lengths to obtain cosmetic items, mounts, and sets of equipment and weapons from every corner of the game, just for the purpose of looking great while they pretend to be AFK just where many people could see them. What else was worth doing in an MMORPG?

It was only last year, in 2014, when Immorality Police's guildmaster Vrbica first came up with an idea for a player-made event during which her people showed off their coolest and rarest collectibles by just walking down the main road in Vir Estia, one after another. It was the unofficial closing ceremony of 2014's Summer Event being held on the very last evening.

This year though, Vrbica outdid herself by convincing the chief Game Master himself, GM_Kaivax, to do something extraordinary as a collaboration: she received a copy of each costume obtainable through event participation and through server donations, and distributed it among her "models" to show off on the very beginning of the event in June. Every such item, of course, was tracked and then deleted immediately from everyone's inventory after the show. This worked as both a community event and an advertisement of server's donation rewards, an arrangement in which everyone wins. Such was the privilege of unofficial, community-driven game servers.

With September came the return to school for many adventurers. It has been a few years since Sl4y had last gone to any school, but he vividly remembered not liking it there and vastly preferred his adult life and his corporate job. He even got to use a paper guillotine regularly and had the keys to open every door in the building giving him a feeling of real power.

Despite the guild's success and the momentary boost to everyone's morale, Sl4y's optimism was rather stifled though he kept the dourness to himself.

Eightblades had finally returned from his long trip. PowerOverwhelming promised to welcome him with a kick to the genitals (in real life, he assured) for logging out with Power's mining speed gloves before leaving for three weeks and refusing to share account credentials so that he could retrieve them himself. Belixner was also back to regular play, but she became even more belligerent in guild chat, sparking drama for no reason from time to time.

As Sl4y checked the roster and compared it to the guild log, he noticed Bokkie had left the guild without saying a word two weeks ago. This was to be expected from Lonecow's buddy, but still felt like Sl4y's own failure. By pure accident, Sl4y noticed Doomcaster has been spending most of his time on an alt character outside the guild.

Sl4y also remarked that Dereky was still absent in the game but regularly visited the forums, while the brothers Pjj and Arastina have been showing up from time to time but only for brief moments, and never joined any activities. Sl4y tried to guess what could be the reason here. *Do they still want to play,* Sl4y wondered, *just not with this guild anymore? If so, why not just leave?* Sl4y wondered if there was anything he could have done to keep them in the guild and active. The guild's Greeks founded Havoc together with Pvro, and the few that still played preferred to stick to themselves for the most part. They either drifted away from the game or did their own little thing rather than jump guilds. *What keeps them here? Loyalty? Sentiment? How long will this last, and how do*

I keep it going? Sl4y's new bad habit was checking if Venetia was still there at least once a day; he was the one person Sl4y would hate the most to stop seeing regularly. Eventually Sl4y realised such surveillance was immature at best and just talking to the man would be much better at putting his worries to rest. *I just have to actually do it rather than only think about it.*

And Pvro, Sl4y realised one morning before work, *I don't believe he will be back for real.*

At least slowah seems happy though. Apparently Arabesque really did not mind being the bait that one time and found it exciting, and she even survived it after all to see the end of it. However, slowah thought she did not really appreciate the one-of-a-kind memory she made yet, and that was after him trying to explain it. *Girls don't know what's good,* he had said.

But in summary, Sl4y was tired of the situation.

Slam1go was not idle, and would not give up his server forum bragging rights easily. If Havoc could no longer rely on the most skilled players they had in the past, then new elites had to be created. He was, however, not going to wait weeks or months for that to happen naturally.

He had been hard at work but outside the game. He finished creating a new section in Havoc's forums. Sl4y had given him the full moderator privileges to make it happen, so there was at least something the *OfFiCeR hEehEe* was good for. The section was the brain-child of himself and 415, the two least helpful people in Havoc, and was intended to provide help. In this supposedly elitist guild, Slam1go saw character builds so bad he suspected their owners even used keyboards to turn around.

415 and Slam1go School of Unfucking Your Build, read the name. Then he created two sub-sections: *Request help,* and *Knowledge Base.*

Inside the former he posted a thread: *Welcome!* where he wrote: *Tired of your dogshit Trainer Hunter build? Come here and ask questions or post your character build for review. 415 and myself will advise you, suggest improvements, and link the gear you should have.*

In the latter, he posted: *Coming soon: a handbook for every class and spec useful for organised PvP. We need a class expert for Witch Doctor and Scholar, contact me if you think you're one.*

How the two elitist-theorycrafting-minmaxers would agree on any topic related to stat and skill distribution or optimal itemization was anyone's guess, but Slam1go was confident that if it came to a dispute he could easily out-post 415 so there was that.

Now, he thought, *how do we make people actually want to use it?*

'...because it's back to school time,' she groaned.

^_Miko_^'s subtle voice contrasted strongly with the dry, no-nonsense tone of Sapphire, a second-rarest guest in the Havoc girls' club only after Belixner. Vizovia checked the guild window to see what the latter veteran was doing, and as expected, she was in a 5v5 PvP arena, likely with Venetia, Prast and Sarevoc, likely knee-deep in blood and screaming curses. Vizovia imagined Belixner in real life and pictured a two-metre tall hunk of a woman with face paint and braided blond hair, blue eyes, a shield in one hand and axe in another, screaming her lungs off while standing on the bow of a drakkar. In her free time, Vizovia was sure, Belixner probably transported fallen Vikings to Valhalla, although she did not even know why she had assumed Belixner was Nordic at all. Did someone tell her so? She could not remember.

Vizovia was torn between being curious about their only female Veteran and being scared of her. *As if Sapphire wasn't scary enough.*

^_Miko_^ was more hushed than normal, as if afraid to be overheard. It was quite likely in fact, since she was explaining how her parents had limited her gametime until she proved she could maintain decent grades at school.

'I know how that feels…' Vizovia muttered.

'Wouldn't be a problem if school was only PE, then I'd smash it,' the youngest girl added. 'But nooo, literature. Who needs that?' To Vizovia, such rants sounded almost comical when whispered by a fifteen or sixteen year old, although she well remembered being in ^_Miko_^'s place. It was less than three years ago, but Vizovia felt she had grown up a lot since then. She added another manga volume to her shopping cart online while the conversation went on.

'Do you need help with anything?' asked Sapphire. Paper shuffling sounds could be heard when she spoke.

'No,' replied ^_Miko_^ automatically.

'Riiiiight,' said Ma_Ris knowingly. 'It's Maddie's third year of school. I'll be helping her with maths for sure. Maybe I will open an in-game school?' she giggled. 'Picture this: a group of lowbies sitting around me in a tavern room somewhere as I explain the lesson of the day. We could do voice chat and screen sharing too. Weird idea, huh?'

'You're good at maths?' asked ^_Miko_^.

'Uhum! I tutor people as a side job. Kids, students, adults.'

'Mom said she will get me a tutor too…'

'Hey, listen,' jumped in Sapphire. 'Being tutored is no shame. Know what's a shame? Being uneducated,' she spoke with that seriousness she sometimes switched to without any warning. 'MaMa here says she knows math. I could help you with biology, chemistry and some physics, and, you know what, forget I said anything. You staying up until 2 AM waiting for me might be a problem,' Sapphire said all that in one breath.

'Thanks for trying,' ^_Miko_^ laughed.

'It worked with Sl4y,' said Sapphire, resigned.

'Hah, you helped him do homework?' asked Ma_Ris with enthusiasm over learning new fun little trivia.

'Yes,' Sapphire admitted bluntly. 'And he wrote essays for me. He said he couldn't explain how to write essays, so he just did them for me. Those were the days.'

'...but I thought you both were like… twenty-five-ish?' asked Vizovia.

'Yes, and?'

'...'

'They knew each other before AltAr, Vee,' clarified Ma_Ris.

'Anyway, I was saying,' Sapphire continued. 'I'm sure we can find someone for every subject in the guild. Just think about all the languages we have here – Beli is from Greece I think I think, Eightblades and PowerOh are Italian, Slam1go Polish, Money is Spanish I think. Just be careful with Sl4y. He's a literature and history nerd, and if you ask him about those things, he won't shut up about it and will keep sending you links to check out. At least math people don't do that.'

'Heh,' reacted Ma_Ris.

'Gee, girls, thanks for making me feel even dumber!' ^_Miko_^ snickered.

'So young, so sarcastic!'

'Yes, I'm so proud!' agreed Sapphire.

Later that night when everyone else went to sleep, Sapphire admired her in-game storage, as she did regularly. The treasures she had forcibly ripped from the random number generator's clutches which now would be put to a much better use, such as looking good in her stash. But September brought change to her life as well, one she had been very carefully not thinking about until now. The clock on her phone told her it was well past one in the morning. She suppressed her urge to put on her rollerblades and go out for night skating. Instead, she sighed, and reached for her biochemistry book. It was a really thick, expensive, and certainly very entertaining thing for a brick. She opened it and skimmed through the first chapter lazily, then paused. She stared blankly out the window to the night sky as dots were being connected in her head.

She went back to her computer, and logged onto AltAr. The hour was late (by other people's standards), but the person she meant to chat with would often still be on, although in various stages of dozing off. In fact, it was even normal for her Canadian friend living in the Netherlands to stop responding in the middle of the conversation as she fell asleep without warning. Sapphire whisped her once to no effect, but waited a few minutes wondering how and why that one thought even crossed her mind in that moment. She tried again.

[01:23] [To: Anzu_]: asdf

[01:23] [Friend] Anzu: oh hi

[01:23] [To: Anzu_]: got a moment?

[01:23] [Friend] Anzu: I'm not going anywhere with you, I'm on a touchpad atm

[01:23] [To: Anzu_]: I only need some gossip:P

[01:23] [Friend] Anzu: then shoot before I drop

[01:23] [To: Anzu_]: you said you have a new girl, the one who knows old stuff?

[01:24] [Friend] Anzu: yeah, what about her?

[01:24] [To: Anzu_]: where did you say you ffound her?

[01:24] [Friend] Anzu: I picked her up as a random for mobbing nagas for us one time

[01:24] [Friend] Anzu: then we talked, I liked her, I invited her, and that's it

[01:24] [Friend] Anzu: didn't even know she was female then

[01:24] [To: Anzu_]: did she look like she wanted to be taken in?

[01:24] [Friend] Anzu: hmm

[01:24] **[Friend]** Anzu: dunno, maybe, I didn't notice anything odd about her

[01:25] **[Friend]** Anzu: that thick french accent would make it super hard for her to blend in the crowd:D

Both women were silent for a moment, before Anzu asked the same question Sapphire asked herself.

[01:25] **[Friend]** Anzu: why, do we know her from somewhere?

Sl4y needed to think.

He was in the exotic coastal town of Hellesvyand, but the ever-festive mood of both the place itself and the players frequenting it contrasted with his own current frame of mind. There was a place he was going to, but his Priest had not crossed the town's gate yet.

He took a deep breath, rubbed his eyes, then rested his chin on his palm. He was not annoyed, or sad, but a combination of multiple issues nagged at him. He was stressed, under pressure, and wanted out of it.

The guild chat rolled in the bottom corner of his screen, perfectly illustrating the very matter he intended to solve and he read the conversation from the outside.

[00:11] **[Guild]** Maxitaur: what's the big deal? GvG is just a part of the game, not the whole game

[00:12] **[Guild]** Prast: I didn't take you for such a quitter Slam1go

[00:12] **[Guild]** Faystus: would be nice if greeks hadnt bailed out already lol

[00:12] **[Guild]** Belixner: would be nice if you stfu

[00:12] **[Guild]** Slam1go: bruh wtf, im, not quitting -_- all I'm saying is that I joined guild for good GvG and I'm not getting it now so fuck off, thanks

[00:12] **[Guild]** Azarus: wtf Beli he's not wrong tho

[00:12] **[Guild]** Slam1go: @prast I am putting in a ton of work, dont take that tone with me k?

[00:12] **[Guild]** Faystus: yeah wtf?

[00:12] **[Guild]** Venetia: excuse me…

[00:12] **[Guild]** Intervene: can you people chill out?

[00:12] **[Guild]** Intervene: Pvro is fuck knows where, but Sl4y is doing what he can

[00:12] **[Guild]** Intervene: there is no way that will satisfy everyone

[00:12] **[Guild]** Ò_Ó: let the man work

[00:12] **[Guild]** Intervene: ^

[00:12] **[Guild]** Belixner: work on what? there's nothing he can do, shit's fucked and I'm not the only one thinking that

[00:12] **[Guild]** Intervene: who else then?

[00:12] **[Guild]** Azarus: ^ I'm guessing people who aren't even here to speak for themselves

[00:12] **[Guild]** Belixner: I don't really want this conversation anymore

[00:12] **[Guild]** Faystus: yeah it's hard to argue with absent people

It's been two days since their little triumph of thwarting You Never Wipe Alone's ploy, but several weeks since they ended a GvG evening with Havoc's colours flying over a capital city, and such conversations as this were becoming more frequent. Havoc was, historically and traditionally, the winning guild. It was no secret many members joined for this reason. *This has to stop, one way or another,* he said to himself. *This can't be good for anyone, even those who don't care about GvG.*

He took a deep breath. *All right,* he thought, and went to withdraw something from his storage.

Elsewhere, Sapphire was also paying attention. There was a time, not long ago, when such displays of negative emotion and uncertainty would not be an almost daily occurrence. She wanted to help the guild, but even more so she wanted to help one specific person in it whom she noticed was not participating in the conversation, and she knew what it meant when he was not saying anything for a while. She was not good with words, and saying things such as *it's gonna be fine* was so cringeworthy to her she would rather keep her mouth shut. She could not make the veterans log in more. Maybe she could try to play better for her part, pick up the slack for others, but not by much.

But maybe she could trigger something inside Sl4y. Maybe there was a lever she could pull, even if it made things worse rather than better. Perhaps it would do nothing at all. In such situations she did what she would always do: *whatever I want.* So she broke the seal on the emergency lever.

She typed a nickname in the chatbox, then a message, and sent it. The recipient was online and active, so the message was delivered.

Hey, long time no see, the message read.

Someone, somewhere, read the message and pondered their options for a while. A reply was sent, and a conversation was had. A decision was made. Now was the time. As Sl4y did at around the same time, a different but likewise precious item was withdrawn from personal storage, and activated with a heavy heart.

[00:21] [To: Venetia]: hey, got a moment?

[00:21] [Whisper] Venetia: for?

[00:21] [To: Venetia]: I need your help. Can you come to Hellesvyand for a moment?

[00:21] [Whisper] Venetia: ok, when I finish this bg

[00:21] [To: Venetia]: ok, I'll wait

Sl4y twirled his thumbs waiting for the master of Warlocks to finish his battleground match. Fireworks went up and illuminated the night sky from time to time, players in various stages of undressing went by around him, some of whom he even recognized. It seemed that for people who hang out in this place midnight was the peak hour.

[00:24] [Whisper] Venetia: ok, coming

Sl4y sent a party invite to the guild's Veteran as he waited for him to show up, thinking about what he was about to say. After another few minutes, the grim figure finally rolled into his screen on a skeletal armoured warhorse. The eyeless darkness of the Warlock's hood looked down on the standing but dismounted character of Sl4y, before the newcomer too dismissed the steed. They switched to party chat and Sl4y was about to raise a topic, but he was momentarily amused by random people throwing beneficial spells on Venetia and Sl4y when they passed by him; but more so on Venetia, Sl4y noticed. *Seeing that never gets old*, he thought.

'What are we doing?' asked Venetia.

'Just talking,' said Sl4y.

'Eh? We could do that by pm.'

'Sorry, I need to have your attention :)'

'Ah,' Venetia said knowingly. 'Something serious.'

'I don't suppose you have any idea what Pvro is planning to do about us?' Sl4y asked.

'No, I don't', Venetia admitted. 'But you know Pvro was never someone to make plans. He does what he wants.'

'Has he ever been this inactive before? You've been here far longer than me.'

'Hmm. He has had breaks, we all have breaks sometimes.'

'Okay but did he tell you guys before he would be absent like that?'

The Warlock master thought for a while before answering. 'He always told Trill, and he told us, I think. Memory of that is not good.'

Sl4y sighed. 'I just want to know what to do -_-'

'With what?'

'The guild.'

'What is there to do?' Venetia asked.

Sl4y was taken aback for a moment. Of all the things he thought Venetia would say, he did not expect him to not see any problems at all. Was this a misunderstanding? Sl4y chose his next words carefully.

'I don't see your friends around much lately.'

'Yes, and? You're worried about me? :p'

'Haha, always. But seriously – Pjj, Arastina, Lonecow, Bokkie, Trillex, Sarevoc, Doublehead – they were the core of the guild for a long time, and we don't have them anymore. Some of our best players, and you can see that in the cities, on the flag poles. They're not our flags on them. We don't win castles anymore. Not having them hurts us. Everyone sees it, inside and outside.'

'But that is not a problem. You thinking about it as a problem is a problem.'

'...explain.' Sl4y had a strange feeling of losing ground in a conversation. Venetia was taking him in an unexpected direction.

'They are not your responsibility. They are adults, they choose what to do with their time. They chose to do something else. That's normal. They played for 6 years or more. Everyone can get bored after 5-6 years of doing something.'

'But not you?' Sl4y asked. This was perhaps the real question he wanted to ask Venetia in this conversation.

'No :) I still have fun here.'

'Fuck, that's a relief,' Sl4y admitted honestly. 'Some load off my mind.'

'Also, since everyone thinks I'm some sort of a wise old master, I will tell you a secret. You ready?'

'Yeah, hit me.'

'Fuck winning. The goal is never to win. It's to keep playing.'

Sl4y mulled over the thought that Venetia had implanted in his mind. *The goal is never to win,* that sounded to Sl4y as paradoxical, given Havoc's reputation over the years that came with winning a lot.

'That goes against what this guild actually did,' Sl4y pointed out.

'This is just my opinion. Not everyone thought like me. And look where it brought us, hm?'

'OK, so your buddies are their own people, they do what they want. Like Pvro, actually. But doing things in the game requires groups. We're still a guild, we do things together, and we need Pvro to do things for us so that we all can work as a group. I mean, come on, we're Havoc, we're supposed to be the cool guys. It's a fucking shame how we look now.'

'But who cares how we look? We never did.'

'No?'

'We never asked for any reputation, it just happened. Trying to look good makes us look bad. Who cares what others think about us?'

Sl4y absorbed the oldest remaining Veteran's point of view in silence. He had no answer to that question, but it did not require one. Then Venetia asked a real question of his own.

'So what are you going to do?'

'I don't know,' Sl4y repeated. 'Why do I have to do anything? Why don't you lead Havoc? You're one of the founders etc. I see now you understand things better than me.'

'The reason is obvious, in front of you,' Venetia said bluntly. 'You asked yourself the questions I wouldn't bother with.'

'So you're happy with where we're going?'

'There are new things happening, and they're good. That new Mage, Vissovia? She led a raid recently with some other new guy. Slam1go has interesting GvG ideas that Pvro or Doublehead never had. People propose things, post ideas, discuss things. I see fun chats in the guild, international banter etc. We always had some of them, but they are still fun now, so it's good.'

'No, optimism aside,' Sl4y took a stand. 'We have a guild for a reason, playing MMO's solo is pointless. Some people are on board for GvG, and we're not delivering it. We need a success. We need to do something. You, I, Slam1go, and others who care.'

'Then do something, you don't need my permission.'

'Even if it's to make a new guild?'

Sl4y finally voiced the idea he had been brewing in his head for a couple of days, and felt relieved having finally spoken about it. The opinion of the Greek man before him, or his avatar at least, mattered greatly to him.

'Hmmm,' was all Venetia said for a few moments. 'I don't know how this will work. But it's probably the best idea at the moment.'

'But it feels terrible… I mean, I haven't been here half as long as you did. You and Havoc are almost synonyms - Venetia from Havoc, the Warlock boss, trademark. There are others too. There's a lot of history in the name. How can we leave something like that behind?'

'You said playing MMO's solo is pointless. Guild matters, but a guild is people, not pixels or numbers. What's the point of having a legendary guild with no people in it?'

Sl4y said nothing. It was not exactly a point that he had not thought of himself, but having it said by someone else, especially Venetia, was very different.

'Good point,' he said eventually. 'So you stick with us for the time being?'

'Yes. It's hard, but we can always just go back if Pvro returns.' That was another argument that Sl4y had thought of, and though he liked the practicality of it, there was a pang of guilt in it too.

'In that case, I have something for you,' the Priest said.

Sl4y right-clicked on Venetia's nameplate and opened a trade window. He dragged something from his inventory to the new grid, and accepted the trade for nothing in return. For Venetia it was a very clear sign that he was being offered a gift.

Enchantment: Eldritch Gift

'Consider it a gift from the guild,' Sl4y said. 'Take it.'

'Holy fuck,' was all Venetia had to say for a moment. He accepted the deal, and stood there dumbfounded.

'How??' he asked. 'Why?'

'It's not from me, that much I can tell you :p' Sl4y said. 'But the gifter and I think you will use it better than anyone else.'

'You have no idea,' the Veteran said.

He hid himself in his little place near Hellesvyand, just outside the town, so that nobody could look up his location. Not that anyone was looking for him, but in his mind he felt the need to isolate himself to consider his options in some sort of solitude. He knew it was perhaps counter-productive to do it with the game still open in front of him, *but the problems are here so the solutions must be here too,* he thought.

This was one of his favourite places, but it's been a while since he visited it. He decided not to hang out in it again in a bad mood after his time, lest he ruin it for himself by association with negative feelings. Fortunately, the meeting with Venetia had calmed him a little, or maybe even pleased him, and he felt slightly more confident in the course of action he was considering to take.

He opened the Guild interface and displayed all current members, including whoever was offline, taking the tally of the names he thought he could trust the most. Intervene, slowah, Sapphire, and now Venetia would follow. Slam1go too, probably, and so would Ma_Ris, and with her also Vizovia and little ^_Miko_^. Gaav too, especially since his generous donation to Venetia. BATS... who knows? Eightblades, Power... the list went on. Belixner would be a problem, and perhaps also Agnelei who enjoyed the Havoc brand a lot, having written many of the PvE playbooks of the guild. In all, there were about forty people still playing regularly, and a quarter of that he knew well and trusted. As for the rest... and by the way, he also needed to propose or discuss a new name, symbols... and how would they get a website and forums as decent as Havoc's? And-

He noticed a stranger approaching him in his outdoor retreat, seemingly coming straight at him though unhurried, unmounted. He had no idea who this stranger was. Lyonni, read the nameplate over their head, but that did not ring any bell to him, though the <Execute> tag told him this could be someone he knew, after all. And then, when she filled his screen some more and he could see the character's visual details, with just one look at her from up close, he knew. His calm and confidence was gone like the wind.

A Priest and an Assassin sat together side by side on a fallen mossy log, gentle breeze swaying the trees and the bushes. Two pairs of identical gold eyes were directed at something far away, maybe something from another life, while their owners awkwardly wondered what they should say.

'You put on the eyes, I see,' he said.

'Mhm. We won them together, after all,' replied the character in a tightly fitting, black combat outfit.

'I haven't forgotten. You must be on the same account now, then.'

'Yes.'

'And you've been playing for months now, and haven't logged on Aura even once. Even by accident. I would have seen the last login info update. Admirable willpower and precision.'

'I didn't even know for sure if you were still playing until this month, but it was as you said. Right as always.'

'Am I?' asked Sl4y sadly. 'I wish that was the case like 4 years ago.'

'Don't.'

He thought she was going to elaborate, but he waited in vain. He could not let it go by like that.

'Why not?'

'There was nothing you could do about it. It was my decision.'

'Selfish,' he commented harshly.

'My life, my choice.'

'*I* thought of us as *us*, though.'

'Your mistake.' If the previous response was a slap, this was a stab. His heart sank a little reading it.

'You don't mince words, do you -_-' he said.

'Nope.'

'Did you come here just to salt the wound?'

'I don't think so.'

Silence fell again, and neither of the two silhouettes against the night sky moved. The hour was late, tasks awaited in the morning, but that was irrelevant for the time being. Nobody was in a hurry. Nobody was going anywhere. The moment lasted. Were this real life, Sl4y would have proposed going for a walk.

'How did you know I was here?' he asked, instead of pushing the previous topic.

'You're a sentimental fool, that's how.'

'Heh.'

'Are you upset I left?' asked the hooded female.

He wrote a response, but deleted it instead of sending. Then he wrote another.

'I was at the time. I moped a lot, but that was long ago. Now I am only upset that you left without saying a word.'

'It was cruel, I know.' Sl4y noted the distinct absence of *sorry* in her words.

'And you still did it?'

'I wasn't good at making decisions back then, but somehow I made it. It was hard for me too, you know?'

Another minute of silence passed by while he typed his question, then deleted it. He typed it again, changed a few words, deleted it again. Eventually, he sent nervously:

'I may never have the courage to ask you again. Why?'

He immediately regretted asking, and was increasingly anxious the longer she typed the response. Perhaps she was rethinking messages too. Eventually, she said:

'It's hard to explain. I don't know. I was confused. I needed to grow up, and you were too close to let me.'

'I would have given you space if you told me you needed it.'

'That's the problem: I knew you would. You'd do anything I asked. You'd give me anything I wanted. But I was 18, in love over the internet, and terrible at knowing what I really wanted. Or understanding my feelings for that matter, but you were all in. I had to go.'

He pondered it for a moment. *No, you didn't,* he wanted to say.

'Perhaps we were both immature,' he typed instead.

'That was only one of the reasons though.'

'What were the others?'

'They don't matter.'

'If you say so.'

Silence.

'I thought we would never talk again.'

':)'

'Even if I don't know why you came to talk now.'

She was not taking the hint to explain. He had to ask.

'Why reveal yourself now?'

'Sapphire busted me. Said she would let you know if I don't go talk to you myself.'

'Bless that woman. I should buy her flowers IRL.' Sl4y meant every word he said, and he would remember to actually do that one day. 'So, you did not want to talk to me then?'

'I don't know,' she said after an extremely long time. 'I was scared for sure.'

'Of what? Me?'

'Mhm. Of your reaction.'

'Why? Am I so terrible?'

'Maybe you are. People can change over four years. You did change, I think. It seems to me you used to be a happier person.'

'Gee, I wonder what happened to that?'

'Still sarcastic though :)'

'Oh, you noticed?'

She ignored the jab. 'And I heard quite a few mean things about you around here.'

'They're all true,' he said.

'The one about stealing someone's girl too?'

'Yes, but the girl was slowah incognito. Sigh, I wish I had his problems instead.'

'So what are the problems?' she asked, and the fact she even asked was precious to him.

'There are two,' he began. 'I'm going to steal a guild from my friend, that's one. You, that's two.'

'I see. Let me help with one of them, then.'

[Lyonni wants to register you as a friend. Accept / Reject]

END